6-
C

Frye Street
& Environs

Frye Street & Environs

The Collected Works of Marita Bonner

. . .

Edited and Introduced by

Joyce Flynn

and

Joyce Occomy Stricklin

Beacon Press · Boston

Beacon Press
25 Beacon Street
Boston, Massachusetts 02108

Beacon Press books
are published under the auspices of
the Unitarian Universalist Association of Congregations.

94 93 92 91 90 89   2 3 4 5 6 7 8

Text design by Christine Leonard Raquepaw

Library of Congress Cataloging-in-Publication Data
Bonner, Marita, 1899–1971.
Frye Street & environs.
(Black women writers series)
1. Afro-Americans—Literary collections.
I. Flynn, Joyce.   II. Stricklin, Joyce Occomy.
III. Title.   IV. Title: Frye Street and environs.
V. Series.
PS3503.0439 1987   810'.8'0896073   87-47450
ISBN 0-8070-6300-2

Contents

Contents

A Portrait of My Mother

Joyce Occomy Stricklin

When my future sister-in-law's cousin married a student from the Ivory Coast of Africa, my father and mother and brothers and I were invited to the ceremony at City Hall.

We dressed carefully, paying close attention to the slight sense of intrigue we all felt. It was the early 1960s and we were just beginning to come face to face with our distant African heritage. We wanted the groom somehow to know that we knew our common black background.

I wore a short-sleeved black linen dress that had no pockets; it was fitted in the bodice and hung straight from the waist to the hem. I didn't wear earrings then, as I do now, or a hat, and I had on little makeup. My mother suggested I wear a necklace. I didn't. I thought the effect was perfect, lean and hollow like the works of African sculptors I had recently seen.

That day my two brothers dressed in the brown, tan, and mustard and red, white, and blue colors that Mother had chosen for them early in their lives. She selected their colors with as much imagination and joy as she had taken in choosing our names. William Almy Junior (Billy) received his name from our father because he was the oldest and because he and our father were born in the middle of September. But it was Mother who decided that the somber tones of autumn matched Billy's sensitive, quiet moods; even to this day he wears those same subtle, subdued colors. The suit he wore that day to the wedding was a finely tailored brown suit, one that hung easily from his narrow, slightly stooped shoulders. He was particularly eager to look dapper because he was soon to marry the cousin of the bride.

Warwick Gale Noel (Gale), the younger of the two, gleamed with the health, wholesomeness, and correctness our mother had instilled in us daily. His skin was bright with the glow of vitamins, oatmeal, gallons of milk, cod liver oil, and roast beef. His cavityless teeth sparkled from an overabundance of calcium. Mother always said that during the time she carried him she had once bitten into a soft section of an orange and her tooth cracked—an indication that the calcium was being taken from her system and absorbed by baby Gale. He has always had perfect teeth. That day his bright smile and dazzling white shirt sparkled against his navy blue suit; he didn't wear a red tie. Gale had been born near the fourth of July. Mother always called him by his middle name. She had given him the last name of Dad's paternal grandmother, Warwick—the last name of one of her distant aunts—Gale, and her own mother's maiden name, Noel. She thought he would be the last child.

Billy and Gale stood very tall that day of the wedding, and moved with a youthful elegance perhaps not unlike young African princes.

Dad was not at all smitten with the emerging African connection. He was too much a gentleman, steeped in his personal New England–Narraganset Indian history to wonder how his grey eyes and light-toned complexion could connect with Africa. Nothing changed. He wore his every-day, every-night, all-occasion brown suit to the wedding that day. It didn't matter how many times he had it on: it always looked new. Maybe that was because his shoes were always polished and his hair freshly cut and his shirt newly laundered so that the frayed edges of his trousers and suit jacket were unnoticed; or perhaps it was his inbred good manners and quiet intelligence that made you forget whatever it was he wore. But despite his dignity, and on special occasions only, Mom called him Biddy. That wedding day she called him Biddy, maybe because their wedding had taken place in a similar city hall thirty-two years before.

Mother accepted our burgeoning African linkage the way she embraced everything from raising her children to talking to a stranger in the German meat market—with every fiber of her being. When I was two years old, I remember Mom and I standing at the corner of the oak table, which is now in my dining room, waiting to hear Kate Smith sing "Hands across the Table" on the Breakfast Club. It was about nine o'clock in the morning and Mom was dressed formally in pumps and hose and a woolen crepe dress, and as Kate Smith began singing on the radio, Mom and I held hands and sang along. I knew then and have always known that Mom was there for me. I realize now how special and respectful was the treatment I received as a child.

Young feelings and decisions were taken seriously in our house. When I was four years old, I told my parents that I didn't like nursery school. I didn't cry or fuss; I just didn't want to go back. Mother listened to me very carefully and decided not to send me back to nursery school. She had just begun to work outside the home again but stopped to stay with me. When I did go to school, I was to start kindergarten. I was required to have a physical examination before entering the neighborhood public school. This was my first physical examination, and Mom stayed next to me during each medical procedure. She protected her children physically, mentally, and morally and yet created a household life in which we were encouraged to spend time alone regularly and develop our independence. She had seen worldliness and steered us away from the disheartening blandness of living only for material goals. Yet she instilled a type of worldly poise: we were to be catlike, always able to land on all fours. Balance was taught to us like the common courtesies of thank you and please.

The day of the wedding, I could sense Mom's excitement. She chose to wear one of her classroom dresses, one in which she taught the mentally handicapped in the last of the many teaching jobs she held in her life. She believed in her students and was convinced that lack of love and attention were the most serious handicaps they faced. She spent her evenings talking on the telephone to their parents, encouraging the parents to have confidence in their own intelligence and that of their children.

Her woolen crepe dress for the wedding had a jewel neckline and three-quarter-length sleeves much like the others she had worn all my life. She always said it was the accessory or accent that moved anything beyond the ordinary. That day she carried her navy gloves and a kid handbag. She wore a "good" pair of oxfords, the dressy kind with mesh lattice work on the instep, and a blue hat.

I have seen that blue only once since then, when my husband and I stood on the black sand beaches of Guadeloupe and looked into the Caribbean Sea. It was a clear, pure blue, with no green, yellow, or white shafts of light to alter the perception of infinite depth.

The hat was small and round, shaped somewhat like an inverted shallow bowl hugging the round part of the head, the way an adult's hand cups the head of an infant. She wore it slanted toward the right side, over the right eye. It was secured with a black hat pin. A feather was attached to the hat, spiraling over its circumference and over her hair beneath like a flash of light on the wet plumage of a swift, long, tropical bird. It was a brilliant association with Mom's gentle brown complexion.

The wedding ceremony took place in a greenish-gray room in City Hall. The bride wore a light-colored dress and the groom wore dark trousers and a light jacket. The environment seemed somber for a marriage ceremony, especially for someone of African descent accustomed to bright, gay weddings with dancing and singing. The groom later remarked to my mother that the most exciting part of the celebration was the feather on her hat.

Introduction
Joyce Flynn

Now, walking along Frye Street, you sniff first the rusty tangy odor that comes from a river too near a city; walk aside so that Jewish babies will not trip you up; you pause to flatten your nose against discreet windows of Chinese merchants; marvel at the beauty and tragic old age in the faces of the young Italian women; puzzle whether the muscular blond people are Swedes or Danes or both; pronounce odd consonant names in Greek characters on shops; wonder whether Russians are Jews, or Jews, Russians—and finally you will wonder how the Negroes there manage to look like all men of every other race and then have something left over for their own distinctive black-browns.
There is only one Frye Street. It runs from the river to Grand Avenue where the El is.
All the World is there.

From the Foreword to "A Possible Triad on Black Notes"

The Frye Street that anchored a fictional universe in Chicago functioned as a daring symbol of the diversity, novelty, and opportunity available in cities like Chicago and Detroit, meccas for black migration from the South in the decades surrounding World War I. The architect of Frye Street, Marita Bonner (1899–1971), was one of the most versatile early twentieth-century black writers. Her contributions to *The Crisis* and *Opportunity* between the two world wars include essays, reviews, plays, short stories, and fictional narratives published in several parts. The focus of much of her work—urban life in the interwar period—probably stemmed from her residence in three urban centers: Boston, where she was born and educated; Washington, D.C., where she worked for eight years; and Chicago, where she moved after her marriage to William Almy Occomy in 1930 and lived for forty-one years, raising her three children, William Almy, Jr., Warwick Gale, and Marita Joyce Occomy.

Bonner's works offer the perspective of an educated black female consciousness on a rapidly changing America between the two world wars. She focuses on black Chicagoans and their neighbors, internal immigrants from the South or immigrants from Europe, as they deal with discrimination and the brutalized exhaustion of the working poor. Bonner's vision of Chicago contrasts sharply with that of Theodore Dreiser or of her own contemporaries James T. Farrell and Richard Wright. In her evocation of the cramped apartments in which mothers attempt to protect their children from the streets, she anticipates the heroine and architectural focus of Ann Petry's *The Street* (1946). Bonner's cityscapes capture the terrible cost of life on the northern urban frontier.

On the multi-ethnic Frye Street of Bonner's Depression fiction, black residents mingle with immigrants but watch the newcomers obtain better jobs and their children better futures. But "Frye Street (black)" saw no promise equal to the possibilities offered "Frye Street (white)." The black working mothers of Bonner's Chicago stories battle against poverty, gangs, and prejudice, but too often find that their children are destroyed while the parents are absent, working the long hours at low wages that are the share allotted them by prejudice in the new city.

Bonner's preparation for writing included the finest schooling then available, and that opportunity inspired her lifelong commitment to those less fortunate. She was one of four children born to Jospeh Andrew and Mary Anne (Noel) Bonner. She was raised in the Boston area and educated locally, attending Brookline High School, where she acquired musical training and the beginnings of her fluency in German. Upon entering Radcliffe College in 1918, she concentrated in English and comparative literature, winning admission to Charles T. Copeland's exclusive writing seminar. During Bonner's college years, black students at Harvard and Radcliffe were not allowed dormitory accommodations, but like the majority of women students enrolled, Bonner commuted from home. While still a college student, Bonner taught at a nearby Cambridge high school; after her graduation in 1922, she continued her teaching career, first in the Washington, D.C., area and later in Chicago. At Radcliffe, Bonner was active in campus activities such as the Radcliffe song competitions, which she won in 1918 and 1922. She continued her studies in musical composition and in German literature, which would be important influences on her later literary career.[1]

Literary Apprenticeship: The Early Sketches and Stories

Though Bonner had shared some of her writing with Radcliffe colleagues through the Copeland writing seminar and the Radcliffe songwriting competition, her first published works—"The Hands" and the autobiographical essay "On Being Young—a Woman—and Colored"—appeared in the black journal *The Crisis* in 1925, when she was living and working in Washington, D.C., and a member of Georgia Douglas Johnson's "S" Street salon. A poet, playwright, and composer thirteen years Bonner's senior, Johnson forged a lifelong friendship with the new arrival from Boston and involved her in regular Saturday night gatherings that included over the years such authors as Langston Hughes, Countee Cullen, Alain Locke, Jessie Fauset, S. Randolph Edmonds, Willis Richardson, May Miller, and Jean Toomer.[2]

These early pieces, as well as others published in the 1920s, are notable for their brevity, their original perspective on the unfolding action, and their striking imagery that unites theme and tone. In addition, they demonstrate Bonner's early interest in telling the stories of the black working class, stories largely neglected in the writings of her Afro-American contemporaries such as Jessie Fauset and Nella Larsen. Bonner's attempts to find the genre and narrative techniques most suited to her work proceeded unevenly through stories and sketches published between 1925 and 1928. During the twenties, she tended to shape essays, fiction, and even plays as personal meditations, making it difficult to classify her work generically. Bonner characteristically employed the second-person pronoun "you" in the narration that frames her stories and plays.

"The Hands: A Story" and "On Being Young—a Woman—and Colored" provide the sensitive perspectives of black female narrators. Observing the lives of the black masses, both women try to bridge the gap, if only in imagination. A very brief story, "The Hands," is framed by the opening meditation of a narrator who boards a bus and becomes fascinated by the work-roughened hands of an older male rider. She creates a whole imaginary world of work, love, and family served by those hands, described in terms of alligator scales and nodes on a branch. The narrator imagines the man's simple hard work, devout religion, and family life. The ending of this touching vignette of the worker repeats the narrator's dual fantasies: one about "snakes, peopling the forest" (likened to a jungle in the story); the other about "Christ-in-all-men."

These fantasies comment obliquely on the two-dimensional treatment of blacks in American literature. One aspect of this treatment was an exoticism with hints of the jungle or the tropics as exemplified in a number of early twentieth-century works, including Vachel Lindsay's "The Congo" (1914), Eugene O'Neill's *The Emperor Jones* (1920), and Countee Cullen's "Heritage" (1925). Another was the portrayal of dutiful, religious, excessively humble characters, a tradition dating back to nineteenth-century fiction and abolitionist tracts and updated in Bonner's day in O'Neill's *All God's Chillun Got Wings* (1924).[3] In "The Hands" Bonner seems to be expressing skepticism about romantic racialism of either kind.

Though less technically skilled than Bonner's later work, "The Hands" shows the same consciousness of class differences represented in "On Being Young—a Woman—and Colored." This autobiographical piece conveys skillfully and openly its author's sense of comparative privilege and obligation as well as her ambivalence about living in segregated Washington, "flung together . . . in a bundle" with other blacks "because of color and with no more in common." She feels obligated to identify with the black poor, even though that identification leads to entanglement in what she calls "the seaweed of a Black Ghetto."

Introduction

The essay also explores a dichotomy seen in many works by
Afro-American writers: the dichotomy between inner reality and
socially sanctioned racial and gender roles. Bonner laments the
fact that, like all black women, she is seen primarily as "a gross
collection of uncontrolled desires." Viewing her own situation,
she is determined to wait, with Buddha-like composure, until
"time is ripe" for her to rise to her full stature.

The breadth of Bonner's reading and her tendency to present
new angles on old subjects are evident in the two pieces from the
1920s that focus on male artist-heroes. "Nothing New" (1926) is
Bonner's first story with an explicitly Chicago setting. The story's
account of would-be painter Denny Jackson's collision with the
society around him touches on a number of themes that the
author would continue to develop: ties between white and black,
thwarted youthful aspiration, and the complexities of racial
intermixture. In "Nothing New" Bonner introduces her key
symbol of the Frye Street neighborhood as multi-ethnic cosmos,
an urban universe shared by Irish, Chinese, Russian, Jewish,
French, German, Swedish, and Danish immigrants, as well as
blacks, many themselves recent arrivals from the South. In
introducing Frye Street, Bonner uses the familiar second-person
narration of her early work:

> You have been down on Frye Street. You know how it
> runs . . . from freckled-faced tow heads to yellow Orien-
> tals; from broad Italy to broad Georgia; from hooked nose
> to square black noses. How it lisps in French, how it
> babbles in Italian, how it gurgles in German, how it
> drawls and crawls through Black Belt dialects. Frye Street
> flows nicely together. It is like muddy water.

But this image of Frye Street's ethnic groups "flowing nicely
together" is marred by two violent episodes that divide the
neighborhood into black and white. The protagonist Denny has
two collisions with the racially unjust society that surrounds the
comfortable ethnic cocoon of integrated Frye Street. The first of
these involves his crossing an imaginary racial divide in a public
park; the second, and more dangerous, involves his choice of a
white lover. He defends his right to love Pauline, a white art

student. In both these encounters, Denny refuses to heed repeated warnings to stay on his own side of an invisible color line. (Bonner's inspiration for the story of Denny's life and death may have derived from accounts of the much-publicized 1919 Chicago race riots. The days of violence were precipitated by the drowning of young Eugene Williams. While swimming, he had strayed from the unofficially black Twenty-seventh Street beach to the unofficially white Twenty-ninth Street beach, but could not approach the shore because of stone-throwing whites.)[4]

Bonner's Chicago stories of the thirties and forties would assume the background of episodes such as those experienced by Denny in "Nothing New." They would deal with Chicago as a fallen world both in terms of race relations and the doomed aspirations of the city's black immigrants from the South. Her last two stories published in the twenties—"One Boy's Story" and "Drab Rambles"—anticipate this development.

In "One Boy's Story" (1927), her only short story with a male narrator, Bonner continues the exploration of color issues. Told by a young black boy, the story treats the classic theme of the identity crisis that mixed racial origins create. (Bonner shared this interest in mulatto characters with such contemporaries as Nella Larsen, Jessie Fauset, Georgia Douglas Johnson, Paul Green, and Langston Hughes.) Donald, the young narrator—illegitimate child of a southern black woman and a white father—comes to a tragic awakening concerning his illegitimacy and the identity of his white father. Through Donald's absorption in a book of legends, Bonner evokes not only the biblical tale of David and Goliath, but the classical tragedies of father-son conflicts in the myths of Oedipus and Orestes.[5] The story's denouement is a paradigm of literary silencing and the dangerous truth that cannot be spoken: Donald, having unknowingly killed his real father, is wounded by his mother in a strange accident that results in the amputation of his tongue. Donald's recollections become blurred with the tales he has read:

a forked whip . . . I am Orestes with the Furies' whips in my mouth . . . I am Oedipus and . . . I cut [my tongue] out for killing my own father.

The maiming of the story's child narrator (and the fact that Bonner chose to publish this story under a pseudonym)[6] suggests both the pain and the forbidden quality of such distorted family relations.

One month later Bonner published "Drab Rambles" in *The Crisis*. The narrative frames two portraits, one male and one female, of black city dwellers in the final stages of being crushed by the economic slavery and racism they have encountered. The exact location of their city is unspecified, although there are similarities between Peter Jackson of Sawyer Avenue and the Georgia-born Chicago parents of Denny Jackson in "Nothing New." Both protagonists in "Drab Rambles" face destruction from a power structure that gives them few opportunities for employment: the man in the first sketch faces death from overwork, and the young woman in the second confronts either dismissal from her job or an unwanted liaison with her white employer that could produce a second yellow child for her to support. (The young mother's first child takes her name from her mother and is called Madie Frye.) The narrator of "Drab Rambles" elevates such mixed-race children to mythic status, asserting the black Everyman through the figure of the mulatto: "I am all men tinged in brown. I am all men with a touch of black. I am you and I am myself."

Other early pieces were less focused and less successful. "The Prison-Bound" (1926) is interesting as an early treatment of Chicago's impact on a simple black woman from the South, a situation later explored in "The Whipping" (1939) and "Reap It As You Sow It" (1940–41). A short essay, "The Young Blood Hungers" (1928), lacks a concrete central image, and its repeated phrases fall short of what was apparently intended to be a haunting refrain effect. But the essay's militant content and apocalyptic tone link it to the early stories and sketches and to Bonner's 1928 dramatic masterpiece *The Purple Flower*.

Experimental Plays

In Washington, influenced by Georgia Douglas Johnson and other playwriting members of the "S" Street salon,[7] Bonner attempted three plays: *The Pot Maker: A Play to be Read* (1927), *The Purple Flower* (1928), and *Exit, an Illusion* (1928). All three dramas feature elaborate stage directions couched in Bonner's second-person narration and innovative structures built around a central metaphor. *The Purple Flower* is generally regarded as Bonner's masterpiece and has been hailed by Margaret Wilkerson as "perhaps the most provocative play" written by a black woman during the first half of the twentieth century.[8] Bonner had deplored the lack of a theater for black Washington residents in her 1925 autobiographical essay. Theater historian Addell Austin has established that Bonner was a member of the Krigwa Players in Washington,[9] but Bonner's own dramas may have been intended for reading rather than performance. The plays were not produced in Bonner's lifetime.[10] All three dramas continue her exploration of the black American as Everyman/Everywoman and are structured as morality plays: the protagonists undergo a testing experience on an imagined stage whose fourth wall is the territory of death, a force personified as the mysterious lover Exit in Bonner's final play.

The test to determine true worth is explicit in the parable of the silver, brass, and tin pots preached by Elias in *Pot Maker*. *The Pot Maker*'s cottage setting suggests its affiliation with the folk-drama vogue in the American theater,[11] but it shares the premise of the urban *Exit, an Illusion*: in both plays the black male protagonist must decide whether to act with love and compassion toward a light-skinned black woman. His personal salvation depends upon his ability to love and, when necessary, forgive others. Both plays are short and suspenseful: in *The Pot Maker* the audience waits for the preacher to discover the flaw in his own wife; in *Exit, an Illusion*, for the arrival of Dot's white lover, who turns out to be Death.

Bonner's allegory of the black quest for freedom and happiness in post-Emancipation America, *The Purple Flower*, combines first- and second-person perspectives to define the "Us's," and sympathetic communal protagonist of the play. The "Us's" are situated on a plain that lies between a looming hill called Somewhere and a distant border called Nowhere, but they wish to climb the hill to reach the purple Flower-of-Life-At-Its-Fullest bloom at the summit. However, small, grotesque, and quick-moving White Devils defend the hill, which bears some relation to the "racial mountain" that Langston Hughes saw as an obstacle to the black artist.[12]

The Purple Flower is set at the time of the most powerful challenge to the White Devils ever mounted, a time of new strategies for the "Us's." The play begins in the "Middle-of-Things-as-They-Are," though this time is interpreted differently by the two groups. It spells the "End-of-Things for some of the characters and the Beginning-of-Things for others." On the surface, the play shares some characteristics with the black pageant movement that began with W. E. B. Du Bois's *The Star of Ethiopia* and continued with the work of such playwrights as Maud Cuney Hare and May Miller.[13] But Bonner explicitly orients the play toward the future rather than the past.[14] While symbolically rejecting the compromise course of Booker T. Washington,[15] *The Purple Flower* may also suggest the struggles of the third world against white colonialism.[16] E. Quita Craig in *Black Drama of the Federal Theatre Era* argues that Bonner's inclusion of drum music seems a deliberate Africanism,[17] an interpretation that lends itself to an international reading of the struggle of the "Us's" to gain the mountain with the purple flower.

The new plan to attain the flower involves the rejection of past strategies and a new blending of black experiences in a cauldron that may be magical. The concoction requires blood, either black or white, "blood for birth so the New Man can live." On one level, the ascent of the "Us's" deals with black aspiration in America and the possible relevance of the myth of the melting-pot, in which all ethnic groups are combined and transformed. On another level, the drama seems to assume a less optimistic solution, the inevitability of violent racial revolution, a theme echoed in "The Young Blood Hungers," published four months later.

Measuring the Black Metropolis: Chicago

When Bonner next examined the melting-pot, it was an on-site inspection of an urban crucible in the North. After moving to

Chicago as a bride in 1930, she took a short break from writing and then began to write and publish fiction exclusively. The subject of her new direction was the variety of black Chicago, its class and color demarcations, its interaction with European and to a lesser extent Asian immigrants, its strained relations between parents and children, and its vulnerability to crushing economic and social forces. She resumed publishing in 1933 under her married name and noted in the introduction to a three-part story called "A Possible Triad on Black Notes" that the piece was part of " 'Black Map,' a book entirely unwritten." Her eldest son believes he heard Bonner refer to the work-in-progress as "Frye Street Trilogy."[18]

During the thirties, Bonner made significant changes in her narrative technique to better convey the complexity of her subjects. The most notable was her new tendency to compose stories in several separately published parts, which allowed her to juxtapose different characters as well as outer and inner impressions of the same character. Her new narrative organization had been antic-ipated by the double narrative in "Drab Rambles," but Bonner intended a work much larger in scope than pairs or triplets of stories: her "Black Map" was planned on a scale comparable to James Joyce's mapping of the Irish capital in *Dubliners*.

The first of the new narratives of Chicago life, "A Possible Triad on Black Notes," was published as three parts in the July, August, and September issues of *Opportunity* 11 (1933). (With the exception of the early "Drab Rambles," published in *The Crisis* in 1927, all of Bonner's multipart narratives appeared in *Opportunity*. As the cultural arm of the Urban League, the magazine's emphasis was sociological and urban, making it especially appropriate for pieces of the cycle.)

Each of the three stories in "A Possible Triad" contains an internal juxtaposition of Chicago lives to supplement the larger juxtaposition of the triple framing. "There Were Three" (July 1933) describes the events that eventually destroy a light-skinned family of three and leaves open the surviving daughter's choice of social streams—black, white, or yellow. The author's foreword speaks of Frye Street as the ultimate ethnic intersection ("All the World is there") and serves as an advance introduction to the second and third stories, which deal with more "respectable" protagonists. In "Of Jimmy Harris" (August 1933), Jimmy, a hard-working and successful immigrant from Virginia, dies of a stroke as his wife Louise stalks his doctor for her next husband. By the final paragraph, the story's opening line, "Jimmy Harris was dying," has come to mean that the protagonist has been dying for the fifteen years since he left love and Luray, Virginia, for Chicago's prosperity. (Bonner steadfastly refused to romanticize the rural Southern pasts of her black Chicago characters, however. The near-starvation of the sharecropping family in "The Whipping," the inhuman adherence to the rules of the color caste by a prominent light-skinned family in "On the Altar," and the family violence of "One Boy's Story" and "Patch Quilt" seem to allow little happiness for blacks rich or poor in the early twentieth-century South.)

In the third story, "Corner Store" (September 1933), Bonner's sole white protagonist, Esther Steinberg, painfully misses her lost German-Jewish ghetto, remembering it as a place with more feeling than the comfortable but joyless life behind her husband's grocery store on Frye Street. Like "Of Jimmy Harris," "Corner Store" deals with marital betrayal and family strife. Esther's husband Anton, long involved with a woman of black and Jewish ancestry, is being blackmailed by his own daughter. Esther is prostrate and sobbing at the story's end, the fabric of her family having been irrevocably torn.

The two-part story "Tin Can" won the *Opportunity* literary prize for fiction in 1933 and was published in that magazine in July and August of 1934. With a more developed plot than most of Bonner's stories, "Tin Can" chronicles the transformation of a high-spirited seventeen-year-old con artist and high school student named Jimmie Joe into an inadvertent murderer. The other members of Jimmie Joe's family have only generic names—"Ma," "Little Brother," and "Pa"—but "Ma" in particular is drawn in detail. A hard-working and religious parent, Ma loses control over her elder son through overwork and fatigue. Images of hollowness reverberate throughout the story: the opening image of the tin can with pebbles, the near-emptiness of Ma's purse, the coffin that Jimmie Joe's twisted corpse cannot properly fill, and the ending's speeding, rattling patrol wagon that carries Ma off to the station house instead of the hospital because she collapses in grief but is thought to be drunk. The hollowness is also metaphorical in its applications: both representatives of authority in the black community, "Black Bass Drum," the principal, and the Reverend Brown, are hypocrites who preach to their impoverished charges virtues that they themselves flout. Jimmie Joe and his friends repudiate these male role models and turn to gangs instead. Like Richard Wright's *Native Son* (1940), "Tin Can" traces the effects of poverty, low expectations, and peer pressure on the development of personality.

"A Sealed Pod," with its image of peas close together but not touching, a metaphor of Frye Street, was published in 1936. It presents further portrayals of Frye Street families in trouble, and focuses on young Viollette Harris, "warmed with an odd mixture of uncontrolled passions and bloods" until she is murdered by the only man she has ever loved, an Italian immigrant named Joe Tamona. Three 1939 stories, "The Makin's," "The Whipping," and "Hongry Fire," also show the city's destruction of children virtually before their parents' eyes. In "A Sealed Pod," Ma Harris comes home from her all-night cleaning job to find Viollette with her throat cut. In the three 1939 stories, David Brown's parents in "The Makin's" are too preoccupied with their own self-destructive habits to do anything but applaud their son's decision to write numbers when he grows up; in "The Whipping," Lizabeth's son dies in a fluke fall when his mother slaps him for repeating a hurtful lie; and in "Hongry Fire" a mother seeing her children on the verge of ruin resorts to poisoning the daughter-in-law who is corrupting them. The innocent suffer more often than the guilty: the innocent Ma Harris returns every morning to an empty house and the wrong man is hanged for her daughter's death. Nothing happens to the irresponsible parents in "The Makin's," but the pathetic Lizabeth in "The Whipping" is accused of murdering her child and is too ignorant to defend or even explain herself. Like Lutie Johnson in Petry's *The Street*, she is ultimately overwhelmed.

Bonner's Chicago fiction does not present the middle-class element of black Chicago as a source of strength or hope for the black working class. In the pseudonymously written "Hate Is Nothing" (1938), Bonner, herself the target of prejudice on the part of Chicago's predominantly light-skinned middle-class matrons, awards a daughter-in-law victory over a mother-in-law whose notion of respectability is based on color rather than behavior. "Black Fronts," published the same year, presents three sketches of the lives of black married women in different strata of Chicago society. The most affluent of the three protagonists, the illegitimate daughter of a washerwoman by a white doctor, is viciously snobbish and color-conscious. Bonner's character Aunt Margaret in "Stones for Bread" (1940) is similarly pretentious, dismissing her less-educated and darker brother with contempt. The grandmother of the heroine in "On the Altar" is the most destructive of Bonner's enforcers of the color code. Mrs. Breastwood annuls her granddaughter Beth's marriage to a darker school classmate without Beth's knowledge. She even goes so far as to hire an obstetrician who will assure that the baby of the match is born dead: "Never can tell about colored babies. . . . Next one might have been a tar-kettle." While Mrs. Breastwood keeps Beth out of town and away from Jerry, she sends back social notices that serve as a bitter satire on color obsession within the black community:

> Mrs. Blanche Kingsman Breastwood and her
> granddaughter, the lovely Elizabeth Grey, dainty blonde
> replica of her mother, Mrs. Louise Grey—are circling the
> states.

Even some of the names (Blanche, Grey) underscore the persistent use of color as a gauge of human worth. Other upper-middle-class practices, including parties, weddings, and card playing, are also satirized.

Fully drawn examples of males in black middle- and upper-middle-class society are rare in Bonner; her caricatures of the principal and the minister in "Tin Can" have already been noted. Similarly, the protagonist of "High Stepper" has earned wealth but not respectability through his gambling house, and thus is scarcely an admirable figure in the community. For positive ideals, Bonner turns to the thrifty working class: the laborer/church deacon who helps others in "Drab Rambles," for example, or unpretentious Dan and Mary, building cleaners in "Stones for Bread," who, in contrast to the rest of the family, seem to represent a positive ideal of tolerance and economic self-reliance.

In her last published story, "One True Love" (1941), Bonner returned to some of the problems of black female aspiration to which she alluded in "On Being Young—a Woman—and Colored." Her heroine Nora changes overnight from "just a butter-colored maid with hair on the 'riney' side" to a determined young woman with a dream. Nora's dedication to studying the law is finally thwarted by exhausting full-time employment combined with color and class prejudice, obstacles Bonner had explored in the earlier autobiographical essay. The love that develops between Nora and Sam, "a runty, bow-legged, dark brown janitor's helper," suggests a *rapprochement* between light-skinned and dark, between the black intelligentsia and their working-class allies. However, this alliance is never tested because the story ends with Nora's death as she struggles to tell Sam that she loves him.

The last story in the Chicago cycle was "Light in Dark Places," completed in 1941. Conveying Bonner's deepening pessimism concerning the fate of young black Chicagoans, the story presents a new worry of growing up black and female in a city: the possibility of rape by a school classmate. Though the protagonist Tina is saved by the blind but quick-thinking grandmother, the reader senses that Tina will be radically altered by the experience. Bonner speculates mid-story on the reasons why black Chicago shapes so many young males like Luke, whose indifference to Tina's well-being is total and whose only motto is "Anything that gives Luke a good time!" She decides that the problems start with the excesses that characterize crowded Chicago:

> Too many young people: too few houses: too many things
> to long for and too little money to spend freely: too
> many women: too few men: too many men weak enough
> to make profit of the fact that they happen to be men:

too few women with something in them to make them
strong enough to walk over weak men: too much liquor:
too many dives: too much street life: too few lovely
homes: life from the start—too many people—too few
houses.

Too many peasants lured out of cotton and corn
fields. . . . Too many neon signs winking promises. . . .

All this slaps a woman—loose.

All this slaps a man loose from every decent bit of
manliness.

After 1941 Bonner wrote rarely, raised her three children, and
taught. Her interest in writing, however, was lifelong: at the
edge of sixty-eight, she mentioned on a Radcliffe alumna
questionnaire that she was currently enrolled in a correspon-
dence course from the Famous Writers School, an ironically
amateur affiliation given her talent and past record of publication and prizes. She never completed to her satisfaction her
planned charting of black Chicago. One reason for this was a
busy work and family life; but her increased intellectual
involvement with Christian Science and her growing despair
concerning the city's effect on the individual may have been
factors in her goodbye to Frye Street.

Marita Bonner died in 1971 of injuries she suffered in a fire in
her Chicago apartment—a city accident of the type she understood so well. But her writing has kept alive an entire world—the
stories and feelings of the black universe coming to consciousness
in northern cities in the decades that separated the world wars.
For that act of imaginative deliverance, future generations will be
grateful.

Notes

1. All information about Marita Bonner's college years was
supplied by Radcliffe archivist Jane Knowles, Radcliffe College.
On Bonner's later career see Joyce Flynn, "Marita Bonner
Occomy (1899–1971)" in *Afro-American Writers from the Harlem
Renaissance to 1940, Dictionary of Literary Biography* 51 (Detroit:
Gale Research, 1987), 222–28, and Diane Isaacs, "Marita

Bonner," in *Dictionary of the Harlem Renaissance* (Westport: Greenwood Press, 1984).

2. For an account of Georgia Douglas Johnson's life and work, see Winona Fletcher, "Georgia Douglas Johnson (1886–1956)," *Dictionary of Literary Biography 51: Afro-American Writers from the Harlem Renaissance to 1940* (Detroit: Gale Research, 1987), 153–64.

3. Some of Bonner's work seems particularly framed to suggest alternatives to O'Neill's plays *The Emperor Jones, The Hairy Ape*, and *All God's Chillun Got Wings*. O'Neill left Harvard one year before Bonner entered Radcliffe.

4. *The Negro in Chicago* was prepared by the Chicago Commission on Race Relations, on which Johnson served in the capacity of associate executive secretary. For background on early twentieth-century black Chicago, see Emmett J. Scott, *Negro Migration during the War* (Carnegie Endowment for Peace, 1920; rpt. New York: Arno Press and the New York Times, 1969), and Allan H. Spear, *Black Chicago: The Making of a Negro Ghetto, 1890–1920* (Chicago: University of Chicago Press, 1967). St. Clair Drake and Horace Cayton's *Black Metropolis: A Study of Negro Life in a Northern City* (New York: Harcourt, Brace, 1945) provides a rich study of a period closer to Marita Bonner Occomy's Chicago cycle.

5. For a discussion of the American mulatto and themes from classical tragedy, see Werner Sollors, "The Mulatto, An American Tragedy?," *Massachusetts Review: A Quarterly of Literature, the Arts, and Public Affairs* 27 (1986):293–316.

6. The pen name used by Bonner here is an amalgam of her own nickname and the first names of her brothers, Joseph and Andrew. She may have felt that a male name was more appropriate to the story's claim to be a boy's autobiographical narrative. On one other occasion, while dealing with in-law stresses, Bonner published a story about conflict between mother and daughter-in-law ("Hate Is Nothing") under a pen name, presumably for reasons of privacy.

7. See Fletcher, "Georgia Douglas Johnson," 154, 158.

8. Margaret Wilkerson, "Introduction" to *Nine Plays by Black Women* (New York: New American Library, 1986), xvii.

9. Addell Austin in conversation, September 1986. Professor Austin interviewed Willis Richardson before his death in 1977 and has amassed considerable information concerning the black theater scene in Washington, D.C., and New York City during the years of the Harlem Renaissance. For background on the Howard University Players and the Krigwa Players, see Austin's "Pioneering Black Authored Dramas," Ph.D. dissertation, Michigan State University, 1986, and Fannie Ella Frazier Hicklin, "The American Negro Playwright, 1920–1964," Ph.D. dissertation, University of Wisconsin, 1965, 34, 178.

10. Errol Hill and I concur on this point. See his discussion of *The Purple Flower* in "The Revolutionary Tradition in Black Drama," *Theatre Journal* 38 (December 1986):419–21.

11. Black and white playwrights were attracted to the folk play. Literary creators of American folk drama included Paul Green, Georgia Douglas Johnson, Lula Vollmer, Willis Richardson, and S. Randolph Edmonds, among others.

12. Langston Hughes, "The Negro Artist and the Racial Mountain," *Nation* 23 (June 1926); reprinted in *The Ideology of Blackness*, ed. Raymond Betts (Lexington: D.C. Heath, 1971), 82–86.

13. An anthology *Plays and Pageants from the Life of the Negro*, ed. Willis Richardson (Washington, D.C.: The Associated Publishers, 1930) presents a sampler of these dramas, which were often the work of black women authors.

14. Hill, "The Revolutionary Tradition in Black Drama," 419.

15. James V. Hatch, "The Purple Flower" in *Black Theater U.S.A.: Forty-Five Plays by Black Americans, 1847–1974*, ed. Hatch and Ted Shine (New York: The Free Press, 1974), 201.

16. Nellie McKay, "What Were They Saying? Black Women Playwrights of the Harlem Renaissance," forthcoming in *The Harlem Renaissance Re-Examined*, ed. Victor Kramer (New York: AMS Press, 1988).

17. E. Quita Craig, *Black Drama of the Federal Theatre Era* (Amherst: University of Massachusetts Press, 1980), 88.

18. Letter from William Almy Occomy, Jr., to Joyce Flynn, October 1986.

Note on the Text

Most of the pieces in this collection were previously published in *The Crisis* or *Opportunity*. Five stories—"On the Altar," "High Stepper," "Stones for Bread," "Reap It As You Sow It," and "Light in Dark Places"—existed only in a worn notebook, along with two fragmentary sketches. At some point in the years between her last publication in 1941 and her death in 1971, Marita Bonner copied the pieces longhand into the notebook with the dates of their original composition. The five complete stories are reproduced here essentially as Bonner wrote them in her final manuscript versions, which are now preserved in the Radcliffe College Archives. Some small changes in punctuation and (in the case of "On the Altar") in the names assigned to characters have been made for the sake of consistency, and gaps or crossed-out words in the manuscript have been indicated by square brackets. Bonner used her best handwriting and apparently glossed the hard-to-read words for the readers she knew would one day find her.

ESSAYS

On Being Young—
a Woman—
and Colored

You start out after you have gone from kindergarten to sheepskin covered with sundry Latin phrases.

At least you know what you want life to give you. A career as fixed and as calmly brilliant as the North Star. The one real thing that money buys. Time. Time to do things. A house that can be as delectably out of order and as easily put in order as the doll-house of "playing-house" days. And of course, a husband you can look up to without looking down on yourself.

Somehow you feel like a kitten in a sunny catnip field that sees sleek, plump brown field mice and yellow baby chicks sitting coyly, side by side, under each leaf. A desire to dash three or four ways seizes you.

That's Youth.

But you know that things learned need testing—acid testing—to see if they are really after all, an interwoven part of you. All your life you have heard of the debt you owe "Your People" because you have managed to have the things they have not largely had.

So you find a spot where there are hordes of them—of course below the Line—to be your catnip field while you close your eyes to mice and chickens alike.

If you have never lived among your own, you feel prodigal. Some warm untouched current flows through them—through you—and drags you out into the deep waters of a new sea of human foibles and mannerisms; of a peculiar psychology and prejudices. And one day you find yourself entangled—enmeshed—pinioned in the seaweed of a Black Ghetto.

Not a Ghetto, placid like the Strasse that flows, outwardly unperturbed and calm in a stream of religious belief, but a peculiar group. Cut off, flung together, shoved aside in a bundle because of color and with no more in common.

Unless color is, after all, the real bond.

Milling around like live fish in a basket. Those at the bottom crushed into a sort of stupid apathy by the weight of those on top. Those on top leaping, leaping; leaping to scale the sides; to get out.

There are two "colored" movies, innumerable parties—and cards. Cards played so intensely that it fascinates and repulses at once.

Movies.

Movies worthy and worthless—but not even a low-caste spoken stage.

Parties, plentiful. Music and dancing and much that is wit and color and gaiety. But they are like the richest chocolate; stuffed costly chocolates that make the taste go stale if you have too many of them. That make plain whole bread taste like ashes.

There are all the earmarks of a group within a group. Cut off all around from ingress from or egress to other groups. A sameness of type. The smug self-satisfaction of an inner measurement; a measurement by standards known within a limited group and not those of an unlimited, seeing, world. . . . Like the blind, blind mice. Mice whose eyes have been blinded.

Strange longing seizes hold of you. You wish yourself back where you can lay your dollar down and sit in a dollar seat to hear voices, strings, reeds that have lifted the World out, up, beyond things that have bodies and walls. Where you can marvel at new marbles and bronzes and flat colors that will make men forget that things exist in a flesh more often than in spirit. Where you can sink your body in a cushioned seat and sink your soul at the same time into a section of life set before you on the boards for a few hours.

You hear that up at New York this is to be seen; that, to be heard.

You decide the next train will take you there.

You decide the next second that that train will not take you, nor the next—nor the next for some time to come.

For you know that—being a woman—you cannot twice a month or twice a year, for that matter, break away to see or hear anything in a city that is supposed to see and hear too much.

That's being a woman. A woman of any color.

You decide that something is wrong with a world that stifles and chokes; that cuts off and stunts; hedging in, pressing down on eyes, ears and throat. Somehow all wrong.

You wonder how it happens there that—say five hundred miles from the Bay State—Anglo Saxon intelligence is so warped and stunted.

How judgment and discernment are bred out of the race. And what has become of discrimination? Discrimination of the right sort. Discrimination that the best minds have told you weighs shadows and nuances and spiritual differences before it catalogues. The kind they have taught you all of your life was best: that looks clearly past generalization and past appearance to dissect, to dig down to the real heart of matters. That casts aside rapid summary conclusions, drawn from primary inference, as Daniel did the spiced meats.

Why can't they then perceive that there is a difference in the glance from a pair of eyes that look, mildly docile, at "white ladies" and those that, impersonally and perceptively—aware of distinctions—see only women who happen to be white?

Why do they see a colored woman only as a gross collection of desires, all uncontrolled, reaching out for their Apollos and the Quasimodos with avid indiscrimination?

Why unless you talk in staccato squawks—brittle as seashells—unless you "champ" gum—unless you cover two yards square when you laugh—unless your taste runs to violent colors—impossible perfumes and more impossible clothes—are you a feminine Caliban craving to pass for Ariel?

An empty imitation of an empty invitation. A mime; a sham; a copy-cat. A hollow re-echo. A froth, a foam. A fleck of the ashes of superficiality?

Everything you touch or taste now is like the flesh of an unripe persimmon.

. . . Do you need to be told what that is being . . . ?

Old ideas, old fundamentals seem worm-eaten, out-grown, worthless, bitter; fit for the scrap-heap of Wisdom.

What you had thought tangible and practical has turned out to be a collection of "blue-flower" theories.

If they have not discovered how to use their accumulation of facts, they are useless to you in Their world.

Every part of you becomes bitter.

But—"In Heaven's name, do not grow bitter. Be bigger than they are"—exhort white friends who have never had to draw breath in a Jim-Crow train. Who have never had petty putrid insult dragged over them—drawing blood—like pebbled sand on your body where the skin is tenderest. On your body where the skin is thinnest and tenderest.

You long to explode and hurt everything white; friendly; unfriendly. But you know that you cannot live with a chip on your shoulder even if you can manage a smile around your eyes— without getting steely and brittle and losing the softness that makes you a woman.

For chips make you bend your body to balance them. And once you bend, you lose your poise, your balance, and the chip gets into you. The real you. You get hard.

. . . And many things in you can ossify . . .

And you know, being a woman, you have to go about it gently and quietly, to find out and to discover just what is wrong. Just what can be done.

You see clearly that they have acquired things.

Money; money. Money to build with, money to destroy. Money to swim in. Money to drown in. Money.

An ascendancy of wisdom. An incalculable hoard of wisdom in all fields, in all things collected from all quarters of humanity.

A stupendous mass of things.

Things.

So, too, the Greeks . . . Things.

And the Romans. . . .

And you wonder and wonder why they have not discovered how to handle deftly and skillfully, Wisdom, stored up for them—like the honey for the Gods on Olympus—since time unknown.

You wonder and you wonder until you wander out into Infinity, where—if it is to be found anywhere—Truth really exists.

The Greeks had possessions, culture. They were lost because they did not understand.

The Romans owned more than anyone else. Trampled under the heel of Vandals and Civilization, because they would not understand.

Greeks. Did not understand.

Romans. Would not understand.

"They." Will not understand.

So you find they have shut Wisdom up and have forgotten to find the key that will let her out. They have trapped, trammeled, lashed her to themselves with thews and thongs and theories. They have ransacked sea and earth and air to bring every treasure to her. But she sulks and will not work for a world with a whitish hue because it has snubbed her twin sister, Understanding.

You see clearly—off there is Infinity—Understanding. Standing alone, waiting for someone to really want her.

But she is so far out there is not way to snatch at her and really drag her in.

So—being a woman—you can wait.

You must sit quietly without a chip. Not sodden—and weighted as if your feet were cast in the iron of your soul. Not wasting strength in enervating gestures as if two hundred years of bonds and whips had really tricked you into nervous uncertainty.

But quiet; quiet. Like Buddha—who brown like I am—sat entirely at ease, entirely sure of himself; motionless and knowing, a thousand years before the white man knew there was so very much difference between feet and hands.

Motionless on the outside. But on the inside?

Silent.

Still . . . "Perhaps Buddha is a woman."

So you too. Still; quiet; with a smile, ever so slight, at the eyes so that Life will flow into and not by you. And you can gather, as it passes, the essences, the overtones, the tints, the shadows; draw understanding to yourself.

7

And then you can, when Time is ripe, swoop to your feet—at your full height—at a single gesture.

Ready to go where?

Why . . . Wherever God motions.

The Young Blood Hungers

The Young Blood sits—back to an Eternity—face toward an Eternity. Hands full of the things ancestry has given—thriving on the things today can give—guided vocationally—inducted spiritually—fed on vitamins—defended against diseases unthinkable—hungry.

The Young Blood hungers.

It's an old hunger. The gnawing world hunger. The hunger after righteousness.

—I speak not for myself alone.

Do not swiftly look and think you see and swiftly say, "It is not, most certainly, a hunger for righteousness this Young Blood feels!"

But it is. It is the Hunger.

Some Young Blood feels it—and then they see if they can out-strip it—if they can get rid of the gnawing—try to dance it off as a man smokes off a trouble—try to float it off on a drunken sea—try to cast a spell on it. Daze it off.

Sometimes the Old Blood perceives the hunger and offers food: "It's the World Hunger," the Old Blood says. "It's the Hunger-After-Righteousness. Take God. Take Him as we have taken Him."

That is what the Old Blood says: "Take God—Take Him as we have taken Him."

And the Young Blood sits still hungry and answers: "Not your God as you had Him."

The Young Blood sits. The Young Blood hungers yet. They cannot take God as the Old Blood takes Him.

Not God sitting at the top of a million worn orthodox steps. God in the old removed far-off Heaven. Not God showering thunder-wrath and stripping man of all Life's compensations to prove him righteous. Not God always offering a heavenly reward for an earthly Hell. Not God poured out in buttered sentences from the pulpit four or fives times a month. Not the Old Blood's God demanding incessant supplication—calling for constant fear.

Not the Old Blood's God—but the God His own Son said that He really is. His own Son, Jesus, who knew Him better than any earth-born creature knew Him. Jesus who said that He was a friendly father who wanted respectful fear and confidential chats and obedience to principle and cooperation and thanksgiving as much as He wanted supplication.—I speak not for myself alone, Lord. The Young Blood hungers.—

The Old Blood argues: "You don't seek God in too-brief garments and too-tinted cheeks—too fancy-free dance steps—too fancy-free Thoughts-about-Things."

Perhaps not—but how?

Up the million steps? Removed? Far? How? How?

The Young does not know. The Young hungers.

The Young Blood hungers and searches somehow. The Young Blood knows well that Life is built high on a crystal of tears. A crystal of tears filled with Illusory Veils of Blind Misunderstand-ings and Blunderings. Enough filmy veils wet with tears, stamped down hard beneath your feet to let you rise up—out—above—beyond.

Just think of the number of veils cast down! Just think of the tears to pack them down hard so you can stand on them.

Yet that is growing.

The Young Blood knows that growing means a constant tearing down of Illusory Veils that lift themselves thin—filmy—deceptive—between you and truth. Veils that flutter breath-thin across things and make you mistake the touch of Heaven for the touch of Hell.

Veils—breath-thin—so thin you feel them rather than see them.

Tearing down Illusory Veils. Jesus called it watching. Such watching that I of myself and you of yourself cannot do it alone. Veils lift themselves sometimes in the still of the night when even the soul is asleep. Eyes that kept Israel and did not slumber nor yet sleep are needed to help with the tearing down.

I speak not for myself alone, Lord. The Young Blood hungers for Eyes to watch.—

All this the Young Blood knows. All this and more.

Young Blood knows that some Truths solidified in Eternity will not rot until Eternity crumbles. Solidified in Eternity. One love perhaps is to be pure and clean or it is not love. When the mists of Half-Lies play around the face of a truth—Lord—the Young Blood hungers.

Solidified in Eternity—Rooted and tipping in Eternity. Young Blood knows this. And yet if you fumble through the mists of Half-Lies-About-Things to feel the Truth-About-Real-Things safe—sound—solid—behind you—are you a crab—a prude—out of step with your age?

Are there no regular drum-beats? Can't you mark your step to one drum that beats from the rim of Eternity up through the Dark Ages—through the Middle Ages—through Renaissances—through Wars and Remakings-of-Worlds—to the same rhythm?

Is there not a pulse-beat you can feel—beating—steady—Bloody Reigns and Terrors and Inquisitions and Torments—up to Hells-of-Republics and back?

Or is it, after all, a new gait for every new day?

A new drum?

A new rhythm?

A new pulse-beat?

A new step?

A new Heaven?

A new Hell?

Today, a Truth. Tomorrow, a Lie.

Everything new. Raw and new. No time to root before the sun sets its first rays of a new day dawning.

The Young Blood hungers for Truth for God. For the God they called Jehovah when Christ was yet to come. Where is Jehovah?—

A brief breath of a paper-weight-dress—slippers—perfumed—curled—rouged even. Can't you toss your soul out—up—beyond the mere room-full of brief breaths of dresses—perfumes—curls—rouge—and walk and talk to God?

Must you come—eyes down-cast—to an altar four or five times a month to meet God of a Sabbath morn? Can you only commune with Him when you take Christ's body and blood on an appointed day from hands not always too free from blood—before eyes that seem to lick out and eat up—lusting for Young Blood? Isn't it the call for God thrilling in the voice of Young Blood when it is lifted in song—no matter the song?

Isn't it God seeking God in the question of Young Blood when it asks: "Do you understand things? Sometimes I am afraid? Do you understand?"

If Young Blood knew how to converse with God—would so many Young feet stumble in the drunken mazes of seeking to find Self—seeking to find Truth—seeking to drown cries within—seeking enchantments to fill hollows within—seeking to catch up with something greater than yourself in a swift mad consuming fire-flash of living?

—It's the gnawing pains.—

Gnawing pains make you toss your body around. Make you toss your body now this way—now that. Young Blood hungers. Young Blood feels the gnawing pains of hunger—you do not know where your body will come—where it will go. All you wish is to toss your self away from the pain gnawing within.

—It's the gnawing pains.—

Can a mote appear to lay blindness across the vision?

Isn't there a part of Young Blood that leapt into being at Eternity and goes on through all Eternity? Isn't there something that sees beyond curls and rouge?

—I speak not for myself alone, Lord.—

Something winding and winding in the rhythmic inanities of a dance, Young Blood hears things beside the music—the feet—the talk—the chaff of laughter.

Sometimes when you teeter to a jazz-band's play voices speak within you and seem to say:

The Young Blood Hungers

You may prance, fool, prance
You may skim, you may slide,
You may dip, you may glide,
But you've lied to yourself,
Oh you've lied—lied—lied.
—Gave a damn for the night—
—Chanced your all upon Today—
But you've lied! Yes you've lied!
—I'm the Voice that never died.

Voices and Hunger. Searchings and Seekings. Stumbling—falling—rising again.

—I speak not for myself alone, Lord! The Young Blood hungers. —Back toward an Eternity. Facing Eternity. Perhaps that is the way in which Young Blood is to sit—back toward an Eternity—face toward an Eternity—hungering.

Perhaps it must be that God must be sought in new ways—new ways—fewer steps—fewer steps—each time there comes Young Blood—each time there comes Young Blood—until they find Him.

A few less steps each time. A few less steps each time.

Soon the top.

Then—no longer Hunger.

Then no longer—Hunger.

—I speak not for myself alone, Lord! The Young Blood hungers.—

PLAYS

The Pot Maker

A Play to Be Read

SETTING:

See first the room. A low ceiling; smoked walls; far more length
than breadth. There are two windows and a door at the back of the
stage. The door is between the windows. At left and right there are
two doors leading to inner rooms.

They are lighter than the door at back stage. That leads into the
garden and is quite heavy.

You know there is a garden because if you listen carefully you
can hear a tapping of bushes against the window and a gentle
rustling of leaves and grass.

The wind comes up against the house so much awash—like
waves against the side of a boat—that you know, too, that there
must be a large garden, a large space around the house.

But to come back into the room. It is a very neat room. There
are white sash curtains at the window and a red plaid cloth on the
table. Geraniums in red flower pots are in each window and even
on the table beside the kerosine lamp which is lit there. An
old-fashioned wooden clock sits on a shelf in the corner behind the
stove at the right. Chairs of various types and degrees of ease are
scattered around the table at center.

CHARACTERS:

The son—"called of God," Elias Jackson
His wife, Lucinda Jackson
His mother, Nettie Jackson
His father, Luke Jackson
Lucinda's lover, Lew Fox

17

As the curtain is drawn, see first the mother; a plump colored woman of indeterminate age and an indeterminate shade of brown, seated at the table. Luke, the father, whose brown face is curled into a million pleasant wrinkles, sits opposite her at the left.

Lew stands by the stove facing the two at the table. He must be an over-fat, over-facetious, over-fair, over-bearing, over-pleasant, over-confident creature. If he does not make you long to slap him back into a place approaching normal humility, he is the wrong character for the part.

You must think as you look at him: "A woman would have to be a base fool to love such a man!"

Then you must relax in your chair as the door at right opens and Lucinda walks in. "Exactly the woman," you decide. For at once you can see she is a woman who must have sat down in the mud. It has crept into her eyes. They are dirty. It has filtered through— filtered through her. Her speech is smudged. Every inch of her body, from the twitch of an eyebrow to the twitch of muscles lower down in her body, is soiled. She is of a lighter brown than the mother and wears her coarse hair closely ironed to her head. She picks up each foot as if she were loath to leave the spot it rests on. Thus she crosses the room to the side of Elias who is seated at the window, facing the center of the room.

It is hard to describe Elias. He is ruggedly ugly but he is not repulsive. Indeed you want to stretch out first one hand and then the other to him. Give both hands to him. You want to give both hands to him and he is ruggedly ugly. That is enough.

ARGUMENT:

When you see Elias he is about to rehearse his first sermon. He has recently been called from the cornfields by God. Called to go immediately and preach and not to dally in any theological school.

God summoned him on Monday. This is Wednesday. He is going to preach at the meeting-house on Sunday.

SCENE I:

As the curtain draws back, expectation rests heavily on every one.

The mother is poised stiffly on the edge of her chair. Her face and her body say, "Do me proud! You're my son! Do me proud."

The father on his side rests easily on his chair;

"Make all the mistakes you want. Come off top notch. Come off under the pile. You're my son! My son."

That sums them up in general too. Can you see them? Do you know them?

Elias *(rising and walking toward the table)*
You all set back kind er in a row like.
(He draws chairs to the far end of the room at right.)
There, there, Ma here! Pa there! Lew—
(He hesitates and Lew goes to Lucinda's side and sits down at once. This leaves Elias a little uncertain but he goes on.)
Now—
(He withdraws a little from them.)
Brothers and sisters.

Mother
M-m-m-m, 'Lias can't you think of nothin' new to say first? I been hearin' that one since God knows when. Seems like there's somethin' new.

Elias
Well, what'll I say then?

Mother
Oh—"ladies and gent'mun"; somethin' refined like.
(At this point, Lew and Lucinda seemed to get involved in an amused crossing of glances.)
But go on then, anything'll be all right.
(The mother stops here and glares at Lucinda to pay her for forcing her into back water. Lucinda sees Lew.)

Elias *(continuing)*
Well Brothers and Sisters! There is a tale I'd like for to tell you all this evening, brothers and sisters; somethin' to cheer your sorrowing hearts in this vale of tears.

Lucinda
What if their hearts ain't happen to be sorrowing?

Father (cutting in)
Boun' to be some time, chile! Boun' to be!
(The son flashes thanks to father. He appears to have forgotten the jibe and to be ignorant of the look of approval too. He is a delightful mutual peacemaker.)

Elias
A tale to cheer your sorrowing hearts through this vale of tears.—This here talk is about a potmaker what made pots.

Lucinda (laughing to herself—to Lew)
Huh, huh; Lord ha' mercy.

Mother (giving Lucinda a venomous glance and rising in defense)
Look here 'Lias, is that tale in the Bible? You is called of God and He ain't asked you to set nothin' down He ain't writ himself.

Elias
This is one of them tales like Jesus used to tell the Pharisees when he was goin' round through Galilee with them.

Mother
Jesus ain't never tol' no tales to Pharisees nor run with them either! Onliest thing He ever done was to argue with them when He met them. He gave 'em good example like.

Elias
Well this'n is somethin' like—wait you all please! Once there was a man what made pots. He lived in a little house with two rooms and all that was in those rooms was pots. Just pots. Pots all made of earthenware. Earthenware. Each one of them had a bottom and a handle just alike. All on them jes' alike. One day the man was talking to them pots—

20

Lucinda (*just loud enough to be disagreeable*)
  What kinder fool was talking to pots?

Elias (*ignoring her*)
  An' he says, "Listen you all. You all is all alike. Each on you
  is got a bottom to set on and a handle. You all is alike now but
  you don' have to stay that away. Do jes' as I tells you and you
  can turn to be anything you want. Tin pots, iron pots, brass
  pots, silver pots. Even gold." Then them pots says—

Mother
  Lias, who the name of God ever heard tell of a minister saying
  pots talked. Them folks ain't goin' to let you do it.

Elias
  Ma! Then the pots said, "What we got to do?" And the man
  he told them he was goin' to pour something in them. "Don't
  you all tip over or spill none of the things I put in you. These
  here rooms is goin' to get dark. Mighty dark. You all is goin'
  to set here. Each got to set up by hisself. On his own bottom
  and hold up his handle. You all is goin' to hear rearin' and
  tearin.' Jes' set and don't spill on the ground." "Master, I got
  a crack in me," says one of them pots, "I got a crack in me so's
  I can't hol' nuthin." Then the man took a little dirt and he
  spit on it and put it on the crack and he patter it—just as
  gentle like! He never stopped and asked "How'd you get that
  crack" and he patted it—just as gentle like! He some folks
  would have done. He stooped right down and fixed the crack
  'cause 'twas in his pot. His own pot. Then he goes out.
  Them rooms got so dark that a million fireflies couldn't have
  showed a light in there. "What's that in the corner?" says one
  of the pots. Then they gets scared and rolls over on the ground
  and spilled.

Lucinda
  Uhm.
  (*She sees only Lew again.*)

Elias (still ignoring her)

It kept getting darker. By 'n by noises commenced. Sounded like a drove of bees had travelled up long a elephant's trunk and was setting out to sting their way out thoo the thickest part. "Wah, we's afraid," said some more pots and they spilled right over.

For a long time them rooms stayed right dark and the time they was dark they was full of noise and pitchin' and tearin'—but pres'n'y the dark began leaving. The gray day come creepin' in under the door. The pot-maker he come in; "Mornin' y'all, how is you?" he asks.

Some of them pots said right cheery, "We's still settin' like you tol' us to set!" Then they looked at their selves and they was all gol'.

Some of them kinder had hung their heads but was still settin' up.

The pot-maker he says, "never min', you all, you can be silver. You ain't spilled over."

Then some of the pots on the groun' snuk up and tried to stand up and hol' up their heads. "Since you all is so bol' as to try to be what you ain't, you all kin be brass!"

An' then he looked at them pots what was laying on the groun' and they all turned to tin.

Now sisters and brothers them pots is people. Is you all. If you'll keep settin' on the truth what God gave you, you'll be gol'. If you lay down on Him, He is goin' to turn you to tin. There won't be nothin' to you at all. You be as empty as any tin can. . . .

Father

Amen, amen.

Elias

'Tain't but just so long that you got to be on this earth in the dark—anyhow.

Set up. Set up and hold your head up. Don' lay down on God! Don' lay down on Him! Don' spill on the groun'. No matter how hard the folks wear and tear and worry you. Set up and don' spill the things He give you to keep for him. They tore him—but He come into the world Jesus and He went out of it still Jesus. He set hisself up as Jesus and He ain't never laid down.

(Here, Lucinda yawns loudly and gives a prolonged "Ah-h-h-h-h!")

Elias

Set up to be gol' you all and if you ever feels weak tell God, "Master I got a crack in me." He'll stoop down and take and heal you. He won't ask you how you got cracked. He'll heal you—the pot-maker done it and he warn't God. The pot-maker he didn't blame the pots for bustin'. He knows that pots can bust and God knows that it wouldn't take but so much anyway to knock any gol' pot over and crack it an' make it tin. That's the reason He's sorry for us and heals us.
Ask Him. And set. Set you all. Don't spill on the groun'. Amen.

(There is a silence. The father looks along the floor steadily. Elias looks at him. Lucinda sees Lew. The mother sees her son. Finally Elias notes Lucinda has her hand in Lew's and that they are whispering together. But Lew releases her hand and smiles at Elias, rising to his feet at the same time.)
Lew (in a tone too nice, too round, too rich to be satisfactory)

Well, well folks! I'll have to go on now. I am congratulating you, sister Nettie, on such a son! He is surely a leadin' light Leadin' us all straight into Heaven.

(He stops and mouths a laugh.)

I'll be seein' you all at the meetin'—good night.

(He bobs up and down as if he were really a toy fool on a string.)

Ah—Lucinda—ah—may—I—ask—you—for—a drink of water if—ah—it do not bother you?

(The tone is hollow. There will be no water drunk though they may run the water. Lucinda smiles and leaves behind him giving a defiant flaunt as she passes Elias. This leaves the other three grouped beside the table.)

Father

That is a right smart sermon, 'pears to me. Got some good sense in it.

Mother

But them folks ain't goin' to sit there and hear him go on to tell them pots kin talk. I know that.

(A door bangs within the room in which Lucinda and Lew have disappeared. Lucinda comes out, crosses the stage, goes into the room at right. A faint rustling is heard within.)

Mother *(calling)*

'Cinda what you doin' in that trunk? Tain't nuthin' you need in there tonight

(The rustling ceases abruptly—you can almost see Lucinda's rage pouring in a flood at the door.)

Lucinda *(from within)*

I ain't doin' nothin—

(She appears at the doorway fastening a string of red beads around her throat.)

Mother

Well, if you ain't doin' nothin' what you doin' with them beads on?

Lucinda *(flaring)*

None of your business.

Mother

Oh it ain't! Well you jes' walk back in there and rest my best shoes under the side of the bed please, ma'am.

Father

Now Nettie, you women all likes to look—

Mother

Don't name me with that one there!

Elias

Ma don't carry on with 'Cinda so.

Mother

You ain't nothin' but a turntable! You ain't got sense enough to see that she would jam you down the devil's throat if she got a chance.

Lucinda

I'm goin' long out of here where folks got some sense.
(She starts off without removing the shoes.)

Mother

Tain't whilst to go. I'm goin' callin' myself. Give me my shoes.
(Lucinda halts at the door. There are no words that can tell you how she looks at her mother-in-law. Words cannot do but so much.)

Lucinda (slinging the shoes)
There.
(Elias picks them up easily and carries them to his mother. She slips them on, and, catching up a shawl, goes off at back followed by her husband. Lucinda stamps around the room and digs a pair of old shoes up from somewhere. She slams everything aside that she passes. Finally she tips one of the geraniums over.)

Elias (mildly)
Tain't whilst to carry on so, Lucinda.

Lucinda

Oh, for God's sake shut up! You and your "tain't whilst to's" make me sick.

(Elias says nothing. He merely looks at her.)

Lucinda

That's right! That's right! Stand there and stare at me like some pop-eyed owl. You ain't got sense enough to do anything else.

(Elias starts to speak. Lucinda is warmed to her subject. What can he say?)

Lucinda (even more rapidly)

No you ain't got sense enough to do anything else! Ain't even got sense enough to keep a job! Get a job paying good money! Keep it two weeks and jes' when I'm hoping you'll get a little money ahead so's I could live decent like other women—in my house—you had to go and get called of God and quit to preach!

Elias (evenly)

God chose me.

Lucinda

Yas God chose you. He ain't chose you for no preachin'. He chose you for some kinder fool! That's what you are—some kinder fool! Fools can't preach.

Elias

Some do.

Lucinda

Then you must be one of them that does! If you was any kind of man you'd get a decent job and hold it and hold your mouth shut and move me into my own house. Ain't no woman so in love with her man's mother she wants to live five years under the same roof with her like I done.

*(Elias may have thought of a dozen replies. He makes none.
Lucinda stares at him. Then she laughs aloud. It is a bitter
laugh that makes you think of rocks and mud and dirt and
edgy weather. It is jagged.)*

Yes you are some kinder fool. Standing there like a pop-eyed
owl.
(There follows the inevitable.)

The Lord knows what I ever saw on you!

Elias *(still evenly)*
The Lord does know Lucinda.
*(At that Lucinda falls back into her chair and curses aloud in
a singsong manner as if she were chanting a prayer. Then she
sits still and stares at him.)*

Lucinda
Elias—ain't you never wanted to hit nobody in your life?
*(Before he can answer, a shrill whistle is heard outside the
window at left. Lucinda starts nervously and looks at the
window. When she sees Elias has heard the sound she tries to
act unconcerned.)*

Lucinda
What kinder bird is that whistlin' at the window?
(She starts toward it. Elias puts out a hand and stops her.)

Elias
Tain't whilst to open the window to look out. Can't see
nothin' in the dark.

Lucinda
That ain't the side that old well is on is it? That ain't the
window is it?

Elias
You ought to know! Long as you been livin' here! Five years
you just said.

(There is a crackle of bushes outside the window close to the house. A crash. Then a sound of muttering that becomes louder and louder. A subdued splashing. Lucinda starts to the window but Elias gets there first. He puts his back to the wall.)

Lucinda

Somebody's fallin' into that well! Look out there!

Elias

Tain't whilst to.

Lucinda

Tain't whilst to! Oh, God—hear um calling! Go out there! Tain't whilst to!

(She tries to dart around Elias. They struggle. He seizes her wrists and drags her back. She screams and talks all the time they struggle.)

Call yourself a Christian! The devil! That's what you is! The devil! Lettin' folks drown! Might be your own mother!

Elias

Tain't my mother!—You know who it is!

Lucinda

How I know? Oh, go out there and save him for God's sake. *(The struggles and the splashing are ceasing. A long-drawn "Oh my God" that sounds as if it comes from every portion of the room, sifts over the stage. Lucinda cries aloud. It is a tearing, shrieking, mad scream. It is as if someone had torn her soul apart from her body. Elias wrenches the door open.)*

Elias

Now Cindy, you was goin' to Lew. Go 'long to him. G'long to him.

Lucinda (trying to fawn at him)

Oh! No! Elias, Oh Master! Ain't you no ways a man? I ain't know that was Lew! I ain't know that was Lew.—Oh, yes I did. Lew, Lew.

(She darts past Elias as if she has forgotten him. You hear her outside calling, "Lew, Lew." Full of mad agony, the screams search the night. But there is no answer. You hear only the wind. The sound of wind in the leaves. Elias stands listening. Then he closes the door. All at once there is the same crackling sound outside and a crash and a splash. Once more Cindy raises her voice—frightened and choked. He hears the sound of the water. He starts toward the door. "Go 'long to Lew," he shouts, and sits down. "You both is tin." But he raises himself at once and runs back to the door. "God, God, I got a crack in me too!" he cries and goes out into the darkness. You hear splashing and panting. You hear cries. "Cindy give me your hand! There now! You is 'most out." But then you hear another crash. A heavier splashing. Something has given away.

One hears the sound of wood splitting. One hears something heavy splashing into the water. One hears only the wind in the leaves. Only the wind in the leaves and the door swings vacant.

You stare through the door. Waiting. Expecting to see Elias stagger in with Lucinda in his arms perhaps. But the door swings vacant. You stare—but there is only wind in the leaves.

That's all there will be. A crack has been healed. A pot has spilled over on the ground. Some wisps have twisted out.)

The Purple Flower

TIME:
  The Middle-of-Things-as-They-are. (Which means the End-of-Things for some of the characters and the Beginning-of-Things for others.)

PLACE:
  Might be here, there or anywhere—or even nowhere.

CHARACTERS:
  Sundry White Devils (They must be artful little things with soft wide eyes such as you would expect to find in an angel. Soft hair that flops around their horns. Their horns glow red all the time—now with blood—now with eternal fire—now with deceit—now with unholy desire. They have bones tied carefully across their tails to make them seem less like tails and more like mere decorations. They are artful little things full of artful movements and artful tricks. They are artful dancers too. You are amazed at their adroitness. Their steps are intricate. You almost lose your head following them. Sometimes they dance as if they were men—with dignity—erect. Sometimes they dance as if they were snakes. They are artful dancers on the Thin-Skin-of-Civilization.)

  The Us's (They can be as white as the White Devils, as brown as the earth, as black as the center of a poppy. They may look as if they were something or nothing.)

SETTING:
  The stage is divided horizontally into two sections, upper and lower, by a thin board. The main action takes place on the upper stage.

30

The Purple Flower

The light is never quite clear on the lower stage; but it is bright enough for you to perceive that sometimes the action that takes place on the upper stage is duplicated on the lower. Sometimes the actors on the upper stage get too vociferous—too violent—and they crack through the boards and they lie twisted and curled in mounds. There are any number of mounds there, all twisted and broken. You look at them and you are not quite sure whether you see something or nothing; but you see by a curve that there might lie a human body. There is thrust out a white hand—a yellow one—one brown—a black. The Skin-of-Civilization must be very thin. A thought can drop you through it.

SCENE:

An open plain. It is bounded distantly on one side by Nowhere and faced by a high hill—Somewhere.

ARGUMENT:

The White Devils live on the side of the hill. Somewhere. On top of the hill grows the purple Flower-of-Life-at-Its-Fullest. This flower is as tall as a pine and stands alone on top of the hill. The Us's live in the valley that lies between Nowhere and Somewhere and spend their time trying to devise means of getting up the hill. The White Devils live all over the sides of the hill and try every trick, known and unknown, to keep the Us's from getting to the hill. For if the Us's get up the hill, the Flower-of-Life-at-Its-Fullest will shed some of its perfume and then there they will be Somewhere with the White Devils. The Us's started out by merely asking permission to go up. They tilled the valley, they cultivated it and made it as beautiful as it is. They built roads and houses even for the White Devils. They let them build the houses and then they were knocked back down into the valley.

SCENE:

When the curtain rises, the evening sun is shining bravely on the valley and hillside alike.

The Us's are having a siesta beside a brook that runs down the Middle of the valley. As usual they rest with their backs toward

31

Nowhere and their faces toward Somewhere. The White Devils *are seen in the distance on the hillside. As you see them, a song is borne faintly to your ears from the hillside.*

The White Devils *are saying:*

> You stay where you are!
> We don't want you up here!
> If you come you'll be on par
> With all we hold dear.
> So stay—stay—stay—
> Yes stay where you are!

The song rolls full across the valley.

A Little Runty Us
  Hear that, don't you?

Another Us *(lolling over on his back and chewing a piece of grass)*
  I ain't studying 'bout them devils. When I get ready to go up that hill—I'm going!
    (He rolls over on his side and exposes a slender brown body to the sun.)
  Right now, I'm going to sleep.
    (And he forthwith snores.)

Old Lady *(an old dark brown lady who has been lying down rises suddenly to her knees in the foreground. She gazes toward the hillside)*
  I'll never live to see the face of that flower! God knows I worked hard to get Somewhere though. I've washed the shirt off of every one of them White Devils' backs!

A Young Us
  And you got a slap in the face for doing it.

Old Lady
  But that's what the Leader told us to do. "Work," he said. "Show them you know how." As if two hundred years of slavery had not showed them!

Another Young Us

Work doesn't do it. The Us who work for the White Devils get pushed in the face—down off of Somewhere every night. They don't even sleep up there.

Old Lady

Something's got to be done though! The Us ain't got no business to sleep while the sun is shining. They'd ought to be up and working before the White Devils get to some other tricks.

Young Us

You just said work did not do you any good! What's the need of working if it doesn't get you anywhere? What's the use of boring around in the same hole like a worm? Making the hole bigger to stay in?

(There comes up the road a clatter of feet and four figures, a middle-aged well-browned man, a lighter-browned middle-aged woman, a medium light brown girl, beautiful as a browned peach, and a slender, tall, bronzy brown youth who walks with his head high. He touches the ground with his feet as if it were a velvet rug and not sunbaked, jagged rocks.)

Old Lady *(addressing the Older Man)*

Evenin', Average. I was just saying we ain't never going to make that hill.

Average

The Us will if they get the right leaders.

The Middle-Aged Woman—Cornerstone

Leaders! Leaders! They've had good ones looks like to me.

Average

But they ain't led us anywhere!

Cornerstone

But that is not their fault! If one of them gets up and says, "Do this," one of the Us will sneak up behind him and knock him down and stand up and holler, "Do that," and then he himself gets knocked down and we still sit in the valley and knock down and drag out!

A Young Us (aside)
Yeah! Drag Us out, but not White Devils.

Old Lady
It's the truth Cornerstone. They say they going to meet this evening to talk about what we ought to do.

Average
What is the need of so much talking?

Cornerstone
Better than not talking! Somebody might say something after while.

The Young Girl—Sweet (who just came up)
I want to talk too!

Average
What can you talk about?

Sweet
Things! Something, father!

The Young Man—Finest Blood
I'll speak too.

Average
Oh you all make me tired! Talk—talk—talk—talk! And the flower is still up on the hillside!

Old Lady
Yes and the White Devils are still talking about keeping the Us away from it, too.
    (*A drum begins to beat in the distance. All the Us stand up and shake off their sleep. The drummer, a short, black, determined-looking Us, appears around the bushes beating the drum with*

strong, vigorous jabs that make the whole valley echo and re-echo with rhythm. Some of the Us begin to dance in time to the music.)

Average

Look at that! Dancing!! The Us will never learn to be sensible!

Cornerstone

They dance well! Well!!
(The Us all congregate at the center front. Almost naturally, the Young Us range on one side, the Old Us on the other. Cornerstone sits her plump brown self comfortably in the center of the stage. An Old Us tottering with age and blind comes toward her.)

Old Us

What's it this time, chillun? Is it day yet? Can you see the road to that flower?

Average

Oh you know we ain't going to get up there! No use worrying!

Cornerstone

No it's not day! It is still dark. It is night.
(For the sun has gone and purple blackness has lain across the Valley. Somehow, though, you can see the shape of the flower on top of Somewhere. Lights twinkle on the hill.)

Old Us *(speaking as if to himself)*

I'm blind from working—building for the White Devils in the heat of the noon-day sun and I'm weary!

Cornerstone

Lean against me so they won't crowd you.
(An old man rises in the back of the ranks; his beard reaches down to his knees but he springs upright. He speaks.)

Old Man

I want to tell you all something! The Us can't get up the road
unless we work! We want to hew and dig and toil!

A Young Us

You had better sit down before someone knocks you down!
They told us that when your beard was sprouting.

Cornerstone (to Youth)

Do not be so stupid! Speak as if you had respect for that beard!

Another Young Us

We have! But we get tired of hearing "you must work" when
we know the old Us built practically every inch of that hill and
are yet Nowhere.

First Young Us

Yes, all they got was a rush down the hill—not a chance to
take a step up!

Cornerstone

It was not time then.

Old Man (on the back row)

Here comes a Young Us who has been reading in the books!
Here comes a Young Us who has been reading in the books!
He'll tell us what the books say about getting Somewhere.
  (A Young Man pushes through the crowd. As soon as he
  reaches the center front, he throws a bundle of books.)

Young Man

I'm through! I do not need these things! They're no good!

Old Man (pushes up from the back and stands beside him)

You're through! Ain't you been reading in the books how to
get Somewhere? Why don't you tell us how to get there?

36

Young Man

I'm through I tell you! There isn't anything in one of these books that tells Black Us how to get around White Devils.

Old Man (*softly—sadly*)

I thought the books would tell us how!

Young Man

No! The White Devils wrote the books themselves. You know they aren't going to put anything like that in there!

Yet Another Old Man (*throwing back his head and calling into the air*)

Lord! Why don't you come by here and tell us how to get Somewhere?

A Young Man (*who had been idly chewing grass*)

Aw, you ought to know by now that isn't the way to talk to God!

Old Man

It ain't! It ain't! It ain't! It ain't! Ain't I been talking to God just like that for seventy years? Three score and ten years— Amen!

The Grass Chewer

Yes! Three score and ten years you been telling God to tell you what to do. Telling Him! And three score and ten years you been wearing your spine double sitting on the rocks in the valley too.

Old Us

He is all powerful! He will move in his own time!

Young Us

Well, if He is all powerful, God does not need you to tell Him what to do.

Old Us

Well what's the need of me talkin' to Him then?

Young Us

Don't talk so much to Him! Give Him a chance! He might want to talk to you but you do so much yelling in His ears that He can't tell you anything.

(There is a commotion in the back stage. Sweet comes running to Cornerstone crying.)

Sweet

Oh—oo—!

Cornerstone

What is it, Sweet?

Sweet

There's a White Devil sitting in the bushes in the dark over there! There's a White Devil sitting in the bushes over in the dark! And when I walked by—he pinched me!

Finest Blood (catching a rock)

Where is he, sister?

(He starts toward the bushes.)

Cornerstone (screaming)

Don't go after him son! They will kill you if you hurt him!

Finest Blood

I don't care if they do. Let them. I'd be out of this hole then!

Average

Listen to that young fool! Better stay safe and sound where he is! At least he got somewhere to eat and somewhere to lay his head.

Finest Blood

Yes I can lay my head on the rocks of Nowhere.

(Up the center of the stage toils a new figure of a square-set middle-aged Us. He walks heavily for in each hand he carries a heavy bag. As soon as he reaches the center front he throws the bags down groaning as he does so.)

An Old Man

'Smatter with you? Ain't them bags full of gold.

The Newcomer

Yes, they are full of gold!

Old Man

Well why ain't you smiling then? Them White Devils can't have anything no better!

The Newcomer

Yes they have! They have Somewhere! I tried to do what they said. I brought them money, but when I brought it to them they would not sell me even a spoonful of dirt from Somewhere! I'm through!

Cornerstone

Don't be through. The gold counts for something. It must!

(An Old Woman cries aloud in a quavering voice from the back.)

Old Lady

Last night I had a dream.

A Young Us

Dreams? Excuse me! I know I'm going now! Dreams!

Old Lady

I dreamed that I saw a White Devil cut in six pieces—head here *(pointing)*, body here—one leg here—one there—an arm here—an arm there.

An Old Man

Thank God! It's time then!

Average

Time for what? Time to eat? Sure ain't time to get Somewhere!

Old Man *(walking forward)*

It's time! It's time! Bring me an iron pot!

Young Us
> Aw don't try any conjuring!

Old Man (louder)
> Bring me a pot of iron. Get the pot from the fire in the valley.

Cornerstone
> Get him the pot!
>> *(Someone brings it up immediately.)*

Old Man (walking toward pot slowly)
> Old Us! Do you hear me. Old Us that are here do you hear me?

All the Old Us (cry in chorus)
> Yes, Lord! We hear you! We hear you!

Old Man (crying louder and louder)
> Old Us! Old Us! Old Us that are gone, Old Us that are dust do you hear me?
>> *(His voice sounds strangely through the valley. Somewhere you think you hear—as if mouthed by ten million mouths through rocks and dust—"Yes—Lord!—We hear you! We hear you"!)*
>
> And you hear me—give me a handful of dust! Give me a handful of dust! Dig down to the depths of the things you have made! The things you formed with your hands and give me a handful of dust!
>> *(An Old Woman tottering with the weakness of old age crosses the stage and going to the pot, throws a handful of dust in. Just before she sits down again she throws back her head and shakes her cane in the air and laughs so that the entire valley echoes.)*

A Young Us
> What's the trouble! Choking on the dust?

Old Woman
> · No child! Rejoicing!

Young Us
   Rejoicing over a handful of dust?

Old Woman
   Yes. A handful of dust! Thanking God I could do something
   if it was nothing but make a handful of dust!

Young Us
   Well dust isn't much!

Old Man (at the pot)
   Yes, it isn't much! You are dust yourself; but so is she. Like
   everything else, though, dust can be little or much, according
   to where it is.
      (The Young Us who spoke subsides. He subsides so
      completely that he crashes through the
      Thin-Skin-of-Civilization. Several of his group go too. They
      were thinking.)

Old Man (at the pot)
   Bring me books! Bring me books!

Young Us (who threw books down)
   Take all these! I'll light the fire with them.

Old Man
   No, put them in the pot. (Young Us does so.) Bring me gold!

The Man of the Gold Bags
   Here take this! It is just as well. Stew it up and make teething
   rings!!
      (He pours it into the pot.)

Old Man
   Now bring me blood! Blood from the eyes, the ears, the whole
   body! Drain it off and bring me blood! (No one speaks or
   moves.) Now bring me blood! Blood from the eyes, the ears,
   the whole body! Drain it off! Bring me blood!! (No one speaks

or moves.) Ah hah, hah! I knew it! Not one of you willing to pour his blood in the pot!

Young Us *(facetiously)*
How you going to pour your own blood in there? You got to be pretty far gone to let your blood run in there. Somebody else would have to do the pouring.

Old Man
I mean red blood. Not yellow blood, thank you.

Finest Blood *(suddenly.)*
Take my blood!
(He walks toward the pot.)

Cornerstone
O no! Not my boy! Take me instead!

Old Man
Cornerstone we cannot stand without you!

An Old Woman
What you need blood for? What you doing anyhow? You ain't told us nothing yet. What's going on in that pot?

Old Man
I'm doing as I was told to do.

A Young Us
Who told you to do anything?

Old Man
God. I'm His servant.

Young Us *(who spoke before)*
God? I haven't heard God tell you anything.

Old Man
You couldn't hear. He told it to me alone.

Old Woman

I believe you. Don't pay any attention to that simpleton! What God told you to do?

Old Man

He told me take a handful of dust—dust from which all things came and put it in a hard iron pot. Put it in a hard iron pot. Things shape best in hard molds!! Put in books that Men learn by. Gold that Men live by. Blood that lets Men live.

Young Us

What you supposed to be shaping? A man?

Old Us

I'm the servant. I can do nothing. If I do this, God will shape a new man Himself.

Young Man

What's the things in the pot for?

Old Man

To show I can do what I'm told.

Old Woman

Why does He want blood?

Old Man

You got to give blood! Blood has to be let for births, to give life.

Old Woman

So the dust wasn't just nothing? Thank God!

Youth

Then the books were not just paper leaves? Thank God!

The Man of the Gold Bags

Can the gold mean something?

Old Man

Now I need the blood.

Finest Blood

I told you you could take mine.

Old Man

Yours!

Finest Blood

Where else could you get it? The New Man must be born. The night is already dark. We cannot stay here forever. Where else could blood come from?

Old Man

Think child. When God asked a faithful servant once to do sacrifice, even His only child, where did God put the real meat for sacrifice when the servant had the knife upon the son's throat?

Old Us (*in a chorus*)

> *In the bushes, Lord!*
> *In the bushes, Lord!*
> *Jehovah put the ram*
> *In the bushes!*

Cornerstone

I understand!

Finest Blood

What do you mean?

Cornerstone

Where were you going a little while ago? Where were you going when your sister cried out?

Finest Blood

To the bushes! You want me to get the White Devil?
(*He seizes the piece of rock and stands to his feet.*)

44

Old Man

No! No! Not that way. The White Devils are full of tricks. You must go differently. Bring him gifts and offer them to him.

Finest Blood

What have I to give for a gift?

Old Man

There are the pipes of Pan that every Us is born with. Play on that. Soothe him—lure him—make him yearn for the pipe. Even a White Devil will soften at music. He'll come out, and he only comes to try to get the pipe from you.

Finest Blood

And when he comes out, I'm to kill him in the dark before he sees me? That's a White Devil trick!

Old Man

An Old Us will never tell you to play White Devil's games! No! Do not kill him in the dark. Get him out of the bushes and say to him: "White Devil, God is using me for His instrument. You think that it is I who play on this pipe! You think that is I who play upon this pipe so that you cannot stay in your bushes. So that you must come out of your bushes. But it is not I who play. It is not I, it is God who plays through me—to you. Will you hear what He says? Will you hear? He says it is almost day, White Devil. The night is far gone. A New Man must be born for the New Day. Blood is needed for birth. Blood is needed for the birth. Come out, White Devil. It may be your blood—it may be mine—but blood must be taken during the night to be given at the birth. It may be my blood—it may be your blood—but everything has been given. The Us toiled to give dust for the body, books to guide the body, gold to clothe the body. Now they need blood for birth so the New Man can live. You have taken blood. You must give blood. Come out! Give it." And then fight him!

Finest Blood
I'll go! And if I kill him?

Old Man
Blood will be given!

Finest Blood
And if he kills me?

Old Man
Blood will be given!

Finest Blood
Can there be no other way—cannot this cup pass?

Old Man
No other way. It cannot pass. They always take blood. They built up half their land on our bones. They ripened crops of cotton, watering them with our blood. Finest Blood, this is God's decree: "You take blood—you give blood. Full measure—flooding full—over—over!"

Finest Blood
I'll go.
(*He goes quickly into the shadow. Far off soon you can hear him—his voice lifted, young, sweet, brave and strong.*)
White Devil! God speaks to you through me!—Hear Him!—Him! You have taken blood: there can be no other way. You will have to give blood! Blood!
(*All the Us listen. All the valley listens. Nowhere listens. All the White Devils listen. Somewhere listens.*
Let the curtain close leaving all the Us, the White Devils, Nowhere, Somewhere, listening, listening. Is it time?)

Exit, an Illusion

A One-Act Play

Foreword
(Which presents the setting, the characters, and the argument)

The room you are in is mixed.

It is mixed.

There are ragged chairs with sorry sagging ragged bottoms.—There are lace curtains with sorry ragged holes—but all over the chairs are scattered clothes, mostly lingerie of the creamiest, laciest, richest, pastel-crepe variety.

Everything is mixed.

Dishes are pushed back on the table. They may be yesterday's dishes or they may be today's. But dishes are pushed back and the tablecloth is rumpled back. A pair of red kid pumps are on the edge of the table. Your eyes skip from the scarlet omen of their owner's hasty death— omen, if the bottom still holds in superstition—

Shoes mixed with dishes on the table.

Newspapers, pillows, shoes and stockings are scattered across the floor, making a path straight to an exquisite dressing-table of the variety type. This stands at the extreme right of the stage.

There is a window at right back—nearly at the center—through which you see snow falling. Directly beside the window there is a door which must lead into an inner hall. It is not stout enough to be an outer door. It is the brownish sort of nondescript door that shuts a cheap flat off from the rest of the world.

On the left side of the room is an open couch-bed. The sheets and blankets depend almost to the floor in uneven jags. Easily, then, you can see the figure of a woman lying there. Her hair which is a light brown—lies with a thick waving around her head. Her face—thin—is almost as pale as the sheets. She is sleeping with an arm hung over the side of the bed. Even though she keeps tossing and twitching as if she would come awake, she holds her arm over the side.

Down on the floor on the same side, lying so that her arm falls across him—there is a man. A part of his face shows against the bed-clothes and you can see he is blackly brown with the thin high-poised features that mark a "keen black man."

You can see at a glance that his slender body is cast for high things. High things. High things of the soul if the soul is fully living—high things of the flesh if the soul is fully dead.

He is Buddy.

The girl is Dot.

You are in their flat.

They are most assuredly not brother and sister.

Neither are they man and wife.

The room is mixed.

—Dot suddenly leans over the side toward Buddy. You wonder how she awakens so easily.

Dot

Well Buddy I got a date. I got to get gone. Buddy! Buddy!
(She leans over further and shakes him.)

Buddy

Hunh—hunh? What say, Dot? *(He wakes up.)* What say Dot? *(He yawns.)* Uh-uh! Guess I was sleep. What say?

Dot

I say I got a date, Buddy.

Buddy *(fully awake at once)*

Date? Where you think you're going keeping a date sick as a dog and with the snow on the ground!
(He looks toward the window.)
Snowing now! Where you think you're going?

Dot

I got a date I tell you!

Buddy

An' I tell you you ain't going to keep it!

Dot

Aw cut that stuff! How long since you thought you could tell me when to go and when to come! Store that stuff!

Buddy

I ain't storing nothing! You ain't going, I say.

Dot

Aw Buddy I been knowing the guy all my life! Played with him when I's a kid! Been on parties with him since I been going around!

Buddy

Aw don't try that old friend stuff! What's his name?

Dot

Exit.

Buddy

Exit? Exit! Where'd he get that! off the inside of a theayter door? Exit! Exit! What's his other name or is that the onliest one he got?

Dot

Mann. Exit Mann. That's his name. Yeah—
(She hesitates and seems to be uncertain.)

Buddy

Well it sure is a rotten name! Must be hiding from the cops behind it!
(Dot takes this opportunity to rise from her couch. The filmy night garments cling to her almost as closely as her flesh. You see she is not curved. You see she is flat where she should curve, sunken where she should be flat. You wish she would lie down again but she gets up—almost falls back—takes hold

49

of the back of the chair and passes across the room to the dressing table.)

Buddy

Look at you! 'Bout to fall down! You better lay down again.
(Dot has begun to brush her hair before the dressing table. She brushes rapidly with strokes that grow vigorous as if each one made some new strength start up in her.)

Dot

Aw let me alone! I'm going out!
(Buddy sits on the floor and watches her. She rouges her cheeks and paints her lips and begins to powder heavily with white powder.)

Buddy

You ain't fixin' to go out passing are you?

Dot

Aw don't ask so many fool questions!

Buddy *(growing angry)*

Don't get too smart! Guess there's something after all in what the fellers been saying 'bout you anyhow.

Dot

What your nigger friends been saying now?

Buddy

Nigger friends? You're a nigger yourself for all your white hide!

Dot *(shrugging)*

I may not be—You'd never know!

Buddy

Aw shut up! You'd like to think ya was white! You'd have never lived with niggers if you'd a been all white and had a crack at a white man!

(Dot starts to speak—changes her mind—and paints her lips again.)

Buddy *(after a second's silence)*
   Take some of that stuff off!

Dot
   I can't! Mann likes a woman like me to paint up so I'll flash out above the crowd.

Buddy
   Mann! what's Mann got to do with the way you look! Look here you! You been running 'round with this fellow Mann?
      (He plunges to his feet and lunges toward her.)
   Is he the white feller they been seeing you out with for the past three months?

Dot
   They? What they? Some more of your—!

Buddy
   Don't call them niggers again you half-white—
      (Dot catches him by the shoulder and pushes him away.—She selects a piece of clothes out of a drawer.)

Dot
   I told you in the beginning I been knowing this guy all my life! Been out with him!

Buddy
   Is he white?

Dot
   I don't know!

Buddy
   You don't know! Where'd you meet him?

51

Dot

Aw for God sake shut up and let me alone! I never met him! This is the last time I'm going to tell you I been knowing him all my life!

Buddy

Naw I ain't lettin' you alone! Naw I ain't letting you alone! This is the guy the fellers been telling me about! This is the guy! Ol' lop-sided lanky white thing! Been hanging around you at all the cafes and dances and on the streets all the time I'm out of the city! I'm out of the city—working to keep you— you hanging around with some no count white trash! So no count he got to come in nigger places, to nigger parties and then when he gets there—can't even speak to none of them. Ain't said a word to nobody the fellers say! Ain't said a word! Just settin' 'round—settin' 'round—looking at you—hanging around you—dancin' with you! He better not show hisself 'round here while I'm here!

Dot

He can't never come when you're here.

Buddy

You right he can't come here. Can't never come! He better be afraid of me.

Dot

He ain't afraid of you. He's afraid of your love for me.

Buddy (laughing shortly)

Aw for crap sake! My love! He ain't afraid of my love! He's afraid of my fist!

> (*Dot does not seem to hear him now. She talks to herself— "It's almost time! It's almost time!" Buddy hears her the second she speaks.*)

Almost time for what?

Dot

Him to come!

Buddy

Who?

Dot

Exit!

Buddy (cursing)

He ain't coming here! He ain't coming here! I'll knock his head clean off his shoulders if he comes here!

Dot

He's coming!

Buddy

I'll kill you 'fore he gets here and then kill him when he comes!

Dot

Aw Buddy—don't take on so! If you love me he can't come in between your love and come to me!
    (Buddy curses until his veins are swollen—packed full of the poison of the curses.)

Buddy

Damn you! Damn you! Trying to throw this "your love" stuff out to cam'flage and hide behind. I tol' you when we were fussing before you went to sleep that I didn't believe you when you said everybody was lying on you! You said everybody was lying and you was tellin' the truth! Say you ain't never been with other men! Naw I don't love you!
    (He breaks off and rushes to a drawer and snatches out a mean, ugly, blue-black, short pistol.)

Dot (screaming and overturning her chair)

Aw Buddy—Buddy don't! You love me!

53

Buddy

Shut up!!
> (He lifts the gun as if he were going to bring it down—raking
> her with fire the length of her body. He stops-)

'Naw I don't love you! Half-white rat!

Dot (crawling to her knees away from him)

Then he's got to come! I got to go with him!

Buddy

Yas he's got to come! And when he comes I'll fix you both!
Get up!
> (He prods her with his foot.)

Get up! Get up and dress to go out before your Exit is here!
Exit! Exit! I'll Exit him when I get through with you!
> (Dot completes her powdering then she suddenly reaches her
> hat down from a hook above the table. It is a smart black
> turban. It is black crepe and is wound and wound around.
> She snatches up a sealskin coat that has been lying on another
> chair and begins to put it on.)

Buddy

You must be foolish! What you putting the coat on over the
night-clothes for?

Dot

I ain't got time to put no more on.

Buddy

Aw yes you got time, sister! Put on all you want! I ain't going
to run you off before he gets here! You ain't going 'till your Exit
comes!

Dot

This is all I need—all I need! I'm ready.

Buddy

You're ready—where's your friend? Can't go without him!

Dot

He's here! *(She points.)* There he is.

(And close behind Buddy you see a man standing. He is half in the shadow. All you can see is a dark overcoat, a dark felt hat. You cannot see his face for his back is turned. You wonder how he came there. You wonder if perhaps he has not been there all the while.)

Buddy *(starting back as he sees the man)*

You're a regular sneak, ain't you! Ain't enough to sneak in and take a man's girl while he's out workin'! Got to sneak in his house! Sneak in on him when he's minding his business!

(The man does not move or answer. Dot's color is bright. Her eyes glow in the semi-shadow. The lights in the room seem dimmer somehow. Dot is breathing so that the fur mounts and slides—mounts and slides on her bosom. She keeps wetting her lips as if they were drying out. She starts across the floor toward him but pauses and draws back almost at once.)

Buddy *(still talking to the man)*

Turn around and say something! Turn around and say something! They say all you do is hang around niggers' places and keep a still tongue! *(To Dot:)* Go on over! Go on up to your Exit. Go on so you can go off the way I am sending you off. Go off like you lived! lying in some man's arms—then lying to me. *(As if to himself:)* That's the way to die anyhow: jus' like you lived!

Dot *(rubbing a hand across her face)*

Buddy! *(gasping)* Buddy! Say you love me! I don't want to go! I don't want to go with him!

(Buddy's answer is an inarticulate wild roar: "Get on to him! Get on over to him! With a scream and a quick run Dot crosses the little space and as quickly the man opens his arms and draws her to him without turning around.)

Dot (*crying smothered against the coat as if she were far away*)
Buddy—Buddy—Buddy! Do you love me? Say you love me before I go!
(*As she cries out the man begins to walk toward the back door. Buddy curses and fires at the same time. A stray shot strikes the light. It goes out. Buddy scratches a match and you see the man standing in the doorway—about to cross the threshold. His back is still turned but as you look he slowly begins to turn around.*)

Buddy
Mann? Mann!! Dot! Dot!
(*At that the man turns fully and you see Dot laid limp—hung limp—silent. Above her, showing in the match light between the overcoat and the felt hat are the hollow eyes and fleshless cheeks of Death. But almost at once the light flares back. You see the room as it was at first. Dot on her couch with her arms hanging over the side—Buddy lying beside the couch. The red shoes on the table.*)

Dot (*struggling awake*)
Buddy!
(*You can hear a rattling in her throat. A loud rattling. The rattling of breath soon to cease.*)
Buddy!!! Buddy!! Aw God, he can't hear me!—Buddy, do you love me? Say you love me 'fore I go! Aw—ah—ah—!"
(*The rattling is loud—loud. It stops on a high note. She stretches rigid and is still. The room is quiet an instant. You think you hear the rattling, though.*)

Buddy (*striving in his sleep*)
Exit!! Mann!! Exit! (*He pauses—then cries aloud:*) You lied! Naw I don't love you! (*He cries so loudly that he comes fully awake and sits up swiftly.*) Say Dot—I had a—! Dot! Dot!! Oh my God! (*He touches her.*) My Dot! (*And he leans over her and begins to cry like a small boy.*) Oh Dot! I love you! I love you!

CURTAIN

SHORT STORIES

The Hands: A Story

I saw his hands as soon as I skipped on the car at Vesey Avenue. Dark Brown, gnarled, knotted, bumping arm, in quirky knots like old brown bark on a cherry tree.

I skipped on the car real quickly. I wanted to cry, so I skipped. Someone had hurt my feelings and I wanted to cry—but I would not. I stared at everyone opposite me.

I am not rude. I can stare at people without their noticing me. Women only glance at me in pity or in grim scorn. Men never see me; so I stare safely.

You see, I am tallish and my bones poke out in subduable angles. I have no complexion—no hair. Of course there are some features and something atop my head, but the one is not complexion and the other not hair. My clothes look well when they are not on me. I have good taste in selecting things but I cannot wear them well. Nothing seems to belong to me, nor I to anything. I guess I am merely unfortunately ugly.

There are games I have to play by myself when I feel particularly ugly, particularly unfortunate.

I tried them all as soon as I had sat in my seat, for tears were coming up from behind, from each side and from below my eyes and I was breathing in quick rushes—with long pauses in between—around lumps in my throat, that kept rising and sinking like mercury in a thermometer. I plunged headlong into my first game: Being-where-I-was-not. . . .

There was all around me a crushing dark forest with a crooked ribbon of water in its midst. There was a cheese-colored moon and a wind playing a flighty dance rhythm through the trees. Vines draped low to the water's edge and the cold black slender loops of snakes were strung like bracelets on the boughs of trees. Spicy flowers and fruit and the tanging odor of crushed green leaves and water, too, still in its basin. Snakes—and no people snakes. Where were the people? I in the forest and the forest peopled by snakes. . . .

One of the mercurial lumps caught my breath and choked me out of my game. I started unmolested and struggled over another lump into my second game: Christ-in-all-men.

The lumps were closer together now—almost consolidating. Christ-in-all-men.

In the woman in the corner with the purple-scarlet painted cheeks and the purple blotched lips and the hungry restless light quick-snapping like fox-fire, in her eyes!

Maybe the tears were run together. I could not see Christ-in-all-men there.

Then I saw the hands: dark brown skin laid in thin grey-rimmed patches, like an alligator's back. Joints jutting like nodes on a bough; hands laid carefully, one on the other on blue denim trousers.

Working hands. Hands that had toiled.

Christ-in-all-men. Christ, the carpenter.

Now the game could be played in earnest. . . .

He started to work when he was seven. Ran errands, lugged coal, lugged oil, lugged washing, sold papers. In the summer when the sun baked the flesh on your hands; in the winter when the blood stands still in your hands; when the wind blows.

Went to school sometimes and labored hard to keep the pen from wavering between the round end fingers.

Worked after school: Labored as hard with shovel as with pencil. Ran elevators; shoveled coal; washed windows; scrubbed; dug.

Graduated from "grades" and "got a job."

Worked.

Up at five; swallowed coffee.

Slumbered down town, through a city half asleep, half

preparing to go to bed. Scraped square-toed across a wharf, across a plank, down into a ship.

A strange ship that never moved, never went anywhere. Just stood at the wharf like a Christmas toy, with its insides fractured. All around, other ships whisked, frittered, floated—according to their bulk—in and out.

This one stood unashamed and motionless while you shoveled and shoveled and shoveled until the step from bin to boiler seemed a pit in which your feet were fastened. Until the blood in your arms and the blood in your head met together and your heart seemed crowded out of it all.

Shoveled until sooty sweat stood in pools on the floor and shrank the few garments on your back into a back that shoved them off at once with the hard quiver of muscles. Shoveled and shoveled—until it was dinner time.

Sometimes he washed his hands; sometimes he did not. Days there were when he went above; then there were days when he dragged to a pile of coal close by the bin and sat to eat.

Slices of bread, half a loaf thick. Slabs of meat too wide to swallow well. Cold coffee in a flanked bottle—something sweet at the end.

Perhaps a snatch of sleep; perhaps a friendly smoke—then the shovel.

The feel in the handle for the "good grip" and then from bin to boiler—from boiler to bin until six.

World in dim twilight when he went down; world in dim twilight when he came up.

Home. At first one narrow room with a trough bed, a jig-saw mirror and a gas-light with an asthmatic flaw in it. A light that sputtered and flickered to hide from the hateful brassy brown paper on the wall and the piece of shade at the window that was pretending to be what it wasn't.

He washed his hands now and spread vaseline on spots where the skin wore thin. Then he set forth into a world deliciously dark now. To dance halls, where violins and pianos wooed melody, syncopation and one another with a breath-taking seduction. Where made a deal wood floor glassy and an over-robust figure a pleasing armful and made your teeth show whether you would or not.

Shovels were shovels; with music, lights, perfume and gay colors, a mere poke in the ribs worthy of a deep-seated laugh. A brown face, ashy with white powder and dyed with too-bright rouge make your breath draw in twice to once coming out.

Sometimes he played at pool and cards.

Sometimes it was lodge night and he added new dignity as carefully as he adjusted his white apron.

At church he took collection, balancing the basket carefully between thumb and forefinger. One night in June there was a revival and all the lost found Christ and themselves. As usher he helped most of them to and from the forward bench—politely ministering, protecting, urging on at once.

One slight brown girl, crying as if she had truly melted in tears wavered up from a back seat. His sturdy hands steadied her and their strength only made her cry the more.

He guided her into a bench and looked down into her round, plump, seal-smooth face with its tilted eyes too far apart and a nose, flat and yet up-turned. A face full of the strangely unrelated features found only in a race as marred by tampering, crossing and back-crossing as the Negro.

"Don't worry, Christ ain't hard to find if you're looking for Him," the hands said.

"I'm afraid of everything! Life. Religion. Help me! Where is God? Where is Christ? Tell me! What shall I do to be saved?" pleaded the eyes.

Of course, it was but a second, but he felt very, very strong and knowing and weak and awkward all at the same time. He withdrew rapidly and came back to be sick just as rapidly after the service—and stayed.

Patted her arm one dazing night as she mouthed almost in a whisper: "I do."

Patted her when she trembled into the unspeakable uncertainty of birth.

Patted little brown cheeks, wreathed in smiles. Wiped snubbed brown noses and patted young heads flung care-free and unknowing; high.

Shoveled. Sometimes with soul out of the ship and at home.

The Hands

Shoveled desperately, almost frantic with fear lest they lay him off at the wrong time.

Shoveled the children out of two rooms into four. Out of grades into high school. Out of gingham and into crepe-de-chine.

Shoveled and dreamed about some day with its hours of ease, its house with a yard and garden; its plenty to eat; its plenty to drink and something in the bank to put 'him and her away decent.'

Shoveled, patted, soothed, smoothed, steadied souls welcoming back from the fearsome darkness of the unknown and Judgment.

Shoveled, patted, smoothed, smoothed—steadied.

Laid carefully one upon the other on a lap of blue denim.

Snakes, peopling the forest. Christ-in-all-men.

Which game, Oh God, must I play most? . . .

The Prison-Bound

—"God help the prison-bound this evenin'
Them within the four iron walls—"

From a prayer heard in a country church

It was supper time.

There was salt in Maggie's tea cup. She had not put it in there. She was choking on it.

—Did you every try to swallow salt tears with food? It will choke you.—

Maggie did not know how the salt got in there. She had not put it in the tea and Charlie had not lifted his eyes from the plate since he had sat down. The salt was there, though.

Maggie held the cup to her lips and her eyes on a spot on the wall behind Charlie. The spot was greasy like all the rest of the wall.

It was greasy and dingy; yellow and cracked. It was smoked up to a sooty ceiling. It made even the window and the glimpse of house tops through the window greasy.

That's all the kitchen was anyhow. Greasy no matter how you scrubbed and dug.

Grease and soot and waterbugs always covered the kitchen. That's what everybody on the three floors above her and the three floors beneath her said. If you lived in a colored tenement you had to take grease and soot and waterbugs along with a constant "break-down" of things.

Yesterday the stove had smoked a little. Today it smoked a little more. Six months from now it would fill the whole room with smoke when you lit it.

The sink was stopping up. The zinc under the stove curled up and tore your skirts when you passed. Little crumblings of things

64

that nobody fixed. Charlie would not. He was too tired when he came home. Always too tired. And the agent said the owner was abroad.

Abroad? Somewhere. Not there.

Everything was breaking down. Even Charlie himself looked broken down humped over his plate.

Why didn't he straighten up some time? His arm thrust out of a sweater with a flannel shirt showing beneath, plied back and forth, up and down, from plate to mouth.

His hands were even greasy and fat. His fingers almost overlapped. They used to be slender and strong. His very shoulders were like young hams. There was no sink, no slender hollow between his neck and shoulders. You could not lay your head there now. He was fat and greasy. Greasy like kitchen wall.

The fork beside his plate could not puncture the rolls of fat. Even Death himself would have to play with his ribs a half hour before he could find his way between them.

How long had Charlie looked like this? Six months? Six years? Must have been longer.

It must have been more than six years when he had begun to "call on her." She hadn't been so fat herself then. He came to call. That was all. There had been nothing compelling or acute about the calling. He had come dryly, placidly, consequentially.

He had squatted in the middle of a chair. Squatted in the middle of sentences that always began and always ended alike. Somehow or other they had married. Squatted in two rooms. Squatted in these. Now he worked in a mill.

She wished that they could get up. Move up. She looked out of the window. Even move up into one of the trees.

She wanted to be at the top of one of those trees. Maybe a leaf. She was a leaf. A leaf greening, drinking in the sun. Shaking on a thread of stem. Charlie—was squatting over his plate. Blind to everything. Blind like a mole.

She cried to him silently: "Mole! Mole! Can't you see the sun? Can't you see the rain? Gold and plenty around you?"

Blind to everything. Only after the rain and sun have become strength and sap—lost their freshness and become a something else—like warm love turned to tepid tolerance—does the mole answer. He sniffs and smells but never sees, and he answers, "Yes, leaf—I see it."

And he squats at the roots and thinks he is in the tree-tops with the leaf. He thinks his eyes are wide open and he is happy—.

Charlie ought to quit squatting. He ought to see. —She set the cup down.

—One iron wall.—

She wondered why he did not say anything. She could talk. He called her ignorant lots of times though. "You ain't never been higher than the fifth grade in Dexter County schools. You ought to learn up here. This ain't down home," he'd say.

She could talk about things though she never talked to people. All the women round about bore themselves with such assurance it shamed her. She hung out of the windows and watched them.

"You ain't nothin' but lazy," Charlie told her. "Stay in out them windows."

But she looked and held silent talks with the women who passed. Watched each one as she passed. Talked gayly to her if her eyes were gay. Talked soothingly and peacefully if their eyes stared through everything and saw nothing.

Told the women who passed below her things about herself too. How she would like a gas log in the parlor instead of that coal stove with the broken door. But Charlie grumbled like a whole hive of bees if she asked him to pay the gas bill. She wanted curtains and a new hat and carpet. The place could look nicer. —A long iron wall—.

This was a town where you could not go to the theatre if you were colored. Nobody wanted to sit next to you.

Pushed out, the colored people had one of their own. Charlie said no decent man took his wife there.

Still the woman across the hall—the one who could laugh until tears came to your eyes while you listened to her—that woman said her husband took her and he had even beaten a man once for looking at her too pleasantly.

She laughed all the time. She even made Charlie laugh. Maggie couldn't. Once the other had even laughed at Maggie herself. Laughed when she told her what Charlie had said about the theatre.

Laughed and called her green and countrified. Well, maybe that woman wasn't decent as Charlie said and she had better let her alone like he told her too. She'd never go over the hall into her house though she thought she had heard him laughing in there once. Still, he was a man and she, a woman.

Why didn't he look up? Or laugh, even? The kitchen walls were so greasy. She wanted to see some others. It was too cold to sit in the parlor. The fire was out all the time. It was silly to go to bed as soon as you have eaten. You might die of acute indigestion before morning.

She sat back and closed her eyes. Charlie looked up swiftly. Saw her face, swollen and shiny beneath the tears. Tears streaming down into her tea cup. The sight sickened him suddenly.

Why did she cry? Why didn't she say something? If he asked a question she acted like she had to get her mind together to answer. And then she only said, "Yeah—!"

Women were not supposed to be so soft. Supposed to be soft, but not so soft you could knock a rock through them without their saying a word.

She asked for things, too, as if she were afraid to ask. Why didn't she wheedle things from him? Put her arms around him?

Why couldn't he have a victrola and folks dropping in? Why didn't she dress and fix up the place? The kitchen walls were greasy. Maggie's face. Maggie's clothes—Maggie—.

Oh well! Things he couldn't walk out of. Could not walk around. Or walk beside. Iron walls.

He pushed his chair back.

Maggie raised her eyes slowly. Maybe he would talk to her now. Tell her something someone said. What they had said and what they had done. Where they had been. How he felt when they said it. Where they went to make people laugh like the woman across the hall.

He went into the bedroom. She heard him walking around. Walking heavily and slowly. Maybe he was tired. Tired enough to sit down and talk.

He called from the hall: "Guess I go 'long out. Least till you can stop cryin'."

The salt choked her. She'd been crying, then. She set her cup down. She wiped her eyes.

She'd wash the dishes and wipe up some of the grease. Might not be so bad tomorrow. Tomorrow—.

God help the prison-bound—
Them within the four iron
walls this evening!

Nothing New

There was, once high on a hillside, a muddy brook. A brook full of yellow muddy water that foamed and churned over a rock bed.

Halfway down the hillside the water pooled in the clearest pool. All the people wondered how the muddy water cleared at that place. They did not know. They did not understand. They only went to the pool and drank. Sometimes they stooped over and looked into the water and saw themselves.

If they had looked deeper they might have seen God.

People seldom look that deep, though. They do not always understand how to do things.

They are not God. He alone understands.

You have been down on Frye Street. You know how it runs from Grand Avenue and the L to a river; from freckled-faced tow heads to yellow Orientals; from broad Italy to broad Georgia, from hooked nose to square black noses. How it lisps in French, how it babbles in Italian, how it gurgles in German, how it drawls and crawls through Black Belt dialects. Frye Street flows nicely together. It is like muddy water. Like muddy water in a brook.

Reuben Jackson and his wife Bessie—late of Georgia—made a home of three rooms at number thirteen Frye Street.

"Bad luck number," said the neighbors.

"Good luck number," said Reuben and Bessie.

Reuben did not know much. He knew only God, work, church, work and God. The only things Bessie knew were God, work, Denny, prayer, Reuben, prayer, Denny, work, work, work, God.

Denny was one thing they both knew beside God and work.

Denny was their little son. He knew lots of things. He knew that when the sun shone across the room a cobwebby shaft appeared that you could not walk up. And when the water dripped on pans in the sink it sang a tune: "Hear the time! Feel the time! Beat with me! Tap-ty tap! T-ta-tap! Ta-ty-tap!" The water sang a tune that made your feet move.

"Stop that jigging, you Denny," Bessie always cried. "God! Don't let him be no dancing man." She would pray afterwards. "Don't let him be no toy-tin fool man!"

Reuben watched him once sitting in his sun shaft. Watched him drape his slender little body along the floor and lift his eyes toward the sunlight. Even then they were eyes that drew deep and told deeper. With his oval clear brown face and his crinkled shining hair, Denny looked too—well as Reuben thought no boy should look. He spoke:

"Why don't you run and wrestle and race with the other boys? You must be a girl. Boys play rough and fight!"

Denny rolled over and looked up at his father. "I ain't a girl!" he declared deliberately.

He stared around the room for something to fight to prove his assertion. The cat lay peacefully sleeping by the stove. Denny snatched hold of the cat's tail to awaken it. The cat came up with all claws combing Denny.

"My God, ain't he cruel," screamed his mother. She slapped Denny and the cat apart.

Denny lay down under the iron board and considered the odd red patterns that the claws had made on his arms. . . . A red house and a red hill. Red trees around it; a red path running up the hill. . . .

"Make my child do what's right," prayed Bessie ironing above him.

People are not God. He alone understands.

Denny was running full tilt down a hillside. Whooping, yelling, shouting. Flying after nothing. Young Frye Street, mixed as usual, raced with him.

There was no school out here. There were no street cars, no houses, no ash-cans and basement stairs to interfere with a run.

Out here you could run straight, swift, in one direction with nothing to stop you but your own lack of foot power and breath. A picnic "out of town" pitched your spirits high and Young Frye Street could soar through all twelve heavens of enjoyment.

The racers reached the foot of the hill. Denny swerved to one side. A tiny colored girl was stooping over in the grass.

"Hey, Denny!" she called. Denny stopped to let the others sweep by.

"Hey, Margaret!" he answered, "What you doing?"

Margaret held up a handful of flowers. "I want that one." She pointed to a clump of dusky purple milkweeds bending behind a bush.

Denny hopped toward it.

He had almost reached it when the bush parted and a boy stepped out: "Don't come over here," he ordered. "This is the white kids' side!"

Denny looked at him. He was not of Frye Street. Other strange children appeared behind him. "This is a white picnic over here! Stay away from our side."

Denny continued toward his flower. Margaret squatted contentedly in the grass. She was going to get her flower.

"I said not to come over here," yelled the boy behind the bush.

Denny hopped around the bush.

"What you want over here?" the other bristled.

"That flower!" Denny pointed.

The other curved his body out in exaggerated childish sarcasm. "Sissy! Picking flowers." He turned to the boys behind him. "Sissy nigger! Picking flowers!"

Denny punched at the boy and snatched at the flower. The other stuck out his foot and Denny dragged him down as he fell. Young Frye Street rushed back up the hill at the primeval howl that set in.

Down on the ground, Denny and the white boy squirmed and kicked. They dug and pounded each other.

"You stay off the white kids' side, nigger!"

"I'm going to get that flower, I am!" Denny dragged his enemy along with him as he lunged toward the bush.

71

The flower beckoned and bent its stalk. On the white kids' side. Lovely, dusky, purple. Bending toward him. The milky perfume almost reached him. On the white kids' side. He wanted it. He would get it. Something ripped.

Denny left the collar of his blouse in the boy's hand and wrenched loose. He grabbed at the stem. On the white kids' side. Bending to him—slender, bending to him. On the white kids' side. He wanted it. He was going to have it—

The boy caught up to him as he had almost reached the flower. They fell again.—He was going to get that flower. He was going to. Tear the white kid off. Tear the white hands off his throat. Tear the white kid off his arms. Tear the white kid's weight off his chest. He'd move him—

Denny made a twist and slid low to the ground, the other boy beneath him, face downward. He pinned the boy's shoulders to the ground and clutching a handful of blonde hair in either hand, beat his head against the ground.

Young Frye Street sang the song of triumph. Sang it long and loud. Sang it loud enough for Mrs. Bessie Jackson—resting under a clump of trees with other mothers—to hear.

"I know them children is fighting!" she declared and started off in the direction of the yelling.

Halfway she met Margaret, a long milkweed flower dragging in one hand: "Denny," she explained, holding it up.

"I knew it," cried his mother and ran the rest of the way. "Stop killing that child," she screamed as soon as she had neared the mob. She dragged Denny off the boy. Dragged him through the crowd under a tree. Then she began:

"Look at them clothes. Where is your collar at? All I do is try to fix you up and now look at you! Look at you! Even your shirt torn!"

"Just as well him tear that for what he said," Denny offered.

This approximated "sauce" or the last straw or the point of overflow. His mother was staggered. Was there nothing she could do? Unconsciously she looked up to Heaven, then down to earth. A convenient bush flaunted nearby. She pulled it up—by the roots.

— On the white kids' side. The flower he wanted.—

God understands, doesn't He?

It had been a hard struggle. Reuben was still bitter and stubborn: "What reason Denny got to go to some art school? What he going to learn there?"

"Art! Painting!" Bessie defended. "The teachers at the high school say he know how to paint special like. He'd ought to go, they said."

"Yes, they said, but they ain't going to pay for him. He ought to go somewhere and do some real man's work. Ain't nothin' but women paddin' up and down, worryin' about paintin'."

"He's going all the same. Them teachers said he was better—!"

"Oh, all right. Let him go."

And Denny went to the Littler Art School. Carried his joyous six-foot, slender, brown self up on Grand Avenue, across, under, the elevated towers—up town. Up town to school.

"Bessie Jackson better put him on a truck like Annie Turner done her Jake," declared colored Frye Street. "Ain't no man got no business spendin' his life learnin' to paint."

"He should earn money! Money!" protested one portion of Frye Street through its hooked noses.

"Let him marry a wife," chuckled the Italians.

"He's going to learn art," said Denny's mother.

Denny went. The Littler School was filled with students of both sexes and of all races and degrees of life. Most of them were sufficiently gifted to be there. Days there when they showed promise. Days there when they doubted their own reasons for coming.

Denny did as well and as badly as the rest. Sometimes he even did things that attracted attention.

He himself always drew attention, for he was tall, straight and had features that were meant to go with the blondest hair and the bluest eyes. He was not blond, though. He was clean shaven and curly haired and brown as any Polynesian. His eyes were still deep drawing—deep telling. Eyes like a sea-going liner that could drift far without getting lost; that could draw deep without sinking.

Some women scrambled to make an impression on him. If they had looked at his mouth they would have withheld their efforts.

Anne Forest was one of the scramblers. She did not know she was scrambling, though. If anyone had told her that she was, she would have exploded, "Why! He is a nigger!"

Anne, you see, was white. She was the kind of girl who made you feel that she thrived on thirty-nine cent chocolates, fifteen-dollar silk dress sales, twenty-five cent love stories and much guilty smootchy kissing. If that does not make you sense her water-waved bob, her too carefully rouged face, her too perfumed person, I cannot bring her any nearer to you.

Anne scrambled unconsciously. Denny was an attractive man. Denny knew she was scrambling—so he went further within himself.

Went so far within himself that he did not notice Pauline Hammond who sat next to him.

One day he was mixing paint in a little white dish. Somehow the dish capsized and the paint flowed over the desk and spattered.

"Oh, my heavens!" said a girl's voice.

Denny stood up: "I beg your pardon." He looked across the desk.

Purple paint was splashed along the girl's smock and was even on her shoes.

"Oh, that's all right! No harm done at all," she said pleasantly.

Nice voice. Not jagged or dangling. Denny looked at her again. He dipped his handkerchief into the water and wiped off the shoes.

That done, they sat back and talked to each other. Talked to each other that day and the next day. Several days they talked.

Denny began to notice Pauline carefully. She did not talk to people as if they were strange hard shells she had to crack open to get inside. She talked as if she were already in the shell. In their very shell.

—Not many people can talk that soul-satisfying way. Why? I do not know. I am not God. I do not always understand—.

They talked about work; their life outside of school. Life. Life out in the world. With an artist's eye Denny noted her as she talked. Slender, more figure than heavy form, moulded. Poised.

Head erect on neck, neck uplifted on shoulders, body held neither too stiff or too slack. Poised and slenderly molded as an aristocrat.

They thought together and worked together. Saw things through each other's eyes. They loved each other.

One day they went to a Sargent exhibit—and saw Anne Forest. She gushed and mumbled and declared war on Pauline. She did not know she had declared war, though.

"Pauline Hammond goes out with that nigger Denny Jackson!" she informed all the girls in class next day.

"With a nigger!" The news seeped through the school. Seeped from the President's office on the third floor to the janitor down below the stairs.

Anne Forest only told one man the news. He was Allen Carter. He had taken Pauline to three dances and Anne to one. Maybe Anne was trying to even the ratio when she told him: "Pauline Hammond is rushing a nigger now."

Allen truly reeled. "Pauline! A nigger?"

Anne nodded. "Denny Jackson—or whatever his name is," she hastened to correct herself.

Allen cursed aloud. "Pauline! She's got too much sense for that! It's that nigger rushing after her! Poor little kid! I'll kill him!"

He tore off his smock with a cursing accompaniment. He cursed before Anne. She did not matter. She should have known that before.

Allen tore off the smock and tore along the hall. Tore into a group gathered in a corner bent over a glass case. Denny and Pauline were in the crowd, side by side. Allen walked up to Denny.

"Here you," he pushed his way in between the two. "Let this white girl alone." He struck Denny full in the face.

Denny struck back. All the women—except Pauline—fled to the far end of the room.

The two men fought. Two jungle beasts would have been kinder to each other. These two tore at each other with more than themselves behind every blow.

"Let that white woman alone, nigger! Stay on your own side!"

Allen shouted once.—On your own side. On the white kids' side. That old fight—the flower, bending toward him. He'd move the white kid! Move him and get the flower! Move him and get what was his! He seized a white throat in his hands and moved his hands close together!

He did move the white kid. Moved him so completely that doctors and doctors and running and wailing could not cause his body to stir again. Moved him so far that Denny was moved to the County Jail.

Everything moved then. The judge moved the jury with pleas to see justice done for a man who had sacrificed his life for the beautiful and the true. The jury moved that the old law held: one life taken, take another.

Denny—they took Denny.

Up at the school the trustees moved. "Be it enacted this day— no Negro student shall enter within these doors—."

The newspapers moved their readers. Sent columns of description of the "hypnotized frail flower under the spell of Black Art." So completely under the spell she had to be taken from the stand for merely screaming in the judge's face: "I loved him! I loved him! I loved him!" until the court ran over with the cries.

Frye Street agreed on one thing only. Bessie and Reuben had tried to raise Denny right.

After that point, Frye Street unmixed itself. Flowed apart.

Frye Street—black—was loud in its utterances. "Served Denny right for loving a white woman! Many white niggers as there is! Either Bessie or Reuben must have loved white themselves and was 'shamed to go out open with them. Shame to have that all come out in that child! Now he rottenin' in a murderer's grave!"

White Frye Street held it was the school that had ruined Denny. Had not Frye Street—black and white—played together, worked together, shot crap together, fought together without killing? When a nigger got in school he got crazy.

Up on the hillside the clear water pooled. Up on the hillside people come to drink at the pool. If they looked over, they saw themselves. If they had looked deeper—deeper than them-

selves—they might have seen God.
But they did not.
People do not do that—do they?
They do not always understand. Do they?
God alone—He understands.

One Boy's Story

I'm glad they got me shut up in here. Gee, I'm glad! I used to be afraid to walk in the dark and to stay by myself.

That was when I was ten years old. Now I am eleven.

My mother and I used to live up in the hills right outside of Somerset. Somerset, you know is way up State and there aren't many people there. Just a few rich people in big houses and that's all.

Our house had a nice big yard behind it, beside it and in front of it. I used to play it was my fortress and that the hills beside us were full of Indians. Some days I'd go on scouting parties up and down the hills and fight.

That was in the summer and fall. In the winter and when the spring was rainy, I used to stay in the house and read.

I love to read. I love to lie on the floor and put my elbows down and read and read myself right out of Somerset and of America—out of the world, if I want to.

There was just my mother and I. No brothers—no sisters—no father. My mother was awful pretty. She had a roundish plump, brown face and was all plump and round herself. She had black hair all curled up on the end like a nice autumn leaf.

She used to stay in the house all the time and sew a lot for different ladies who came up from the big houses in Somerset. She used to sew and I would pull the bastings out for her. I did not mind it much. I liked to look at the dresses and talk about the people who were to wear them.

Most people, you see, wear the same kind of dress goods all the time. Mrs. Ragland always wore stiff silk that sounded like icicles on the window. Her husband kept the tea and coffee store in

Somerset and everybody said he was a coming man.

I used to wonder where he was coming to.

Mrs. Gregg always had the kind of silk that you had to work carefully for it would ravel into threads. She kept the boarding house down on Forsythe Street. I used to like to go to that house. When you looked at it on the outside and saw all the windows and borders running up against it you thought you were going in a palace. But when you got inside you saw all the little holes in the carpet and the mended spots in the curtains and the faded streaks in the places where the draperies were folded.

The pale soft silk that always made me feel like burying my face in it belonged to Mrs. Swyburne. She was rich—awful rich. Her husband used to be some kind of doctor and he found out something that nobody else had found out, so people used to give him plenty of money just to let him tell them about it. They called him a specialist.

He was a great big man. Nice and tall and he looked like he must have lived on milk and beef-juice and oranges and tomato juice and all the stuff Ma makes me eat to grow. His teeth were white and strong so I guess he chewed his crusts too.

Anyhow, he was big but his wife was all skinny and pale. Even her eyes were almost skinny and pale. They were sad like and she never talked much. My mother used to say that those who did not have any children did not have to talk much anyhow.

She said that to Mrs. Swyburne one time. Mrs. Swyburne had been sitting quiet like she used to, looking at me. She always looked at me anyhow, but that day she looked harder than ever.

Every time I raised up my head and breathed the bastings out of my face, I would see her looking at me.

I always hated to have her look at me. Her eyes were so sad they made me feel as if she wanted something I had.

Not that I had anything to give her because she had all the money and cars and everything and I only had my mother and Cato, my dog, and some toys and books.

But she always looked that way at me and that day she kept looking so long that pretty soon I sat up and looked at her hard.

She sort of smiled then and said, "Do you know, Donald. I was wishing I had a little boy just like you to pull out bastings for me, too."

"You couldn't have one just like me," I said right off quick. Then I quit talking because Ma commenced to frown even though she did not look up at me.

I quit because I was going to say, "Cause I'm colored and you aren't," when Ma frowned.

Mrs. Swyburne still sort of smiled; then she turned her lips away from her teeth the way I do when Ma gives me senna and manna tea.

"No," she said, "I couldn't have a little boy like you, I guess."

Ma spoke right up, "I guess you do not want one like him! You have to talk to him so much."

I knew she meant I talked so much and acted so bad sometimes.

Mrs. Swyburne looked at Ma then. She looked at her hair and face and right down to her feet. Pretty soon she said: "You cannot mind that surely. You seem to have all the things I haven't anyway." Her lips were still held in that lifted, twisted way.

Ma turned around to the machine then and turned the wheel and caught the thread and it broke and the scissors fell and stuck up in the floor. I heard her say "Jesus," to herself like she was praying.

I didn't say anything. I ripped out the bastings. Ma stitched. Mrs. Swyburne sat there. I sort of peeped up at her and I saw a big fat tear sliding down her cheek.

I kind of wiggled over near her and laid my hand on her arm. Then Ma yelled: "Donald, go and get a pound of rice! Go now, I said."

I got scared. She had not said it before and she had a lot of rice in a jar in the closet. But I didn't dare say so. I went out.

I couldn't help but think of Mrs. Swyburne. She ought not to cry so easy. She might not have had a little boy and Ma might have—but she should have been happy. She had a great big house on the swellest street in Somerset and a car all her own and some one to drive it for her. Ma only had me and our house which wasn't so swell, but it was all right.

Then Mrs. Swyburne had her husband and he had such a nice voice. You didn't mind leaning on his knee and talking to him as soon as you saw him. He had eyes that looked so smiling and happy and when you touched his hands they were soft and gentle as Ma's even if they were bigger.

I knew him real well. He and I were friends. He used to come to our house a lot of times and bring me books and talk to Ma while I read.

He knew us real well. He called Ma Louise and me Don. Sometimes he'd stay and eat supper with us and then sit down and talk. I never could see why he'd come way out there to talk to us when he had a whole lot of rich friends down in Somerset and a wife that looked like the only doll I ever had.

A lady gave me that doll once and I thought she was really pretty—all pale and blonde and rosy. I thought she was real pretty at first but by and by she seemed so dumb. She never did anything but look pink and pale and rosy and pretty. She never went out and ran with me like Cato did. So I just took a rock and gave her a rap up beside her head and threw her in the bushes.

Maybe Mrs. Swyburne was pale and pink and dumb like the doll and her husband couldn't rap her with a rock and throw her away.

I don't know.

Anyhow, he used to come and talk to us and he'd talk to Ma a long time after I was in bed. Sometimes I'd wake up and hear them talking. He used to bring me toys until he found out that I could make my own toys and that I liked books.

After that he brought me books. All kinds of books about fairies and Indians and folks in other countries.

Sometimes he and I would talk about the books—especially those I liked. The one I liked most was called "Ten Tales to Inspire Youth."

That sounds kind of funny but the book was great. It had stories in it all about men. All men. I read all of the stories but I liked the one about the fellow named Orestes who went home from the Trojan War and found his mother had married his father's brother so he killed them. I was always sorry for the women with the whips of flame like forked tongues who used to worry him afterwards. I don't see why the fairies pursued him. They knew he did it because he loved his father so much.

Another story I liked was about Oedipus—a Greek too—who put out his eyes to hurt himself because he killed his father and married his mother by mistake.

But after I read "David and Goliath," I just had to pretend that I was David.

I swiped a half a yard of elastic from Ma and hunted a long time until I found a good forked piece of wood. Then I made a swell slingshot.

The story said that David asked Jehovah (which was God) to let his slingshot shoot good. "Do thou lend thy strength to my arm, Jehovah," he prayed.

I used to say that too just to be like him.

I told Dr. Swyburne I liked these stories.

"Why do you like them?" he asked me.

"Because they are about men," I said.

"Because they are about men! Is that the only reason?"

Then I told him no; that I liked them because the men in the stories were brave and had courage and stuck until they got what they wanted, even if they hurt themselves getting it.

And he laughed and said, to Ma: "Louise he has the blood, all right!"

And Ma said: "Yes! He is a true Gage. They're brave enough to put their eyes out too. That takes courage all right!"

Ma and I are named Gage, so I stuck out my chest and said: "Ma, which one of us Gages put his eyes out?"

"Me," she said—and she was standing there looking right at me!

I thought she was making fun. So I felt funny.

Dr. Swyburne turned red and said: "I meant the other blood, of course. All the Swyburnes are heroes."

I didn't know what he meant. My name is Gage and so is Ma's so he didn't mean me.

Ma threw her head up and looked at him and says: "Oh, are they heroes?" Then she says real quick: "Donald go to bed right now!"

I didn't want to go but I went. I took a long time to take off my clothes and I heard Ma and Dr. Swyburne talking fast like they were fussing.

I couldn't hear exactly what they said but I kept hearing Ma say: "I'm through!"

And I heard Dr. Swyburne say: "You can't be!"

I kind of dozed to sleep. By and by I heard Ma say again: "Well, I'm through!"

And Dr. Swyburne said: "I won't let you be!"

Then I rolled over to think a minute and then go downstairs maybe.

But when I rolled over again, the sun was shining and I had to get up.

Ma never said anything about what happened so I didn't either. She just walked around doing her work fast, holding her head up high like she always does when I make her mad.

So I never said a thing that day.

One day I came home from school. I came in the back way and when I was in the kitchen I could hear a man in the front room talking to Ma. I stood still a minute to see if it was Dr. Swyburne though I knew he never comes in the afternoon.

The voice didn't sound like his so I walked in the hall and passed the door. The man had his back to me so I just looked at him a minute and didn't say anything. He had on leather leggins and a sort of uniform like soldiers wear. He was stooping over the machine talking to Ma and I couldn't see his face.

Just then I stumbled over the little rug in the hall and he stood up and looked at me.

He was a colored man! Colored just like Ma and me. You see, there aren't any other people in Somerset colored like we are, so I was sort of surprised to see him.

"This is my son, Mr. Frazier," Ma said.

I said pleased to meet you and stepped on Ma's feet. But not on purpose. You know I kind of thought he was going to be named Gage and be some relation to us and stay at our house awhile.

I never saw many colored people—no colored men—and I wanted to see some. When Ma called him Frazier it made my feet slippery so I stubbed my toe.

"Hello, son!" he said nice and quiet.

He didn't talk like Ma and me. He talked slower and softer. I liked him straight off so I grinned and said: "Hello yourself."

"How's the books?" he said then.

I didn't know what he meant at first but I guessed he meant school. So I said: "Books aren't good as the fishin'."

He laughed out loud and said I was all right and said he and I were going to be friends and that while he was in Somerset he was going to come to our house often and see us.

Then he went out. Ma told me he was driving some lady's car. She was visiting Somerset from New York and he would be there a little while.

Gee, I was so glad! I made a fishing rod for him that very afternoon out of a piece of willow I had been saving for a long time.

And one day, he and I went down to the lake and fished. We sat still on top a log that went across a little bay like. I felt kind of excited and couldn't say a word. I just kept looking at him every once in a while and smiled. I did not grin. Ma said I grinned too much.

Pretty soon he said: "What are you going to be when you grow up, son?"

"A colored man," I said. I meant to say some more, but he hollered and laughed so loud that Cato had to run up and see what was doing.

"Sure you'll be a colored man! No way to get out of that! But I mean this: What kind of work are you going to do?"

I had to think a minute. I had to think of all the kinds of work men did. Some of the men in Somerset were farmers. Some kept stores. Some swept the streets. Some were rich and did not do anything at home but they went to the city and had their cars driven to the shop and to meet them at the train.

All the conductors and porters make a lot of scramble to get these men on and off the train, even if they looked as if they could take care of themselves.

So I said to Mr. Frazier: "I want to have an office."

"An office?"

"Yes. In the city so's I can go in to it and have my car meet me when I come to Somerset."

"Fat chance a colored man has!" he said.

"I can too have an office!" I said. He made me sore. "I can have one if I want to! I want to have an office and be a specialist like Dr. Swyburne."

Mr. Frazier dropped his pole and had to swear something awful when he reached for it though it wasn't very far from him.

"Why'd you pick him?" he said and looked at me kind of mad like and before I could think of what to say he said: "Say son, does that guy come up to see your mother?"

"Sure he comes to see us both!" I said.

Mr. Frazier laughed again but not out loud. It made me sore all over. I started to hit him with my pole but I thought about something I'd read once that said even a savage will treat you right in his house—so I didn't hit him. Of course, he wasn't in my house exactly but he was sitting on my own log over my fishing places and that's like being in your own house.

Mr. Frazier laughed to himself again and then all of a sudden he took the pole I had made him out of the piece of willow I had been saving for myself and laid it across his knees and broke it in two. Then he said out loud: "Nigger women," and then threw the pole in the water.

I grabbed my pole right out of the water and slammed it across his face. I never thought of the hook until I hit him, but it did not stick in him. It caught in a tree and I broke the string yanking it out.

He looked at me like he was going to knock me in the water and even though I was scared, I was thinking how I'd let myself fall if he did knock me off—so that I could swim out without getting tangled in the roots under the bank.

But he didn't do it. He looked at me a minute and said: "Sorry, son! Sorry! Not your fault."

Then he put his hand on my hair and brushed it back and sort of lifted it up and said: "Like the rest."

I got up and said I was going home and he came too. I was afraid he would come in but when he got to my gate he said: "So long," and walked right on.

I went on in. Ma was sewing. She jumped up when I came in.

"Where is Mr. Frazier?" she asked me. She didn't even say hello to me!

"I hit him," I said.

"You hit him!" she hollered. "You *hit* him! What did you do that for? Are you crazy?"

I told her no. "He said 'nigger women' when I told him that Dr. Swyburne was a friend of ours and came to see us."

Oh Ma looked terrible then. I can't tell you how she did look. Her face sort of slipped around and twisted like the geography says the earth does when the fire inside of it gets too hot.

She never said a word at first. She just sat there. Then she asked me to tell her all about every bit that happened.

I told her. She kept wriggling from side to side like the fire was getting hotter. When I finished, she said: "Poor baby! My baby boy! Not your fault! Not your fault!"

That made me think of Mr. Frazier so I pushed out of her arms and said: "Ma your breast pin hurts my face when you do that!"

She leaned over on the arms of her chair and cried and cried until I cried too.

All that week I'd think of the fire inside of the earth when I looked at Ma. She looked so funny and she kept talking to herself.

On Saturday night we were sitting at the table when I heard a car drive up the road.

"Here's Dr. Swyburne!" I said and I felt so glad I stopped eating.

"He isn't coming here!" Ma said and then she jumped up.

"Sure he's coming," I said. "I know his motor." And I started to get up too.

"You stay where you are!" Ma hollered and she went out and closed the door behind her.

I took another piece of cake and began eating the frosting. I heard Dr. Swyburne come up on the porch.

"Hello, Louise," he said. I could tell he was smiling by his voice.

I couldn't hear what Ma said at first but pretty soon I heard her say: "You can't come here any more!"

That hurt my feelings. I liked Dr. Swyburne. I liked him better than anybody I knew besides Ma.

Ma stayed out a long time and by and by she came in alone and I heard Dr. Swyburne drive away.

She didn't look at me at all. She just leaned back against the door and said: "Dear Jesus! With your help I'll free myself."

I wanted to ask her from what did she want to free herself. It sounded like she was in jail or an animal in a trap in the woods.

I thought about it all during supper but I didn't dare say much. I thought about it and pretended that she was shut up in a prison and I was a time fighter who beat all the keepers and got her out.

Then it came to me that I better get ready to fight to get her out of whatever she was in. I never said anything to her. I carried my air-rifle on my back and my slingshot in my pocket. I wanted to ask her where her enemy was, but she never talked to me about it; so I had to keep quiet too. You know Ma always got mad if I talked about things first. She likes to talk, then I can talk afterwards.

One Sunday she told me she was going for a walk.

"Can I go?" I asked her.

"No," she said. "You play around the yard."

Then she put her hat on and stood looking in the mirror at herself for a minute. All of a sudden I heard her say to herself: "All I need is strength to fight out of it."

"Ma'am?" I thought she was talking to me at first.

She stopped and hugged my head—like I wish she wouldn't sometimes and then went out.

I stayed still until she got out of the yard. Then I ran and got my rifle and slingshot and followed her.

I crept behind her in the bushes beside the road. I cut across the fields and came out behind the willow patch the way I always do when I am tracking Indians and wild animals.

By and by she came out in the clearing that is behind Dr. Somerset's. They call it Somerset's Grove and it's named for his folks who used to live there—just as the town was.

She sat down so I lay down in the bushes. A sharp rock was sticking in my knee but I was afraid to move for fear she'd hear me and send me home.

By and by I heard someone walking on the grass and I saw Dr. Swyburne coming up. He started talking before he got to her.

"Louise," he said. "Louise! I am not going to give anything up to a nigger."

"Not even a nigger woman whom you took from a nigger?" She lifted her mouth in the senna and manna way.

"Don't say that!" he said. "Don't say that! I wanted a son. I couldn't have taken a woman in my own world—that would have ruined my practice. Elaine couldn't have a child!"

"Yes," Ma said. "It would have ruined you and your profession. What did it do for me? What did it do for Donald?"

"I have told you I will give him the best the world can offer. He is a Swyburne!"

"He is *my* child," Ma hollered. "It isn't his fault he is yours!"

"But I give him everything a father could give his son!"

"He has no name!" Ma said.

"I have too!" I hollered inside of me. "Donald Gage!"

"He has no name," Ma said again, "and neither have I!" And she began to cry.

"He has blood!" said Dr. Swyburne.

"But how did he get it? Oh, I'm through. Stay away from my house and I'll marry one of my own men so Donald can be somebody."

"A nigger's son?"

"Don't say that again," Ma hollered and jumped up.

"Do you think I'll give up a woman of mine to a nigger?"

Ma hollered again and hit him right in his face.

He grabbed her wrists and turned the right one, I guess because she fell away from him on that side.

I couldn't stand any more. I snatched out my slingshot and pulled the stone up that was sticking in my knee.

I started to shoot. Then I remembered what David said first, so I shut my eyes and said it: "Do thou, Jehovah (which is God today), lend strength to my arm."

When I opened my eyes Ma had broken away and was running toward the road. Dr. Swyburne was standing still by the tree looking after her like he was going to catch her. His face was turned sideways to me. I looked at his head where his hair was brushed back from the side of his face.

I took aim and let the stone go. I heard him say: "Oh, my God!" I saw blood on his face and I saw him stagger and fall against the tree.

Then I ran too.

When I got home Ma was sitting in her chair with her hat thrown on the floor beside her and her head was lying back.

I walked up to her: "Ma," I said real loud.

She reached out and grabbed me and hugged my head down to her neck like she always does.

The big breast-pin scratched my mouth. I opened my mouth to speak and something hot and sharp ran into my tongue.

"Ma! Ma!" I tried to holler. "The pin is sticking in my tongue!"

I don't know what I said though. When I tried to talk again, Ma and Dr. Somerset were looking down at me and I was lying in bed. I tried to say something but I could not say anything. My mouth felt like it was full of hot bread and I could not talk around it.

Dr. Somerset poured something in my mouth and it felt like it was on fire.

"They found Shev Swyburne in my thistle grove this afternoon," he said to Ma.

Ma look up quick. "*Found* him! What do you mean?"

"I mean he was lying on the ground—either fell or was struck and fell. He was dead from a blow on the temple."

I tried to holler but my tongue was too thick.

Ma took hold of each side of her face and held to it, then she just stared at Dr. Somerset. He put a lot of things back in his bag.

Then he sat up and looked at Ma. "Louise," he said, "why is all that thistle down on your skirt?"

Ma looked down. So did I. There was thistle down all over the hem of her dress.

"You don't think I killed him, do you?" she cried, "you don't think I did it?" Then she cried something awful.

I tried to get up but I was too dizzy. I crawled across the bed on my stomach and reached out to the chair that had my pants on it. It was hard to do—but I dragged my slingshot out of my pocket, crawled back across the bed and laid it in Dr. Somerset's knees. He looked at me for a minute.

"Are you trying to tell me that you did it, son?" he asked me.

I said yes with my head.

"My God! My God!! His own child!!!"

Dr. Somerset said to Ma: "God isn't dead yet."

Then he patted her on the arm and told her not to tell anybody nothing and they sat down and picked all the thistle down out of the skirt. He took the slingshot and broke it all up and put it all in a paper and carried it downstairs and put it in the stove.

I tried to talk. I wanted to tell him to leave it so I could show my grandchildren what I had used to free Ma like the men do in the books.

I couldn't talk though. My tongue was too thick for my mouth. The next day it burnt worse and things began to float around my eyes and head like pieces of wood in the water.

Sometimes I could see clearly though and once I saw Dr. Somerset talking to another man. Dr. Somerset was saying: "We'll have to operate to save his life. His tongue is poisoned. I am afraid it will take his speech from him."

Ma hollered then: "Thank God! He will not talk! Never! He can't talk! Thank God! Oh God! I thank Thee!" And then she cried like she always does and that time it sounded like she was laughing too.

The other man looked funny and said: "Some of them have no natural feeling of parent for child!"

Dr. Somerset looked at him and said: "You may be fine as a doctor but otherwise you are an awful fool."

Then he told the other man to go out and he began talking to Ma.

"I understand! I understand," he said. "I know all about it. He took you away from somebody and some of these days he might have taken Donald from you. He took Elaine from me once and I told him then God would strip him for it. Now it is all over. Never tell anyone and I will not. The boy knows how to read and write and will be able to live."

90

So I got a black stump in my mouth. It's shaped like a forked whip.

Some days I pretend I am Orestes with the Furies' whips in my mouth for killing a man.

Some days I pretend I am Oedipus and that I cut it out for killing my own father.

That's what makes me sick all over sometimes.

I killed my own father. But I didn't know it was my father. I was freeing Ma.

Still—I shall never write that on my paper to Ma and Dr. Somerset the way I have to talk to them and tell them when things hurt me.

My father said I was a Swyburne and that was why I liked people to be brave and courageous.

Ma says I am a Gage and that is why I am brave and courageous.

But I am both, so I am a whole lot brave, a whole lot courageous. And I am bearing my Furies and my clipped tongue like a Swyburne and a Gage—'cause I am both of them.

Drab Rambles

I am hurt. There is blood on me. You do not care. You do not know me. You do not know me. You do not care. There is blood on me. Sometimes it gets on you. You do not care I am hurt. Sometimes it gets on your hands—on your soul even. You do not care. You do not know me.

You do not care to know me, you say, because we are different. We are different you say.

You are white, you say. And I am black.

You are white and I am black and so we are different, you say. If I am whiter than you, you say I am black.

You do not know me.

I am all men tinged in brown. I am all men with a touch of black. I am you and I am myself.

You do not know me. You do not care, you say.

I am an inflow of God, tossing about in the bodies of all men: all men tinged and touched with black.

I am not pure Africa of five thousand years ago. I am you—all men tinged and touched. Not old Africa into somnolence by a jungle that blots out all traces of its antiquity.

I am all men. I am tinged and touched. I am colored. All men tinged and touched; colored in a brown body.

Close all men in a small space, tinge and touch the Space with one blood—you get a check-mated Hell.

A check-mated Hell, seething in a brown body, I am.

I am colored. A check-mated Hell seething in a brown body. You do not know me.

You do not care—you say.

But still, I am you—and all men.

I am colored. A check-mated Hell seething in a brown body.

Sometimes I wander up and down and look. Look at the tinged-in-black, the touched-in-brown. I wander and see how it is with them and wonder how long—how long Hell can seethe before it boils over.

How long can Hell be check-mated?

Or if check-mated can solidify, if this is all it is?

If this is all it is.

The First Portrait

He was sitting in the corridor of the Out-Patients Department. He was sitting in a far corner well out of the way. When the doors opened at nine o'clock, he had been the first one in. His heart was beating fast. His heart beat faster than it should. No heart should beat so fast that you choke at the throat when you try to breathe. You should not feel it knocking—knocking—knocking—now against your ribs, now against something deep within you. Knocking against something deep, so deep that you cannot fall asleep without feeling a cutting, pressing weight laid against your throat, over your chest. A cutting, pressing weight that makes you struggle to spring from the midst of your sleep. Spring up.

It had beat like that now for months. At first he had tried to work it off. Swung the pick in his daily ditch digging—faster—harder. But that had not helped it at all. It had beaten harder and faster for the swinging. He had tried castor oil to run it off of his system. Someone told him he ate too much meat and smoked too much. So he had given up his beloved ham and beef and chicken and tried to swing the pick on lighter things.

It would be better soon.

His breath had begun to get short then. He had to stop oftener to rest between swings. The foreman, Mike Leary, had cursed at first and then moved him back to the last line of diggers. It hurt him to think he was not so strong as he had been. —But it would be better soon.

He would not tell his wife how badly his heart knocked. It would be better soon. He could not afford to lay off from work.

He had to dig. Nobody is able to lay off work when there is a woman and children to feed and cover.

The castor oil had not helped. The meat had been given up, even his little pleasure in smoking. Still the heart beat too fast. Still the heart beat so he felt it up in the chords on each side of his neck below his ears. —But it would be better soon.

It would be better. He had asked to be let off half a day so he could be at the hospital at ten o'clock. Mike had growled his usual curses when he asked to get off.

"What the hell is wrong wit' you? All you need is a good dose of whiskey!"

He had gone off. When the doors of the Out-Patients Department opened, he was there. It took him a long time to get up the stairs. The knocking was in his throat so. Beads of perspiration stood grey on his black-brown forehead. He closed his eyes a moment and leaned his head back.

A sound of crying made him open them. On the seat beside him a woman held a baby in her arms. The baby was screaming itself red in the face, wriggling and twisting to get out of its mother's arms on the side where the man sat. The mother shifted the child from one side to the other and told him with her eyes, "You ought not to be here!"

He had tried to smile over the knocking at the baby. Now he rolled his hat over in his hands and looked down.

When he looked up, he turned his eyes away from the baby and its mother. The knocking pounded. Why should a little thing like that make his heart pound. He must be badly off to breathe so fast over nothing. The thought made his heart skip and pound the harder.

But he would be better soon.

Other patients began to file in. Soon the nurse at the desk began to read names aloud. He had put his card in first but she did not call him first. As she called each name, a patient stood up and went through some swinging doors.

Green lights—men in white coats—nurses in white caps and dresses filled the room it would seem, from the glimpses caught through the door. It seemed quiet and still, too, as if everyone were listening to hear something.

Once the door swung open wildly and an Italian came dashing madly through—a doctor close behind him. The man threw himself on a bench: "Oh God! Oh God! I ain't that sick, I ain't so sick I gotta die! No! You don't really know. I ain't so sick!"

The doctor leaned over him and said something quietly. The nurse brought something cloudy in a glass. The man drank it. By and by he was led out—hiccuping but quieter.

Back in his corner, his heart beat smotheringly. Suppose that had been he? Sick enough to die! Was the dago crazy, trying to run away? Run as he would, the sickness would be always with him. For himself, he would be better soon.

"Peter Jackson! Peter Jackson. Peter Jackson. Five, Sawyer Avenue!" The nurse had to say it twice before he heard through his thoughts.

Thump. The beat of his heart knocked him to his feet. He had to stand still before he could move.

"Here! This way." The nurse said it so loudly—so harshly—that the entire room turned around to look at him.

She need not be so hateful. He only felt a little dizzy. Slowly he felt along the floor with his feet. Around the corner of the bench. Across the space beside the desk. The nurse pushed open the door and pressed it back. "Dr. Sibley?" she called.

The door swung shut behind him. Along each side of the room were desks. Behind each, sat a doctor. When the nurse called "Dr. Sibley," no one answered, so Jackson stood at the door. His heart rubbed his ribs unnecessarily.

"Say! Over here!"

The words and the voice made his heart race again. —But he would be better now. He turned toward the direction of the voice, met a cool pair of blue eyes boring through tortoise-rimmed glasses. He sat down.

The doctor took a sheet of paper. "What's your name?"

His heart had been going so that when he said "Peter Jackson," he could make no sound the first time.

"What's your name, I said."

"Peter Jackson."

"How old are you?"

"Fifty-four."

"Occupation? Where do you work?"

"Day laborer for the city."

"Can you afford to pay a doctor?"

Surprise took the rest of his breath away for a second. The question had to be repeated.

"I guess so. I never been sick."

"Well, if you can afford to pay a doctor, you ought not to come here. This clinic is for foreigners and people who cannot pay a doctor. Your people have some of your own doctors in this city."

The doctor wrote for such a long time on the paper then that he thought he was through with him and he started to get up.

"Sit down." The words caught him before he was on his feet. "I haven't told you to go anywhere."

"I thought—," Jackson hung on his words uncertain.

"You needn't! Don't think! Open your shirt." And the doctor fitted a pair of tubes in his ears and shut out his thoughts.

He fitted the tubes in his ears and laid a sieve-like piece of rubber against his patient's chest. Laid it up. Laid it down. Finally he said: "What have you been doing to this heart of yours? All to pieces. All gone."

Gone. His heart was all gone. He tried to say something but the doctor snatched the tube away and turned around to the desk and wrote again.

Again he turned around: "Push up your sleeve," he said this time.

The sleeve went up. A piece of rubber went around his arm above the elbow. Something began to squeeze—knot—drag on his arm.

"Pressure almost two hundred," the doctor shot at him this time. "You can't stand this much longer."

He turned around. He wrote again. He wrote and pushed the paper away. "Well," said the doctor, "you will have to stop working and lie down. You must keep your feet on a level with your body."

Jackson wanted to yell with laughter. Lie down. If he had had breath enough, he would have blown all the papers off the desk, he would have laughed so. He looked into the blue eyes. "I can't stop work," he said.

The doctor shrugged: "Then," he said, and said no more.

Then! Then what?

Neither one of them spoke.

Then what?

Jackson wet his lips: "You mean—you mean I got to stop work to get well?"

"I mean you have to stop if you want to stay here."

"You mean even if I stop you may not cure me?"

The blue eyes did go down toward the desk then. The answer was a question.

"You don't think I can make a new heart, do you? You only get one heart. You are born with that. You ought not to live so hard."

Live hard? Did this man think he had been a sport? Live hard. Liquor, wild sleepless nights—sleep-drugged, rag-worn, half-shoddy days? That instead of what it had been. Ditches and picks. Births and funerals. Stretching a dollar the length of ten. A job, no job; three children and a wife to feed; bread thirteen cents a loaf. For pleasure, church—where he was too tired to go sometimes. Tobacco that he had to consider twice before he bought.

"I ain't lived hard! I ain't lived hard!" he said suddenly. "I have worked harder than I should, that's all."

"Why didn't you get another job?" the doctor snapped. "Didn't need to dig ditches all your life."

Jackson drew himself up; "I had to dig ditches because I am an ignorant black man. If I was an ignorant white man, I could get easier jobs. I could even have worked in this hospital."

Color flooded the doctor's face. Whistles blew and shrieked suddenly outside.

Twelve o'clock. Mike would be looking for him.

He started for the door. Carefully. He must not waste his strength. Rent, food, clothes. He could not afford to lay off.

He had almost reached the door when a hand shook him suddenly. It was the doctor close behind him. He held out a white sheet of paper: "Your prescription," he explained, and seemed to hesitate. "Digitalis. It will help some. I am sorry."

Sorry for what? Jackson found the side-walk and lit his pipe to steady himself. He had almost reached the ditches when he remembered the paper. He could not find it. He went on.

The Second Portrait

By twelve o'clock, noon, the washroom of Kale's Fine Family Laundry held enough steam to take the shell off of a turtle's back. Fill tubs with steaming water at six o'clock, set thirty colored women to rubbing and shouting and singing at the tubs and by twelve o'clock noon the room is over full of steam. The steam is thick—warm—and it settles on your flesh like a damp fur rug. Every pore sits agape in your body; agape—dripping.

Kale's Fine Family Laundry did a good business. Mr. Kale believed in this running on oiled cogs. Cogs that slip easily—oiled from the lowest to the highest.

Now the cogs lowest in his smooth machinery were these thirty tubs and the thirty women at the tubs. I put the tubs first, because they were always there. The women came and went. Sometimes they merely went. Most all of them were dark brown and were that soft bulgy fat that no amount of hard work can rub off of some colored women. All day long they rubbed and scrubbed and sang or shouted and cursed or were silent according to their thirty natures.

Madie Frye never sang or shouted or cursed aloud. Madie was silent. She sang and shouted and cursed within. She sang the first day she came there to work. Sang songs of thanksgiving within her. She had needed that job. She had not worked for ten months until she came there. She had washed dishes in a boarding house before that. That was when she first came from Georgia. She had liked things then. Liked the job, liked the church she joined, liked Tom Nolan, the man for whom she washed dishes.

One day his wife asked Madie if she had a husband. She told her no. She was paid off. Madie, the second, was born soon after. Madie named her unquestioningly Madie Frye. It never occurred to her to name her Nolan, which would have been proper.

Madie bore her pain in silence, bore her baby in a charity ward, thanked God for the kindness of a North and thanked God that she was not back in Culvert when Madie was born, for she would have been turned out of church.

Madie stopped singing aloud then. She tried to get jobs—dishwashing—cleaning—washing clothes—but you cannot keep a job washing someone's clothes or cleaning their house and nurse a baby and keep it from yelling the lady of the house into yelling tantrums.

Madie, second, lost for her mother exactly two dozen jobs between her advent and her tenth month in her mother's arms.

Madie had not had time to feel sorry for herself at first. She was too busy wondering how long she could hold each job. Could she keep Madie quiet until she paid her room rent? Could she keep Mrs. Jones from knowing that Madie was down under the cellar stairs in a basket every day while she was upstairs cleaning, until she got a pair of shoes?

By the time she went to work in Kale's Hand Laundry, she had found the baby a too great handicap to take to work. She began to leave Madie with her next door neighbor, Mrs. Sundell, who went to church three times every Sunday and once in the week. She must be good enough to keep Madie while her mother worked. She was. She kept Madie for two dollars a week and Madie kept quiet for her and slept all night long when she reached home with her mother. Her mother marvelled and asked Mrs. Sundell how she did it.

"Every time she cries, I give her paregoric. Good for her stomach."

So the baby grew calmer and calmer each day. Calmer and quieter. Her mother worked and steamed silently down in Kale's tub-room. Worked, shouting songs of thanksgiving within her for steady money and peaceful nights.

June set in, and with it, scorching days. Days that made the thick steam full of lye and washing-powder eat the lining out of your lungs. There was a set of rules tacked up inside the big door that led into the checking-room that plainly said: "This door is never to be opened between the hours of six in the morning and twelve noon. Nor between the hours of one and six p.m."

That was to keep the steam from the checkers. They were all white and could read and write so they were checkers.

One day Madie put too much lye in some boiling water. It choked her. When she drew her next breath, she was holding her head in the clean cool air of the checking-room. She drew in a deep breath and coughed. A man spun across the floor and a white hand shot to the door. "Why the hell don't you obey rules?" He slammed the door and Madie stumbled back down the stairs.

A girl at the end tub looked around. "Was that Mr. Payne?" she asked.

Madie was still dazed; "Mr. Payne?" she asked.

"Yah. The man what closed the door."

"I don't know who he was."

The other laughed and drew closer to her. "Better know who he is," she said.

Madie blinked up at her. "Why?"

The girl cocked an eye: "Good to know him. You can stay off sometimes—if he likes you." That was all that day.

Another day Madie was going home. Her blank brown face was freshly powdered and she went quietly across the checking-room. The room was empty it seemed at first. All the girls were gone. When Madie was half across the room she saw a man sitting in the corner behind a desk. He looked at her as soon as she looked at him. It was the man who had yanked the door out of her hand, she thought. Fear took hold of her. She began to rush.

Someone called. It was the man at the desk. "Hey, what's your rush?" The voice was not loud and bloody this time. It was soft—soft—soft—like a cat's foot. Madie stood still afraid to go forward—afraid to turn around.

"What, are you afraid of me?" Soft like a cat's foot. "Come here."

—Good to know him—

Madie made the space to the outer door in one stride. The door opened in. She pushed against it.

"Aw, what's the matter with you?" Foot-steps brought the voice nearer. A white hand fitted over the doorknob as she slid hers quickly away.

Madie could not breathe. Neither could she lift her eyes. The door opened slowly. She had to move backwards to give it space. Another white hand brushed the softness of her body.

She stumbled out into the alley. Cold sweat stood out on her.

Madie second had cost her jobs and jobs. She came by Madie keeping that first job.

Madie was black brown. The baby was yellow. Was she now going to go job hunting or have a sister or brother to keep with Madie second?

Cold perspiration sent her shivering in the alley.

And Madie cursed aloud.

Not in my day or your tomorrow—perhaps—but somewhere in God's day of meting—somewhere in God's day of measuring full measures overflowing—the blood will flow back to you—and you will care.

A Possible Triad on Black Notes

Foreword

Now, walking along Frye Street, you sniff first the rusty tangy odor that comes from a river too near a city; walk aside so that Jewish babies will not trip you up; you pause to flatten your nose against discreet windows of Chinese merchants; marvel at the beauty and tragic old age in the faces of the young Italian women; puzzle whether the muscular blond people are Swedes or Danes or both; pronounce odd consonant names in Greek characters on shops; wonder whether Russians are Jews, or Jews, Russians—and finally you will wonder how the Negroes there manage to look like all men of every other race and then have something left over for their own distinctive black-browns.

There is only one Frye Street. It runs from the river to Grand Avenue where the El is.

All the World is there.

It runs from the safe solidity of honorable marriage to all of the amazing varieties of harlotry—from replicas of Old World living to the obscenities of latter decadence—from Heaven to Hell.

All the World is there.

There Were Three

There were three of them.

There was Lucille, there was Little Lou, there was Robbie.

Lucille was the mother of Little Lou and Robbie. She was fat, but most certainly shapely and she was a violet-eyed dazzling blonde. But something in the curve of her bosom, in the swell of her hips, in the red fullness of her lips, made you know that underneath this creamy flesh and golden waviness, there lay a black man—a black woman.

Little Lou and Robbie had a touch of their mother's blondness matched with an ivory tinted flesh in the girl and shaded to a bronze brownness in the boy.

Lots of the women of Frye Street, the colored women—the white women—looked at Robbie's lithe slenderness, small features, and black eyes, with a measuring, waiting, stalking look. Robbie was but sixteen.

"Ku Kaing told me I was the prettiest girl on Frye Street!" Little Lou told Lucille once with the bubbling vanity of flattered fourteen. "And Mr. Davy, that funny Scotchman who keeps the grocery store, said I could be his cashier when I grow up! And Sam Taylor . . ."

"Don't tell me nothing that feather-bed said!" Lucille had screamed. Then she shot out at Robbie, "Why the hell can't you keep care of your sister when I am out working all night?"

Things were like that at number 12 Frye Street where they lived. There were silk sheets on the beds, there was silk underwear in abundance in the bureau drawers, there were toilet waters, perfumes and flashy clothes. But sometimes there was no dinner or no breakfast. And unless Robbie or Little Lou took up the broom, the house was always unswept. Moreover, you continually ran the possibility of sitting down on anybody's hat.

A father?

Nobody gave a thought to such a person.

"You're all mine the both of you!" Lucille had told them once, and neither one of them had ever pushed in behind this for more.

Every night at six thirty Lucille made Little Lou run the bath tub full of warm water.

"Put in half a cup of bath-salts, baby!" Lucille would call from her bedroom while she was undressing.

Little Lou would search out a bottle of heliotrope, jasmine or rose-verbena and drop the crystals daintily in. She would lean way over the steamy tub and sniff with a hungriness at the warm scent as it swept up.

After she had splashed, powdered and partly dressed. Lucille always called the other two into her room to talk. They knew at the call that their mother had put on her dress and was doing her nails and finishing her face.

"You all keep in the house and off the streets while I'm at work, you hear?" she usually began.

"Yes, mama," they never failed to reply readily.

But Robbie stayed out on the corner of Grand Avenue up by the "Toot Sweet Music Shop" with as much of his gang as was not working, until 11 o'clock.

Little Lou went on visits up and down Frye Street, with this girl—with that. But they never left the house until Lucille had finally cocked her hat, settled her complexion to a suitable finality, and silked out to her taxi—to go to work.

"What kind of woman got to go to work dressed better than Sheba when she visited King Solomon and ridin' in a taxi?" Mrs. Lillie Brown who lived at number 14 often asked her husband.

The question was purely rhetorical. The women like Mrs. Brown who waddled wearily beneath a burden of too much of what was not needed in Life—and did not know how to escape it—had already settled the answer among them. To them, Lucille was that flamboyant symbol of uncleanness that always sets the psalm-singers of all earth into rhapsodies.

But Lucille taxied out of Frye Street every night and remained within doors and in bed of a day, so that neither the full chorus nor the free-tones and embellishments of the rhapsodies ever reached her.

It was one of these evenings in April when even a city river tries to smell of spring. The three were shut up in Lucille's room.

"—And you two stay in the house!" Lucille had finished as usual, but she was looking at her buffer when she spoke.

Little Lou and Robbie stared at each other.

"I wish I could go up-town and hop bells with Sammy Jackson at the Sumner!" Robbie remarked after a while.

"You stay down here and stay out of hotels!" Lucille blazed. She hurled the buffer back on her dressing table. "I don't want you 'round no hotel! White women are the devil! Ruin you!"

"They haven't ruined Sammy!" protested Robbie.

"No! The colored women done that for him, 'fore he left Frye Street," retorted his mother.

"Sammy doesn't chase after girls Ma! He always hangs with the gang up to the music store."

"Stay in here and let Sammy alone!" his mother fired. "You hear me?"

"Yes!" Robbie lowered his eyes as he answered.

Before either one of them could speak again, Lucille's taxi tooted, and with a kiss for Little Lou, the mother went to her work.

Little Lou leaned on the bureau gazing absently in the mirror listening to the diminishing chugs of the taxi.

"You going?" she turned to Robbie with the question when the last sound had been lost in the roar of the El.

"You bet!" answered her brother. He swung his leg down from the trunk where he had been sitting. "I got Sammy to ast the man if I could work in a guy's place tonight and believe me I'm going. Get swell tips!"

"Bring me some strawberry ice-cream!" Little Lou begged.

"Sure! I am gonna make two dollars tips!" Robbie expanded.

"We can go to the show!"

"You mean I can!"

"I'll tell if you don't give me some money!"

"Go ahead!"

Robbie swaggered off and out of the house with that, but both of them knew that Little Lou would get a part of the money.

It was a happy Robbie that perched in the midst of the bell-hops at the Sumner two hours later. By that time he had carried two bags, made fifty cents, cursed a little with the boys and already promised the captain that he would gamble below stairs with the bunch when the night was finally over. Robbie felt as smart as his cerise uniform.

"You kin make the next run up-stairs kid!" the captain had offered in a glow of approval.

This new kid was promising. Gave signs of being a good fellow.

Robbie kept an eager eye on the little black register above their seat. When number 740 showed a sudden white eye, Robbie was on his feet before the little plunger had been pushed up to make the board black again.

"Two Silver Sprays for 740!" ordered the captain from his 'phone.

Robbie nodded and flew out into the kitchen to get the tray and the bottles.

"Where you going boy!" the elevator man queried as he closed the doors behind Robbie.

"740!"

"Aw that's a regular souser, that dame! She always gets her sweeties to start the evening by letting her swim in liquor! That's about the sixth bottle of Silver Spray I see go up there tonight!"

"Hot night!" observed Robbie as he stepped off.

"For some folks!" the other called after him and shot the car down again.

In his little flurry of excitement, Robbie found himself following the numbers of the rooms in the wrong direction at first. He reversed his march and stopped to catch his breath before he knocked at 740.

"Come in!" called a woman's voice.

Steadying the tray against the door, Robbie slid into the room.

"Over here by the bed!" the woman spoke again.

Robbie closed the door with his foot and kept his eyes on his bottles as he headed in the general direction of the voice.

He had almost reached the table when the bed came within his range of vision. It sort of swam up between the bottles he was watching so closely.

A pair of plump bare legs protruded between a pink comforter and the sheet. A broad creamy thigh showed through a black satin negligee. Robbie halted.

The door which led into the bath flung open quickly.

"How much boy?" demanded the man who stepped forth.

Robbie sat down his tray. "A dollar and a half, sir," he replied turning around.

"Wait'll I get my trousers!" the man ordered and walked across the room.

Robbie saw that he must have just bathed for he wore only a silk bathrobe. Even his slippers were lacking.

Robbie stole another look toward the bed.

The woman there had been lying on her side with her back

toward the boy, but now she began to stir and finally turned over on her back, drawing the comforter up well all around her.

Her movements among the covers drew the boy's eyes once more.

A pair of violet eyes peering sleepily through tangled blond hair, met his.

Perspiration prickled out all over Robbie.

"Mama!" he whispered hoarsely. "Mama."

"Oh! Jesus!" cried the woman in the bed loudly.

"Mama? Mama!" Robbie began shouting. He tore at the bed clothes. "Mama!!!"

There was a rush of feet across the room.

"Here! what the hell do you mean, you little nigger!" shouted the man as he ran.

Now Robbie was by the window.

It was April.

Even a city river opens up to Spring.

The window tried to draw Spring in, opened as it was, seven stories above the city pavement.

The man rushed up behind Robbie.

The man struck Robbie to knock him down.

The window was open.

. . . A woman on the third floor said that the boy was screaming for his mother as his body hurtled through the air.

But it was an accident.

It was an accident that could not possibly find its way into the daily papers.

There was a note, though, that a bell boy had lost his balance and fallen to his death while opening a window in the Sumner. There was further note that no parents had yet come to claim the body.

That was all to that.

But—there were three.

Now, up at McNeil Institute where those people stay whose wealthy connections can prevent them from being assigned to an ordinary asylum, there is a stout blonde woman patient with violet eyes.

Sometimes she screams: "Take your yellow hands off! Off!

Off!"

Again she cries: "Don't smother me—don't smother me—black feather bed!"

Or even: "Take your dirty white hands off! Off! Off!"

Nobody knows what she means.

It's a color fixation, some people say.

But—there were three you see.

Sometimes I wonder which door opened for that third.

Of Jimmy Harris

Jimmy Harris was dying.

"Can't believe it!" said the "boys."

. . . Every night the "boys" gathered in the Valet de Luxe tailor shop. A day was not completed properly unless the colored men of Frye Street—those who were through with the flesh-pots up-town and just as through with wives with whom they had lived some several years—did not gather in Jimmy's shop from eight until ten. They call themselves the "Boys," but every single one of them was well beyond thirty-five. Indeed, Pop Gentry, the one who told the nastiest jokes, strutted the most vibrant impromptu dances, drank the most, cursed the loudest, was sixty.

Rain, sleet, wind, family wars, could not keep one of the "boys" away from the De Luxe.

Of a night—except Sundays—every chair and piece of chair, every box, and even the cutting tables were filled with colored men of all sizes and varieties. Some of those temporarily devoid of funds, stood around half-dressed and pressed their own trousers while they guffawed and bantered.

Jimmy Harris had a seal-smooth skin coupled with the straight cast features and hair of a natural smooth waviness that constitutes "a good-looking brown." The clothes which he made for himself sat on his medium-sized figure neatly. He was usually amiable, knew how to listen when the gang wanted to do the talking, had a reputation for good living and money, and minded his business.

Everybody liked Jimmy.

He always sat cross legged on one of the big black tables, stitching—stitching—stitching—while the others talked.

"Nigger! don't you never lay off workin'?" Pop Gentry asked this more than once. "Them pantsies an coatsies'll all be 'round here waiting for somebody to wear and yo'll be wid de worms an daisies, boy! How 'm I talkin'!" he would end in a shout of laughter, and slap Jimmy on the back or any handy portion of his anatomy before he sat down.

Usually Jimmy would smile and murmur, "That's right," before he lapsed into silence and went on stitching—stitching—stitching.

It was Pop Gentry who had carried Jimmy's head and shoulders when he pitched head first off of his table one night and laid quiet on the floor in their midst.

"My God! the boy got a stroke!" somebody had chattered after the first dazed moment of speechless surprise.

"It's his liquor maybe!" someone else had suggested.

"Jimmy can carry his 'thout laying on the floor and pavements!"

"Git a doctor!" Pop had shouted.

"Cerebral hemorrhage! Put him in bed at once!" the doctor had ordered.

"No hope, I am afraid!" he added.

. . . "Can't believe it," sobbed his mother adjusting an ice bag over Jimmy's temples. "I can't believe God's goin' take my boy home yet! He's not but thirty-eight!"

She wiped her eyes on a huck towel which she had in her hand. Then she walked to the window. Seemed as if there could be a little less light in the room.

Would it be all right to lower the lace-edged window shades a few fractions of an inch?

That Louise—Jimmy's wife—was such a durn fool about her house.

"Don't break my John Haviland china! Use the jelly glasses to drink out of! You'll chip my hand-etched goblet! Don't take an ice pick to get the ice cubes out of the Frigidaire! If you slam that oven door, you'll upset my thermostat!" she made Jimmy's mother sweat blood for every hour spent visiting at his house.

"Marm Harris" would have preferred to remain in Luray, Virginia, in her own modest five rooms where a body could feel at home and eat with elbows on the table dressed only in a cotton kimona if the urge seized her.

But she never felt easy about Jimmy.

She never felt easy about Jimmy up in the big city on Frye Street with a tailor shop and a blonde wife who said she was colored—and Mary Linn, staying single all the fifteen years that had elapsed since Jimmy forgot her for Louise.

And though she hated Frye Street, hated Louise, hated the smoothness of Jimmy's home, Marm would bundle up herself every year and go north to Jimmy's.

One night in the dark solitude of their bed-chamber, Louise had tried a plaintive air of long suffering affliction.

"Does your mother have to visit you this year again?" she had asked.

"My mother can come any time she wants and stay as long as she wants! The other bedroom is for her!"

"Oh, oh! I did not know that!" Louise had retorted stiffly. "I thought that was the spare-chamber!"

"Spare hell! It's Ma's!"

Louise had been surprised into silence at the violence of Jimmy's retort. She usually swung the reins of their life together skillfully in one hand. Jimmy had never balked before.

It would not do to carry things to open battle. Sniping is more annoying than straight line firing.

The old lady would find her visit "spare hell."

But Marm came and came again and came when Jimmy was sick and Louise had wired that she herself was unable to take care of him.

"I can't believe Jimmy is dying!" Louise cried to Doctor Whetbone. She sat well in the center of the green satin love-seat which made some visitors unwelcome to her parlor.

"Well, dear lady, I am very sorry but I can offer no hope!" Doctor Whetbone repeated.

"Gosh! A lanky bronze colored man with deep set gray eyes is a heart ache, believe me!" thought Louise watching the doctor.

Whetbone leaned easily against the mantle.

He was one of those tall men who never sat down unless it was absolutely necessary. Some people said that he stood up so you could see how well his suit fitted him across the shoulders, how well his shoes fitted his feet, how well he himself fitted into any surroundings under any circumstances—in short—what a patrician he was.

That was what some people said.

People say a lot of things about a reasonably decent looking man who can earn a comfortable living and is still single at 34.

Louise widened her eyes until water flowed into them. "What'll I do?" she lifted her voice and her eyes piteously to Dr. Whetbone.

"Now—now," countered the physician. "Just try to realize that you have done your best for him—kept your home beautifully for him!" he made a sweeping gesture of the room.

"Oh, yes," murmured Louise.

"You tried to make him take more rest and better care of himself!" continued Whetbone soothingly.

"Yes, I made him put in oil-heat so he would not have to shovel coal and buy a car so we could go out for nice rides in the evenings together, and buy an electric refrigerator so I could always keep milk and vegetables fresh for him!"

"Yes, yes!" finished the Doctor. "Let's run upstairs and take a look at him."

And Jimmy, fastened inside of his body by a tongue that could no longer speak, saw Louise standing close beside the doctor at his bedside.

Saw her lift and lower her eyes as she talked to him.

Why were they smiling at each other?

He watched them.

The doctor left the room presently.

Louise went to the bureau and smiled into the mirror at herself pinching first her arm, then her cheek, fluffing out her hair, smoothing down her black satin dress.

Then she went out of the room too.

She did not look toward the bed again.

"Oh, I can't believe it! Jimmy can't be dying!" a tall thin brown woman cried aloud.

She was walking up a country road in Luray.

"God don't take him! Oh God!!" she stopped and knelt on a bank that was tangled with rose vines and dead leaves.

But she had stopped and cried and prayed on rose banks for fifteen years—and Jimmy had married Louise and stayed up north on Frye Street and waxed and prospered—though he had no children.

Presently she rose from the rose-vines and went walking on crying and praying.

But God must despise a sniveler.

She had cried and prayed for fifteen years.

Jimmy Harris was dying.

Pain thundered down across Jimmy Harris.

Back and forth it avalanched, dragging him down, sucking him deeply under.

Once he fought through, came up out of the thundering to find himself in his own bed—in his own room. The lavender electric clock on the bureau was flanked by the lavender and green figurines that supported Louise's boudoir lamps there. But everything looked new, distant.

"God!! I've been sick!! Sick!!" Jimmy told himself.

He sent his thoughts here, there, into himself to seek out the sick spot, the weak spot.

But before he had found it, pain tumbled back angrily, smotheringly, sucked him under, dragged him down, pulled,—pulled—pulled—.

"I can't fight back! I can't get up over this pain mountain over me!" Jimmy cried within.

He began to sink straightway.

That is what they call being reconciled to die. They call it reconciled when pain has strummed a symphony of suffering back and forth across you, up and down, round and round you until each little fibre is worn tissue-thin with aching. And when you are lying beaten, and buffeted, battered and broken—pain goes out, joins hands with Death and comes back to dance, dance,

dance, stamp, stamp, stamp down on you until you give up.

"I can't believe it!" Jimmy cried to himself—and all of the time the Two were dancing, dancing, stamping, stamping.

"I can't believe it! I'll get up! Go out! Go to work! Finish! Finish! Stitch! Stitch!"

—What was that uprooting like a tree in a windstorm?

—What was that bright glowing in his eyes?

—What was that loosing—tearing loose—uprooting—shedding—?

"He's gone!" exclaimed Dr. Whetbone walking to the bed.

"Gone!" sobbed Marm, kneeling beside the bed.

Louise sat on the steps outside of the room. She had not been able to stay in the room while Jimmy Harris had been breathing, breathing, breathing so that it sounded as if the room were filled with many tubs of water draining off with that gurgling of water settling to waste.

Jimmy Harris was dead.

I guess he'd been happy, though.

He had had his hands on what he wanted.

Corner Store*

"Some more lachs, Anton? A little matzos and wine? A pickled tomato?" A quiver of appeal, entirely too searing for so simple a thing as an invitation to dally with more food, ran through Esther Steinberg's voice.

Anton Steinberg shook his head vigorously in denial. His hands and mouth were full of lebkuchen. He shook his head because he did not wish more food, nor did he wish to recognize the seeking in Esther's tone. He lowered his eyes so that he would not have to see his wife.

Her flabby body, slouched in faded grey house dress and muffled in ragged black sweater, was as dismal as the pallor of her

*As originally published, this part of "A Possible Triad on Black Notes" carried the following heading above the title "Corner Store": "Three Tales of Living/From 'The Black Map'/(A book entirely unwritten)"

flaccid face. Esther's only beauty had been a head of black hair that seemed to spring in aliveness in each curl.

Working from dawn until midnight for seven years behind the counter of Steinberg's Grocery-Market on Frye Street, had made an old woman of Esther at thirty-nine.

Anton crammed crumbs of gingerbread hastily into his mouth, wiped his hands on the apron which he never removed for the noon lunch served in this kitchen in back of their store, and rushed out as the bell tinkled in the shop.

As soon as she was alone, Esther drew a sibilant sobbing sigh and covered her face with both hands.

"Teach me what I should do, Gott!" she prayed in a hoarse whisper.

"Say something, ma?" called a girl's voice suddenly from a room within.

Esther snatched down her hands and crouched lower in her chair. She said nothing.

A sound of yawning came now from within, then all at once, pushing aside the gunny-sacking which served as a drapery between the two rooms, Meta, daughter of Esther and Anton, stood in the door. She rubbed her eyes and stretched with the elastic abandon of seventeen years.

"Who are you talking to, ma?" she queried again.

Esther shook her head. "Nobody. I—I was—I was wishing I was back in the old country. In the ghetto," she finished timidly with a swift look at her daughter's face.

Meta made a rapid gesture, shrugged her shoulders and shaking her black hair out around her, began combing it with quick strokes.

"Oh for God's sake ma! What do you want to be back in that old mud hole for with nothing but Jews, Jews, before you, behind you and beside you? You ought to be glad to get to a free country, for heaven's sake!"

Esther looked first at Meta's high-heeled patent-leather pumps, then at her gun-metal chiffon stockings drawn over nicely-turned legs. Her red flannel dress caught her snugly across the bosom and at the hips, but its vivid color brought out the blackness of her curly bob the rich red of her lips and the soft moulding of her delicate, oval face. Jewish girls in the Old World did not dress this way.

"You ashamed to be a Jew?" Esther demanded harshly.

"No, ma! but for pete's sake, I should think you'd be glad papa is making good money and spending it here like you never could back there!"

"I want to be near a nice Schule and have nice Jewish neighbors!" persisted the mother with a sort of stubborn sullenness.

"Then you don't want the new auto and the fur coat and the flats that we own on the West Side?"

Esther made an exclamation like a cat when it spits. "Tcha! We got just as good in the old country—!"

"Like fun! don't you think I remember those old cold stone houses with no heat and nothing else in them! Why do you want to go back to a place where dirty German kids wait around to throw mud on you when you go out? No! Give me Frye Street!"

Meta dropped down to the table and helped herself to some of the smoked salmon.

Her mother drew back into her corner—drew back into herself.

Anton's heavy step sounded in the little hall outside the kitchen. He scowled as soon as he saw his daughter.

"You up, you Meta! What for do you sleep all the day when I want that you should help me with the Saturday rush?"

Meta wiped her fingers on a piece of wax paper and licked one daintily. "Don't you think I go to sleep, maybe?"

"Why don't you sleep nights instead of racing the streets? That's what I want to know!"

An angry flush swept the girl's face. "Yah!" she mocked. "Why don't I go to the Schule at night—Monday—Tuesday—Thursday again like you! You!! At the Schule—"

Her pertness trailed off into a frightened silence. The vein in Anton's left temple was standing out like a rope. His face was swollen a dark purple.

"Du—du—!" he choked and lifted his hand.

"Anton! Anton!" shrilled Ester. "Strafe nicht!"

Meta stared back at her father. But she did not flinch.

115

The bell on the door of the shop jangled.

No one moved.

"One comes to buy!" Esther urged in Jewish.

"A customer comes, Anton!" she repeated as he did not move.

Her husband hung an instant on the threshold, then with a snort that was almost a snarl, he went back up the passage to the store.

"Gott! Was fur ein' Mann!" Esther chattered in an agony of fear. "Ever since we got to this place he becomes more cold to me! Now he wants to hit you, Liebschen!"

"If he hits me I'll run off to get married, right away." Meta burst forth passionately.

"Ja! David Sorbenstein is one nice boy. Me and papa chose him for you ourselves! Goes to the Schule every week and stays bei the shop of his Vater." Esther garbled Jewish and such English as she knew. "Ach solche ein' Knabe!"

"David Sorbenstein is a fat greasy slob! A dumbell! He makes me sick! I wouldn't marry that guy!"

"Meta! he'd make such a goot husband! Such an industry—"

But Meta shook her shoulders impatiently and switched David's virtues to scorn as fast as Esther could tell them off.

"I'd run off to marry Abe Brown!" Meta declared.

"A goy—a Gentile?" Esther could not believe herself.

Meta nodded. "He isn't all goy. His grandfather is a Jew and his mother is colored. Schwartze!"

"Ein' Schwartze! Du mein' lieber Gott!" Esther laid her face on her arm and wept aloud and loudly.

Anton came running back again. "Was ist geschied'? Na! Na, Esther," he cried as he came.

He rubbed his hands soothingly across his wife's hair.

"Du!" he glowered at Meta across Esther's bowed head.

"Ein' Schwartze! Meta!" screamed Esther.

Anton's eyes hung in Meta's. "Du?" the word was a gasp.

His face whitened. Meta shook her head. "Only Abe," she whispered.

Something desperate oozed out of Anton's face. Vast relief grew there.

"Na na! Esther!" he began again. "Nichts! Nichts! Es gibt nichts! Du musst dass nicht! Meta don't mean nothing! She wouldn't marry no Gentile. She wouldn't marry no Schwartze!"

The bell on the shop rang loudly.

"I'll go!" Anton announced briskly, and he was out and back by the time Esther's wails had subsided to an incessant hiccoughing.

"Now mama! Now mama! Our little girl will make bei Yom Kippur mit Sorbenstein's boy a nice marriage!"

"I won't!" Meta shouted.

"Aah—aah!" began Esther in a rising tone of lamentation.

The shop bell rang.

"You go mama! Wait on the custom! Papa will talk to Meta!" Anton ordered.

Esther moved on heavy feet forward to the store. Early twilight was falling thickly over everything. Esther turned back to fumble for the switch box.

"Anton! Anton?" called a woman's voice softly from somewhere near the door.

Esther's hand froze uplifted as it reached the switch. Who was this woman who dared to stand in her store calling Anton by his name with that soft, urgent, intimate lift of the voice?

Esther shot on all of the lights and stepped out on to the floor.

Standing by the butcher block, was a woman. Her limbs curved heavily beneath a pink cotton house dress, her black hair shone in a series of braids coiled high around a lovely head. On first glance, she was Semitic. It was not until Esther was upon her that she saw that she was a colored woman.

"You want something?" demanded Esther brusquely.

"No—" the other replied hesitatingly.

Heavy steps padded from the rear. "I'll attend the custom, mama!" Anton nearly shouted as he bounded forward.

"Mama—mama!" he gabbled. "Meta wants that you should come there. She will tell you something."

"Noch der schwartze? (Is it still to be the black man)" his wife queried.

"Moglich! We must be patient, though after a little—ver- leicht—David Sorbenstein! We'll see! Nun!"

117

Esther sped along the hall to the kitchen but Meta was back in the inner room talking on the telephone.

—"So listen, Abe darling,—I just told him that you were Ella's nephew and that you knew already about his going to the "Schule"—ha! ha!—every night. And he says to me, 'Well, maybe then I'll talk to mama and tell her to wait a little, but don't you do nothing about marrying, yet awhile!'—What? Sure! He's crazy about her! She's out there now! Ella's out in the store talking to him now—What? Sure! Makes a swell whip to hold over papa!"

Standing in the kitchen, Esther stared slowly around her, listening. As the words bore into her, she began to stare wildly, shaking her head from side to side—side to side.

This wasn't Meta talking!

That was not Anton outside!

This room was not home. Only stone houses in ghettoes are homes.

The narrow kitchen with its barren huddled air was closing her in.

—"She's out there now! Yah! Ella!!"—

—"Anton?" a woman's voice had called softly with a caress in it that searched like a gentle hand seeking to find something loved in a dark place. . . .

Esther tore back up the hall toward the store.

Anton stood beside his block, a cleaver trailing idly from one hand talking, talking, looking down into the woman's face.

There they stood.

Close together.

Her head tilted back, her eyes veiling, then lifting.

Esther rushed back and standing in the hall between the shop and the kitchen—she lifted up her voice and screamed and screamed.

She caught hold of the sacking. It tore down from its place between the doors. She fell as it ripped and lay prone on the floor, the sack cloth around her and screamed and screamed.

"Like a wild thing in a forest, you holler!" Anton came running to swear at her.

"Like one who moans for Israel!" replied Esther—and lay and sobbed in her sack cloth.

Tin Can

1

*"For my people have committed two evils: they
have forsaken me, the fountain of living
waters—and hewed them out cisterns, broken
cisterns, that can hold no water."*

Jeremiah

Take an empty tin can.

Stand it up.

Drop two or three hard jagged pebbles in it.

Knock the tin can down. The pebbles will rattle-rattle-rattle.
You can hear each little rock pattering its own little rattle, its
hollow rattle, when the can is shaken and knocked down.

You can hear each hard rattling—like undigested thoughts—
hollow.

Hollow.

Jimmie Joe was dancing. There are no words in any language
under the sun rich enough in color, movement and sound to
make you see a young black boy lilting a slim seventeen-year-old
body through a dance.

Right now, Little Brother sat hunched up on his own cot
watching. The holes in his cotton union suit were as wide as his
mouth as his eyes danced with Jimmie Joe.

"Yappy-titty yap-yap! Skee-dad-dad!" chanted Jimmie Joe. He
slid a neat step up into the corner between his own bed and the
bureau and began "falling-off-the-log" to get out again when the
sound they had both been praying would not come before the

119

dance had finished—tore from below stairs.

"You, Jimmie Joe! You, Little Brother!" It was Ma, standing at the foot of the stairs. "You all stop that racket and get them clothes on and get down here 'fore I comes up there!"

"Unh-unh!" exclaimed Little Brother on two tones. He dropped his knees at once and began to wiggle his black-brown feet into stockings and shoes.

With the dance rhythm on him, Jimmie Joe had to tap his mood out to a finish. He circled the room like some barnyard fowl, his arms moving in an exaggerated flapping.

Little Brother tore his eyes from his square toed scuffed boots long enough to take in Jimmie Joe's neat suede oxfords, black trousers, black belt, white sweater and white shirt with its black bow tie.

"You all right, boy!" he worshipped in an awed tone. "Jes wait'll ma let's me git to them Sunday night dances! I'll show you some steps every Monday, too!"

Panting a little, Jimmie Joe stopped in front of the mirror to straighten the bow tie. "She ain't *lettin'* me git there yet! I jes goes on my hardness, boy!"

Little Brother hoisted his garnet corduroy slacks on over his chunky body. "You all right, boy!" he breathed again.

"Y'all want me to come up there with this clothes stick?" Ma's voice had a real edge on it now.

That meant it was near seven then and that Ma was fidgety to get breakfast on the table and get out so that she could get the eight o'clock car to go to work.

That edge in Ma's voice pried Little Brother up from his seat on the side of the cot and even unfastened Jimmie Joe from his place, glued as he was in a close gazing at himself before the mirror.

Ma got up at half past five every morning and made the fire in the kitchen and cooked breakfast and cleaned up as much of the house as she could get at at that time in the morning.

"I always believes in leavin' my house clean every day!" she told Jimmie Joe and Little Brother many a time. "You never know what day somebody's gonna bring you back home from a accident! And what'd I feel like if the house was dirty and the beds not clean and me not clean underneath my clothes!"

Ma worked from five-thirty to seven, thus. Then she gave the boys their breakfast and ate her own—usually walking back and forth from her bedroom to the kitchen as she ate—dressing so she could catch the eight o'clock car and go and do her day's work.

She would be at work when the boys came back from school. She would be at work when they came home to supper. Ma never came back from her "Rich white folks"—as Little Brother called them—until well after eight o'clock.

And though her steps would usually be slow by then and her breathing hard, she always washed and ironed and mended and cleaned up some more.

The only time Jimmie Joe and Little Brother saw her to talk to her on week days was the time in the morning when she was walking back and forth, drinking a sip of tea, putting her dress on, eating a fork full of grits, putting her hat on—gnawing a piece of bread and telling Jimmie Joe how much to spend for dinner and how to fix it—all at the same time.

"You, Jimmie Joe!" Ma yelled this morning as soon as the two reached the kitchen door. "How come you can't never bring no coal in like I done tole you so's I can fix the fire every morning?"

"Unh-unh!" bleated Little Brother. He scurried to a seat at the table and sat back mentally to watch Jimmie Joe wiggle out of a tight place.

Nobody could ever corner *his* brother!

"I tol' Little Brother to git the coal last night, Ma!" Jimmie Joe yelled back as loudly as his mother had spoken.

"Heah! Don't you holler at me, boy!" Ma snatched up the coal shovel and held it, batwise, pressed against her left shoulder.

Little Brother breathed noisily.

Jimmie Joe did not flinch. "Little Brother didn't bring it in, Ma! I tole him to do it while I was at Lucas's last night—studyin'!" Jimmie Joe repeated as if the shovel had not been there.

"Dat boy kin sure lie!" Little Brother marvelled to himself. "I ain't heard you!" he apologized aloud on a whining note to Jimmie Joe.

Ma said nothing to this. Jimmie Joe slid into a chair, kicked

Little Brother slyly under the table, and began to shovel up hominy grits and gravy.

"Don't forgit to thank God for them vittles!" Ma exploded next. "I 'clare you is going to the devil fas' as you kin make it, Jimmie Joe!"

Jimmie Joe lowered his head over the plate an instant, then raised his head and voice in his own defense.

"I always says my blessing, Ma! You just come jumping on me this morning 'fore I got in here good 'bout something Little Brother didn't do and made me fergit! Ain't I been going to church every Sunday like you tole me?"

"You aint been there no Sunday nights! You better not be hanging 'round no dance halls on Sunday nights like Anna Lucas's boy. I bet I'll take the hide off you ef I hears you been there!"

Jimmie Joe eeled into another tangent.

"I got to get another book today for English, Ma!"

"What the name of God you got to buy so many books for? Ain't I given you money to buy six English books this year and this ain't but March? What them teachers think I is?"

Jimmie Joe slid into a closer position. "But I got to have it or Miss Thomas'll flunk me and you know Pa says he'll take me out of school if I flunk English again!"

That silenced Ma. She and Pa fought a constant war over the fact that Jimmie Joe and Little Brother went to school. Pa maintained a colored boy did not need high school—like Jimmie Joe was getting—nor even junior high school—where Little Brother was—to do the kind of work a colored man could get to do. All you needed was a little reading so you could find a "Help Wanted" sign and get on the right street cars and a little numbering "so's these sheenies" could not cheat you in the stores! And you could get that much—while you had your diapers on!

But Ma—like all women—had her ear tuned to the melody that might be someday, somewhere.

"Them boys may be big Negroes someday! Can't never tell!" she'd always countered.

So Jimmy Joe knew which note to sound.

"That boy sure kin lie! He ain't got to get no book." Little Brother kept telling himself. His thoughts wriggled through him so rapidly that he began to gobble his food.

"Little Brother! You chew that food 'fore you chokes to death!" Ma ordered.

"Yas'm!" Little Brother was meek.

"He sure God is dumb!" sneered Jimmie Joe to himself. He studied Little Brother's round blobby face in contempt. "No stuff in him! That guy will never be smart!"

"The book'll be six bits, Ma!" Jimmie offered next, his eye on the clock.

"Six bits! You mean seventy-five cents! What kinder book you got to get now!"

This was a crack that could be widened. Jimmie Joe began to work on the opening. "Shakespeare!"

"Ain't that what you got the las' time!"

"Aw yes, Ma! But that guy wrote a whole lot of stuff! You gotta read some this year and some next year too!"

"Well you gotta *earn* some of the money yourself this year and next year too! I 'clare I ain't got no seventy-five cents for no books this day!"

Ma flung her tea-cup from her to the ledge on the back of the stove, gave a hurried glance at the clock which was indicating quarter of eight and fled to the bedroom for her hat and coat.

Little Brother laid his fork down to watch Jimmie Joe. Would he be defeated?

Ma came charging out of the bedroom. "Aw, I ain't got no time to argue with you," she called back to Pa—who was still in bed. She snatched up her pocket-book from the place where it had been hanging on the knob of the sideboard door.

"You, Little Brother! You bring that coal in tonight!"

"Amen!" chanted Jimmie Joe, sotto voce.

"Shut up!" Ma stopped for a momentary battle of eyes. "And, Little Brother, you put them sugar loaf cabbages to soak in salt and water, when you get home! Don' cook 'em for an hour! Jes let 'em soak so's the bugs and worms will die out of them! Then put it in that water what I cooked the ham knuck in yestiddy!"

"Yas'm!"

"Y'all behave in school!"

"Yas'm!" in chorus.

"And you come in the house at five—both of you!"

"Yas'm!" final chorus!

"Bye!"

"Bye!"

And Ma was gone.

Ma hurried up Tenth Street, around the corner and stood under the "El" waiting for a cross town surface car. Through the city streets' flecky, dirty mounds of snow Spring had forwarded a subtle something into the morning air.

Ma looked in a shop window at herself. "I 'clare I gets fatter every year! Who'd think I weighed jes' ninety-seven when I married Pa! I ought to git me one of those new satin hats this week. This thing is a mess!"

She passed on a little farther.

Krönen's Swedish Bakery, fresh in a coat of light blue paint on the woodwork and bedecked inside with pink crepe paper napkins—had a pyramid of pink and yellow cakes in the window.

Ma stopped short.

"Believe I'll git me one of them cakes for lunch today!" she decided, suddenly reckless, and she went in.

"Nice day!" grinned Mrs. Krönen as she drew the cake in from the window. "Anything else?" she seemed to beg it as she started wrapping the cake.

"No!" Ma grinned back. She opened her pocketbook.

One lone nickel and three pennies rolled in there as she shook it.

Where was the ninety cents that she had put back in there after she had put a dime in church last night? She had broken a dollar!

Her mind made a frantic hurdle forward. Where would Tuesday's and Wednesday's dinner come from if she had no money?

Maybe the ham knuck would hold out if they ate fried potatoes and onions with it.

Then her mind hurdled distractedly back.

She couldn't give the woman five cents for a cake and then

124

walk to work. She'd never get there!

She jangled coins fiercely again, trying to concoct ninety cents out of a nickel and three pennies.

—"Ma! I gotta get a book this morning! Six bits!"—

Jimmie Joe had it.

Mrs. Krönen held out the cake.

Sweat hung in huge beads on Ma's face and neck, itched along her body.

Jimmie Joe stole!

"I guess I can't take the cake!" Ma panted.

Mrs. Krönen's smile froze and faded.

Ma stumbled out, slamming the door behind her.

Jimmie Joe was a thief.

In the meantime scrocking his heel plates grandly in the midst of his gang, Jimmie Joe was advancing on the High School.

Situated as it was in the middle of the Black Belt of that big northern city, nobody called the school the colored high school, but everything in it from top to bottom, from janitor to principal was some one of the varieties of Negro. The School Board sent all the colored children from every district there. The School Board appointed colored teachers with the proper qualifications to this one high school.

By licking the boots of those above him and kicking the backs of those below, and by never walking upright where it would gain him a point to crook his spine physically and morally, the black principal gained and held his job.

It was of him Jimmie Joe and his gang talked that morning.

"Wonder what tune that old Black Bass Drum is going to be playing in assembly this mornin'."

Three boys sang aloud in derision, "The Character building program! Blah! Bloo! Wah!"

"Aw—!" One scraped his feet and cursed.

You have seen Jimmie Joe's gang in every Negro section of every city of any size in the world. They range from sixteen to nineteen—they range from coal black to it-takes-a-second-glance-to-tell light. They are all neat and well dressed after their own particular pattern of heel-plated oxfords, wide trousers, foppish overcoats, gay sweaters and lumberjackets and pastel-toned felt hats.

And like Jimmie Joe, most of them had sounded every note in the scale of living except the whole note of legitimate marriage. All the half-tones and chromatic inversions of indecent living they had played, until an overlay of boredom, such as might weight the jaws of a forty-year-old rounder, masked the youth in their faces before they were twenty.

So—scraping their feet cursing, gibing at each other and at groups of boys and girls they passed, they reached the building just as the bell rang.

"Hell! I ain't going to no home room!" exploded Jimmie Joe at the sound. "Come on, George!" He singled out one rangy fair youth who was his special confrere. "Let's grab us a smoke in the Auto Paint Shop!"

"Yeah!" asserted George, swinging off from the larger group with Jimmie Joe. "I sure don't feel like hearing that character stuff today! I get damn sick of that Black Bass Drum telling you how much manners and stuff he's got, and honest to God, when I used to work in his office on the switchboard, I've seen that nigger plug in his 'phone so he could listen to the teachers talk when they got an outside call!"

"Aw he ain't got nuttin—!" began Jimmie Joe—but just as they swung around the next corner there met them face to face, the principal.

He skinned back his lips in what he took to be the proper degree of cordiality to students whose parents were not his social equal.

"Mawnin!" muttered George and Jimmie Joe.

The man passed on, swaying an overstuffed figure from side to side on rubber heels. What character he might have once had, had long been swallowed up in a morass of petty littleness, snobbishness and downright silly conceit. He prided himself on three things: that he was a leading Negro—that is to say, he had been placed at the head of a school—; then, he could never cease to marvel that though his own skin was jet black his children had managed to be born with tawny skins, slightly darker than their fair mother's. Finally, he could not forget that he was the first black man born in a certain college town to graduate from a famous college.

Anything that did not contribute to these conceits, simply did not exist to the Black Bass Drum.

You could not make him understand that something besides formal platform speeches should be done about the fact that there was a gang of boys in his school who stole everything from everybody. No teacher could persuade him that instead of sending on inflated reports full of empty embroidered phrases— saying absolutely nothing—to the higher ups—somebody ought to appeal to someone to stop the growing menace of the spread of social diseases among students. He closed his eyes to the annual crop of unmarried mothers in the senior class, blamed the teachers because the general scholarship was unspeakably low— and never admitted that he had any vital part in all of these problems but to lead where his narrow soul dictated.

He was not so much a black bass drum as he was just the fool ostrich, sticking his head into a hollow hole—the height and depth of his particular brain capacity—while an overwhelming world and ocean full of a million new conditions were sweeping up on him.

Bells were ringing at regular intervals all over the building as George and Jimmie Joe took their furtive way toward the paint shop. As they passed groups of students scurrying in cockroach fashion up and down the corridors, Jimmie Joe seemed to be on a restless lookout for someone. He would cut short whatever he was saying to George to stare into this group—then that.

"This nigger sure has got a bad case of Caroline," George thought to himself—but he said nothing of what he thought, aloud. "If she jus' doesn't happen by till we get to the paint shop, we'll get a smoke!"

And then Caroline met them face to face.

There is no accounting for the Carolines of this world—not that they are all called Caroline. Their names never matter really. What does matter is that they are all compelling, all glamorous, all undeniably attractive to all men of all types and all ages.

This Caroline was not fair. She would have been just another white girl if she had been. Instead, she was a golden reddish brownish shade. She was dimpled and smooth and clear. Her eyes were black and thick-lashed and her mouth took rouge with a pouting insouciance. She dressed beautifully, neatly, smartly and daintily, though she got her clothes by the nastiest possible means.

And her love affairs—or affairs of sex, it would be far better to call them—had given her a subtle languor as well as a confident seductive dash—and a body well filled with unmentionable disease.

At the sight of her, Jimmie Joe stood stock still. So did the world, so far as he was concerned. He did not even answer George's "See you later!" as he plunged on.

2

"Jimmie Joe!" Caroline crescendoed on all the nearest delightful tones of the scale. "I was thinking about you," which she wasn't. "Come on and carry my books up to my locker and then walk down to the assembly hall with me!"

Dumbly Jimmie Joe swung around, dumbly Jimmie Joe went down to the assembly hall and followed his section up the aisle to their usual seats, though he had not meant to be there.

The Black Bass Drum rapped out his usual monotonous roundel of so much palaver to an audience that was only younger than he—chronologically.

"Character is everything. I never forget my fellowman! It's easier to be good than to be bad!"

There were no new arrangements of words. It was all so empty, so vacant, so useless, so futile. Nobody—nobody—nowhere by talking from a platform can make you really know things that need to be induced gently, firmly, carefully, steadily into the essence of you every moment of your life. It's too late when fourteen years or more of haphazard, slap-dash, hit-or-miss, grab-bag living has snatched you through the lowly life of poor colored homes in black sections.

There was nothing new in it all. His audience dozed or ruminated or plotted and planned as peacefully as if they had all been seated by a placid pool, letting the ripples ruffle its surface—unheeded.

Jimmie Joe sat plunged in a daze of joy that was to cost him one F in English, the first period for inattention and two the second and third periods in General Science for staring out of the window instead of into a microscope. Caroline was going to eat lunch with Jimmie Joe at recess.

The eighty-two cents of which Ma had been relieved, was going to buy two hot-dogs, two pieces of strawberry meringue pie and two ten cent boxes of vanilla ice cream.

For the hot-dogs, pie and ice cream, Jimmie Joe was going to have the privilege of sauntering by Caroline's side down the streets near the school as they ate.

All the gang would see him.

All the gang would know, accordingly, that Jimmie Joe had money from somewhere because no male could talk to Caroline long without a moneyed backing of some sort.

All the school would see and know straightway that Jimmie Joe was a man of parts.

Dazed back in the midst of his seat as he waited through three periods and three F's for the fourth period and recess and Caroline, Jimmie Joe's only regret was that the eighty-two cents had not been eighty-two dollars.

It was the second Sunday in April when Ma first mentioned the theft of the eighty-two cents—and that indirectly.

Ma did not go to work on Sunday.

She got up at six o'clock, took her bath in the tin wash tub in the kitchen, straightened her hair with an old knife and crimped it with a hot fork before she waked the boys to breakfast.

Sunday morning she always sat between them at the table. Pa never got up to eat unless they had breakfast nearer ten o'clock than nine.

This particular morning, though, Ma served the boys at nine.

The three were, thus, alone.

"Y'all is goin' to church with me this mornin'!" Ma announced after she had bowed her head and thanked a good Father for the victuals.

Jimmie Joe shot an oblique glance up from his plate. He was swallowing his food to clear a way to mouth his lie that would get him out of the ordeal.

Ma was ahead of him, though.

"I want you to go especial, Jimmie Joe! I ast the Reverend to speak on young liars and thieves!"

This was too much for Little Brother. He swallowed half a pancake in one whop and had to be smacked on the back.

Ma gave Little Brother a drink of coffee, but she was not through with Jimmie Joe.

"A lots of us women of the church what has no count chillun has been astin the Reverend to for God's sake do somethin' 'bout the lyin' and thievin' and nasty dirty mess they all is up to! So today he is talkin' and you all is going!"

Jimmie Joe was as meek as Little Brother after that. Ma could lead them both through the extra shining up that meant Sunday dressing—down the street—round the corner to the Holy Christian Saints of the Redeemer Church.

The Holy Christian Saints of the Redeemer was a split from the Anointed Lambs of the Most High.

The Anointed Lambs poured forth their unction on the corner of First Avenue and Second Street in the store that had been King Solomon's Pawn Shop. The split had taken up the broken lease of a tailor shop across the way. There was a great deal of friendliness between the congregations, but the Reverend Mr. Shinn, who led the Lambs no longer spoke to the Reverend Cato Seneca Brown who led the Saints.

Reverend Shinn said he had brought Cato Seneca Brown up from the foothills of Georgia, put the first pair of shoes he had ever owned on his feet—put the first piece of meat he had ever tasted which was no part of a hog, into his mouth, clothed him, got him a job, let him act as assistant pastor of the Lambs when the Spirit had called this Cato from dusting the floors in Leoin's Furniture Store and given him a fair part of the Sunday collection.

But that is the point where Reverend Brown split with Reverend Shinn. He said that what he received was no fair part of the profits. Nobody but God knew how many dollars the

Lambs laid into their shepherd's hand every Sunday.

And after vainly trying to find out the exact amount and after trying still more vainly to get more for himself—Reverend Brown had left Reverend Shinn.

And though only one hundred and fifty Lambs had left the fold with him—Reverend Shinn went blind whenever Reverend Brown came near him.

Ma and the boys went in to Reverend Brown.

"Been introduced to the Father, Son and Holy Ghost!
Ah cry ho—ly, unto de Lord!"

The hymn bellowed out to meet the three as they opened the door to come in. Little Brother looked more dejected at once. Jimmie Joe's face took on a leaden mask that was supposed to be poise but was a most uncomfortable pose.

Ma, more buxom and perspiring than usual in a black straw bucket hat and black satin coat strewed with monkey fur—or monkeyed furs—bowed and smiled her way up the aisle to the third row from the front.

As she reached the chairs there, she drew severely back and let her two boys file in first.

"Lord! Look at Little Brother!!" hoarse whispers chorused up as they sat down.

Little Brother shot a miserable glance backward.

Three little girls who were in his class at school were teetering and tittering in the row behind.

"Got lard and tea on his naps this morning!" giggled one.

"Got powder on too! I kin smell it!"

Little Brother crumpled in his chair, bent double with steaming confusion.

Jimmie Joe unfroze to find he was looking directly on the semi-side of Caroline's head. She sat against the wall with the heavy black woman who was her mother.

A sort of pleasant haze fell on Jimmie Joe at once. He could sit there and stare at Caroline as long as he pleased.

The Reverend Brown advanced majestically from his ebony throne at the back of the platform as the hymn died out.

"My er—friends!" he began in a rumbling of awfulness. "My

er—friends? I never hear that beauteous melody of that grandiose hymn floating on the air around me, but I am not reminded of my beloved, revered, honored and respected mother back in that humble cabin of ours in the foothills of Georgia!"

"Amen! Das de way!" yowled Caroline's mother.

Jimmie Joe cringed in clammy embarrassment for Caroline. But she kept her thick lashed eyes fastened on the Reverend Brown. If she heard her mother's outcry, no tremor of her body revealed the fact.

"And it's to you young upstarts, you young devils, you young Jezebels—who have no respect for man, mother or God—that I want to talk this morning!"

"Yas, sir, Jesus!" sang Ma on high C.

A deafening salvo of "Amens" and "Do Mercy Father" rocked the room for the next few minutes. It took the Rev. Brown two drinks of water and a general hand shaking from the entire deacon board before he could go on to his next sentence.

And he did go on—blasting—smothering—damning.

And the hungry still were hungry.

And a heavier darkness settled on those who walked in shadows. No light was lit. No fulfillment of visions, long tarrying, was promised.

There was vengeance and the paying of an eye for an eye and the promise of superlative damnation for iniquities.

No love—no mercy—no telling of a great enfolding love that works no ill.

And Sadie Montgomery sat in the back row and shivered and shook but decided to keep up her affair with Mary Lou Jones's husband. For if Hell so certainly faced her, why not carry the memory of tenderness and gentle love down with her into the eternal fire? Why not carry the kisses and caresses that had branded her for a thousand thousand years of burning—instead of the kicks and fists of her own husband—Jake?

And Caroline, slant-eyed, looked at the preacher and thought how much money such a good talk would draw from the niggers—and how much, as a consequence she would be able to leave at the various shops on her "Will calls."

Jimmie Joe saw her. Watched her eyes lingering on the man as he panted and ranted, back and forth across the platform.

Jimmie Joe saw—and knew what it all meant.

He shivered too, and looked at Caroline and then looked at the minister.

"Old fool! Old cheater! I wish I had your drag!" Jimmie Joe cursed within himself.

And Ma sat there and screamed out, "Aw Jesus" and felt Jimmie Joe tremble. "Gawd! Let thy Spirit rest on us dis mawnin!" she prayed aloud in contrapuntal style to the preaching.

And when she felt Jimmie Joe shiver, she thought her answer had come.

The Wild Cat Social Club was dancing. With multi-colored crepe paper streamers and hanging baskets of artificial flowers on the ceiling, a clash-banging, rocketing jazz band on the stage, and with the floor comfortably packed with smooth-stepping young Negroes, the Wild Cats were passing a pleasant Sunday evening.

Jimmie Joe and his gang were a part of the Wild Cats, but some dozen older boys who were through with school—for various reasons—and who worked, were the backbone of the club's treasury. They paid for the hall, paid for the orchestra, bought the liquor.

"Them niggers try to run everything," George had growled in a complaint more than once.

"They got the best go! They got the most dough!" Jimmie had replied.

He had never felt the claws of the older Wild Cats too sharply.

But tonight when the Wild Cats were giving their semi-annual formal—when Caroline had lushed in, in a peach colored satin that looked as if it had been poured on her figure, and had jangled her apple-green bracelets and necklaces in the face of Dan Grey, president of the Wild Cats, something deep had scratched Jimmie Joe.

Caroline had chattered with Jimmie Joe with just the proper degree of casual aloofness as she neared Dan. Then, just as the three came fully face to face, she twinkled, dimpled, and stretched out both hands to Dan.

"Hell—o!" she cooed.

"Movie stuff!" sneered Jimmie Joe as he watched her.

Caroline sidled and angled and nodded and enfolded Dan in talk, patterning her every action—as they all did—after the only examples of the niceties of living that any of them ever saw.

The movies!

Unconsciously, too, as she mimed and copied, Jimmie puffed up in the role of the offended, jealous sweetheart. He withdrew a few paces and stood, feet apart, hands in pockets, watching the dancers with a to-hell-with-you scowl.

"Unh-unh! Ole Caroline's done got Jimmie Joe's goat time they gits here!!" tittered Sammy Raines into the ear of his partner.

Sammy Raines was one of these runty black boys who have a perpetual grin and joke for Life. No one in the hall was happier just to pirouette, jazz, dip and glide in the warmth and light and amidst gay dresses and colors and folks he knew—than Sammy.

Jimmie Joe frowned and cursed within. He wanted Caroline to hurry up so they could begin to dance. The orchestra was pulsing through one of those soul disturbing rhythmics that Negro orchestras concoct.

Dan tapped Jimmie Joe suddenly on the arm. "I'll take the next dance with the little lady, bud!" Dan announced.

Jimmie Joe's rage nearly knocked him down.

She wouldn't let him walk in with her in full view of the gang and dance off, leaving him standing alone!

He looked at Dan's suave Japanesy yellow face. Then he looked into Caroline's eyes.

She would. He saw that as he looked at her.

She did.

Jimmie Joe cursed his way through the laughing dancers who had been watching this by-play.

George danced his girl to the edge of the crowd and plunged into the dressing room after Jimmie Joe.

"Hey, feller!" he greeted Jimmie Joe gravely. "Some?" He offered Jimmie Joe a drink of gin.

Jimmie Joe grabbed the flask and swallowed and swallowed.

George watched him in silence. He could have knocked Caroline's face in with joy.

The gin down, Jimmie Joe began to feel worse.

"What the hell you gimme that stuff for?" he swore at George.

"Aw, come off and get out on the floor!" was George's reply. They swaggered back to the hall.

Sammy Raines was ducking past the door with a tall fair girl.

Jimmie Joe caught the rhythm of the dance, took two or three steps alone, parallel to Sammy, and then neatly pushed Sammy away and whirled the girl on without a backward look.

Sammy laughed aloud. "Well excuse me, Mr. Nigger, for livin', please!" he called and chuckled off to find another girl— any girl who could dance—just so she could dance!

Jimmie Joe found no pleasure in the gyrations of the dance. He kept glimpsing a peach satin frock on the only real form in the hall, swishing around in undulations of joy.

Jimmie cut in on another boy in the next dance.

Here, he met opposition, though.

"Here, nigger! Don't try that stuff with me!" blazed the boy. "You ain't got guts enough to get your own girl. Stay away from mine!"

George and Sammy Raines separated Jimmie Joe and the lad before their clinch had blossomed into a scuffle.

"You better not start no fighting with some of these niggers, Jimmie Joe!" warned George. "Those that ain't all busting out with bad liquor and knives have guns on 'em! For God sake—let 'em alone!"

Jimmie Joe drained George's flask of gin this time. "That damn fool says I ain't got the guts to go git Caroline!" he was almost sobbing as he finished.

"Aw let that gal go to Hell!" George blazed.

Jimmie Joe smashed wildly at George's face.

Sammy Raines got in between them.

"Heah! Heah!!" he grunted. "You all will mess up de man's furniture. Lay off dat mess!"

George, flaming red, panted in a corner, glaring at Jimmie Joe, puffing in his.

"Whyn't you swing on Dan!" George taunted. "Ef you're so

damn hot to fight—go git him!"

Jimmie Joe tore away from Sammy's clutch and shot out of the door toward the hall once more.

George's rage oozed out of him. He stared open mouthed first at the door through which Jimmie had disappeared, then at Sammy.

"God, Sammy!" George breathed presently. "He ain't going after Dan, is he? Why that nigger totes a gun and a knife even when he's in bed!"

Pale now, George fled out toward the hall, with Sammy bow-legging behind.

On first glance, the dance seemed to be progressing as merrily as ever.

Up in a corner though where a peach satin dress was crushed close to Dan's navy blue figure, George and Sammy could see Jimmy Joe's head over the crowd. In silent rushes, George and Sammy threaded and waded a way around the outskirts of the hall. And they reached that far corner just when Jimmie snatched Caroline by the shoulders and wrenched her away from Dan's arms.

It was George who saw Dan's hand drawing back toward his hip.

It was George who knocked a couple down, hurdled over them as they kicked on the floor—and it was George who snatched at his own hook-shaped knife and thrust it into Jimmie Joe's right hand.

And Jimmie Joe, the gin scorching his brain, broiling with a desire for revenge, consumed with the lust to hurt, to bleed, to bruise and cut as he himself had been hurt, bled and cut— brought the knife down with this full behind it, into Dan's side.

The coroner said Dan had been stabbed *a dozen times!*

But Jimmie Joe cried out in Ma's arms that he had only brought the knife down once.

A doctor in court said that that one lunge up into Dan's side had cost him his life. "Cut the left ventricle!" he declared.

Grey-faced the "Gang" listened while the older Wild Cats told a story of Dan's superb manhood. Gene Terry, the club treasurer, broke down and wept on the stand when he swore that Dan was stabbed to death, but that he had had no knife in his own hand or on his person.

"Oh I gave Jimmie Joe the knife he had myself. He never even owned one!" mourned George as he heard. But he said nothing.

Jack Sullivan, the cop who had first reached the hall after the murder swore, too, that no gun nor knife had been on Dan's body.

The gang sat grey-faced because they knew that those older Wild Cats had taken Dan's gun and unstrapped his knife from the leather band on his wrist before they called the police.

And the younger gang said nothing. According to "Crafty Detective Stories" and the movies—the sort of things all of them lived by—the younger portion of a gang did not peach on the older heads.

The older Wild Cats meant to claw Jimmie Joe to death for robbing their ranks of the one and only Dan Grey.

When all had been told, when Caroline had had her hysterics and her fainting spell and been fanned—as she told her part in it all, the judge rose up.

"You young lawless creatures who take a life with as cool an indifference as you tear a piece of paper—must be blotted out for the good of humanity!"

The jury rose up, too, and went out.

"Aw Jesus!" Ma had screamed out once during that crucifying hour while the jury was still gone. "Ha' mercy! Ha' mercy Lawd!"

And she had cried and cried on Pa and even the bailiff had patted her shoulder to comfort and quiet her.

Her rich white folks had supplied a lawyer for Jimmie Joe. The woman of the house had said that somehow she felt responsible since Ma was in her cellar washing and ironing or around her house cleaning, instead of being at her own home to talk to Jimmie Joe all his life when he had needed someone somewhere near at hand to talk to.

The jury filed back.

"Guilty, First Degree!" They said.

Everyone felt so helpless when they said that Jimmie Joe's life must be given because he had taken a life himself.

The judge felt tangled. His own son had a way of going to the wrong places with the wrong people.

Jimmie's lawyer was not sure whether Jimmie Joe was normal. "He knows so doggone little about anything real!" the man was thinking as he gathered up the papers of the case he had lost.

Ma screamed all the way out of court as they led Jimmie Joe away. She screamed all night while Pa and Little Brother and some of the members of the Holy Christian Saints had eddied with Reverend Brown, around her bed.

"Call on God!" urged one old lady. "Das de way, chile! He'll heah you!"

And Ma had called out into the night loudly—loudly.

They sang, too, for Ma, 'Take the Name of Jesus with you!" in that sort of harmony which makes you want to fall on your knees, lay your head in the seat of your chair and shed bitter tears—tears whose bitterness could eat through the thickest armour plate scales of sophistication. Tears that would eat down to the place where the real you staggers at a world that travels under two faces, a world that teaches that the devil is the nearest possibility and God—only an impossible remoteness—

So taught, then, this God could not hear. They took Jimmie Joe, fastened him, hooded him, poured electric fire through his body until his heart burst within him.

And he had screamed all the while like a baby in a dark room. "Ma! Oh—Ma!"

They buried his burnt twisted black brown young body—

—"What could we do?" mourned the gang. "We could not squeal on the Wild Cats."

—"I gave my pal my knife when Dan was going to get him! I couldn't let him kill Jimmie Joe!" George mourned aghast.

—"Jesus? What was it I didn't do?" Ma cried in the wash-tub, dragging her mind back from the memory of a screaming cry of "Ma! Oh—Ma!" Dragging her mind back from the thought of a twisted burnt body, a body so twisted they could not straighten it, even in the coffin.

Better to scrub a million floors and plod back home on dog-tired feet to cook, clean and scrub there, if only there would be once more a slim black brown boy, dancing, jigging, joking, eating—instead of that dead empty silence that drowned everything there now. Little Brother crawled into bed every night before eight now with a scared look on his face all the time. Pa sat up in a corner with his head and shoulders—his very soul—hung down.

Pa didn't have any scrubbing or tubs or any God to help him. He could not go up and ask his God—like Ma could—what it was he should have done.

—"Ma! Kin I have six bits?" he had asked.

And he had taken it.

Nobody snitched money from her now.

It lay safe in her pocket book.

—But a slim black-brown body lay twisted and burnt in its casket. It was twisted and burnt so that they could not straighten it out—even in the casket.

One morning—thinking all this—Ma turned the corner to wait for her car by Krönen's bakery.

Pink cakes pyramided in the pale blue background of the window.

And Ma—flooded with a rush of bitter sorrow—fell on the sidewalk in a faint.

"Where the devil do you 'spose these nigger women go to get drunk so early in the morning?" the driver of the patrol wagon asked the cop as they loaded Ma in to take her to the station house.

They rattled off down the street with Ma.

They rattled just like the stones in a tin can.

—Don't you wonder, sometimes, with a feeling like a knife in your heart, why Life serves up stones—hard stones—throws stones into Tin Cans—so that they only rattle, rattle, with a hollow sound when the winds of Living knock them down and shake them?

A Sealed Pod

It was one fine funeral.

No matter what Frye Street might think of all the incidents that led up to it, the funeral itself—with curly plumes saluting the winds from the four corners of the white automobile hearse, two rusty black open carriages entirely buried under flowers, two perspiring doctors fanning Ma, applying smelling salts to Ma's nose—a long line of automobiles filled with crepe-hung Negroes—the funeral itself, stirred the mind, uprooted the feelings, shook the soul.

And all this was as it should be. When they were burying a girl who had been cut to death, it ought to be done so you remembered it.

"Viollette Aurora Davis was as sweet and tender as her name!" the Reverend Johnson Harris had quavered as he opened the obituary.

He had known how sweet and tender Viollette could be.

A floodtide of moans ebbed up from the packed church to second all this.

Viollette's mother—Ma—had lifted her cry above the entire assembly, "Do mercy, Jesus! Have mercy Lord! Aw Father! Aw, Jesus, Aw!"

The two doctors fanned Ma, they soothed Ma, they supported Ma between them.

They had known Viollette's sweetness and tenderness, too.

Ma was alone in the world now. With Viollette gone, she had no one else except some cousins who had come in from the country for the funeral.

Frye Street (black) wept and wailed all through the obituary, the hymns, and had uttered a full symphony of lamentation when they passed around to take a last look at Viollette.

"My God, Old lady Davis'll never git over it!" one mourner had sniffed. "Jes' to think! Comin' home findin' your one and only child carved like any beef steak! Dead in her bed! My God!"

"Twarn't nobody but that Davie Jones!" Ma had screamed right out once.

That is what everybody in Frye Street agreed on.

Dave Jones it had been who killed Viollette!

Hadn't he boasted openly in Jimmie Harris's "Valet de Luxe" tailor shop—right out in front of everybody on that fatal Tuesday night—that he was going to spend a "Pleasant evening with Frye Street's Violet!"

And when Pop Gentry had advised him to go on home to Susie, his lawful wife, hadn't Dave spat and cursed in reply, "Mind your business, ole nigger! When both my feet gits to hanging in the grave like yours is, I'll spend my nights at home!" Those men who were Pop Gentry's best friends all swore and testified to this at the inquest.

Dave was arrested—though he cried he was innocent.

Dave was convicted—though he swore he was guiltless.

Dave was hanged—crying and praying, swearing that his hands were absolutely clean of Viollette's blood.

And Susie, Davie's short, fat, square little wife, had followed him through the maze of court trials and cells—up to the very death chamber.

Then she had taken her two children and disappeared from number 15 Frye Street the day Dave died.

Some folks say she went back "Down home."

Others say she ran off uptown where the Negroes did not know her.

Pat McKeagh who drove the city refuse wagon that carried the muck of Frye Street to the river, swore he saw Susie throw her two babies in the river and then fall in herself.

But Pat was always drunk and swearing he saw things.

"Maybe she did once!" sighed Esther Weinstein, wife of Anton, who kept the Corner Store Grocery Market. She drew a breath that sobbed and touched her breast. "Maybe she did, that Susie, throw herself in the river! So much trouble! Such a heaviness! Such a stone here!" and she smote her breast many times.

"God rest her soul!" murmured Mary Sugnee and crossed herself.

"Ain't no good Christian girl like Susie Jones done no such a thing! That McKeagh's just a drunk mick! Ain't nobody what held up her church and her pastor like Susie always has—flung her soul away fur no no-count nigger man!" Ma Davis herself pronounced this—and Frye Street black, stood to a man, behind this opinion.

Christian girls didn't kill themselves.

And it was not Dave who had killed Viollette.

Dave Jones told the truth when he died, crying, "Honest to Gawd, y'all! I didn't do it!"

Frye Street, as you know, runs from Grand Avenue where the "L" is to the big river that skirts the city. It runs from Heaven to Hell (as I have already told you) with its little brick houses—too filled with every race on the earth.

Strange things can happen there.

Strange things.

For instance, black Ma Davis who lived in number nine had had a daughter, Viollette Aurora—as blonde and fair and apparently Nordic as Ma was concentratedly negroid.

Strange things can happen in Frye Street.

Ma scrubbed all night in the office buildings down town and left number nine to eighteen-year-old Viollette.

And Viollette—warmed with an odd mixture of uncontrolled passions and bloods, entertained a varied assortment of men of every race every night.

The men flowed in and out. Viollette did not care who they were or why, usually.

Only one man had she ever loved—and only this one had really loved her.

That was Joe Tamona, twenty-two-year-old Italian boy. He and Viollette made a handsome pair—he with his swarthy complexion and flashing black eyes—she, kitten-soft with the golden flesh and golden hair that marks the mixed-blood blonde.

Joe would have married Viollette in spite of the black men—and the white men—not to mention the Orientals.

But Joe had a knack of flashing a knife as quickly as he flashed his eyes. One night in a pool room, he and Andy Laughlin had an argument over a shot.

Joe's knife flashed.

Andy was dead when they picked him up.

Joe had disappeared from Frye Street that very night as completely as if he had died.

"Gone to sea"—some of the folks on Frye Street said. The police chose to believe so, too.

But Joe—after pelting wide-eyed with fear to Viollette—had borrowed some clothes from her and made her call a taxi—made her swear eternal love that would wait for his return—and then had ridden off uptown.

The police could not find Joe. He changed his name, "forgot" how to speak English and lived with a group of old country Italians on the outskirts of the city—fully forty miles from Frye Street.

Now Joe hankered for his Viollette. He could not forget the cool arrogance of her—strangely joined to the abandoned passion which could possess her.

One April night, Joe, feeling safe since twenty-two months had gone by, since he had done for Andy Laughlin—and gone scot free—went back to Frye Street.

He went back in a taxi—got out a little above number nine and started to ring the bell. However, he caught a glimpse of Ma Davis charging around in the "front" room. Joe changed his mind and drew back in a shadow to watch.

Ma was calling aloud, "You Viollette? Gal? Where de devil you put my hat! It's nigh on seven-thirty and I ain't found it yet! Where is it, I says!"

Joe could hear Viollette answering faintly from somewhere upstairs. "Here it is, Ma!"

Joe had watched the old lady go out of the room again—for the shades were up and the lamp was lit. He shrank bank into the doorway of number eleven as Ma sailed by on her way to work.

Watching Ma out of sight and stepping cautiously, Joe was again approaching Viollette's door, when a man swung suddenly from the opposite direction—and leaped eagerly up the steps of number nine.

Cursing under his breath, Joe curved far out to the curb and passed on by. He sauntered a little beyond the house, doubled, and went back.

The shades at the windows were still undrawn. Peering in, Joe recognized Dave Jones as the man. His breathing altered as an overwhelming surge of desire swept over him at the sight of his Viollette.

Afraid to linger in the street, Joe decided on a bold stroke. He tried the outer door of number nine, found it open, crept in the hall, took off his shoes and passed the door of the front room which was closed. He crept upstairs to the room which he knew was Viollette's and hid himself in her closet.

That Dave Jones would be going home pretty soon, then Viollette belonged to him, Joe Tamona.

Hadn't she promised with tears in her eyes on that night nearly two years ago when he had run away—to remain truly his until such a time as he should come back to her!

Dave Jones would be going soon.

The closet was small. The closet was airless. Joe took a swig of gin and opened the door a crack.

He must have fallen asleep. Sounds and lights in Viollette's room awakened him. "Davy!" It was Viollette's voice! "Dave, darlin, why don't you let Susie go on back down South. She's too big a dumb-bell for this man's town! And you know I'm really in love with you!"

Joe leaped to his feet. A dress on a coat-hanger clattered to the floor.

"What's that?" demanded Dave.

"Aw, jes' one of them big hoss rats that bust around this place all night! Forgit it!—Say, . . . listen!"

And Viollette slammed the closet door without looking in.

Joe trembled, knife in hand, ready to burst forth.

Then his brain steadied a little. He could not cut both their throats at once. The girl would scream while he was finishing Dave.

That would not do.

Knife in hand, Joe crouched down again, pulled the dresses and clothes around him and waited.

Joe sat there all night.

Joe sat there and heard Dave with his Viollette.

More gin put Joe to sleep again—but he kept his knife in his hand.

It was a scraping sound that aroused him this time. Someone was moving a chair.

"Better get home early, honey!" Joe heard Viollette cooing in a sleepy voice. "Ma'll be here soon now! It's most five o'clock! The old lady'd raise the devil if she found you!"

They laughed together—a comfortable, smug crescendo.

Joe, trembling to his knees, could hear Dave walking back and forth.

"Aren't you going to kiss your Viollette again before you go!"

Joe gripped his lips in his teeth, gripped his knife closer, braced his rubber heels against the wall to keep himself from splitting the door wide in the silence that followed.

"Come on! I'll let you out, Davie boy!" Viollette said finally. "When are you coming back? See me tonight again?"

The man laughed the tender caress tone of a man who would give you anything. "Maybe! Can't never tell!"

Their voices trailed off. Joe could hear their feet on the steps.

Now

Presently Viollette came back alone. Yawning and stretching in luxurious abandon, she perched on the side of the bed to shake off her slippers before she cuddled back for the peaceful sleep Ma always found her in every morning.

Viollette stretched, Viollette yawned, Viollette was drawing the covers up cozily when Joe burst open the door. . . .

Ma's feet hurt her that morning. She came crawling up from the five o'clock car.

"Look heah, conductor!" she had pleaded. "No need to carry me pas' my corner! Leave me off on the wrong side this once, for

145

God's sake! My feet's 'bout to kill me!"

The conductor knew Ma by sight, so he rang the bell for emergency stop and let the old lady off on the corner where there was no white post.

"Thank you, and thank you, Jesus!" Ma called back fervently as she climbed down.

She eased herself along the street. It was too early for many people to be out, but Ma spied Teresa Tamona as she passed number 24—a black shawl on her head—her pallid face pressed against the window.

"What the name of the Lawd ails that Eye-talian dis early in the mornin'? Ever since that boy of hers been gone, she been settin' by the windows, watching out for him! Always seeing him, and 'feelin' him! and all that kinder mess!!"

Ma groaned on by. As she drew near to number nine, the sun shot a few rays up over the house opposite.

"My eyes must be gittin' worser! 'Pears like to me that gal Viollette's done left the door wide open!"

The door was open.

Ma uttered an alarmed cry. "What's the matter with that gal!"

Feet forgotten, she tore up the stairs. "Heah's Me!" she shouted, standing in the lower hall. "Git up from there, gal! What de devil you leave this front door settin' wide open for all night? I ain't got nuthin' now but I don't want nobody to steal that!"

She waited.

There was no answer.

Not a sound came from the bedroom above. Ma's anger took fire from the pain in her feet.

"You Viol—lette! You heah me!! I bet if I come up there you'll answer me!"

A blanket of complete silence covered the house.

Ma pulled herself up the stairs, strode along the hall—pushed into Viollette's room.

Ma fell downstairs screaming.

Ma screamed all the way out to the sidewalk and laid down flat in the middle of the street. "Aw Jesus! Aw Gawd! Aw Jesus! Aw Gawd!" She screamed over and over.

Teresa Tamona and Anton Weinstein, who kept the grocery market, came running to Ma first.

"Du mein lieber Gott! Was ist geschien!" Anton shouted as he puffed up. ("Dear God! What has happened?")

"You seen something perhaps?" Teresa panted, her face more pale than ever.

Ma raised her head and her voice.

"My Viollette! Cut!! Cut to death!! Aw Jesus!" Ma laid back down in the mud.

"Gott!" stammered Anton who knew Viollette.

Teresa sat down on the curb. "I thought maybe you see my Joe!" she said sadly.

Others came running.

The door of number 15 where Dave Jones lived with his Susie— flew open.

Dave and Susie had been having an argument.

"What the devil you got to do with where I was las' night?" Dave had cursed suddenly and struck Susie.

Screaming, Susie ran downstairs and out into the street.

She stumbled and fell and lay near where Ma Davis had fallen.

Dave heard the uproar—followed Susie—and reached the crowd just as Jimmie Harris, who owned the "De Luxe" tailor shop, came up.

"Viollette Davis been cut to death!" one Negro stammered.

Dave staggered and paled.

"Dave spent the night with Viollette—" Jimmie began loudly.

"Ain't nobody seen my Joe?" queried Teresa Tamona all at once. "Nowhere?"

That is what started all.

Dave was tried.

Dave was hanged.

Nobody—not even Teresa—saw Joe Tamona run out of number nine, down Frye Street, toward the river.

A tramp freighter with a flat end was swinging down the river when Joe reached the shore. He took a big leap—and was on it.

And everything and everybody in the case was side by side—like peas in the pod.

But the pod was sealed.

And the peas did not touch each other.

Black Fronts

Front A

He was a lawyer. He had not had a case since 1932. This was 1935.

Ma and Pa had crossed the Alps of effort, carrying an elephantine load to advance him. Luther had quit high school in his junior year to go to work in a foundry so Big Brother could be a lawyer. Henry had taken a janitor's job after he finished grammar school because he could get $125 a month and they could send Big Brother to law school.

When Big Brother was a lawyer they would all be rich!

Big Brother went through law school. Big Brother passed the state bar. Big Brother did a fair-to-middling business among the razor-cutters and crap-shooters.

"I'll hit a big gun some day!" he would promise. "Just wait! Then I'll be in the dough!"

But he met Miss Rinky Dew first. Miss Dew had come to the big city to go to business college. She said that her father was a doctor down in the little southern town that had loosed her upon the city.

She never mentioned her mother. Perhaps because her mother was a big, black, bandanna-bound washwoman. Her father was the white doctor in the town.

You know Rinky. The skin of civilization which covers the black world has been erupting her type for years.

They have no back—no middle—all front. No genuine intelligence, no real education, no super-saturation of a rich over-flow of true culture. Nothing but an extra wave to the hair—an extra flop to the powder puff—an avalanche of self-conscious "ings" and "ists" (in the presence of the lesser lights) just to show how close "dis" and "dat" still are.

Rinky was one of those still so bedazzled with their own fresh varnish of diction and degrees that they cannot discriminate between those born to the manor and those born to the gutter. In short, too weighted and freighted with claptrap and blank rot to offer soil suitable for the culture of anything but the weeds of Living.

When she first came to the big city, she held herself a little aloof. She finished the business college and went to work for Big Brother.

She was well aware that Big Brother eyed her warmly. And a lawyer's wife surely was on a par with a doctor's daughter!

Gradually the aloofness melted.

Gradually Big Brother was entwined until he unravelled himself before a preacher.

As befitted what Rinky considered a doctor's daughter should have, their bedroom set cost $750.

It made everything else in Pa's and Ma's home look shame-faced and outmoded.

Rinky made the whole family look shamefaced and outmoded.

By the time Big Brother was two months beyond the altar, he was moving the $750 bedroom set out of Pa's and Ma's flat, with $3,200 worth of furniture added to it to match the $750 layout.

Before long there was an automobile.

After Big Brother had moved his Rinky, the family did not see him so often. Once in a while he'd drop in on Saturday night— with an excuse for Rinky's absence—a hungry look toward the supper table—and a grateful murmur for the few dollars Ma would pinch off and slip to him when nobody was looking.

Came 1929.

Everybody in the world—with the exception of a few natives still naked in their jungles—knows what happened in 1929.

1929 began stripping Big Brother and his Rinky. The over-carved walnut dining room set followed the baby grand piano down the back stairs one Monday morning. Big Brother's suite of offices shrank to desk space in an insurance firm. The table-top range joined the hegira and took the typewriter, the automatic ice box, the vacuum cleaner and all the lamps on the light bill along with it.

The landlord grew insistent. The landlord grew insulting. The landlord leeched on the front door like a nightmare.

Big Brother and his Rinky took a shambled house near Ma and Pa.

"We're taking a studio," Rinky broadcasted, and proceeded to angle the residue of the $3,950 worth of furniture until the studio atmosphere was more apparent.

There came still further shrinkage and lopping off. Rinky manoeuvered a job as a typist with the Relief Commission. The $75 she earned there each month appeased the landlord intermittently—reduced the grocery bill occasionally—and kept her lawyer-husband sitting in his desk space from 1932 to 1935—waiting.

Luther and Henry lost their jobs. They moved their families in with Pa and Ma. All three families went on relief.

That meant that three coal orders, three grocery orders, three twenty-four-pound bags of flour and three boxes of canned goods went to Pa and Ma's each month.

With a little juggling and rearranging, the three families were adjusted. They had enough to eat. The house was warm. Ma found a roomer who worked in a private family but who " 'preciated a good home." The twelve dollars a month Ma got for the room meant money for church, movies, and a new pair of stockings once in a while.

Less than $100 a month was not so much at Big Brother's. He took to coming over to Ma's on Sunday morning just before breakfast.

Rinky would have a cup of tea and a cigarette and stay in bed.

Sometimes Big Brother lugged a basket of coal and a basket of food back from Ma's.

He could not go on relief.

He was a lawyer!

He had to keep up his front.

So did Rinky. She had to have her hair "done" and buy a new dress "on time" monthly.

"Can't let the folks think I'm ragged," she'd say to herself as the debts mounted.

Every once in a while she and Big Brother gave a splashing party. The liquor and sandwiches cost them several semi-square meals.

But they would have their "gang" over to the "studio" and holler and shriek shady witticisms to cover the hollows inside of their bodies and inside their thoughts.

"I want one of those new rose lamé backless dresses for the next formal!" Rinky frequently shouted. She knew while she was saying it that there was no money for lamé dresses, no money for formals, no money for rent, nor food, nor clothes, nor anything else she wanted or had to have.

But she shouted and everybody else yelled with her to keep from being blotted out and smothered.

All the time the shouting and the drinking and the cackling was mounting, Rinky would be thinking, "My God! The rents are almost due again! My God! What will I do! What can I do!"

But then she would laugh louder and drink one more whiskey-sour and caress somebody else's husband just to show that she was smart and up-to-date, carefree, prosperous and a leading light—some few steps beyond Luther and Henry and their wives whom she never invited to her Sunday nights.

And when the gang and the whiskey and the sandwiches were gone, Rinky and Big Brother would lie in bed and rehearse the party, each bolstering up the other's confidence in the thickness of their smoke-screen of pretense which they were spreading before their tattered notions of living.

Then—finally—Big Brother would lie quiet so Rinky would think he was asleep and would stare out into the darkness and wonder, "How long will it be before I can earn even ten dollars a month again? Or even a dollar a week? When will I ever be able to pay Ma back all I owe her?"

And Rinky, breathing evenly so Big Brother would believe she was asleep, would be lying there, wracking her mind, trying to find a place to pinch off one more dollar to send a gift of some sort down home to her mother. It was not to be so much a gesture of affection as it was to be an indication of unlimited largess and affluence such as befitted a lawyer's wife whose husband had an office in the main colored business block in the main street of the colored section of a big city up North.

She did not dare think forward to the day when the landlord and the grocer and all the rest of them would not accept a part of their money, but would demand it all. There was nothing to which she could think back.

Nothing.

So—she only could cover—hide herself—away from life— beneath her front.

Front B

(The Top of the Design)

Yas'm! I'll jes' iron out these heah damp things and leave the rest 'til tomorrer! Whyn't you go lie down an rest? I kin look out after these babies! When I go to Mis' Bowers, she jes' leave everything to me and lies down and reads a book! She shore is one nice lady! An' ain't her husband lovely to her! Jes' buys her everything and gives her plenty! She pays good, too! Two fifty a day and carfare! She always gives me something to carry home, too. Her husband—he been to college. He's a fine doctor, too!

Ain't your husband never went to college?

Yas!?

Then how come he ain't a doctor or a preacher?

He study "business!"

What he got to go to college to study business for? These Jews on every corner—they makin' money all day and all night with Sunday th'owed in and they ain't never need to study no business! They can't hardly read but they shore can figger the dough outa your pockets into their'n. There's you 'phone ringing! (Thank God that telephone did ring! Git her out a here! Always doin' something aroun' the kitchen! Must be scared I try to *take* something! What she got for anybody to take? Po' as Job's turkey, her! She ain't got nuthin' to take! Sure hope she stays out there so's I can git a little sugar and flavorin' to make that cake for Reverend's birthday! Ole Miss Lewis, she think she the only one can bring Reverend anything! She *so rich*, and they gonna read out the names of those that gives a gift this time . . . !)

Heah, you little devil! Leave that iron cord alone. I bet I'll smack yore head off!

What? Your mama don't let nobody hit you?

I'll bet I'll give you to the boogy man!

Ain't no boogy man!

Don't say "Ain't!!"

You is the mannish somethin' I ever see for three years old!

Here comes yore ma! She callin' you! Better g'long! (Certainly glad them little devils is out of the way! Make you sick! Tryin' to be white! Don't say "Ain't." Don't say "Bust!" Don't say "Yas mam," say "Yes, Mrs. Jones!" All that foolishness! Gotta feed them brats spinach and carrots and fresh eggs in the winter time and special milk and God knows what all—an she wearin' cotton stockings! I bet I'd feed them kids some bread and gravy and git myself somethin' if I was her! She ain't got as much stuff in her house as my Ruthie has! Dan—he pay fifteen dollars down and git Ruthie five rooms full of furniture with a radio throwed in! Talk about she don't buy on the 'stallment plan! How anybody going to get a house full of furniture 'less they ask for credit? Whyn't she leave them little fools with somebody and go on out an' teach—she s'posed to have so much edjucation! Course, Mrs. Bowen, she don't need no money 'cause she got plenty and he make a lot all the time. This pore gal ought to try somethin! Her husband can't be makin' so much. Always talkin' 'bout she don't want to leave her children! Bet she can't get no school to teach in this town! Talk about she always wanted to do somethin' else that won't take her from home! Hope she ain't thinkin' of takin' up sewing! That dress she make herself look like something the devil give his wife! Wish she'd leave them brats to me! They wouldn't be able to set down when I got through wid them! These napkins shore is pretty! Guess I'll take one to put on the flower table in the pulpit! They don't need no six napkins for two people no how! I'll jes'—Lawd! she comin!)

Yas'm! I forgot and left the iron settin' on the napkin while I was fixin' my stockin'! I shore am sorry it scotched! Maybe ef you puts a little flour paste on it, it'll come out! Only five napkins! Only

five? Guess the laundry lost one for you! That's what comes of
sending your stuff to the wet wash! I always says a woman ought
to wash her own things ef she ain't sick abed! (Hope that stung
you!) What! I standing on the napkin? Where? (Ain't that the
dog-beatenest! Wish she'd a stayed out 'a here!) Well . . . !
Gettin' on to five o'clock! Guess I better start gettin' ready to
get home! Doctor Bowen, he always drive me home when I
work at his house. Y'all ain't got no car, has you?

My daughter Ruthie, she got a Cadillac! Yeah!! Dan, he pays
his boss so much every week out of his salary for his ole car!
They got the swellest car in their block! (You'd think anybody
with all de edjucation they 'sposed to have would have a car!
Her husband look like a half-dead fool to me anyhow! Tippin'
his hat to me on the car, then settin' in a seat all by hisself like
he ain't never knew me!) It's two dollars and a quarter. Yas'm.
I tol you on the phone that day you call me at Mrs. Bowers' it'd
be a quarter extra when the clothes need to be ironed! Two
dollars any other day. Mrs. Bowers always pay me extra when I
iron things, 'thout saying nuthin! (She better find another
quarter! Ef she so broke, she don't need nobody doin' no work
for her! Some women gits so *helpless* 'cause they got a couple of
babies! I ain't but ten year oldern what she is an I'm 'bout to be
a grandmother! I'se married when I'se fifteen! Ain't no sense to
no woman going to school and all that foolishness like she say
she been when all she going to do anyhow is have babies
and housework on her hands. She too soft anyhow! He kissin'
her goodbye every morning like he was going to Yoorup and
pattin' her head like she was a baby 'stead of an old hard
woman!)

Yas'm! Thank you! Guess I'll be gettin' along! (Hope she go
out again! I think I'll take Ruthie some of that fancy underwear!
She thinks I been workin' for rich white folks and they always has
somethin' you can take home! Don' want nobody know I been
workin' for colored! Shore be glad when this depression business
is over and the white folks'll turn loose the money again and I can
work like I wants to! Aw, she ain't never going out! Let me git
out a here!)

Goodby, y'all!

Front B
(The Bottom of the Design)

Why doesn't she hurry up and finish that ironing and go home? It's too much to keep concocting little jobs that will keep me busy around the kitchen while she's here! But if I don't stay, everything we own will go home with her. Two teaspoons and the butterknife last time! I can't take a weekly inventory, and—) Junior! Take your fingers out of that sugar bowl! Baby! Don't hit the window with the milk bottle! Why not play with the clothespins! See? Nice! (Between her brick-bat insinuations and these babies—it's a wonder that I don't loop-the-loop out of that window and mushroom somebody's hat! I ought to get rid of her—but she *does* do some of the things that I hate to do—when she feels like it!)

Junior! I told you to let the sugar alone! Suppose you and baby go into your room and play! Say excuse me to Mrs. Jones when you step over her feet, sonny! You *don't want to!* (Is this the point where I use the hairbrush or reason with him? God! why isn't there a Glossary of Living with all the proper answers for mamas indicated with red ink, or red lights, or red buttons or something? Or did everything I ever learned fail to teach me how to dive for the answers in my soul quick enough? Thank God the telephone is ringing! Time out from the maelstrom!)

Oh, hello! Your call is just interrupting round two with that curse you wished on my house! I thought you told me she was a splendid worker? She ought to be with Ali Baba's gang! Who was Ali Baba? Don't you remember the old story of the forty thieves—the way they had to simmer them in oil to stop them from stealing? What? You knew she took things from you? How did you stop her?—You let Nature take its course? How many shirts did you say she took? Well, Nature can't course in my house! My husband doesn't own that many shirts.

I'm too fretty? Have to pay for what I don't want to do? I don't mind paying, but I can't give away the shirts off of his back just to keep her, can I?

No, I don't want to talk about your club. Crazy? Losing poise? I suppose I am. These children and that woman are poised on my nerves so—

Of course, I want to hear about your new dress! Mm! Mm!! Sounds lovely. Listen. The children have gone back to the kitchen! I'll just have to go! I'll call you later!

The iron is scorching that napkin, Mrs. Jones! (She's stolen one napkin while I was gone! Always snipping and nipping at what I haven't got then stealing what I do have! How can I search her?)

You're standing on the napkin! Yes, under your left foot. (Thankful am I, too, that it's five o'clock! If she takes the whole house while I am out of the room getting her money—I don't care! I'm just going into the living room and sit down with myself for five minutes! Wonder if I'll ever reach the place, once more, when I can sit down quietly a little while every day?

It's time to pay her! How many extras can she find today? How many days can I stand this? Well—it's time to unlock my nerves—open the door—meet the pain again.)

I'll call you when I want you again! (That pile of clothes does look small!) I'll call you! (If I *do*, it will be my final bid for a sanatorium or the "dark house" or "my long sleep.")

Good night!

Hate Is Nothing

The door would not open.

Lee's key hung in the lock. She pushed against the door with the fur coat that was slung over her left arm.

It would not yield.

She rattled the knob. And with the sudden perversity of old doors in old houses, the door swung wide.

Roger—Lee's husband—was coming down the stairs with the measured leisureliness that always marked his every move.

"Hey, ole Injun!" she started to greet him, but a door creaked open somewhere toward the back of the house.

That meant her mother-in-law was listening.

That meant her mother-in-law was standing somewhere between the kitchen and the inner hall.

In the shadow.

Listening.

Why didn't she walk out where they both could see her? Why did she have to stay out of sight—keep silent—and listen?

"Where were you all morning, Lee?" Roger asked and walked toward her.

Lee left the door and met him.

"I've been in jail!" Lee said distinctly so her voice would carry back in the shadow between the kitchen and the inner hall.

Roger moaned. "Anything left of the car?"

"The car? I wasn't in an accident. The car is all right. I was in a morals case—morals court or whatever you call it when you are taken out of a raided house!"

That banged the door shut.

That made the door bang shut in the shadow between the kitchen and the inner hall.

Roger said nothing. He took the coat gently from Lee's arm and stood aside so she could go upstairs. When he had laid the coat on the arm of the chair by the table, he came upstairs too. His steps were unhurried.

Lee was in her room, tossing off her hat, tearing off her gloves. She breathed in deeply and let her eyes rest on the color and loveliness that made the room.

"This is one place where Hell isn't! It has not brimstone in here yet!" Lee thought.

She touched a chair, a shade, fussed with her hair, then dropped back on the couch.

Roger closed the door carefully.

Lee turned her eyes up to the ceiling so that she would not see Roger.

There were times when she loved him for his calm immobility.

But when there was a tale to tell that carried her in quick rushes before everything—a speck of dust in the winds of Life— she never looked at him. He always made her impulses seem bad taste with his patience and aloofness.

Right now he sat silent.

There were no rays of disapproval pricking against her, but she could sense that he had gone deeper within himself. He was not reaching out to her.

"I ain't approved!" Lee commented racily to herself.

Then she began to talk.

"I couldn't sleep last night," she began then waited.

Her husband did not say anything.

She started again, "My mind was hurtling and racing and hurdling and hopping and skipping—so I got up at half past four—"

She stopped once more. He had told her where the keys to the car were before she went—so he knew all that.

He knew everything, too, that had kept her awake.

They had been reading—Lee had gone so far into what she was reading that she sensed rather than saw that Roger had dug a pencil out of a vest pocket and was scribbling—

He had spoken all at once. "Lee! Don't you think you spend too much money on the house?"

He had had to say it twice before she really heard him.

But she finally asked "Why? I am spending no more than usual!"

Roger had tapped the pencil on the paper for a moment. "Well—," he seemed to be searching for words. "My mother said that she thought that we spent altogether too much!"

A geyser of angry words had roared inside of Lee's mind. "Tell your mother to end her visit that started six months ago and go home! Tell her that I did not spend nearly so much money until she decided to cook the meals alternate weeks!—And since she serves her Roger the fatted calf in every form from roast through salad and stew in her cooking weeks—my own menus have to be anemic assemblings of what I can afford! She blasts the hole in my household money—and I sweep up the dust! Tell her to go home!"

The geyser only roared inside. Lee only answered aloud soberly, "I'll look into it."

Then she had to grip her toes down in her slippers to keep from rushing out of the room at once to search out his mother—and tell her all the things that six months of pricking and prying had festered in her soul.

Lee did not go.

At thirty-three Lee was still struggling with impulse—for impulse had tangled her once in the barbed wires of an unhappiness that still—nine years after—was hard to heal.

With her eyes still on her book, Lee could see all of that unhappiness—her first marriage—spread out before her.

That first husband had drunk all of the time, yet Lee had never seen him reeling.

In the morning he would grab a cigarette in one hand, his bathrobe in the other and he would go and mix a drink.

That lit the devilish quirk in his eyes that some people called personality.

Lee had once thought that it was charm. Later she learned it was a tip of a flame from the hell-fire of the fastest living.

He drank in the morning, then he would go to see his patients and attend clinics.

Drunk—but not staggering. Only too gay, too cocky, too glib to be entirely sober.

Lee hated it. She had been afraid not for him, but for the people he treated. A drunken doctor with needles and knives in his hands!

But nothing had ever happened. His touch was too devilishly sure. Still the fear had shadowed all her life with him.

That whole marriage had been uneasy from the start—stable as the shadow of a leaf. He had already lived three years for every year of his chronological age. But the keen edge of his excitement of living had cut new paths for her away from the conservative reserve of life as she had known it for twenty-two years—away from her Self—away from the sorrow that had given her no rest after both her parents had been swept away from her.

For awhile her impulses outstripped his insatiable hunger for good times, until finally, so awed by the teeth of his sensuality that her soul retched when she heard him leaping upstairs (for he could never seem to walk) Lee loosed herself suddenly from him.

"I am good to you, Lee! Why can't you stay?" he had pleaded at first.

(Good to you, Lee! Good because I never knocked you down! Never bruised or hurt you with my fists! But I say nothing of the blows I have hammered on YOU!)

"Why can't you stay Lee?" (Stay and blot out more of your real SELF every time we quarrel and curse each other! Stay and blot out your Self! See if I can't make you and God lose each other!)

"I love you, Lee. There is something different about you! You are not stale-surfaced like most of these sisters! Stay with me!"

He had called Lee all the refreshing things like wildrose and seabreezes—and then he had gone off to stay with the stale-smooth-surfaces.

—Perhaps to test the surface tension of stale surfaces.

It was too much for Lee. You cannot live twenty odd years with the Ten Commandments then drown your Self in liquor and mad kissing in one year of unreal living.

Anyhow—who has ever been able to soak a wild rose in whiskey, flail it to straw on the threshing floors of fleshly lust, and then care for the rose—the straw—tenderly.

Lee cut herself away.

He fought to get her back. But by knowing the right persons here and there the marriage was annulled.

People called Lee odd.

Odd. The flavor of something foreign to You grafted on to your life.

You cannot lose both your parents at twenty-two—be married and divorced at twenty-four—anneal the surface of a second marriage so that your background, your pride, your prejudices, your likes and dislikes are fused to those of another so there will be no seams nor cracks that are loose enough to separate into chasms between you—and be a "placid pool of sweet content."

The tense aching spots left by the two-edged sword of sorrow—the fearful doubt and shattering devastation of a disgusting love—stoke fires of unrest in you that will not cool to ashes no matter how many tears you pour over it all.

"It won't break me to lose you!" he had sneered at the last.

God did that breaking.

One night, following a lonely country road home from a gay carouse, his car turned over and pinned him underneath. Only ashes and charred metal were left next morning.

Some people say another man's wife was with him, but it was never known. It was all hushed up, erased by the sleight-of-hand coups of a society that whitewashes the crimson of Babylon with the blandest perfumes of deceitful sophistry.

It did not matter.

Lee had never loved him truly and intensely as she did Roger. But what woman who has been close enough to a man to have been his wife could hear that his funeral pyre had been lit one drunken midnight on a lonely road without a shudder? Who could have lain in the arms of a weak fool and not burned with remorse because she had left him as she had found him—a weak fool?

Lee shuddered and wondered what the Great One had said to a man who had lived for and by all the things He had told men to leave alone?

What has God said to a man who—drunk with all the excesses of living—had met Death on the run?

Just because a jumble of creeds have created a mist that blurs the simple boundaries of the Way, men who live as he had lived, think Truth lies smothered under the dust of centuries of men's willfulness—blotted out so that a God cannot even know the Way.

Cannot know the Way—or still see every man.

There could be, then, no mild ordinary wonder about painful things in a mind that had suffered as Lee's had.

If Roger's mother told him when Lee was not present that his wife spent too much of his money—and said nothing to Lee—she meant to cause trouble.

Trouble.

The first shadow of Hell once more across Lee's path of living.

Lee had thrown her book from her and left the room where she and Roger had been reading.

"Is she trying to turn him from me? It's a slow process—this turning a person away from someone else! A paw here! A claw there! A knife thrust there! Some wicked tonguing everywhere!"

Lee had run a warm bath to sooth herself. All the unspoken bitterness fretted her still, though.

—Was the snake curled up in the center of Eden from the very start—or did she just happen to come and visit one day? And when she had observed the love, the loveliness, the peace and plentitude, did she decide that all this was too good for a poor fool like Lee—and straightway begin her snakiness?

By three o'clock in the morning Lee had worked over a dozen-dozen unpleasant situations that had been set up during the past six months. They all chained together and led to what?

Now it happened that Lee's mother-in-law hated her. Mrs. Sands belonged to that generation of older Negroes most heavily cursed by the old inferiority hangover left from slave days.

She was one of those who believed that when an exceptional Negro is needed for an exceptional position—or when a colored man in an exceptional position marries—only the nearest approach to a pure Caucausian type is fit or suitable.

Mrs. Sands had never forgiven Roger, her only son.

He had raised her hopes to great heights when she saw him, an exceptional colored man in an exceptional position—and then he had dashed her sensibilities by bringing home a brown-skinned wife whose only claim to distinction was good breeding.

Not that Mrs. Sands conceded good breeding to Lee. To her the most necessary ingredient for anything that set a person apart was the earlier or later earmarks of bastardy.

Mrs. Sands hated Lee.

As long as the contacts between the two women had been limited to casual visits, there had been enough frosty smiles and felt-covered nippy remarks on the one hand and smothered annoyance on the other to pass for polite courtesy.

But when the frost and nippiness became a daily portion, the world inverted itself and what had been harmony and peace began to crack, and hell peeped through.

It was deep down. Only women know about claws sunk so deeply in an enemy's flesh that they are out of sight.

The surface skin—the civilized covering—is unbroken.

So small a thing as "my mother says we spend too much"—was like a fuse that might lead to one stick of dynamite—or it might lead to a whole mountain range of high explosives.

By four o'clock in the morning, hot-eyed and restless, Lee crawled out of bed. She lifted herself carefully so she would not waken Roger.

His breathing was even, steady and placid.

The very calmness of his sleep fretted her. She hurried into her slippers and crossed the hall to her own room.

Even here ugliness had stalked her.

"Why do you need satin chairs in a room that you use every day?" Mrs. Sands had asked her once.

"Because I love lovely things around me every day," Lee had retorted.

Had she been trying to make Roger think her extravagant even then?

What was she trying to do? Why was she always picking, twisting, prying, distorting the most ordinary things of their life together?

"I am going out! I can't stay in this place. I'll drive out on the river road," Lee decided suddenly.

She pulled on a black corduroy suit—yellow sweater—a yellow felt hat—caught up her fur coat.

She felt in her bag. Roger must have the keys to the garage. She opened the bedroom door again and went in.

Roger spoke suddenly through the darkness. "Lee?"

"Yes."

"The keys are in the gray tweed vest in the closet."

She turned on a small light, opened the closet door, inserted swift fingers and found the keys.

"Be careful!" Roger said and held out one arm.

That meant that he expected to be kissed.

Lee did not want to kiss anybody. She began a struggle to enter her coat drawing nearer to the door all the while.

"I am just going to take an early drive! Can't sleep!" she offered from the doorway.

Roger shifted his position in the bed.

"You live too intensely, Lee!" he replied and yawned.

"Some more of Mama's talk!" Lee's mind clicked. "We can't all take life in cow-like rhythmics!" she shot at him.

Then she raced down the stairs, crossed the kitchen and went out to the garage.

The city slid away behind her and the twists and turns of the broad road beside the water made her forget herself for awhile.

It was not until she had run as far out as the little colored settlement—Tootsville—that she stopped. And then she had only stopped because the paved road ended where Tootsville began.

Deep yellow streaks were showing to the east where the sun was coming up out of the river mists. The tar-paper and tin houses of Tootsville looked so inadequate and barren of any beauty that Lee began to wish that she had driven in another direction.

But what was the need of trying to leave ugliness? It had to be seen through—and lived through—or fought through—like her own troubles.

Tears gathered swiftly in her eyes and she laid her head on her arms, crossed on the wheel and cried for a long time.

Lee had raised her head to wipe her eyes when she saw, running toward her, a colored woman so stout that she might have been running off of a comic strip.

Though the fog of a wintry morning was just beginning to rise from the water, the woman was dressed only in a cotton housedress, a ragged sweater and a huge pair of felt bedroom slippers.

Stumbling and slipping grotesquely in the muddy road, she came abreast of Lee's car.

"It must be pretty terrible, whatever it is, to drive you out in those clothes on a morning like this," Lee thought to herself. She ran the glass down swiftly in the door beside her and called to the woman, "Need any help?"

For an answer the other woman wrenched at the back door of the car. Lee pivoted and unlocked the door.

She sat silent and waiting while the woman lay back against the cushions and puffed.

"Jesus sure sent you to help me!" the woman managed finally. "I got to go to the lockup! Annie Mae is in there!"

Lee turned her ignition key and put her gloves on. "I am sorry I don't know where the lock up is. Can you tell me?"

"O, sure, honey! You just go back down that away apiece and turn at Sis Jones's house and cross the railroad track and it's right nigh to the preacher's!"

"May God forgive us," Lee prayed to herself. "Suppose you tell me as I drive along. Get up front with me."

The woman began to outshout the motor. "Willie Shack, he come busting up to my door talking about my Annie Mae! She and Lee Andrew Miller both been put in the lockup! I keep telling that gal to let Lee Andrew alone! She ain't but eighteen and here now they gits into one of them raids last night and now she in jail this Sunday morning! I gonna stop at the preacher's if God helps me and see if he can't go up to the lockup with me!"

"Will he bail your daughter out?"

"Naw! I can do that myself!" She patted her bosom with the palm of her hand. "Got my rent money here! Landlord, he have to wait! The reverend he gonna marry them two right in the lockup so when some of these nosey niggers says to me long about next week—'Seems like I heard somebody say your Annie Mae was in the lockup lass week!'—Then I can bust right back and say, 'You liable to hear 'bout anything child! Meet Annie Mae's husband!' Then they'll heish! See?"

"I see," Lee told her.

"Here's de preacher's! Let me git out!" And she was out on the pavement and up the stairs before Lee had warped the car into where a curb should have been.

The Reverend must have been accustomed to being roused at dawn to minister to his flock. He came out surprisingly soon neatly dressed in a frock tail coat.

No one asked Lee her name, so she did not offer it. She merely drove off and pulled up before a two story tin shack that sat directly on the ground.

"Here's where that fool gal is!" the mother burst forth. "Git out Reverend! Gawd have mercy! Much as I tried to do to raise that gal decent! That Lee Andrew Miller! Dirty dawg!" She muttered to herself as she waddled up the stairs.

Lee locked the car and walked in behind her.

A dirty slouch of a white man was sitting half asleep in a chair tilted against the wall.

The chair crashed down as the woman and her minister walked in.

"What you want?" the man in the chair growled.

The Reverend was the spokesman. "We want to see about the lady's daughter, Annie Mae Smith."

"When did she git in?"

"Last night, mister!"

"Hey Jim," roared the man from his chair. "Second back!"

There was a sound of doors opening, of feet stumbling and an undersized black girl, shivering in a cheap velvet crumpled dress, came walking out.

"This must be Lee Andrew," Lee thought as a swaggerish black man followed the girl.

Annie Mae was blinking dazedly. "Morning, Reverend," she offered sheepishly. " 'Lo ma!"

Ma sniffed and spoke not a word.

The man who had been asleep in the chair yawned to his feet

and moved over to an old desk. "Couldn't you find no better place to take your girl, Willie?" he growled at the black man.

"Naw, sir." Lee Andrew accepted the "Willie" and all the rest of it with an apologetic grin.

"All right! That little visit will cost you fifteen bucks!"

Lee Andrew dug deep in a pocket and dragged forth a crumpled mass of dirty bills. He flung a ten and a five down on the desk with a more-where-that-came-from swagger.

"Why the hell didn't you make your boy friend take you somewhere else?" was the next demand—this time of Annie Mae.

She could only grin dazedly. She seemed to be wincing in fright, more from her mother than the officer.

"Fifteen bucks, too, sister!"

Lee Andrew dug deep again, swaggered a little more, but could only produce ten dollars in singles. Mama bustled forward and laid three dollars more on the desk. But there were still two dollars missing.

A panicky hiatus followed. No one seemed to know what to do.

"There are five dollars remaining for my table next week in my bag!" Lee calculated to herself. "If I risk two of them on this girl, I'll have to serve Roger tinted broths for dinner! And his mother—!"

Lee drew out the five-dollar bill.

As he made the change, the man at the desk swept Lee with his eyes.

"Who are you? The dame that was running the joint?"

Before Lee could select the worst of the retorts that avalanched through her, the Reverend spoke. "She is just a lady what helps the community at times!" he supplied smoothly.

The other man made no reply. He made a great show of writing with a scratching pen.

From the place where she was still fastened with rage, Lee could see what he wrote.

"Willie Lee Miller—five dollars. Annie Mae Smith five dollars." He wrote beside the two names.

"Dirty thief!" Lee had to choke the words deep in herself.

But already the mother and the minister, with much whispering and bustling were pushing Lee Andrew and Annie Mae to the back of the room.

And standing right there in the ugliness and the dirt, the minister began: "Dearly beloved! We are gathered to unite this man and woman in the bonds of holy wedlock!"

Holy wedlock.—

Tears crowded into Lee's throat. She looked at the mother. She was grinning joyfully. Lee Andrew smirked. Annie Mae was still dazed and frightened.

Lee could feel that old tangle of barbed wire eating into her flesh. Her first marriage.—A runaway affair. A justice of the peace. Liquor on *his* breath.

Drunken fingers gripping tight—eating down into the flesh of her arms the way barbed wire does when it is settling for a grip.

Settling for a grip that always digs a scar too deep for eternity to ever fill again.

Lee told Roger all this.

Even as she talked there was a knocking at the door. A soft knocking, but a sharp insistent rupture of the peace in the room.

"It is time for dinner! Roger? Roger!! Your dinner will be cold!"

It was his mother calling Roger for dinner. Calling Roger for dinner from his wife's room as if she were not there. All the prongs of ugly thoughts pricked Lee at once. "In my own home— she means to omit me!"

Roger stood up hastily. "Glad you could bail Annie Mae, Lee, but we'll talk about it all after dinner. It is time to go down, so we had better hurry." He left the room.

Lee did not follow him at once. She stood up and took off the jacket of her suit.

"I'd rather go out again. I can't sit to the table with her!" Lee stood alone with herself again.

But she had gone out hours before. She had driven fast and far and come back with still no peace in her.

"Oh there's no need to run and to think and talk to myself! I'll stay in! I'll eat dinner! Wrong things can't whip you around in

Arabian cartwheels forever! There is a place where they have to stop! Things have to stop! Gouging into you! Something will turn it all aside and there'll be peace and no more whipping and gouging! I'll go down!"

She freshened her face.

She would have to step aside—let go of her own thoughts— push them aside and rest the case with herself and God.

It was the point where no human mind could unravel or untangle the snarls of her life. Only a greater mind could untangle—unravel—could go before her and straighten the crooked places.

Lee went down stairs.

Roger's mother was preening herself excitedly in the chair opposite her son. Lee sat at the side of the table.

As a guest should have sat—Lee sat at her own table.

The mother began to talk. "Lauretta Jones is having a little tea—a sort of wedding reception—for her son Henry and his bride this afternoon!"

"Oh did they finally work up to launching the bride?" Lee asked. "There was some talk the last time I heard as to whether she would be accepted."

An angry red crept over the older woman's face. "Any connection of the Jones family is most certainly the best this city can offer! Why Lauretta's husband, Atty. Henry Lyon Jones, represents the third generation of lawyers in that family! And Lauretta was a *Brewster* before she married! The Brewsters can trace their name back to the old aristocrat who owned their grandmother! The Jones family is certainly one colored family that can claim aristocracy, I can tell you! Acceptable? Any Jones is accepted!"

("The man who owned their grandmother." Lee's mind echoed. "Aristocratic!")

"Must is!" declared Roger. "If Miss Lauretta's darling Henry never went to jail for petty larceny—then they really must be exceptional! Why Lee, when we were all living in the frat house back at college, that guy would swipe anything hockable from anybody's room! Overcoat—watch—fountain pen—typewriter—

anything! He even took my cuff links! Some that had belonged to mother's grandfather!"

Mrs. Sands' red glow deepened. "Roger, you must never tell that! It might get to poor Lauretta's ears and it would hurt her so! I just believe that you lost them yourself."

"I couldn't have lost them myself! I never wore them. I always kept them in my case!"

"Maybe the women who cleaned up stole them. Those ordinary Negroes are such petty thieves! I'll never believe Henry took them."

("The *man* who owned their grandmother! The Brewsters trace their *aristocratic* names to him. Now—! those *ordinary* Negroes!" Lee repeated this all to herself.)

"I wouldn't believe it either if Atty. Jones hadn't had to come up to school every year and pay off different guys for the stuff old Henry had swiped during the semester! I mean things they saw afterward in a pawn shop themselves! Everybody knew about Henry!"

Lee spoke suddenly. "Well, I don't understand why they are laying the red rug and elevating the canopy for Henry's Pearl— isn't that her name? They surely shut the door in Ann's face when she married six years ago! Mrs. Jones's daughter Ann certainly deserves as much as her son Henry!"

Mrs. Sands' voice took a higher note: "But look at what Ann married! Some *janitor's* son! And they say his mother was a perfect Aunt Jemima. Why poor Lauretta nearly died! She was so afraid Ann would have a child that she didn't know what to do! Why there has never been anybody as colored as Ann's husband in any of the Jones family for generations!"

"Yet when Ann's husband bought up half the Negro district a little later, poor Lauretta began to ride everywhere everyday in one of her son-in-law's cars," finished Lee drily. "I won't be at the tea this afternoon! All of Ann's friends—her real friends—those who went to see her all the years when Miss Lauretta wouldn't— swore we'd never go to anything that the Jones tribe might give for Henry's wife. She and Henry lived together for two years before they finally decided to get married! Ann has really never forgiven her mother."

"Oh, you say the worst things, Lisa!" (Mrs. Sands never called Lee by her short name.) "Why shouldn't a girl forgive her mother—the one who gave her life?"

"And what a life! They tell that she always nagged Ann to death! Anyhow—why should a mother shut the doors of her home in the face of her daughter because she chose to marry a man blacker than her mother would have chosen for her son-by-marriage?"

Mrs. Sands drew her lips in with an I-won't-push-this-fool-argument sneer. "I shall want you to drive me to Lauretta's after dinner, Roger," she told him after a slight pause. "Lauretta expects you! She and I were girls together!"

"Roger," Lee asked, "do you care to meet a bride who spent two years as a wife before she was finally married?" Mrs. Sands' red paled to a gray. Roger laughed.

"Don't be so shocked, mother! That was town talk all the years Henry was supposed to be off on that tour for an intense study of business. Of course everybody who spent those years hashing over this situation is going to fall into Miss Lauretta's this afternoon! They'd be afraid to stay away for fear someone might think they didn't belong!"

"And they want to add a deceitful simper to the hee-haw chorus they'll all be pouring out to draw attention to the loveliness of their cliques—to see if they can perfume away the stench around the bride's past!" Lee laughed.

Mrs. Sands laid her fork down. "Really, Lisa, if you are going to carry on this objectionable talk at the table, I'll have to excuse myself. Lauretta Jones is my best friend"—with a cross between a snort and a sniffle—"and anyone dear to her is dear to me."

Roger's voice curved gently across to his mother: "But mother!" he laughed apologetically. "Lee is only stating plainly what every durn one of them there will *know* this afternoon! Lee is just separating the marrow from the bones for us."

(So! I am at the point that he needs to explain me to her! Upstairs will be better for me after all. At least there won't be any prejudiced ignorance in my own room! She can have the chair—the room—Roger—and everything!) Lee thought to herself. "Sorry," she said aloud coolly to the mother, "the truth always

172

will be the light, but light really blisters certain types of skin! I'll take a cup of tea upstairs in my own room."

Her chair went back in one swift push . . . —"If you'll excuse me!"

—So the cartwheels were still there.

—So this was not the time to straighten the crooked path.

Lee went out of the dining room to the small inner hall, where there was a cabinet of glass and dishes.

"I'll take my tea-pot and use my best small cloth upstairs. Maybe the touch of elegance will take my mind off of things."

She opened the drawer where the linens were and reached into a special corner where the cream damask lunch-cloth stayed.

It was not there.

Only two large table-cloths were left in the drawer.

"I know it isn't in the laundry! What on earth has happened to it!" Lee spoke aloud to herself.

She drew out an old stool and stood up to open the cabinet door.

Lee owned a tea set of cut glass with black inlay, a lovely Victorian ornate thing that had been her great-grandmother's. That grandmother had been a seamstress for a wealthy group that had brought her gifts from every country they had visited.

Lee kept the tea set on a top shelf where nothing could possibly hurt its old-fashioned loveliness.

She climbed up on the stool.

The top shelf was bare.

Lee stared at the empty space.

Roger's voice reached her; "Lee! Telephone! It's Mrs. Jones! She's having some sort of hysteria on the wire! She says Henry's new wife just dropped two of your cups—Say! You ought not to jump off of that chair like that! You will break your neck in those heels.

Lee pushed Roger out of the way and threw the dining room door wide open.

Mrs. Sands was still in her seat. Something in Lee's face made her half rise.

"You gave Mrs. Jones my tea set!" Lee did not speak loudly at first. "You took my grandmother's tea set—without asking me!"

The older woman dropped back. Her ready sneer rode her features. "Surely anything in my son's house is mine too!"

"There are some things in your son's house—(which happens to be my house too)—that do not belong to your son! That tea set was mine! You had no right to touch *one thing* in here without asking me!"

"Asking *you?* I am his *mother!*"

"And I am his *wife!*"

This was one of the spots where life left no words to fight with.

But *eyes* can carry a battle forward.

Roger spoke. "Answer the phone, Lee!"

"Throw the phone and everything else out of the window!" Lee told him. ("Any fool could have said something wiser!" Lee told herself.)

And she ran all the way upstairs to the couch in her room.

She heard Roger come up the stairs soon after.

He walked into his room. There was a sound of his closet door opening. He came out into the hall again and walked along the hall.

"Don't let him come in here!" Lee prayed to herself.

But the door opened. She kept her face buried on the couch. She could hear him cross two of the small spaces between the rugs. Then he stood still.

"I am going after your tea set, Lee," he said after a moment of silence.

There wasn't anything to say now. There was nothing to say unless you meant to use your words as a hatchet to hack out the roots of bitterness.

And Lee was too tired to hack. She'd spent too much strength trying to keep from blasting roots at the wrong time.

She kept her face turned to the pillow and waited.

Lee waited to hear Roger walk across the two small spaces between the rugs again. That would have meant that he was going out of the room.

But the sound did not come.

She twisted over suddenly.

Roger stood looking out of the window, his face in profile to her. Tense lines furrowed deep with a bitterness within, were drawn around his mouth. He stared far before him with the glaze of sadness you see in a person who has had to look a long time—alone—at some deep wound life has gashed in him.

"Why—*he* has seen how hatefully highhanded his mother can be—before this!" Shot swiftly through Lee's mind. "He has seen her do things this way before! *Her own* way! And to hell with you—your sense—your sensibilities—your property—or even your own soul! He has seen this all his life."

She started to rush over to him and throw her arms around him. But if she did that, the glazed sadness and the tense bitterness might run together. Then things might be said that could never be unsaid.

She would have to put her mind . . . and not herself—between him and the thing that was hurting him.

That thought made her able to drop her feet to the floor.

"I'll go with you, Roger," she suggested. "There's a detour on the river road that I saw this morning. You might miss it in the dark. Better wear a heavy coat. It's damp over there near the water."

She began to talk lightly while she powdered her nose, touched her lips and her cheeks, put on her hat and coat.

Then she ran downstairs ahead of him.

Passed the dining room door.

Talking—talking—lightly—lightly—lightly—spinning a gossamer of light talk so that there would be no chance for even one weighted word.

There are some cancerous spots in people's lives that no one ever wants to touch.

She did not wait for Roger to answer. She did not want him to answer, until the lines in his face were softer.

There are some cancerous spots in people's lives that no one ever wants to touch. Never.

She shook the door of the car a dozen times before she realized it was locked and that Roger was digging in his pockets for the keys.

They were ten miles out on the River road before Roger spoke: "You take much better care of me than I do of you, I am afraid,

Lee!" was all he said.

It was enough, though.

His face was not bitter, drawn, hard and old now. He was himself once more.

It was enough.

She had blurred, then, some of the saw-toothed edges of hatefulness that must have eaten into him before this.

"Why *she* meant to go! *She* wanted to go to the tea! And we forgot her!" Lee remembered suddenly.

"We forgot her!"

And the fear of the hate that had seemed so strong—so full of power?

"I even forgot to be afraid while I was trying to help Roger get back into himself!"

And if you can forget the fear of a hate—walk out even for one second from under the shadow of the fear—that means it is nothing.

Nothing.

No hate has ever unlocked the myriad interlacings—the *front* of love.

Hate is nothing.

The Makin's

Little David remembered that he wanted ten cents when Mrs. Summers, the lady next door, tossed an empty tomato can out of her kitchen window.

The can hit the scarecrow fence that pretended to separate her yard from David's. Then it struck against David's house before it lay still.

"Teacher, she say not to throw cans and mess in the yard! She say we oughta plant grass and flowers instead! I forgot to ast Ma for my dime to git me some seeds like she said!"

He went into the kitchen. Ma was sitting on a chair between the stove and the sink. Her kinky bob stood up like a half-blown thistle pod all over her head.

The dishes left from last night piled the breakfast dishes up to the shelf over the sink, where the lamps sat.

Ma was reading, "Let Me Tell All," so David had to yell to make her hear him.

"Ma, ma!! The teacher she says for all the kids to git a dime and buy seeds! She says you should pitch the cans and paper and stuff out of your back yard and plant the seeds!

Ma grunted. "Huh-huh," and turned a page.

David waited. "Well, where's the money, Ma?" he yelled again.

Ma's book went down. "Money? What you talking 'bout, boy?"

"I told you and you said yes, Ma!"

"You done tole me what!"

"I done tole you teacher say to git a dime from your Ma and buy some seeds and plant them in your yard! And you says yes!"

"I ain't said nothin'. I ain't heard you askin' for no dime."

"You said huh-huh when I asked you!"

"Well, who the devil got any money to buy seeds? I sure God ain't goin' to buy no seeds! These teachers always got some fool notion! They ought to give you the seeds if they want you to have them! Here, Here!" Ma felt in the pocket of her pajamas and drew out a piece of paper. "Here! Take this number and this quarter down to Mr. Ed in the barber shop. Don't you lose it, neither, 'cause God knows I'd skin you if 609 was to hit today and you lost this last quarter I'm playing on it!"

David took the paper and the quarter and tried again.

"I can't git no seeds then, kin I, Ma?"

Ma always carried a cigarette behind her ear the way a clerk carries a pencil. She took her cigarette down now, reached expertly up on the lamp shelf and got a match without getting up out of her chair. She began to puff as she opened her book again.

She found her place, "I betcha you better git along out o' here," she yelled and grabbed a cup out of the dishes piled in the sink as if she meant to throw it at David.

The yell and the cup set David in motion. If he ran out of the back door again, he would be in line for a direct blow. So he curved and shot forward toward the front of the house. He heard the cup hit the kitchen door. He could already smell that sweet sickening smoke from Ma's cigarette.

"Them cigarettes sure make that gal mean!" David had heard Marm, his grandmother, say about his mother.

A burst of singing came down to him suddenly from upstairs where Marm had her room. That meant she was having a praying meeting this morning.

"Maybe she'll give me a dime for some seeds," David thought, and started upstairs.

> *"Glory, glory, hallelujah*
> *When I lay this burden down!"*

Marm was leading the song. David could hear a man's voice take up a verse while the whole room answered in chorus.

"One day, one day, I was walking along!
(When I lay this burden down)
And de element opened and de dove came down!
(When I lay this burden down)!"

David peeked in the door.

Though Marm had on a cotton house dress and her apron, and though this was her own room, she had her hat on. Some half dozen elderly colored people were in the room with her.

Dragged north to the city by that uneasy surge of hope for better times that had fretted their children out of the South, most of them had felt poked and jibed by the strange ways of city living. They had felt alone and unwanted when they sat singly at home. Grouped together now, they counted for something and the fiery spirit of their old-time religion fused them together into a praying band that met daily.

These were not the parents of those young Negroes who can float through a white man's world balanced on some sustaining inner poise. These were those who believed everything they heard and knew that everything they saw was real. Their children seldom bothered to pray nor did they bother the old folks when they prayed.

Little David teetered on the doorsill.

Gramp Dean was beating out the time of the hymn with his cane. Aunt Susie Kiner was weeping loudly, burying her face in her apron. Old Miss Mary snatched up a song as soon as the last "When I lay dis burden down" had faded away. She began to sing loudly:

"I'm trampin!
Trampin
Tryin' to make heaven my home!
(Hal-lee-loo!)"

The room shouted joyously in response.

Marm caught sight of David in the doorway. She bustled over to him.

"What you want, boy?" she asked him and kept looking back into the room.

"I want ten cents, Marm."

Marm's head snapped around. "You want ten cents? Whyn't you Ma give it to you? She know I ain't got no ten cents."

"She ain't tole me to ask you for it!" David explained hurriedly. "I just thought maybe—"

"Well, God knows I ain't got no money. You don't need none nohow. When I was your size if I had a penny I thought I had sumtin. Y'all children in the city git so rich you wants a dime."

The hymn had ended now. Everyone was listening to Marm at the door. Marm had meant to testify to the full and rich presence of the spirit in her life.

The room was listening to her so she at once began to speak to David and everyone else at the same time.

"Y'all so rich in the city you needs a dime. Just want it for some devilment! Ain't no use no children to have so much anyhow. Got so much nowadays—ain't got no time for God!"

"Amen!" Miss Kitty Creesey cried.

Her cry oiled Marm's tongue. "What y'all needs is more God and less dealing with the devil!"

"Yassuh!" Gramp Dean shouted.

He preached the same doctrine to his son Jerry whenever he could get hold of him. Jerry ran a gambling joint and was seldom at home. His only answer to Gramp was that since he kept Gramp off of the charity rolls, surely he was a good son. And God only wanted you to be as good as you could. You couldn't be perfect. So what?

Gramp shouted "Amen! Yassuh, Jesus!" Then he shook hands with those nearest him.

David cringed back from the door. When you're eight years old, you do not want a room full of people shouting amen about you and your relations with the devil.

As David ran back down the stairs and out into the street, he wondered if the devil helped or hindered the planting of seeds in a back yard.

His father, Jack, was coming up the street. David glanced quickly at his face. Frowns creased his forehead and his mouth was in a straight line. That meant it would be better to lay low. David

180

curved way out to the edge of the sidewalk.

" 'Lo, Jack," he offered.

His father spat out in the middle of the street and said nothing.

"Ain't you working today, Jack?" a man called from the steps of the house next door.

"Hell, no!" Jack answered. "Spent my carfare to go way out to that damn place and when I git there they talk about it look like rain and we can't clean no weeds out of no lots!"

"Sure God is awful the way they take your grocery order from you and put you out workin' for a dollar a day, trashing around," the man on the steps declared.

"Jack, gimme a dime!" David could not help trying once more.

Jack turned toward him. "A dime, for what?"

"Some seeds! The teacher, she say—"

"Aw, how the hell you think I gonna give you a dime out of this damn measly dollar a day I get for you to throw away? Here! Go get me two good packages of cigarettes, and if Sam ain't got em, go somewhere's else!"

Jack began to talk to the other man again. "Been buying them a penny a piece all the time when I wasn't working, but now I'll be dogged if I'm gonna let them play me cheap anymore!"

"Damn right!" the other replied and moved up closer to Jack. Maybe he could spin on a web of talk that could hold Jack until David got back. He needed cigarettes himself. Maybe he could bum a few off of Jack.

David moved off down the street. It was four blocks to Mr. Ed's and six blocks to Sam's.

To get to Ed's, you went across Grand Avenue under the "El," passed the "Toot Sweet" Shop with its window full of steel guitars, drums and ukeleles inlaid with mother of pearl. Folks said you could play the horses as well as music in that shop.

Then David stopped and looked in at the knives and diamond rings in Sol's Pawn Palace.

But it was while he was wishing for every pink and yellow cake in the window of Kronen's bake shop that Bennie Jones caught up with him.

"Hi, David!" Bennie cried and slapped David on his shoulder.

"Gonna buy some of those?"

Benny was larger than David. He might belong to that gang of older boys who stopped little children on their way to and from the stores and took their money from them.

David was cautious: "Ain't buying nuthin! No money!"

Bennie produced a quarter. "I got money!" he boasted. "I'm buying something!"

David's eye popped. "All dat yours?"

Bennie laughed scornfully. "I takin' some of it. Ma she say give it to Mr. Ed for 473! But she ain't never goin' hit nothin' so I takes me some of it every day she sends me down there!"

David's breathing became noisy.

Bennie looked at him shrewdly. "Whyn't you eat up a little of your Ma's dough? Ain't she layin' out nothin' today?"

David was eager. "A quarter!"

Bennie swaggered. "Come on, boy! Let me show you de way!" He laughed and swung into the bake shop.

For five cents they each got a bottle of strawberry soda. For five cents they each bought a yellow and pink cake. For five cents more they got ice cream cones.

David gobbled and gulped and looked first up the street and then down as they walked along. He was afraid.

"What you scared of?" Bennie taunted. "Your old lady's hittin' the reefers and she won't know whether the quarter reaches there or not. My Ma, she don't smoke no reefers! She says she ain't fixin' to see no snakes crawling all over her in the bed!"

David choked down a piece of cake so he could answer. "My Ma she ain't seen no snakes in bed neither! I ain't got no snakes in my house! Just roaches and stuff like that!"

Bennie tipped his strawberry soda up to his lips and took a big drink. "You sure is dumb," he told David.

A whistle blew somewhere.

"Gee-min-ity!" yelled Bennie. "Dat's quarter of twelve o'clock. Ma's number had better be in there afore twelve."

He broke into a clopping gallop. David trailed behind him. Mr. Ed greeted them genially. "How are ya, boys?" he asked. "Come in, come in!"

He stopped to roar at a man who was going out of the door.

182

"Going down the line, Joe? Well—tell 'em about me, boy."

"You got everything!" Joe laughed at him.

"How much your Ma send, Bennie?" Mr. Ed asked. "Only a dime? S'matter with Gert? She can't win nothin' with this chicken feed! She'd ought to play a half a dollar every day!"

David watched the sun breaking into a thousand lights on the diamond of Mr. Ed's stickpin.

"Who are you, boy?" Mr. Ed asked David suddenly.

"David Brown! My Ma she sent a dime too."

Mr. Ed looked at him sharply. "Sure she ain't sent a quarter?"

David swallowed and paled. Bennie looked wise and made a great flurry of picking up slips for David. Then he pushed him out of the door ahead of him.

"That guy must be awful rich," David told Bennie as soon as they were outside. "Did you see them sparklers?"

"Boy, he's the richest man in this town! My father say old Mr. Ed got a couple of million, he bet!" Bennie told him. "I'm gonna be rich like him when I'm a man!"

"Me too! I gonna write the numbers when I get big too!" David echoed.

"You too dumb!" Bennie taunted.

"I ain't!"

"You are too. Betcha can't even swear!" To demonstrate, Bennie let loose a group of he-male curses.

David was stumped. He did not know half of that. He stuck his hands in his pockets and hung his head.

Something jingled in his right-hand pocket. Jack's thirty cents was in there.

"What ya got?" Bennie demanded. "Holding out on Mr. Ed and me?"

"Naw. I got to get my pa some cigarettes at Sam's. He's waiting for them!"

And David broke into a run that brought him up breathless to Sam's door. Then, cigarettes in hand, he trotted home.

As he stumbled through the back gate his eyes fell on the garbage, the cans, the paper and trash that littered his back yard.

"Should have bought dem seeds with some of Ma's quarter,"

David said to himself. "But she'd of wanted to know where I got the dime."

There was nowhere he could say he had gotten a dime for seeds. But he could pinch a little from everything she sent to Mr. Ed's every day, and eat it up.

"I'm sure gonna write numbers myself someday," he promised himself.

"You ain't tough enough!" Bennie's taunts still mocked him.

David picked up a can and threw it against another before he went into the house.

"I am, too, tough!" he yelled aloud in an imagined argument with Bennie. "You dirty ole son of a gun!"

There! He'd remembered one thing Bennie had said.

Holding the cigarettes in his hand like a gun he swaggered up the back stairs. A cat crouched on the top steps.

David aimed a kick at it. "Get the hell out of here," he roared. Then he repeated Bennie's man-sized curse.

Ma yanked the door open. "S'matter with you, boy?" she cried.

David cowered, then he swaggered. "I'm gonna be a number writer!" he told his mother.

A delighted laugh came from her. "G'long, boy! Goin' be rich, too! I have to send you down to Mr. Ed's every day. So you learn somethin'!"

David brushed by her and went into the kitchen. "Hey, Jack," he called to his father. "Jack! Gotcha ciggies! . . . You dirty ole son of a gun," he added under his breath, to his own surprise.

His mother's laugh crackled louder. "Boy, you all right!" she screamed at him. "You *all right.*"

The Whipping

The matron picked up her coat. It was a good coat made of heavy men's wear wool and lined with fur. She always liked to let her hands trail fondly over it whenever she was going to put it on (the way women do who are used to nothing).

She shook it out and shrugged her shoulders into it.

"I'll be back home again in time for dinner!" She smiled at the warden as she talked. "Helga will have 'peasant-girl,' for dessert, too!"

The hard lines that creased around the man's eyes softened a little. "Peasant-girl-with-a-veil! Ah, my mother could make that! Real home-made jam, yellow cream!—good! Nothing here ever tastes as good as it did back in the old country, I tell you!"

The woman balanced her weight on the balls of her feet and drew on one of her leather driving gloves. Through the window she saw her car, nicely trimmed and compactly modern, awaiting her. Beyond the car was a November sky, dismal, darkening and melancholy as the walls that bounded the surrounding acres of land which belonged to the Women's Reformatory.

At the end of her drive of thirty-five miles back to the city again, she would go to her apartment that—through warmth of color and all the right uses of the best comforts—seemed to be full of sunshine on the darkest days. She looked down, now, as she stood near the warden and saw her right hand freshly manicured.

Her mother's hands back in the stone kitchen with the open hearth found in every peasant home in Denmark, had always been grey and chapped with blackened nails this time of year. No woman who has to carry wood and coal from a frozen yard can have soft clean hands.

The thought made the matron shrug again. "I like things as they are here—but it would be good to go home some day to visit!"

She hurried a little toward the door now. Nobody lingers in the impersonal greyness of an institution whose very air is heavy with fierce anger and anguish and sorrow, buried and dulled under an angry restraint just as fierce and sorrowful.

She had nearly reached the door before she remembered the colored woman sitting alone on the edge of the bench beside the window. The matron had just driven up from the city to bring the woman on the bench to stay at the Reformatory as long as she should live.

She had killed her little boy.

The judge and the social worker said she had killed him.

But she had told the matron over and over again that she did not do it.

You could never tell, though. It is best to leave these things alone.

"Good bye, 'Lizabeth!" the matron called in a loud voice. She meant to leave a cheerful note but she only spoke overloud. "Be a good girl!"

"Yes'm!" Lizabeth answered softly. "Yas'm!"

And the women separated. One went out to the light. The other looked at the grey walls—dark—and growing darker in the winter sunset.

Everything had been grey around Lizabeth most all of her life. The two-room hut with a ragged lean-to down on Mr. Davey's place in Mississippi where she had lived before she came North—had been grey.

She and Pa and Ma and Bella and John used to get up when the morning was still grey and work the cotton until the greyness of evening stopped them.

"God knows I'm sick of this!" Pa had cursed suddenly one day.

Ma did not say anything. She was glad that they had sugar once in a while from the commissary and not just molasses like they said you got over at McLaren's place.

Pa cursed a lot that day and kept muttering to himself. One

morning when they got up to go to work the cotton, Pa was not there.

"He say he goin' North to work!" Ma explained when she could stop her crying.

Mr. Davey said Pa had left a big bill at the commissary and that Ma and the children would have to work twice as hard to pay it up.

There were not any more hours in any one day than those from sun-up to sun-down, no way you could figure it.

The Christmas after Pa left, Mr. Davey said Ma owed three times as much and that she could not have any flannel for John's chest to cover the place where the misery stayed each winter.

That was the day Ma decided to go North and see if she could find Pa.

They had to plan it all carefully. There was no money to go from Mississippi northward on the train.

John had to get an awful attack of the misery first. Then Bella had to stay home to take care of him.

The day Mr. Davey's man came to find out why Bella and Jim were not in the field, Bella had her hand tied up in a blood soaked rag and she was crying.

The axe had slipped and cut her hand, she told them.

That meant Ma would have to wait on Bella and John.

Lizabeth worked the cotton by herself and the Saturday after Ma laid off, Mr. Davey would not let them have any fatback.

"Y'all can make it on meal and molasses until you work off your debts!" he told Lizabeth.

Ma had said nothing when Lizabeth had told her about the fatback. She had sat still a long time. Then she got up and mixed up some meal.

"What you makin' so much bread to oncet?" Bella asked Ma.

"Gainst our gittin' hungry!"

"Can't eat all that bread one time!" John blared forth. "Better save some 'cause you might not git no meal next time! We owe so much!"

"Heish, boy!!" Ma screamed so you could hear her half across the field. "I ain't owe nobody nuthin'!"

Lizabeth's jaw dropped. "Mr. Davey, he say—!"

"Heish, gal!" Ma screamed again. "I ain't owe nuthin', I say! Been right here workin' nigh on forty years!"

She turned the last scrap of meal into a pan. Then she stood up and looked around the table at three pairs of wide-stretched eyes.

"I'm fixin' this 'gainst we git hungry! We goin North to find Pa tonight!"

You would not believe that three women and a half-grown boy could get to Federal Street, Chicago, from Mississippi without a cent of money to start with.

They walked—they begged rides—they stopped in towns, worked a little and they rode as far as they could on the train for what they had earned. It took months, but they found Federal Street.

But they never found Pa.

They found colored people who had worked the cotton just like they themselves had done, but these others were from Alabama and Georgia and parts of Mississippi that they had never seen.

They found the houses on Federal Street were just as grey, just as bare of color and comfort as the hut they had left in Mississippi.

But you could get jobs and earn real money and buy all sorts of things for a little down and a little a week! You could eat what you could afford to buy—and if you could not pay cash, the grocer would put you on the book.

Ma was dazed.

John forgot the misery.

Bella and Lizabeth were looping wider and wider in new circles of joy.

Ma could forget Pa, who was lost, and the hard trip up from the South when she screamed and shouted and got happy in robust leather-lunged style in her store-front church run in the "down-home" tempo.

John spent every cent that he could lay a hand on on a swell outfit, thirty dollars from skin out and from shoes to hat!

Bella's circles of joy spread wider and wider until she took to hanging out with girls who lived "out South" in kitchenettes.

She straightened her hair at first.

Then she curled her hair. After that she "sassed" Ma. Said she was going to get a job in a tavern and stay "out South" too!"

They heard she was married.

They heard she was not.

Anyway, she did not come back to 31st and Federal.

John's swell outfit wasn't thick enough to keep the lake winds from his misery. He began to have chills and night sweats. The Sunday he coughed blood, Lizabeth got a doctor from State Street.

The doctor made Ma send John to the hospital.

"He be all right soon?" Ma asked after the ambulance had gone.

The doctor looked grim. "I doubt if they can arrest it!"

"Arrest it! Arrest what? John's a good boy! He ain't done nothing to git arrested!"

The doctor looked grimmer. "I mean that maybe they can't stop this blood from coming!"

Ma looked a little afraid. "Well, if they jes' gives him a tablespoon of salt that will stop any bleeding! My mother always—"

The doctor put his hat on and went out. He did not listen to hear any more.

The second fall that they were on Federal Street, Lizabeth met Benny, a soft-voiced boy from Georgia.

Benny said he was lonely for a girl who did not want him to spend all his money on liquor and things for her every time he took her out. That is what these city girls all seemed to want.

They wanted men to buy things for them that no decent girl down home would accept from men.

Lizabeth was glad for just a ten-cent movie and a bottle of pop or a nickel bag of peanuts.

They were married at Christmas. The next year, in October, baby Benny came.

In November John died.

In February of the second year Benny—who had begun to go "out South" in the evening with the boys—suddenly stayed away all night.

Ma had hysterics in the police station and told the police to find him.

"He may be dead and run over somewhere!" she kept crying.

The policemen took their time. Ma went every day to find out if there were any news. Lizabeth went too!

She stopped going after she saw the policeman at the desk wink at another when he told her, "Sure! Sure! We are looking for him every day!"

Mrs. Rhone who kept the corner store asked Lizabeth one morning, "Where's your man? Left you?"

Lizabeth bridled: "He was none of these men! He was my husband!"

The other woman probed deeper: "Who married you? That feller 'round to the store front church? Say! Hee-hee? They tell me he ain't no reglar preacher! Any feller what'll slip him a couple dollars can get 'married'—even if he's got a wife and ten kids "out South," they tell me—!"

Lizabeth shrank back. Benny had been truly married to her!!

This woman just did not have any shame!

But after that Lizabeth grew sensitive if she went on the street and saw the women standing together in gossiping groups.

"They talkin' about me! They saying I weren't married!" she would tell herself.

She and Ma moved away.

The place where they moved was worse than Federal Street. Folks fought and cursed and cut and killed down in the Twenties in those days.

But rent was cheap.

Lizabeth only got twelve dollars a week scrubbing all night in a theater.

Ma kept little Benny and took care of the house.

There was not much money, but Lizabeth would go without enough to eat and to wear so that little Benny could have good clothes and toys that she really could not afford.

"Every time you pass the store you 'bout buy this boy somethin'!" the grandmother complained once.

"Aw I'd a liked pretty clothes and all that stuff when I was a kid!" Lizabeth answered.

The Whipping

"How she buy so much stuff and just *she* workin'!" the neighbors argued among themselves.

"She must be livin' wrong!" declared those who could understand all the fruits of wrong living in all its multiple forms.

Little Benny grew to expect all the best of things for himself. He learned to whine and cry for things and Lizabeth would manage them somehow.

He was six years old in 1929.

That was the year when Lizabeth could find no more theaters to scrub in and there were no more day's work jobs nor factory jobs. Folks said the rich people had tied up all the money so all the poor people had to go to the relief station.

Lizabeth walked fifteen blocks one winter day to a relief station. She told the worker that there was no coal, no food, the water was frozen and the pipes had burst.

"We'll send an investigator," the worker promised.

"When'll that come?" Lizabeth demanded vaguely.

"*She* will come shortly! In a few days, I hope!"

"I got nothin' for Ma and Benny to eat today!" Lizabeth began to explain all over again.

"I'm sorry! That is all we can do now!" the woman behind the desk began to get red as she spoke this time.

"But Benny ain't had no dinner and—"

"Next!" The woman was crimson as she called the next client.

The client—a stout colored woman—elbowed Lizabeth out of the way.

Already dazed with hunger and bone-weary from her freezing walk, Lizabeth stumbled.

"She's drunk!" the client muttered apologetically to the woman behind the desk.

Lizabeth had had enough. She brought her left hand up in a good old-fashioned back-hand wallop.

Everybody screamed. "They're fighting!"

"Look out for a knife!" yelled the woman behind the desk.

Her books had all told her that colored women carried knives.

A policeman came and took Lizabeth away.

They kept Lizabeth all night that night. The next day they said she could go home but it was the third day that they finally set her on the sidewalk and told her to go home.

Home was thirty blocks away this time.

"Where you been, gal!" Ma screamed as soon as the door opened. "You the las' chile I got and now you start actin' like that Bella! Ain't no food in this house! Ain't a God's bit of fire 'cept one box I busted up—!"

"She busted up my boat! She busted up the box what I play boat in!" Benny added his scream to the confusion. "She make me stay in bed all the time! My stomach hurts me!"

Lizabeth was dizzy. "Ain't nobody been here?" She wanted to wait a little before she told ma that she had been in the lock-up.

"Nobody been here? For what?"

"Get us some somethin' to eat! That's what the woman said!"

"No, ain't nobody been here!"

Lizabeth put on her hat again.

"Where you goin' now?" Ma shouted.

"I got to go back."

"You got to go back where?"

"See 'bout some somethin' to eat, Ma!"

Benny began to scream and jumped out of the bed. "You stay with me!" he cried as he ran to his mother. "I want my dinner! I—"

"Heish!" Lizabeth out-screamed everyone else in the room.

Frightened, Benny cowed away a little. Then he began again. "I want to eat! The lady downstairs, she say my mother ought to get me somethin' 'stead of stayin' out all night with men!"

Lizabeth stared wildly at her mother.

Hostile accusation bristled in her eyes, too.

"That's what the lady say. She say—" Benny repeated.

And Lizabeth who had never struck Benny in her life, stood up and slapped him to the floor.

As he fell, the child's head struck the iron bedstead.

His grandmother picked him up, still whimpering.

Lizabeth went out without looking back.

Fifteen blocks put a stitch in her left side. Anger made her eyes red.

The woman behind the desk at the relief station paled when she saw Lizabeth this time. "You will have to wait!" she chattered

The Whipping

nervously before Lizabeth had even spoken.

"Wait for what? Been waitin'! Nobody been there!"

"We are over-crowded now! It will take ten days to two weeks before our relief workers can get there!"

"What's Ma and little Benny going to do all that time? They gotta eat!"

The other woman grew eloquent. "There are hundreds and hundreds of people just like you waiting—!"

"Well I stop waitin'! Benny got to eat!"

Fifteen blocks had put a stitch in her side. Worry and hunger made her head swim. Lizabeth put one hand to her side and wavered against the desk.

This time the woman behind the desk *knew* that Lizabeth had a knife—for her alone! Her chair turned over as she shot up from the desk. Her cries brought the policeman from the next corner.

"We better keep you for thirty days," the police court told Lizabeth when they saw her again.

"But little Benny—!" Lizabeth began crying aloud.

There was a bustle and commotion. A thin pale woman pushed her way up to the desk.

Lizabeth had to draw back. She stood panting, glaring at the judge.

He had been looking at her at first in tolerant amusement. But while this pale woman talked to him across his desk, cold, dreadful anger surged into his eyes.

"What's that you're saying about little Benny?" he demanded suddenly of Lizabeth. "He's dead!"

Lizabeth could not speak nor move at first. Then she cried out. "What happen to him? What happen to my baby?"

"You killed him." The judge was harsh.

A bailiff had to pick Lizabeth up off the floor and stand her up again so the judge could finish. "You whipped him to death!"

"I ain't never whip him! I ain't never whip little Benny!" Lizabeth cried over and over.

They took her away and kept her.

They kept her all the time that they were burying Benny, even. Said she was not fit to see him again.

Later—in court—Ma said that Lizabeth had "whipped Benny's

193

head" the last time she was at home.

"I ain't hit him but once!" Lizabeth tried to cry it to the judge's ears. "He didn't have nuthin' to eat for a long time! That was the trouble."

"There was a deep gash on his head," testified the relief worker. "She was brutal!"

"She brought knives to the relief station and tried to start a fight every time she came there!"

"She's been arrested twice!"

"Bad character! Keep her!" the court decided.

That was why the matron had had to drive Lizabeth to the Women's Reformatory.

She had gone out now to her car. Lizabeth watched her climb into it and whirl around once before she drove away.

"Won't see her no more! She's kinder nice, too," Lizabeth thought.

"It is time for supper! Come this way!" the warden spoke suddenly.

Lizabeth stumbled to her feet and followed him down a long narrow hall lit with one small light.

That relief worker had said she would see that Ma got something to eat.

That seemed to settle itself as soon as they had decided they would send her to this place.

"You will work from dawn to sundown," the matron had said as they were driving up from the city.

She had always done that in Mississippi.

It did not matter here. But she asked one question. "They got a commissary there?"

"A commissary!" The matron was struck breathless when Lizabeth asked this. She had decided that Lizabeth was not normal. She had seemed too stupid to defend herself in court. "She must be interested in food!" the matron had decided to herself.

A slight sneer was on her face when she answered. "Of course they have a commissary! You get your food there!"

Lizabeth had drawn back into her corner and said nothing more.

The Whipping

A commissary. She understood a commissary. The same grey hopeless drudge—the same long unending row to hoe—lay before her.

The same debt, year in, year out.

How long had they said she had to stay?

As long as she lived. And she was only thirty now.

But she understood a commissary and a debt that grew and grew while you worked to pay it off. And she would never be able to pay for little Benny.

Hongry Fire

God—it was good to be lying in the bed at eleven o'clock on Monday morning and hear somebody else on the washboard!

Only thing, Margaret never did wash real clean!

—"I've tried ever since that gal was old enough to work to git her to do things up real finished! Jes' listen to her! Missin' those rubs! Be leavin' the dirt in and everybody'll be laughing at my wash!! First time in my life anybody ever laughed at it, too! Jes' listen—!!—Aw Margaret? You Margaret!" Ma yelled aloud and pounded on the bedroom floor so that Margaret, in the kitchen below, could hear.

Heavy footsteps thudded along the lower hall.

That gal even walked fat!

Steaming and puffing, fatter and blacker for the greasy perspiration that glistened on her broad face, Margaret thrust herself into the room.

—"What you say Ma?"

—"You wash them clothes clean, you hear?"

—"Oh, course I will Ma! You jes' lay there quiet and I'll tend to everything! I gotta get back down stairs 'cause the baby'll be gettin' at that lye water!"

"You puttin' lye water on them clothes!! Don't put none on Pa's Sunday shirts or none on Vernice's fancy underclothes!"

"Aw corse not, Ma! Jes' lay still! You want some of your medicine?"

"No!!"

"Well,—I'll git back down! The baby'll be in the lye water!"

Ma listened until she could hear Margaret and the baby. She began talking to herself again:

196

"Just 'cause the doctor said something about 'cardy-something and said to lay quiet they think I'm sick! What I need with that dark green stuff! Twenty drops of that, and take the yellow stuff to sleep! What ever heard tell of a woman what raised six children and worked all her life all day every day needin' somethin' to make her sleep? I'm jes' going to lay here peaceful and let them take things as they find 'em themselves!"

Ma stared around her. Funny how the furniture looked sort of marked up and dirty!

Somebody ought to wash the marble tops on that bureau and table in soap water. Somebody ought to shut the drawers tight and . . . Her feet were on the floor before she remembered.

"I'm jes' 'sposed to lay here quiet like! Too bad I had to lay right down there in church yestiddy mornin' when the reverend was preachin'! But Lawd! Did seem like I'd never draw a clean breath again! Hope nobody'd be evil enough to think I was drunk! People so mean in their hearts they think anything 'bout anybody!"

The pillows became too hard, too hot, too lumpy and smothering.

The front door struck to downstairs.

That would be Pa, getting back from the foundry. Why did he have to shut the door so noisy? Seemed like the noise was right under her bed.

Ma hung her body half off the mattress and looked at the faded rug under the bed. One spot seemed to sag a little. She pushed it. The end turned up.

"Here's the old hole where Pa took out the hot air heater! Always gonna fix it. Hole still here. I can even see down in the kitchen."

Pa's voice eddied up through the hole.

"Hey, Margaret. Gal. Put the little pot in the big pot. I could eat the half side of a ram I'm so hungry! How's Ma? What the doctor say?"

"Aw. She's all right. Able to eat and tell me what to do. The doctor he say she got to lay still a piece."

They both laughed loudly.

"That's Ma, all right. Guess I better get on up and see her."

Heavy crunching footsteps along the hall.

("Here's that Margaret comin' up behind Pa. Anything to leave that wash tub. Them clothes ought to been out by nine o'clock.")

"Hello Pa. Yeah I'm all right. Be up tomorrow I reckon."

"You better stay there till the doctor say git up."

"Aw my Lawd. You all make me sick. I ain't dying. I ought to know how I feel."

"Luly and Sam be here this afternoon, Ma."

"What they coming for?"

"See how you feel and stay till you are better."

"Aw you make me sick. Who's that slamming that front door again?"

"It's me, Ma!"

"What you doin' home from work Jim?"

Though he was twenty-six and though he had the dirty overalls of a mechanic, Jim dropped on the side of Ma's bed like a child.

Everybody eyed him.

"You lost your job?"

"Aw no, Margaret! I jes' run home a minute to see Ma! Was takin' Mr. Drake's car to be greased."

"Well git them greasy clothes off my clean sheets! What the name of God ails you, boy?"

"Ma!—Artie's married."

Jim said it as if he were dropping a load.

"Artie!!"

Ma snapped up right in the bed. Pa jack-knifed down on the trunk. Margaret's mouth dropped open wide and she let it stay wide.

In spite of that pumping and jumping that started in her left side, Ma spoke first.

"Who says Artie's married? My boy ain't going to take no wife 'thout telling me and Pa! You always talk too much Jim!"

"I ain't jes' talkin'! He is so married! Fellers was tellin' me down the oilin' station."

"Who he marry?"

"Mrs. Fannie's Jule!"

"You mean that gal what kept a sportin' flat over the drugstore? My God!"

"Aw hol' on Pa! How you know where she keep her flat?"

"Aw, Ma! Everybody in town knows about Jule!"

"Ma!"

It was Margaret who saw the tears on Ma's face. "You all stop telling Ma all this stuff!"

"Aw heish! Ef Artie's married I'm the mother what borned him and I'm gonna know about it," Ma panted as she said it.

Margaret stabbed a mean look at Jim. "You always talk too much!"

"Y'all stop that fussin'!"

Ma had to breathe strong to keep going but she talked to Pa. "You say this Jule belongs to Miss Fanny? She bound to be bad then, cause Fanny ain't never been a God's bit of good! Maybe, though, if Artie's married her and he brings her home we can git her to join church!"

"Aw Ma. You don't know that gal!"

"Heish, Margaret! Don't speak light of the church!"

Pa snorted: "That gal's been all over town all her life!"

"Pa! No deacon ought to talk that way! Jim! You tell Artie come home and bring his wife!"

"That means I got to git out of his room! Where'll I sleep—in the attic?"

The front door shook the house. John, the youngest boy, raced into Ma's room.

"Hey, Ma! Ole Artie's married. The kids out at school tole me!"

"That ain't no reason you got to come splittin' in here like any Indian! Don't you learn no manners at the high school?"

"I am an Indian, Old Margaret! Ain't I, Ma? You said your great, great grand-pap lived in a tent and had fifteen wives!"

"I ain't never said no such a lie! I said he married one Indian woman. I said he saw these Indians burn up some town and he run off from slavery with 'em and married one!"

"At's the time ma! At's the time! That ole guy is the one you say said them arrows them Injuns was shootin' had fire on them! Jes' ate up everything in town."

"Hongry fire!" chanted Jim like a child finishing a well-known story. "Hongry fire! Et up everything it hit!"

Ma laid down suddenly. "You all go on out of here! Go on out!"

"Aw Ma!! Better take some of that medicine what the doctor left."

"No!"

"Aw Ma!"

"Well—Pa you fix it! Only don't give me much! 'Bout ten drops'll do! You Jim? Tell Artie come on home!"

And up in the flat over the drugstore, Artie was with his Jule.

"You come on home and stay! Leave your Ma have the flat to herself! She won't be lonesome!"

Jule had a butter-colored skin and hair that was bleached red. She did a lot of things to her eyes and lips and kept putting on layers of rouge.

Artie was still breathing as if the ceremony in the city hall and the taxi ride back to Jule's flat had been a marathon.

"Gee I never thought you'd marry me, Jule! All the guys you could get!" Artie kept saying it in a dazed murmur.

Jule let her lips curve a little. "You're a good guy Artie! But why can't you stay here with Ma and me? Plenty of room!"

"I'm going to take you home! You're my wife and I'll look out for you! See? Honey—!"

Finally Jule said "Aw—! All right!" But she said it slowly and began to pick up things and pack her bag slowly too, as if she did not want to put them in it.

Funny Artie could not see she was glued in her own home!

It was a Monday again. Ma Jones was still in bed.

" 'Pears like to me that doctor don't know what he doing! I been taking that green stuff nigh on four months now and I ain't been outside this room yet! Do look like to me—"

A double chorused shout of laughter cut across her thoughts. Jule was down in the kitchen with Margaret.

"Gal, you sure are dumb! Dumb! Ain't six enough! You don't need no more! Gawd knows you don't, Margaret!"

The hole under the carpet still linked Ma with the family life downstairs. She leaned out of bed swiftly and listened.

"But Jule! I'm scared! Suppose this stuff kills me too."

"Aw take it!! I always use the same thing!"

There was a little silence. Then Margaret began to cough and choke. "Sure tastes bad enough!"

Was that Jule teaching her Margaret to drink? Her Margaret what never had a foot on a dance hall floor and was a married woman with six children at twenty-four? Ma called aloud.

"You, Margaret?"

"Ma'am?"

"You, Margaret? Come up here!!"

"Yas'm."

Two sets of footsteps came along the hall and Margaret stood only a little inside of the door. Jule's eyes peeped sleepily over Margaret's shoulder. She had a green silk kimona around her, but her body was bare. She never did wear any clothes in the house.

"You, Margaret." Ma sat up in the bed. "You been drinkin'?"

"Drinkin'!! No Ma!"

"What was you all doing downstairs?"

Jule eeled in. "Aw Ma! I'se jes' fixing up a little something for Margaret's cold."

"Cold! What you doing lettin' yourself ketch cold, Margaret! You know you told me you thought—!"

"The doctor says he gotta wait another month to make sure!"

"He ain't sure yet? I thought he said you was about four months along!"

"Aw no—Ma!—I—!"

"No Ma, he told Margaret he didn't think nuthin' tall was the matter with her! That's what he tol' her las' time she's there!"

"How you know Jule?"

" 'Cause I went with her! Went with her one night you was sleeping."

Ma laid back again in her pillows. Jule went along the hall to her room. Margaret scrabbled heavily down stairs.

She couldn't remember any time that Jule had gone to the doctor's with Margaret.

There went that front door again. Why couldn't Johnny ever

come in decent—like?—

John's steps pounded up the hall.

Jule opened her door. "Aw Johnny? Johnny? Come here, dear! I want you to reach down this window shade for me!"

And John streaked on past Ma's door without stopping to glance in, though he did yell, "Hey, Ma!"

Ma waited for him to come back. It only took a few steps to cross the room. It only took a minute to stand on a chair and reach the shade—then come out and into her room.

Ma waited.

She heard the chair scrape, she heard the shade roll down— then she heard Jule laughing and laughing and talking as if she was telling some joke that was real funny.

("Wasn't that gal stark naked when she stood in this here door five minutes ago?")

"You, Johnny? Johnny!" Ma sat up in bed to shout it.

"Ma'am!"

John stood outside on Ma's door sill and said again, "Ma'am?"

"You stay out of Artie's room—heah me? Stay on out of there!"

Johnny turned and went down the hall toward the steps. "Yes'm!" he called back from the head of the stairs.

Ma heard him walking down stairs. Ma heard the front door click softly.

Johnny had gone out. Johnny had shut the door. Quietly.

Ma panted back in her pillows. She'd better pray. Her breath came so hard!

("I better get up from heah!")

She took hold of the table by her bed so she could support herself. The bottles of medicine in it clinked and rattled.

"Believe I'll try some of the yaller stuff this time. Get some sleep and stop worrying about these children's foolishness! How many drops the doctor say take? Ten! Don't want too many! He say this stuff kill anyone that takes more'n ten—!"

The street lights were slicing the darkness of her room when Ma opened her eyes again.

Someone was talking downstairs. It was Luly and Sam having their supper.

"I wish them children 'd all eat together at the same time like I always had them! Still I s'pose all them brats of Margaret's are too much with Luly and Sam and Johnny and Pa and Vernice! Don't seem like no family—all eating at different times."

Luly was talking. "I wish we'd go on back home, Sam! Don't seem right to stay here on Pa and Ma all the time!"

Sam must have been chewing. There was a silence before he spoke. "I tol' you I put the stuff in storage! Might as well stay here! Save money!"

"You put my furniture in storage! You ain't never tol' me!"

"I did so! You ain't been listenin' to me!"

A sharp wail cut in all at once.

"Can't you never keep that baby quiet, Luly?"

"His stummick bother him, Sam! All I do is keep looking out after him all the time!"

"Wish to God you'd keep him still! Look like a man could have some peace when he gets home after a day's work!"

"Aw shet up!"

This was Sam and Luly!!

"And another thing, Luly! Why didn't you make me no light bread like I ast you this mawnin'? A man had ought to be able to eat what he wants at his own home? You don't have nuthin' t'all to do all day but 'tend the baby!"

"I tol' you that baby had a stummick ache! I couldn't find no time!"

"Why couldn't your mother keep him? She ain't doing nuthin' but layin' in the bed!"

"Ma's sick! You know the doctor said she'd ought to be quiet!"

"Aw—my mother had the same thing she's got! And she never missed a day at the tobacco factory down home neither! These women get too soft and lazy in these big cities!"

—Her own home!—

Her own daughter!

And her own food—Pa said Sam gave next to nothing toward the food bill.

Making a table of discord out of her food!

And Sam suppose to be such a Christian! Superintendent of the Sunday School. Always rolling his eyes and actin' so sanctified! Like some old nanny goat baa-ing! ("Whyn't Luly sass him back and really shet him up. I'll call her right up stairs, and tell her something—tell her something—")

That sleeping medicine must not have let go of Ma entirely. She dozed again and when she woke up it was to struggle with thumping and bumping that tore loose in her left side every once in a while.

The thumping and the struggling kept up all next day. When Ma saw Luly she forgot whether she had heard her quarrelling with Sam. She wasn't even sure whether it was Luly or Margaret or Vernice.

On Thursday she did ask Margaret what the doctor had said about her.

"Did he say you gonna have another baby, Margaret?"

"Heh-heh! No, Ma! Everything's all right. I come all right again!"

"You come all right again! I thought you tol' me you was 'bout the fourth month."

"I guess it was cold! I guess I caught cold or somethin'!"

Jule had been sitting on the trunk listening. Now she began to laugh and laid back against the wall. She got up all of a sudden and walked out and went into her own room.

"That gal sure laughs like the devil, Margaret!"

"Yes'm! You want anything else, Ma? I gotta go downstairs— see 'bout somethin' I left on the stove!"

Margaret went down the stairs bumping the railing, then the wall. Something surely must be burning! Margaret never walked downstairs fast.

Ma went back to struggling for a clear breath over the thumping in her side in her throat—all over her.

By Saturday morning she seemed to have won the race, but Ma lay more tired than ever in her bed.

"Lawd this house seems quiet! Ain't that Luly's baby hollering somewhere?"

Ma listened and rapped on the floor for Margaret.

"What ails little Sam, Margaret?"

"His stummick Ma! Don't seem to git no better!"

"Whyn't Luly give him some castor oil?"

Margaret took hold of the spread on Ma's bed and began shaking it to fluff it up. "I did, Ma," she answered after a minute.

"I ain't asked you why didn't you try castor oil! I said—why don't Luly use it on little Sam?"

"She ain't here no more!"

"She ain't here!! Ain't Sam and the baby here? Where's she at?"

Margaret lifted an arm toward the window. "She gone! Lef' a letter! Tole Sam—tole him she ain't never loved him or the baby neither 'cause the boy was his'n!"

The pain in Ma's side knocked her to her feet this time.

"Where's my child, Margaret! Where's Luly? Aw—Jesus!"

"Jule say she went on with Dick!"

"Dick? You mean that no 'count trash I stopped her from runnin' with 'fore she married Sam! God help me—"

Jule came running when Margaret screamed. She helped Margaret put Ma back in bed and then she went out to the corner drugstore and called the doctor.

"She can't have any more excitement," the doctor told Pa. "You'll have to see that she's kept quiet! She can't stand another attack like this one!"

"Yas sir!" Pa promised. "You Johnny and you Vernice!" he threatened his two youngest. "You'll act like you got some sense and keep quiet in this house! Heah me?"

"Yas sir!"

Johnny took to hanging around Pete's Pleasure Pool Parlor. Vernice began walking out with Jule. Sometimes she would go down to Miss Fannie's—Jule's mother's—with her.

Vernice was sixteen and had velvety black brown skin. You could tell by her walk that her suppleness would make any dance graceful. Ma had made Vernice join church when she was twelve. She had never danced—a Christian could not dance—and she could only see a movie when she slid off without telling anyone at home.

But she wanted movies and dancing and all the other things anybody sixteen anywhere ever wanted.

She began walking with Jule every evening. She would talk to Jule, too.

"Jule—don't it feel swell to have somebody takin' you places and everything like old Artie does for you?"

"Yeah—I dunno!—sure!"

"Lord! I'd know it was swell!"

"Any girl can get something for herself! Just gotta know how! Now take you—you're too slow! You gotta get hot—get out—get a string of guys crazy about you—then pick the one that's the biggest fool over you for your husband! That's all!"

"Yeah!"

"Say! I know a swell feller! Come down to my mother's with me next Friday—"

"Gal's got to know everything in all the books when she starts percolatin' with a guy like Eddie!" A man told this to Artie in the barbershop.

"You ain't tellin' me nuthin'!" Artie agreed. "Who's Eddie bustin' around with now?"

The other man looked surprised—then he masked his expression with a bland wariness. "Better ask Vernice," he laughed.

Margaret was asleep when Artie jerked her door open.

"Where's Vernice?"

"She went out with Jule!"

"What you let her go out with her for?"

"What you talkin' 'bout, boy? Ain't Jule your wife?"

"Yas Jule's my wife—! You ought not to let Vernice stay out after eleven!"

"What time is it now? Aw she's all right as long as she's with your wife! They say they goin' to Miss Fannie's!"

"Miss Fannie's!! You let Vernice go to Miss Fannie's?"

"How I going to stop her from going to your wife's mother's house?"

"Aw go to hell!"

"Heah! Don't you curse me!"

Sam, already awake with the baby and on fire with a longing to fight the world—came into the room, too.

"What ails y'all? Quit yellin'!"

Pa came out of the kitchen. "What the name of God is the matter with y'all? Heish!!"

"Jule's taken Vernice down to Miss Fannie's!!"

Pa cursed so long and loud that Ma rapped on the floor. "Pa!! Pa!!" her voice sounded as if she were ten stories away from them. "You a deacon! Pa, what's the trouble! I'm gonna come down."

Pa yelled back. "Heish, y'all!! Stay up there, Ma! I'll be up there!"

Everyone trailed Pa up into Ma's room.

"I'm gonna beat Jule for takin Vernice to Miss Fannie's!" Artie shouted at the door.

"Is Vernice down there? Lawd!" Ma had to pant a while, but she fought to keep on talking. "Ain't no sense to beatin' no wife, Artie! Jes' you go down and git the child!"

"I'm gettin' ready to throw that Jule out on the sidewalk and set her trunk on top of her!"

"Aw, Pa, heish! You ain't gonnna do nuthin' of the sort! She could go room somewhere else and get 'round the child better then!"

"Well, I feels like blowin' her brains out 'cause she's the one what sent Luly on to her destruction! Luly never'd of thought 'bout leavin' ef Jule hadn't put her up to it!

"Aw Sam! Don't talk no foolishness! You helped send Luly away your own self!"

"What!!"

"Yas!" Ma's voice rallied to a shout.

"I ain't never sent my lawful wife to no bed of sin!"

"Tain't whilst to argue with Ma, Sam! I'm the head of this house!"

Pa's thunder silenced the room.

"Well—I'm going to tell Jule what I thinks of her!" Margaret offered after a while.

"That'll just be bustin' a hornet's nest." It was odd how Ma could silence the flood of pain long enough to silence each one of them.

"Y'all come on out of here!" Pa shouted at them all. "Ma got to be quiet. Come out!!!"

They herded out still yapping and snapping at each other the way people will do when they are wrought up, bewildered, set on—and cannot see a door or a window or even a crack to get out of their tight spot.

The thumping made Ma get out of bed this time. She was feeling for her slippers when the front door opened.

"Here's Jule! Here's Vernice!" Ma wanted to run downstairs in the instant between the sound of the door opening and its closing to hold Pa and the rest of them back in the kitchen.

The door closed.

Jule laughed and called out, "Artie, Oh! honey! Artie?"

"Heigh, honey!" Artie's answer was slow.

"Artie! I left my little bag you gave me down to Ma's. You run on down there and get it for me! Some of Ma's friends'll be pickin' it up and I don't want to lose it—'cause you gave it to me!"

There followed a long quietness. Then Ma heard the door close again. Artie was going for his Jule's bag.

"What'cha sayin', Pa?" Jule's voice swaggered. She was in the kitchen now. "Gosh that ham sandwich looks good to me, old dad! Gimme a bite! Say, Sammy? Ma says to give your kid some arrowroot in milk."

Ma sat down heavily on the side of her bed.

All of them—every one of them—was scared of that gal!

They didn't dare say anything to Jule! And Jule—just like a fire—was burning holes into the lives of each one of them.

That Margaret would never make heaven. That Margaret had had more than a "cold" that time when she and Jule were drinking something in the kitchen.

Luly had turned to be a bad woman—and Jule had led her, had told her how to get out and to be one!

That gal was a fire—a hongry fire—burning up the house just like them Indian's arrows—burning that town.

And nobody had been able to jump on the house tops and stamp out the fire. It had taken a sudden rain from heaven to do that.

"God! What'll I do? Ef I could only see the reverend—I'd ask him! Vernice ain't never even come upstairs to see me yet!"

The thing that plunged and tore loose in Ma's left side pressed her back against the head of the bed. She wanted to scream out but she was too spent when she could get up again.

She kept talking to herself. "Ain't one of 'em left to be saved for the kingdom after this gal gets through! Not a one of 'em but Vernice and Johnny—and she been after them! God! I wisht there's some way to stop her! Wisht there's some ways to stamp out her fire!"

Jule was laughing on the stairs. Pa was laughing with her. Margaret joined in and Sam said something. They all laughed louder.

"Well—night y'all! Guess I'll be ready to turn in time my Artie gets back," Jule announced.

"Yeah!" (That stupid Margaret!)

"Night!" (Dirty thing! Answering so sure of herself.)

Jule was walking up the steps. Jule was going by Ma's door.

"Aw Jule? Jule!"

" 'Scuse me, Ma! You wake? What you want?"

"Ah—you get me a little water—will you? Got—got to take some medicine."

"Aw sure, Ma! Where's the glass? This here? Whyn't you have a light in here?"

"I kin see all I want with the street lights!"

Ma fumbled under the table. "You get it, Jule? Thanks. Say Jule I got a little peach brandy here Miss Johnson brought me las' week. Don't you want a taste?"

"Aw thanks, Ma! I'll take the bottle in the room so's Artie can have some too. Thanks!"

"Oh, now Jule! I—I—I got some all poured out in here for you! You drink it right here! Then you take the bottle in the room for Artie, too! Wait'll I drop my sleep medicine!"

"Here! You ain't s'posed to take but ten drops of that, ain't you, Ma? You putting in too much, ain't you?

"No! Thirty drops! Thirty-five!"

"Aw no! Wait'll I call Margaret—"

"Aw leave that gal downstairs! Leave them all down there—!! I ain't puttin' in too much—!! How you like that brandy? Drink it all up!! Good for you!"

Jule laughed her loudest! "You all right Ma! Well—I'll take the bottle—get ready for Artie! Gosh, what did Sister Johnson put in that stuff? Got an awful kick! I feel kinder funny already!"

"Yeah, Jule? Have some more! Here—!!"

"Say—Ma! You're s'posed to be a deaconess, too, ain't you! Heh-heh! Well—Good night!"

She went out, leaving Ma's door open. She went along the hall singing.

> *"Oh the dog jumped a rabbit.*
> *Run him for one sol-id mile!*
> *And the rabbit set down! . . .*
> *The rabbit set down!*
> *And hollered like a nat-chul chile!"*

Ma called after her. "Say Jule? Ain't that the piece where the rabbit run the dog? Ain't it?"

"Aw no, Ma! Ain't no rabbit never run no dog! You all right, Ma, but you ain't no jazz baby!"

"No! Well—I jes' thought the rabbit might run the dog this once!"

"Well—see you in the mornin', Ma!"

Ma could hear her humming around her room. She heard her open a drawer—close it. She heard Jule yawn. She heard her move a chair. She heard Jule yawning—yawning. Then she heard her lie down on the bed.

Ma listened.

There was no more humming.

There was no more yawning.

Ma listened.

There could not be any more humming. There could not be any more yawning—yawning—yawning.

Ma emptied the rest of the sleeping medicine in the glass.

Then she pulled the carpet back so that she could see the little square of light from the kitchen—where Pa and Margaret and Vernice were—where they all were.

Then she drank her share.

She wanted sleep. The fire slept.

It was out.

She could have peace now.

Patch Quilt

Sara unrolled a piece of damp clothes from the basket beneath her ironing board and shook it out.

"Another one of them ruffled dresses for Mrs. Brown's Sally. I 'clare I can't iron it today." Sara spoke aloud to herself.

She looked at the clock. Twelve o'clock. She should have known that by the sunshine though it was hard to tell time by the sun in March.

Jim ought to be coming any moment now. Jim ought to be coming home from his new job.

"First time in near three years that Jim'll bring home a pay envelope on Saturday. Shore glad the government made them put some of the colored relief men on the new road job along with the white!" Sara had a habit of talking aloud whenever she was alone. She made a half-hearted swoop with her old-fashioned sad-iron over one ruffle before her on the board.

A whistle blew somewhere.

Sara held her iron up from the board and listened. Then walking swiftly to the rusty iron stove that glowed red hot beneath a burden of six irons, she released the one she held in her hand.

"Shame to waste this fire and these clothes all damped just right to iron but I gotta git ready to make market."

She took the board down from its position between two chairs, tossed the dress back into the basket and went into the bedroom.

"I'm going to get me some of the things I been wanting to eat these three years." Sara planned happily as she put on a clean cotton house dress and her only pair of silk stockings.

"Jim's bringing twelve dollars and I got four or five up in the closet. Guess we'll have chicken and yeller yams and greens and ice-cream—if the freezer is still any good—and two kinds of cake for Sunday dinner! Got to celebrate!"

She broke off talking to herself to listen again. Jim ought to be coming into the house right now. Only took fifteen minutes to get home if he took the short cut.

"Guess he gone down to git his hair cut! Git all prettied up," Sara decided finally.

She went to the cupboard in the kitchen, took down an old tea-pot and drew out four dirty crumped one-dollar bills.

"We can take the ten dollars rent out of Jim's money. I'm going!" she decided recklessly.

She snapped her pocket-book together, unlatched the door and stepped out.

Her house, like all the other houses in the colored district on that hill, stood below the level of the street.

Sara puffed a little as she climbed over the ditch where last night's rain had left a little water.

"Wished they'd let that new road come this side of town," she panted aloud as she came up on the street.

She began to pick the driest spots in the mud to walk through for there were no sidewalks.

"Hi, Sara! Looks like spring's most here!" a voice called.

Sara halted and looked around. A tall, dark colored woman of indeterminate age leaned over the gate of a yard across the road.

"Aw, hi, Miss Susie!" Sara greeted her. She drew nearer to the woman. "I'm 'bout to go to town to make market."

"Jim home yet?"

"Naw, but I can't wait for him to get home! I got right smart buying to do."

"Y'all having company tomorrer?"

Sara drew herself up proudly.

"Naw! Jes' Jim and me but I 'clare I feel like eatin' a good dinner like I used to when times was good! I want ice cream and two kinds of cake!"

The other woman did not answer. Instead she looked off toward the top of the hill.

A white cottage stood there.

"Wonder how Miss Drake is?" Miss Susie said after a pause.

Sara looked surprised. "She sick?"

"Naw! I jes' wondered how she was!"

There was another silence. Sara stirred restlessly and said, "Well! I'll be gettin' along!"

The other woman did not speak again nor did she look at her. Sara walked off down the hill.

Once she looked back, Miss Susie still stood as she had left her, staring down the road after Sara.

"What ails Miss Susie? What she say that 'bout Miss Drake for? She ain't no company of Miss Drake! Jes' said that so's I wouldn't git to tell her what I'se having for dinner! How is Miss Drake!!"

Her mind went back to the house at the crest of the hill, too.

Nobody was Miss Drake's "company."

She lived alone with her two children, Sandy and Marie, and earned her living by sewing for white families of the little southern town of Redmond.

"She sews so much for white folks, she thinks she's white too!" was the common belief among the Negroes of the town. "Always stayin' to herself! Keeping that girl and boy cooped up all the time."

"That gal ain't home all the time! She off somewhere passing, workin' in a white store," town gossip proclaimed.

"How anybody going to pass in Redmond where everybody knows everybody else here!" others countered.

Sara thought of all this as she pushed on down the hill toward the shopping district.

She paused once near a clump of bushes to rest.

The shrubbery shook suddenly and a tawny, freckled-face boy in his teens clambered out.

Sara recognized Sandy Drake by the reddish hair.

"Howdy, Miss Sara!" the boy muttered.

"How are you, Sandy? How's your ma and your sister?"

The boy flushed and stuttered something. Sara could not understand him. She tried another tack.

"How they makin' out with the new road? I see you come 'cross the hill from that away? Ain't they knocked off for the day yet?"

Sandy reddened still more. "Yas'm—er—I guess so! I dunno. Ma sent me out to meet sister."

He plunged on up the hill abruptly.

Sara stared after him. "What ails that little fool? Big as any man and can't talk straight so you can get any sense out of it!"

She watched the boy out of sight and quickening her pace set off down the hill until she reached the base where the colored section ended and Market Street—the main street—began.

She crossed Market Street, lost herself in the midst of the mud and chicken crates, the sidewalk vendors and hawkers, the muddy automobiles and crowds of poor whites and Negroes that made Saturday the most exciting day of the week in that town.

With a sort of giddy triumph Sara acquired her chicken and her yellow yams, her fatback and greens, lemons, sugar, flour and vanilla.

At the end of an hour she found herself outside of the Five-and-Ten at the far end of the market, trying to juggle her packages so the oysters would not spill and with but twenty cents in her purse.

"Guess I'll git me an ice-pick! That other thing is enough to try the devil!"

Ten minutes later, with the ice-pick and a pound of pink jaw breakers added to her pack, Sara started back up the hill.

She was heavy with packages—and not one cent was left to her.

She was tired but she was happy. She crunched the candy noisily.

A broad black woman hung across the fence at the first house she reached.

"Hi, Sara! she called in greeting as Sara came abreast her gate. "Looks like you been doin' right smart buyin'?"

Sara choked hastily over a large piece of candy to make room for a complete answer. "Yas. I been jes' makin' a little market! Spent every bit of fo' dollars for just this one meal, though!" she broke off to giggle and watch the effect of her statement.

The other woman let her eyes sweep up and down Sara's figure.

Then she gazed up the hill toward the top and back down and said, "I hear that one of them travelin' buses done fell over on the new road!"

Startled, Sara forgot to giggle.

"Ain't nobody hurt?" she managed to ask. "You know, Jim's workin' over there."

The other woman shook her head doubtfully. "I ain't heard that. I jes' heard 'bout the bus! Say! Whyn't you cut across the back lots and see?"

Sara shot off without saying goodbye and left the other gazing with veiled eyes after her.

Anxiety and the uneven ground of the fields brought a breathless Sara upon the highway.

A cross-country bus lay on its side in a ditch, a group of people, apparently passengers, and mostly white, stood clumped disconsolately around their bags piled in the road. All the machinery used for excavating the road stood idle. No laborers were in sight.

Uncle Eph, a deaf Negro who claimed to be one hundred and ten, sat on a rock nearby cleaning a red lantern.

Sara approached him.

"Who got hurt!" she screamed, pointing to the bus.

"Ain't nobody hurt," answered Eph mildly.

Relief loosed Sara's giggles again. "That Annie May Jones had me thinkin' all y'all was kilt out here on the job!" she cried.

Eph rubbed his lamp. "I gotta git these things ready for the night. I keeps the lights on this here job at night."

"So Jim told me. Is Jim gone home?"

Eph scrubbed the lamp in his hand and sat it down on the ground. He did not answer this time.

"I reckon Jim's gone on home!" Sara screamed again.

Uncle Eph sat back suddenly, shook his rag out and looked Sara directly in the face.

"Go on up to the tool shed!" he said loudly. Go on up there!"

Sara gaped at him amazed. "Guess the poor soul don't know what I ast him!" She hesitated an instant, thrust her hand in her bag of candy and set two pieces down beside Eph. Then she started off up the hill toward the shed.

The door of the shed was open. Sara peered into the semi-darkness there. She saw nobody and was about to turn back when a sound came from behind the door.

She thrust her head inside, peered around the door.

Something green waved in her face and she heard a low murmuring. "You kin have it all honey. I'm crazy 'bout you!"

It was Jim's voice—Sara's eyes grew accustomed to the gloom. There was Jim's back, and staring with pale stricken fright across Jim's shoulder was Marie Drake. In her hand she clutched a bill.

Sara's bundles hurtled to the ground. Sara's hands snatched up the new ice pick. Sara lunged and struck and lunged and struck again.

Then she ran screaming and crying aloud back into the sunshine.

Right outside of the door she ran straight into the arms of Uncle Eph.

"I hadn't ought to a tol' you honey! I hadn't ought to a tol' you, but I couldn't stand no more to see this deceivin' goin' on!"

The bus driver came striding up the hill.

"What's the matter here?" he demanded with that bustling flimsy authority assumed by cheap whites when they want to impress Negroes.

"She busted her eggs and her flour," Uncle Eph replied laconically. "See?"

He pointed to the ground. The driver glanced indifferently, grunted and turning on his heel, strode back to his own troubles.

When he was out of hearing Eph pushed open the door wide. He saw the ice pick on the ground. He saw the blood on the ice pick.

"Y'all?" Eph shouted.

There was no reply. Eph drew Sara in, closed the door and struck a match to a candle.

Jim lay across the girl, Marie. Blood was streaming from one of her eyes and she lay staring in terror. In her hands she still held the money.

"You ain't dead! Ain't no use pertendin'." Uncle Eph ordered, "Git up."

216

"He's bleeding to death on me!" screamed the girl hysterically and began to cry.

"Shet up! Want all them folks from the bus come here and take you to the lock-up?" Eph cried.

Eph knelt beside Jim—rolled him over a little. He beckoned to Sara who leaned, hands clutched at her throat against the door.

"Ain't dead! Neck cut on the side. I'll get some water and we'll lug him 'cross the fields to Dr. Butler."

Eph stood up, yanked the door open back to its hinges. He pointed to Marie and shouted loudly as if she too were deaf, "Git on out of here! Tell your ma it's best to keep young ones like you tied in their own yard!"

And that is how it happened that Marie Drake dropped out of sight.

"She gone North to school" some people said. "Passin'!!"

But Sandy and his mother knew that Marie sat at home with her left eye closed forever and a deep ugly scar marring her left cheek.

Shame made a wall around the house on top of the hill.

And that is how it happened that Jim Brown had to lay off working—" 'cause a pick fell on his arm"—a useless arm hanging limp, a tendon cut at the shoulder.

Spring passed, the job on the road ended, but the tendon did not heal. Jim sat listless on the porch and gazed back toward the hills that hid the highway. Sometimes he looked up toward the top of the hill.

He did not say anything. He did not even offer to go fishing anymore.

—"And when he did go fishin', that gal was right along with him. He used to come home with scarcely no fish!"

—Like patches in a quilt, Sara could piece the whole story clearly now.

The neighbors had known that day when she went shopping for chicken and oysters, lemonade and a new ice pick. They had known all this.

That is why they had looked at her so. And she thought it was envy.

And from those fishing trips Jim used to come back absent-minded, suddenly irritable, with little red patches—that were made by the imprint of a mouth coated with lipstick—Sara knew now—on his shirt . . . "Berries done that!" he had lied.

"You ought to get right smart insurance from Uncle Sam if that pick fell on him!" the neighborhood declared to Sara.

Sara did not answer. She had to work harder to make ends meet.

Only she and Jim and Marie knew about the ice pick.

And shame, humiliation, and despair froze them to silence.

Uncle Eph knew, of course, but he never told.

Sometimes he felt sorry because he had been the one who had sent Sara to the tool shed.

But he always comforted himself with the thought that he had fed the chicken to his cat.

He could not eat delicacies that had been meant for a feast of rejoicing—and dropped for a maiming—and a slaughter of hopes.

One True Love

When Nora came through the swinging doors between the kitchen and the dining room with the roast, she was just a butter-colored maid with the hair on the "riney" side hurrying to get through dinner so she could go to the show with the janitor's helper, Sam Smith.

By the time Nora had served dessert, though, she had forgotten the show, forgotten Sam—forgotten everything but this: she was going to be a lawyer!

"They" had had company to dinner. ("They" in Nora's family were a Mr. and Mrs. This is not their story—so they are merely "They.")

Company came often enough, but this time everything had been different.

"We are having a noted lawyer to dinner tonight, Nora" Mrs. had said.

Nora had expected a bay window, side-chop whiskers and a boom-boom voice.

When she backed through the door with the roast she saw sitting at the table in the guest's place, a woman. She had been beautifully but simply dressed in black velvet: her hair was cut short, worn brushed up in curls: every inch of her had been smart and lovely.

"This must be the lawyer's wife. Maybe he couldn't git here!"

But then "they" began talking. "Is your law practice as heavy as it was two years ago or do you devote more time to lecturing?" he asked.

"We hear you've been pleading at the Supreme Court!" "she" cut in.

Nora nearly gaped.

This was the lawyer!

All through dinner she noted how nicely the lawyer ate, how pleasant her voice was when she spoke—how direct her eyes were when she looked at you.

"I'm going to get in some kind of school and be a lawyer, too!" Nora declared to the dishes as she washed them.

A knock at the back door cut into her thoughts.

Nora opened it and Sam bristled in.

"Why ain't you through? It's quarter to nine!"

"Whyn't you say good-evenin' and ask me how I feel?" Nora shot back at him. "You always act so ignorant!"

"What you got to talk so mean to me for? Ain't you glad to see me?"

"Can't say that I am if you always going to act so ignorant and degrading!"

"De—who?? S'matter with you, Nora?"

"Nuthin' cept I'm tired and I'm not going to be bothered going to no show tonight!"

"Well who—!" Sam staggered back from the choice of two words to follow his who: "cares" and "wants," decided he did not want to use either. "Well, good night, then!" he finished instead. "Maybe Sadie Jones would like to see a show!"

"Maybe so! She's your kind! Two ignorants together!" Nora flashed back at Sam.

"And maybe I don't need to come back here no more! I won't be seeing you!"

Nora did not even turn around to close the door after Sam. He had to close it himself.

Now Sam was a runty, bowlegged dark brown janitor's helper with a shiny scalp on which his hair grew in kinked patches.

That is what Sam was to the world.

And Sam was just that to Nora, too.

But to Sam, Nora was elegant and beautiful and more desirable than anything ever had been to anyone at anytime.

His, "Maybe I don't need to come back here no more!" frightened him.

Nora forgot it.

He had said it on Wednesday.

He stayed awake all Wednesday night, all Thursday night—all Friday night—hearing himself say over and over again: "Maybe I don't need to come back here no more!"

Suppose Nora thought he really meant just that!

Suppose Nora would never see him anymore!

By Saturday morning, his eyes were so red it upset your stomach just to look at him.

"You ain't taking to drink, is you Sam?" the head janitor asked. "Cause if you is, then I needs another helper 'stead of you!"

"Naw I ain't drinking! Don't feel good!"

"Take a good physic! Do something! You look right bad!"

Sam had said "Maybe I won't be seeing you any more" on Wednesday.

So Saturday night he bought a box of flour water and cocoa chocolates and came and knocked humbly on Nora's back door.

"Want to go to the show?" he asked anxiously as Nora opened the door. "They got that 'Kiss in the Dark' down to the Dream World."

"I don't mind," Nora answered mildly. "I have a lot of things to talk over with you!"

Sam's heart turned completely over. "You mean we—going to get—you going to give up working here and we going to get married? That guy keeps telling me he'll rent them two rooms on Rommy Street for twenty dollars and Levack's got some swell new furniture real cheap!"

Sam was breathless.

Nora was not listening to him. She knew vaguely that Sam was talking so she merely waited until his voice ceased before she began to tell him what was in her mind.

"I've enrolled in the night classes at the City College! I'm taking law!"

"You taking law! How come you taking law?"

"I mean I'm going to study to be a lawyer!"

"You ain't! When we going to get married?"

"I been telling you never! I got to get some education first anyhow!"

"Aw you don't need no education! You know enough to get along with me!"

"Aw Sam! Wait'll I get my hat on!"

As they walked toward the town center, Nora gossiped a bit, " 'They' surely was having a terrible fuss tonight! She really cussed and damned him off the boards!"

"Yeah? What's the trouble?"

"Oh, she went down town and tried to buy up the stores and he got to hollering but she out-cussed him! I don't see why they don't get along lovely! Everything so lovely in their home and he and she both educated."

"What makes you talk so much 'bout this education business now? That ain't what makes a man and woman git on together!"

"Aw Sam you so ignorant! If you are educated you know how to do everything just right all the time."

"Everything like gettin' along with a husband? Naw! You got to love folks! A guy really got to love a girl so he kin pass by the beer gardens and the hot mamas and the sheeny what wants him to lay a dollar on a suit and a watch and a diamond and a God-knows-what-all—and bring the paycheck home to her so they kin go in on it together!"

"Aw paychecks ain't everything!"

"And edjucation ain't everything! You got to love folks more than books!"

"And more than money!"

"Yeah! You got to love folks more than everything to git along and live fifty years with 'em!"

"Who said anything 'bout staying married fifty years?"

"Me!" Sam retorted stoutly. "My grandma did and I'm going to too!"

"You ain't going to do nothing your grandmother didn't do! That's ignorant!"

They reached the theater and no conclusion to the argument, so they went in.

Nora kicked off her shoes and munched chocolates and lived the picture. She felt comfortable and happy in a remote way that there was somebody with whom she could talk and argue good-naturedly—someone who knew enough to pass you his handkerchief at the cry parts.

She was glad—dimly—about all this.

What gave her feelings a real edge was that Monday night she was going to her first class at City College to study law.

City College was not particularly glad to receive Nora.

They endured a few colored students there but they had always been men—men whose background of preparation made professors and students of the lesser type keep their sneers under cover.

But after it was seen that Nora got her superlatives mixed and "busted" when she should have "broken" and "hadn't ought to" came out when she meant "should not have"—quite a few sneers came out in the open.

People like to place you and your desires and tastes where they think your particular color and hirsute growth belong. They do not like to feel that Something-greater-than-themselves can give you the feel for the ermine and satin of living; the air for silver services and a distinct love of beauty that sets you quietly aloof—truly poised beyond the rough wood of living.

If they are above you—culturally—sometimes they shower sneers down at you, forgetting all the while that the thick coats of culture which surround them began once with one coat—thinly applied—sometimes—somewhere—on their own family tree.

If they are below you—culturally—they try to stone you to death—sneer at you until you reach the point where you gladly smother all your ideas and ideals and crawl into a protective shell of sameness so that the mediocre mob will let you alone.

Nora had a touch of this something that made her struggle to get beyond a stove, a sink, a broom and a dust-mop and some one else's kitchen.

She worked hard at her books. She stayed up late to struggle with books full of pages that she had to read ten times over to even begin to get a glimmer of sense from them.

Professors demand more than a glimmer of information. They want things presented as they are and a bit more grafted on to it to show you are really getting an education.

Came the mid-year exams.

Nora snapped at Sam—burnt two steaks and had to buy a third one out of her own pocket one night—trying to untangle torts and contracts. Haggard with overwork and bewildered with subjects for which no preparatory steps had ever been laid in her, Nora flunked all her examinations.

Sam came one Sunday night to carry her over to the colored section of town for a special celebration.

Nora met him at the back door and began to cry.

"They flunked me, Sam! I didn't pass! No need to go celebrating."

"You mean those old fools didn't give you no good mark? Much studyin' and stewin' and strivin' and worryin' and stayin' up nights as you did? S'matter with them folks? I bet if I'se to go down there they'd pass you or sumpin!"

Nora's anger flared: "Why you always have to talk so ignorant, Sam? You can't do nothing! I didn't know enough to pass, that's all."

"Tain't no need to bellow at me all the time! I 'clare you got to feelin' right important since you got your feet inside of that City College! Good enough for you! You bound to fail! You too bigitty!"

"You get out of here! You no kind of friend! Rejoicing at my downfall!"

"Wouldn't fall down—if you'd a married me 'stead of learnin' law all the time!"

"Don't need your love! I can lean on law and be a lawyer too if I wants too, Mr. Sam Smith!"

"Well go on leaning on your busted crutch, then!"

"Aw go on home Sam! My head's achin' fit to bust!"

Sam backed out in a huff.

When he came back the next night and knocked at the door no one answered.

The kitchen was dark.

"Gone to bed! Still mad! Let her stay mad!" Sam growled as he left.

The next night he came again and no one opened the door.

Sam did not come back for two whole days.

When he knocked at the door a strange colored woman opened it.

"Where's Nora?" Sam gasped in surprise.

"Nora? On you mean the maid what was here? Oh she sick!"

"Sick?" Sam shouted and bounded into the kitchen. "Where she at? Whyn't nobody tell me?"

"Who you anyhow?"

"I'm the man what's going to marry huh! Marry Nora! Where she at?"

"Well don't yell so and don't come running in here that-a-way! She ain't here! She in some hospital. Wait'll I ask the lady."

When the woman came back to the kitchen Sam was already running down the back stairs!

"She got pneu-monyer in the City Hospital," the woman called down the stairs after him. "And you might have shut the door if you couldn't wait."

Sam tore up the gangway between the buildings and hired the biggest taxi lurking in front of the apartment house where they worked.

"Steppin' out for a big night, Boy?" the driver jibed as he pushed down the meter.

"I'm going to City Hospital to get my wife—what is going to be. Got to bring her home and take care of her!"

It took a while to find Nora. She was in a public ward somewhere and since pneumonia cases were coming in at that particular season faster than the registrar could list them, no one could locate her for a full half hour.

Beads of real agony dropped from Sam's face when the nurse showed him the elevators.

He found the ward.

And he found a white screen around Nora's bed.

He could not believe this grey-faced woman who lay panting—panting was Nora. Her nostrils flared wide—too wide. Her teeth stuck deep in her lower lip and her eyes stared straight at nothing.

If "they" had said a little more—if someone had said that they would pay for Nora—she would not have been shoved aside and forgotten in a public ward.

Sam raced frantically back to the hall where the night nurse sat.

"Could Nora Jones be put in one of these here rooms to herself? I got every bit of four hundred dollars! Couldn't nobody set by her?"

The nurse glanced at a paper on her desk.

"She can't be moved right now! Perhaps—if she's better tomorrow—maybe!"

You could tell all this meant that nothing nobody could do would help Nora anymore.

Sam went back to the bed and sat behind the white screen. He laid his head beside Nora's and cried.

His love must have reached her somewhere.

Nora's eyes focused on him for a second. "Sam! Sam—" he could hardly hear her. "I've got l—I've got l—!"

It sounded as if she said "law" her breath rasped so and her lower jaw seemed to fall away from the work.

Sam wiped his eyes and grabbed her hand.

"I know Nora! I know you got that old law to lean on! Ef you could of just want something I could a helped you git. Just get well! I'll help you get that law!"

Nora tried to shake her head.

Couldn't he understand!

She had waited and waited to tell Sam that down deep somewhere where she had been lost in pain for so long—there was nothing about books and what they gave you. The only thing she had remembered had been that there was someone who loved her enough to love her even when she was snappish and cross— who came back again and again—no matter what.

And she was glad!

So glad she wanted to tell Sam that she loved him—had love enough for the two rooms he wanted on Rommy Street and enough to try to understand how his grandmother came to stay married fifty years.

Right now Nora was too tired to try to tell him again.

She closed her eyes.

But she closed her eyes carrying with her the love that was in Sam's eyes.

She thought she smiled.

The doctor said the death agony had set her face at that angle.

He wondered too, why that little colored man just sat by that empty bed crying so long. The nurses wanted to prepare the bed for another case.

And Sam sat crying—wishing he had been elegant and wonderful enough to match the wonder in Nora—trying to take something out into his empty world from an empty bed.

On the Altar

Gran was mad.

Beth could see the puffs of wrinkles under each of Gran's ears were glowing red.

"Better take it easy, old darling!" Beth offered briskly as she unfastened the screen door for her. "The thermometer's about 90—and what did the doctor say your blood pressure wasn't—?"

Black taffeta skirts crackled as Gran cleared the porch and landed in the hall. Her breath was almost crackling, too.

Beth gave her time to breathe. "How did you get here so early, Gran? Weren't you tired after my commencement last night?"

Her grandmother did not speak at first. She gave Beth a long look. "Where's your mother?" she asked finally as if her breathing was still difficult.

"Why—why she's not up yet! She and Luther are still asleep, I guess. They were tired out after the excitement."

"*They* were tired out? How does it happen you are up so early? Seems to me you would be the one who would want to rest! Why are you up so early?" Gran repeated.

Something that had been sparkling and blooming free and happy in Beth froze suddenly.

"I—I was looking at my presents and then I promised—to go out with some of the girls from my class on a little picnic. I'll call Mother if you want me to." Beth chattered nervously.

Her grandmother gave her huge weight an elegant turn and swished to the foot of the stairs.

"You won't need to call her! I'm going up to her room!" She answered Beth and began an ascent of the stairs, pulling herself up by the balustrade.

As she reached the first landing, she turned around. "Don't you go on any picnic with *any* girls from your class—until I go home!"

It was an order.

Everybody (those who had never seen her without her upper and lower plates and her extra hair) said that Gran looked like Queen Victoria.

Those extra additions for beauty were not necessary to give Gran the haughty imperious attitude that left no room for a person to dodge.

Beth merely stood still and watched her grandmother out of sight. She wanted to run out of the front door, down the street—anywhere.

Gran must *know*!

Gran must know that she was married!

Gran must have found out that Beth and Jerry Johnson, a tall, slim black boy, the handsomest boy in the class according to even its most prejudiced member—had sneaked off in Jerry's father's truck to the county seat—married—rushed back to their separate homes again.

It had taken two weeks of artful planning to bribe Marion Nichols into asking Louise—Beth's mother—if Beth might spend the weekend with her with a relative who did not exist.

The relative was supposed to be out in the country.

But out in the country had been Jerry, a hired room, and all the heaven on earth that Beth was ever to know in all the years she would live.

Beth thought nobody knew.

Jerry *knew* nobody thought or knew that they were married.

But what is it that ever happens in any corner of any colored town that is not shortly blared and tooted at its loudest on all the horns of gossip?

It happened that an old friend of Gran's thought that she had seen Beth wandering hand in hand through a field in Chestershire.

But it could not have been Beth, she guessed to Gran.

The girl in the field, glimpsed as her car drove by, had been tall and fair just as Beth was. She had even had curly light-brown hair and worn a red sweater just as Beth owned.

229

But it could not have been Beth!

The boy who had his arm around her had been no one Gran's friend could recognize.

He had been a tall black boy.

None of their group had tall black sons.

Gran agreed that Beth *could* not have been in Chestershire that particular weekend. She kept her breathing and her eyes controlled as long as the woman was talking.

But when she had left Gran called Mrs. Nichols to thank her for the lovely weekend that her cousin had given Beth.

Mrs. Nichols was artless: "Cousin! All of my cousins are dead and besides none of my people live in the country!"

Gran had been quick: "Oh I guess it was some other youngster in her group that took Beth off for that weekend." She told Mrs. Nichols calmly. "I'm getting so old that I forget names!" she added.

Then she had talked at length about Grandpa Nichols and his rheumatism, Marion's commencement dress, fringed all the local gossip and hung up.

And though the weather was scorching and though the day was scarcely begun, Gran had put on her best—her stiffest clothes—her stiffest Kingsman manner and gone directly to Louise, her daughter.

"Don't be a bigger fool than you can help, Louise!" Gran said as soon as she entered Louise's bedroom. "Beth has been off out of town staying with some boy."

Louise had been yawning awake childishly lazy—stretching and twisting slowly—in the June light. She turned white and leaned up in bed on an elbow that gave way. She fell back and stared at her mother.

"Don't be a fool, Louise!" Gran repeated in the fine tenor voice she used when she was giving Louise "backbone." "Say nothing to her! Act as if you never heard it! I *did*! I *will*!! God alone knows whether she is married or not."

There is where Louise screamed. She screamed twice.

And Beth downstairs—afraid to come up—bit into her lower lip, to keep from screaming too.

They knew then!

She would go to Jerry at once!

She had run to the telephone and was dialing backwards and forwards when she remembered in the part of the town where Jerry lived, most Negroes had no telephones.

She could not call Jerry.

She would go to him, then! Go to his house and tell him that Gran knew they were married and that no house could ever hold both Beth and Gran if she knew.

Beth began snatching up things and stuffing them into a bag. A compact, a handkerchief, a dress, cold cream—

Gran spoke from the door. "My it's nice to see you packing so soon, but we'll have to wait until I get some more money for our trip."

Beth dropped back on the bed. "Our trip?" she stammered.

"Yes! Louise and I think that after the hard years in school, you'd like a trip with me before you go off to college in September."

"But I don't want to—I mean I can't—"

"Thank your grandmother, Elizabeth! Thank your grand-mother!" Louise screamed from her room.

"Thank you." Beth parroted.

Gran did not answer but turned at once to the steps, talking as she went. "I'll have to get Ruth Correll to stay in the house while I'm away and Louise had better help you get your clothes ready! We shall be leaving next week."

Beth's mother came out of her room and went downstairs behind Gran. Her eyes were red with crying and great bumps swelled her face.

As soon as they were downstairs, Gran dropped her chirruping soprano—the false tone that meant that all was well—and picked up the backbone tenor tone. "You fool! Wash your face! Wear your best outfit! Take her shopping! And don't say *one word*! I'll send John to Chestershire to find out if she's married! Shut up! Stop that crying! She's not *your* baby if she's been some *man's* baby, God knows! For God sake, Louise! Stand up!! And don't you *dare* discuss this with her! I'll take charge of this!"

Gran went out.

Gran never asked where her place was.

231

She took a place for herself—always at the head and well in the lead.

And like so many strong people—or people who declare themselves strong—every other member of the family was weaker—more uncertain of his place.

"John's not got a bit of sense and Louise is a perfect fool!" Gran always declared of her children.

She had named grandpa so many names that by the time he was fifty-five he had been finally persuaded that he was too weak to live and had died.

Arthur Grey, Beth's father, had been pushed away from Louise while Beth and Luther were babies. And while Gran's strength could draw support for her daughter from Arthur, she could never draw him back to a home here Gran could grab the reins so easily from her daughter.

Gran had made herself strong—and since she was not God, she could not see where or when she was steam-rolling across other people's spiritual tracts—tracts that might have blossomed and developed into loveliness and beauty. Tracts that were shriveled, instead, lying fallow.

So Gran left Louise's home that June morning and launched into an immediate coming-out-round-the-country tour for Beth.

She called up all the women she knew who talked most and told them: "Poor dear Beth is so tired after studying so hard to finish that I just think that I shall take her on a little trip and go around to see old family friends! She's getting old enough to go out and away on visits. Maybe I'll leave her at one of the New England girls' colleges!"

"I'll leave her if things do not look just right here!" she added to herself each time she hung up.

With a talking program safely started, Gran outfitted Beth and herself, had an itemized list of each outfit printed in the society column of the colored newspaper and rounded up a few old cronies to see them off exactly one week after graduation.

During that week, Louise had stayed beside Beth day and night.

Each day Beth had had to try on this under her mother's supervision: listen to advice about what to wear when she and

Gran had finally arrived here or there. At night, Louise insisted that Beth's little bedroom was too hot. She had made Beth share her bed.

That is, they both lay side by side staring awake all night. Beth was wondering how she could get out to even mail a note to Jerry. Luther was such a tattler. He would tell Gran anything if she promised him a dollar for the telling.

Louise lay wondering what would happen if she screamed and accused Beth of all the ugliness that lay between them in the darkness.

It was a week full of new clothes that did not give one ounce of thrilling joy—packing and preparing that only placed a heavier weight on hearts already struggling through an unrelieved hell.

When Gran was sailing through the gate to the train, Beth wavered behind her for a moment.

"I forgot to mail this letter!" she told a porter and pushed a letter and ten cents in his hands. "Please mail it for me."

"Certainly, miss." the man grinned and pushed the letter and the coin into his pocket.

It was June when the porter took Beth's letter to Jerry to mail.

The last week in August, he found it in his pocket and remembered to mail it.

And from June to August Jerry had only heard from Beth, his wife, by way of the society columns.

Thus:

"Mrs. Blanche Kingsman Breastwood and her granddaughter, the lovely Elizabeth Grey, dainty blonde replica of her mother, Mrs. Louise Grey—are circling the states."

Gran really circled the states. She paraded Beth here; she exhibited Beth there; she showed her off everywhere.

Beth's clothes were lovely, her face was pinched and peaked.

"You look like an ungrateful monkey to me!" Gran had cried at Beth one day in New York. "Here I've even taken an extra mortgage on my house to give you this trip and you look as if you would rather be in a convent wearing a veil! You did not even touch that wonderful seafood dinner Mrs. Jones had for us last night."

"I'd rather be lazy on a beach in slacks with my husband—eating a hot dog!" Beth nearly answered. "Yes, grandmother," was all she said aloud, though.

New York humidity, four-and-a-half shoes on feet that could easily have worn sixes, and good old-fashioned whalebone corsets, had Gran yelping mad.

She named Beth a few names that ladies ordinarily omit.

All of a sudden, Beth vomited.

Gran stopped short. "Oh my God! I was afraid of that. Three days can be too long! Get out the bags!"

Beth was too sick to get the bags or answer for a moment. "Why do you want our bags? Where are we going now?" she asked as soon as she could.

"Home!" Gran was as terse as she had been talkative a few seconds before. "No where to go now but back home and to Dr. Meade."

So the last week in August found Beth and Gran with Louise—this time—in Dr. Meade's office.

Dr. Meade examined Beth and began that pompous old saw: "Of course it's too early to be entirely sure yet, but we might be reasonably sure in the face of certain indications that—"

Louise leaped to her feet. "You mean Beth is going to have a baby?" Her voice rose higher on waves of hysteria.

Gran started to jump up and take charge but a dull thudding began in her head that silenced her.

Without a check from Gran, Louise went to pieces. "I won't be the *grandmother* of any black bastard!"

That was the only time Beth said anything. "Jerry and I are married! I have my wedding ring." She said it hoarsely and dully.

The doctor stepped in. Gran's pain subsided. She took over.

Louise was quieted. Gran made quite a speech: "I'll take Beth away again. We'll go to Boston. There are few Negroes there and we can get everything corrected and she can go to college from there."

"I want Jerry!" Beth began crying.

Louise filled up for another scream but Dr. Meade headed her off, Gran herded them out to the car—and the society column noted the next week that "That noble dowager, Mrs. Blanche

234

Breastwood and her beauteous grand-daughter are headed out of town for another fling of society before college opens in September."

Up in a little town, far north, where you never saw a Negro very often, Gran found a plain respectable colored family.

"I'd like to take a room here while my granddaughter is waiting for her first child," Gran announced frankly as she rented their room.

Gran never mentioned Beth's husband but she let it be generally supposed that he was dead.

The months passed quickly and quietly. Beth bloomed and Gran seemed to fade somehow, though. She seemed tired all the time.

"I guess I'll go back home and send Louise up to take care of you." She told Beth one day. "The doctor is taking good care of you, though."

"Don't send *her!*" Beth started to say. "All right." She whispered in a tired voice.

Beth did not feel too well.

The doctor was taking good care of Beth. Good care. The child would be born dead. Each time Beth went to see him, the physician inserted a needle in one of her veins.

"Blood-tests," he told Beth once.

After that Gran told her: "You'll never have to be bothered with the brat! I've cashed in the insurance policy I meant to leave you to pay for all this. Thought it would be better to give you a better chance at living now!"

Beth did not care about anything that happened. She wrote long letters to Jerry and Jerry never answered her.

Jerry was off driving a truck in the far west, doing everything he could to drive a girl out of his mind who had been his wife a few days—then walked off and forgot him.

Jerry never heard a word from Beth. His mother never sent Beth's letters to him.

"Who he know up in that town?" his mother had wondered idly when Beth's first letter came.

She had torn the letter open: "My Jerry!" were the words she read.

"Well ain't these gals bold!" his mother had thought. "The baby will be soon," the letter said. "Why won't you write to me, darling?"

"Jesus ha' mercy!" Jerry's mother prayed aloud, "Jesus! A baby! Some gal in trouble! Thank God Jerry ain't here! Bet I'll kill him when he gets here!"

His mother burned that letter and whenever any other letters came from that northern town, she burned them also.

Pretty soon no more letters came anyhow.

It was the seventh month and Beth was not interested enough in living to write letters.

"Gran is sick." Louise wrote her. "I'll be up myself in a couple of weeks."

Gran had been busy back home. She had been to see an old judge who was related to her by a blood that never recognized the tie.

He had searched the records and found that Beth and Jerry had really been married.

"Jerry Jackson." Gran had echoed the name. "Who is he? Never heard of him! Nobody we ever knew! He does not belong to Beth's crowd. I knew all these youngsters before their own mothers were born! Jerry Jackson! I want an annulment!"

It took a little time for an annulment. Gran had to wait.

Births do not wait.

Louise had to take an express north to Beth one weekend.

And one winter dawn in a hard-fought struggle that drew every bit of the skill he could summon—the doctor brought Beth's dead baby into the world.

Louise—foolish Louise—who had pretended that she was calm and had persuaded the doctor to let her help him, went hysterical when she saw the baby.

It was a little blonde boy, the image of Louise's own father—Beth's grandfather—lying dead, there, on the white blanket.

"Oh slap him! Make him cry! Isn't he a darling! Just like my father! Gran must see him!" she cried over and over again to the doctor.

"I can't give life," the doctor replied drily.

Louise's cries roused Beth, still half-asleep under the anesthetic. She opened her eyes—saw the child—tried to cry out—

went back, deeper beneath the sleep of the drug—heavy with the image of her child.

It was finished.

Louise called Gran as soon as she could by long distance.

"Never can tell about colored babies," Gran observed drily. "Next one might have been a tar-kettle. Luther told me about Jerry Jackson. Just some ordinary Negro boy who was in Beth's class at school! She's a sly little fool! Those papers—the annulment—will reach you tomorrow. Sent them special. I'm going to sleep now."

And Gran hung up.

"Where's the baby?" Beth asked Louise as soon as she woke up. "Where's Jerry?"

"The baby is dead!" Louise screamed back at her. "And don't talk to me about any Jerry!"

Beth's hysteria frightened her mother. Louise and the doctor did all they could, but Beth cried often for the baby she had glimpsed only once. She would cry for Jerry, too.

Louise began to be afraid to tell her that she was no longer married to Jerry. She hid the annulment papers under her hats in her bag.

"Let's get back home, Beth!" Louise would worry.

She never read or sewed. She smoked all the time that she was not doing her nails or playing solitaire or wondering what her "gang" was doing at home.

"This is the damnedest town I ever was in. How can anybody live here! These niggers have no society at all! They would be knocked out if they could fall into one of our *formals* or bridges back home!" Here she always laughed smugly. "Let's go home!"

Beth just sat pale and listless in the corner of an arm chair by the window. "All right!" she agreed.

But the doctor begged Louise not to go for a while. He wanted to watch Beth a little longer.

He wanted to watch Beth.

It would not do his medical status any good if something went any further wrong than it already was and another doctor had to examine Beth.

Time passed. Beth grew a little stronger.

One day when Louise was in the midst of one of her "wonder-what-the-gang-is-doing" moods, there was a knock at the door.

It was the man of the house with a telegram in his hands.

"Got stars on it! Somebody's pretty sick!" he told Louise as he passed it to her.

Louise could not open it. Beth had to.

"Gran is dead!" she spoke as if she could not read clearly.

Louise began to scream and cry: "It's all your fault! Worrying Mama to death dragging you up and down the country last summer! You are a nuisance and a worry! Killing my mother this way!"

Beth packed.

Beth got strength enough to go back home, but she was pale.

Louise pulled herself together and explained with an air such as Gran might have used: "Beth takes Mama's death awful hard. Then, too, she's been studying too hard in that old college. I just think I'm going to keep her home this year and send her back next September."

Gran's funeral was a ceremony of dignity and elegance.

Louise put Beth in black, wore plenty herself—launched herself into a season of bridges and quiet affairs to fill the emptiness she felt in her.

Nothing soothed Beth.

She had tried to find Jerry. Had taken a taxi down to the part of the town where Jerry lived. She could never find his house. The city planners had renumbered the streets in that particular locale three times and never eradicated the old sets.

Beth wrote Jerry one last time.

He did not answer.

That next September she went to college.

"I can never forgive you for worrying Mama to death," Louise wrote to her often. "And for what! That bumming Jerry you married is an old truck driver, bumming his way around the west coast! How could you disgrace me so and kill poor Mama"—and on and on.

Beth escaped from her mother by plunging as deep into studying as she could go—brought out some good marks and a quiet listless manner.

On the Altar

"Beth needs to fall in love," Louise's best friend Bessie told her.

Bessie had always been Louise's closest friend. Teaching paid Bessie a salary that with the right amount of pruning here and the proper degree of nurturing there might have amounted to a comfortable living after many years.

But Bessie dressed like a wealthy woman—ate and drank and lived in general like a person with an income instead of a salary—and entertained like an heiress.

She was continually without money and deeply in debt. Bessie had the look of a person who puts a fork in a huge plate of good food, or rubs a finger on some rich fabric or smacks greedy lips on a hit-the-spot-drink—and feels that at last she knew life at its best. But it never was at its best.

But since nothing outside of anyone ever gave life its best tone, Bessie was always slightly anxious, slightly restless, always reaching and seeking.

She always led and Louise trailed joyously behind.

When Louise complained of Beth's listlessness, of Beth's pallid good looks, of Beth's lack of interest in clothes and boys and parties, it was Bessie who advised the remedy.

"Beth needs a good love affair. She took that little mess she was in four years ago too hard! Cliff Robertson—Dr. Cliff Robertson, you know—is beginning to get around a lot now and I'll have a little bunch over some night this week so he and Beth can meet. Let me take her downtown and pick out the dress!"

"But I have no money for a dress right now!"

"I'll put it on my charge at Hoffwit's and you can pay me later," Bessie interposed with the easiness that had placed her in the sea of debt in which she already wallowed.

She set all her plans in motion. She called and invited the man—Dr. Robertson—first: "Just a few friends."

After he had accepted, she mulled over and passed by all the younger attractive women—called up and invited the stouter older ones whose wits and remnants of good looks as well as their very good clothes still made them count.

Then she took Beth downtown to Hoffwit's. And for seventy dollars to be paid some other time, she found a black dress with multicolored sleeves and subtle curving and ultra-fitted. It really made Beth's pallor seem like subdued devilment rather than entirely dead lack of love of living on any level.

Louise was advised to arrive late by the time that "Tootsie" Ross and Lollie Joss had set things to rolling with their good-natured but decidedly fortyish wits.

Louise cursed Beth into the dress, longed to kick her up Bessie's front steps—and yet managed to purr to Cliff as she met him—"My little girl! Just out of college!"

Cliff Robertson was forty-seven. He had been married and had cast off each wife in a true cocoon of fashion as he—he himself—developed.

One wife had put him through medical school—worked day and night—gone without the ordinary comforts of living. "Someday he'll be a doctor and we'll be rich!" She had whipped herself on to the heart-breaking sacrifice with this thought.

Cliff became a doctor.

He became richer.

She was left behind in the town where she had sacrificed while he sought "connections" in a larger city.

He had found the connections.

They had included a leader in the colored society in that city.

He published notice of his divorce from the first wife in a Polish newspaper—published in the native tongue.

That made it legal.

When the one who had been left behind heard—he was on his honeymoon abroad.

After that second wife had had a son for him and eaten her heart out as she watched his greedy selfish search for further advancement—away from her—she died.

The third was his match. She was a widow, wealthy—just as greedy—just as selfish—just as ruthless—just as entirely without conscience as he. It was a tough battle that split the judge's eardrums when he granted the divorce.

And it was this man for whom Bessie had put a seventy-dollar creation of seduction on Beth. It was to this man with much trepidation and the prayer that Beth would "for-God-sake-act-human-this-once" that Louise cursed and prodded her girl-child forward.

Beth's aloofness, Beth's correctly careless style of conduct—were new to Cliff.

You know the rest. You know what followed.

He trotted up and down Louise's front steps like a demented puppy gone heavyweight.

"He has a six-flat building—a gorgeous house—two servants—and those *cars!*" Louise exulted to Beth once.

"He has more bay-windows and back-drops over his collar than any human being I've ever seen!"

Louise went to pieces.

She cursed and cajoled. "Anyone would think you did not have good sense! There isn't a girl in this town who wouldn't be willing to die tomorrow if she could have your looks, your clothes, your background, your chance to marry a man as crazy about you as Cliff is! And look at his money! You can have just about everything! Everything!! I'm not fool enough to tell you to marry a poor guy because you *love* him! Anybody could love anything with as much money as Cliff has."

"He has more layers of puffy paunchiness than he has money! I hate him!" Beth shot back at her.

Louise made an ineffective yank at the telephone on the stand beside her. Maybe she wanted something to throw at Beth.

It was just then that the telephone rang.

No one moved or spoke. Mother and daughter merely stared at each other.

There was a shrilling again. Louise reached out a hand automatically.

It was Cliff. He wanted to take Beth for a drive—and to a club—or to a show and to a club—or anywhere or anything just to get near her.

"My little girl will be thrilled to go," Louise gurgled into the telephone: "Yes! Yes!! At eight? I'll tell her—when she comes in! Good-by." She finished quickly and pushed down on the hook to cut the connection.

Beth had started to reach for the telephone while it was still in her mother's hand.

"I'm renting out the house and going to live with Bessie after next month," Louise said after a second. "It's too damn expensive to heat this place all winter! Luther is going to stay at Arthur's."

That was all she said then. She did not mention Beth.

"I'll get a job and live alone before the month is up!" Beth thought.

That is what she thought. It was a time, though, when it took more than just a degree and inexperience to secure a job in four weeks.

All the time Louise was having her rugs and drapes cleaned and her curtains stretched before she should store them. She harangued Beth hourly: "Marry Cliff! Marry *money*! You won't need to be hunting jobs! You can't earn enough to half feed you, anyhow!"

A stronger person would have broken away and gone to face anything—tried to keep her self. Beth had been heeled and heeled by Louise already crushed beneath the weight of Gran who in turn was weighted and freighted with the most rigid ideas of living. Beth could not face anything—strong.

"We cannot offer you anything definite now—perhaps later!" That was the answer Beth received every place she applied.

Louise's house stripping and daily preachments went ahead at full force.

It was Bessie who advised this strategy. "If Beth will agree to marry Cliff," Bessie said, "why your house will be all cleaned and ready for one gorgeous reception! If she *won't*—"

"She'd *better*!" Louise could not bear the thought of so much slipping away from her.

And she cursed and pleaded the more.

And one day Beth told Louise: "I despise him but if you will only let me alone, I'll marry the old fool!"

Louise screamed, laid across the bed and kicked her heels.

She ran to the telephone.

She called Bernice.

She called Cliff.

And after that she remembered to hug at Beth. She did not hug her. She hugged *at* her.

242

Cliff managed a third mortgage on his home (the other two were paying his alimony) and bought Beth a ring that wrung her heart.

It was so beautiful, so exquisitely lovely it should have meant all the loveliness of love.

She hated him whenever she looked at his ring.

There is no need to waste words on what followed.

The society columns burst forth into a hysteria of redundancy, bad taste and worse writing. They listed the showers and the parties and the details of every gift and every garment and every scrap of food served.

That was the way it would always be.

Things, things, things.

Things given and things taken.

But no peace and no real plenty would there be.

The things mounted up to the grand splurge which was the wedding.

Everyone who was anyone or who thought he was anyone was bidden to the colored Episcopal church.

Up the aisle came flower girls and ring-bearers.

Close on their heels followed twelve bridesmaids and a matron and maid of honor.

Parallel to them came the cream of the race, the hope of tomorrow—the ushers.

Everyone was truly lovely to look at for there is no beauty or distinction to be found anywhere as truly exciting as in a group of these latter-day Negroes.

When Beth trembled down the aisle on the arm of her father, there were audible exclamations. Louise's good taste in dress was superimposed on Beth's good looks. She was so unhappy and excited that she seemed beautiful.

And Jerry—Beth's Jerry—who had pushed his way dressed as he was in dirty truck-driver clothes—past the ushers—closed his eyes on the tears that swam into them.

Up in the third pew from the front on the left, Louise in pink lace and pink horsehair—gripped her fists in their gloves.

Just before the procession had started, Luther had raced up the aisle to his mother so fast that the tails of his formal suit wig-wagged.

"That nigger—that damn nigger—that Jerry Beth was married to—just came in," he panted into his mother's ear.

The pink hat cast such a rosy glow on Louise's face that no one could see how pale she grew.

"Call the police!" she chattered.

"Don't be a fool, Lou!" her friend Bessie whispered. "This is public!"

"Suppose he spoils things!"

"Don't be a fool!" Bessie repeated and nodded Luther away.

Luther wavered uncertainly but he scrambled back up the aisle somehow.

Both he and Louise were drenched in perspiration all during the ceremony.

When the organ sang forth the recessional, Louise leaped slightly in her seat. She would have leaped out of it completely, but Bessie's bulk blocked her.

Beth, on the arm of her husband, saw the tears on her mother's face—and she turned her face away unmoved.

As she neared the door, she saw Jerry.

And all the agony in his eyes above a mouth curved in a derisive sneer—flowed quickly into her own.

She wanted to tear her arm away from her husband and rush out of the place alone.

But layers of fat in a broadcloth sleeve pinned her firmly to Cliff's side.

When Beth walked out into the vestibule into the midst of her bridesmaids, she was a woman whose poise forever was merely to be a frozen agony and a derisive sneer at living.

Cliff and his car swept her to the wedding breakfast.

"Drink something, baby!" he whispered to her. "You are too pale."

Beth drank.

Beth drank heavily for the first time in her life.

It was not the last time.

She drank so much that the high tiers of the wedding cake seemed to shake.

She stood and stooped to it.

The tiny bride and groom that perched on top of the cake skidded suddenly.

The white lace dress fell off of the little blonde doll bride.

She lay curled and naked in a fold of white satin ribbon.

She lay curled and naked like a newborn baby in a curl of white satin-bound blanket.

"It's like a baby! It's like my baby!" Beth screamed.

But nobody heard her.

Everyone was yelling at once at one of Sully Jones's jokes.

Sully had been Cliff's best man. Sully was one of those men whose jokes took their root, blossomed and bore fruit in sex.

When the doll fell, Sully was bellowing, "Well, Cliff has been—and Cliff has done everything but have twins! Why I remember one time—heh-heh!"

"Don't let Sully start remembering," some one shouted. "This might turn into a riot!"

The room rocked with laughter at that joke.

Or maybe it rocked with liquor.

Anyhow, the room rocked.

And Louise beamed and Bessie screamed and finally these two noticed Beth was shrunk back in her chair, staring ahead of her at nothing.

Bessie jumped to her feet.

"I'm going to dress the bride!" she announced.

She and Louise herded Beth upstairs.

As soon as the door had closed the three in Louise's bedroom, Bessie produced a bottle.

"Take some whiskey straight, Beth! Nothing like it to quiet your nerves."

Beth drank it straight.

It took Bessie and Louise to dress her.

Straight whiskey on top of mixed everything else can stun you.

It took Cliff to pull her into his car, dressed beautifully in the height of everything.

"S'matter?" Cliff asked as they drove off. "What you need is something to pep you up. Nothing like good straight whiskey. Here!"

Beth drank it straight.

It took the porter and Cliff to put Beth into the drawing room.

All the porters and bridesmaids shrieked good-bye as the train pulled away.

And the train, gathering speed, clattered on and on crying out a thousand sounds that smothered out everything else—the way a thousand thousand particles of dust smother a coffin and bury it deep.

But so long as pride and the old order had been held firmly in place, I guess it does not matter if an unborn life, a girl's life, a boy's life have been tossed on the altar, consumed in the flames of vanity.

It does not matter if the ashes of their complete ruin have been scattered to the four winds of life-as-man-wills-it.

It does not matter.

High-Stepper

The doctor's hands lingered over his instruments as he placed them back in his bag.

What was the need of using instruments in a case like Sadie Allen's? He took them out of his bag more as a matter of habit. The disease that broke in her body had been held in check by needles long ago.

Only her eyes, staring, blank—empty as the mind in back of them—made you know that Sadie was not entirely herself.

"You had better spend as much time as you can with Sadie!" the doctor said to Jim Allen, Sadie's husband. "These mental cases have odd phases. Some day your presence may help her break into herself!"

Jim Allen said nothing.

He smiled down at his russet tan shoes, let his eyes follow the knife creases in his tweed trousers, then rested them a long time on the diamond-set knife that hung on his watch chain.

Dora had given him that knife. Swell girl, Dora. Always doing something nice for him. Nothing too good for him. Just like her to give him this knife. Real diamonds and real gold if ever there was anything real. And the knife did not even open as other knives usually do. You pushed or tapped lightly on the side and three knives, slender as blades of grass and as sharp as flint and steel could make them—sprang out at once all in the same direction.

Jim Allen pulled his mind back suddenly into the room.

"Have a drink before you go, doctor?" he asked.

The doctor grunted assent and followed him downstairs.

Jim walked ahead still smiling to himself.

What did this fool doctor think he was? He paid him good money—good money every time he crossed the door-sill—to look after Sadie.

If he himself did not stay downstairs, the niggers would run away with his club. He had put Bill Palmer in charge of his pool-room and Al Jones had his eye on every one of the fellows who worked in the bar.

And he had his eyes on Bill and Al all the time and his own fingers on both cash registers every five minutes.

He *had to* stay downstairs.

There was not a colored man on Frye Street—not one who was a real man's man—who did not leave some part of his weekly wages with Jim Allen.

Jim called his place "The Old Sports Club."

That made the fellows feel high-class as if they belonged to some real club with leather chairs and swell rugs and pictures instead of the bare floors, nude posters, and hardwood chairs he offered them.

Jim knew what the men of Frye Street wanted. His place was always full of music going full blast—loud laughter—glasses clinking and pool balls clicking and he himself dressed in all the ultra-furbishings of the old-time sport in the midst. Spats, fawn-colored vests, flowers in his buttonhole, diamonds in his tie—in his watch—and on his hands.

"Why do Negroes think all doctors are rich!" thought the man following Jim. "This man must make as much in a week as I do in three months! He even swaggers 'rich'!"

High-stepper—that is what the fellows called Jim Allen. He lived high, dressed high, acted as if everyone else lived and dressed the same way—and he really got around the good-time spots around town when his own place closed.

Jim ushered the doctor into a quiet corner, served him a beer and went back to his own thoughts.

He would do just as he had been doing.

He would run up once in a while—about once a week—to the room where Sadie was.

Didn't her mother always say: "Sadie always acts kind of restless and uneasy whenever you come up here!"

Mom ought to know. She never left Sadie's side day or night. Not once since the sickness had struck two years ago had Mom left Sadie.

"Heigh, Mom!" Jim liked to boom at Sadie's mother from the door-sill.

Mom hated Jim.

And he knew she hated him.

It would have been easy to slam Sadie—a wife who was not a bit of good to any man—in the county asylum. That would have hurt old Mom plenty.

But that was too easy. It was better to come up late at night after everything was quiet for a while downstairs—talking cheerful and hearty as if everything was all right between them and say: "Guess I'll be stepping out for a little time myself."

Mom always stayed quiet for a moment, hating him as loud as she could with her mouth closed.

Then: "No decent man with a wife what's as sick as Sadie is ought to be out 'stepping' after midnight!" Mom would blaze at him.

That gave him a chance to blaze back at her. "What good is Sadie to me? What the hell kind of wife you think Sadie makes me? She been shut up sick here more'n two years in this place! Damn crazy! You and her both better be glad I don't send her on to the asylum! Most men wouldn't be bothered five minutes with a wife what ain't a God's bit of good to them!"

That always knocked the old lady back in her corner. That shut her up.

She did not want Sadie in the asylum where the colored patients ate the leavings from other folks' plates and slop-pails stood unemptied for days on end beneath beds.

She did not want Sadie there!

And *neither* did Jim want her there. It would not look right to "folks" if a guy that made good money as he made put his wife away.

It *might* hurt his business if he put Sadie in the asylum.

He kept her at home and came and talked to Mom whenever he felt like it. He never talked right out plain about his women: he just let Mom know by every little way and means at his command that some other women had his time, his thoughts, his affections—and his wife merely ate his food and sat under his roof.

And the mother hated him more and more every time he came.

What woman can love a man who has brought the only girl child God ever placed in her arms, first a broken heart, then a broken body—and at last—a broken mind?

The room flooded with hate whenever Jim came into it.

Christ said not to hate, though.

But—Christ—it seems too much to love a man as a son who has brought dirty diseases from the dirty bodies of dirty women to the baby girl you bore—clean: that you brought up—clean: to act—clean: to be finally smothered in an avalanche of uncleanness that breaks the heart, the body, and the mind.

The mother hated Jim.

Jim hated the mother.

And neither of them knew that there lay between them an empty mind—a mind waiting for something to fill it.

They never thought that their hate might fill it.

Sadie's mind was not lost.

No mind can ever be lost. You are just no longer completely always with your self. Instead, you swing back and forth eternally against thoughts of Yesterday and thoughts of Tomorrow: against minds of Never and minds of Always.

Somewhere, somewhere, though, you are bound to come back to your Self.

No one knows just when or where your mind will filter back to you and you will be completely your Self. No one knows what sight, what sound, what propulsion from the spiritual side of living casts the mold and the imprint together once more.

Mom and Jim did not know that emptiness is not. Something fills everything. Mom and Jim did not know that hate is something you may not see—but that you can feel.

And Sadie Allen came from minds of Never to minds of Always—through thoughts of Yesterday, past thoughts of Tomorrow—back suddenly into her Self in a room flooded with hate.

It was through steps like these Sadie came back.

Within herself, Sadie always heard her own mind. Sometimes it reached Minds of Never: thus, once.

"I open a door deep within me, walk down the steps and stand, peering with the light of my mind uplifted, at a river of words that flows constantly, silently, deeply there. Ideas shoal by as beautiful and ugly as any of the variegated things that live in the sea. Why is it people are afraid to lose hold of the light that they can feel and see—and walk out into misty darkness where they can listen to the river of words flowing eternally in them? —Sometimes you hear something no one has heard before."

Sadie knew that this was not her Self. She would not speak aloud. Her own mind was still somewhere trying to find her. Trying to find her—again past minds of Always: thus. She was retching back from the ultimate satiation of a marriage purely of the flesh—fretting uneasily on the smooth glass of a marriage of spirit and mind—foot-worn and soul-weary from pacing the two hell-roads that lay distinctly in her. Both were calling, begging—longing for a sure solid foot to tread them. There is something destructively wrong in being so happy in things of the flesh. Follow one road—you leave the other, the spiritual, too far behind. There is something that makes you feel more dead than alive if you live too much in your mind. Follow the other road and you go completely outside of your body.

It was not her mind. Sadie could not speak aloud yet. She could not speak aloud the things she heard within.

Sometimes she screamed and cried that a rat—two rats—some things that wriggled and slithered like rats—were pouring in thousands across the street toward the house where she was.

They were out of sight now. It must be that they were somewhere searching to find a way into the building—to get upstairs and swarm all over her.

She would scream to her mother and cling to her, hiding her face against her.

Downstairs, some loud-mouthed Negro would kyah-kyah and hyah-hyah in a from-the-toes guffaw. A whole room full of shouts would echo him.

"There! They are in!" Sadie cried to her mother. "Mother! They are after people! Hear them all screaming?"

What use was it for her mother to cry with her and tell her that there were no rats. It was as useless as it was for her to rub Sadie's temples with camphor spirits and rub her face with oil to bring her mind back.

It was all as useless as the foolish things people carry out of a house on fire.

You may laugh at the odds and ends you have saved—but you do not laugh at your only child screaming herself hoarse, clawing the bosom out of your dress—trying to shut out a sight of a horde of rats that were nowhere.

Each time this happened, hate lit a fire that burned higher in Mom. For this was the only thing Sadie ever spoke aloud. The screaming, the crying, the words blotted and blurred with terror and hysteria were all she spoke aloud.

But Sadie's mind always seeking—always swinging back and forth, began to fill with the words of hate that flooded unspoken in Mom and Jim.

Sometimes words are merely a fountain, flooding from the soul—shaping, twisting—gesturing in the Winds of Hate.

Sadie once heard this within herself:

"Words are a fountain—shaping—twisting—gesturing in the Winds of Hate. Shaping in the Winds of Hate that sleep all day in a cave of ugliness and bitterness and wait until night to whip out to shape and make gestures of words that are fountains for more hate. Shaping—now a sword—now a tongue—now a needle—always thrusting, thrusting, thrusting through the Dark—shaping, gesturing and thrusting in the Winds of Hate."

Filled as her room was with such intense thoughts of hate, these words began to spread most often within Sadie.

This was not her mind.

This was not her self.

But once after she had felt these words about Hate floating through her—something hard pressed against her breast. At the same time a scent—a perfume from Yesterday reached her.

Her mind plunged wildly—Love deep through Yesterday. Trying to find her in Yesterday.

There had been this same scent—a scent of faint perfume, clinging as closely to Jim's person as some woman's body had but lately clung to pour this perfume over him.

"What is the odor?" Sadie had asked.

"Oh—some sort of stuff the barber put on my hair!" he lied glibly and had taken Sadie in his arms.

Later he called her Dora when he kissed her.

And her name was Sadie.

Not long after that this awful sickness had begun. And she had been plunged backwards over the precipice of a mind degenerating—carrying with her three straws of memory: the name of a woman—Dora; the scent of some perfume a woman might use; and the dazzle of a diamond-set knife that Jim had once boasted that this Dora had given him.

Sadie pushed against whatever pressed hard against her breast.

It was Jim's diamond knife.

So simple a thing as this had happened. Mom had dropped Sadie's pillows behind the chair where Sadie sat.

And when Jim stooped to pick them up, his knife had pressed against Sadie's breast.

"Mama!" Sadie said aloud suddenly in a normal tone. "Mama! He is hurting me!"

Mom threw a glass she had been holding across the room. "Thank God! My baby is talking! Her mind is come back!"

She ran to Sadie and cried and kissed her again and again.

Jim stared speechless—this time.

"My knife must a mashed against her!" he said after he could get his breath.

He held the knife up by the chair.

It swung around in the light.

"Pretty, pretty!" Sadie began babbling like a child and held out her hands.

To humor her, Jim moved closer to her chair—extending the knife toward her.

The words of Hate made one more great surge within her.

The dazzle of the diamonds.
The scent of the perfume.
The woman's name—Dora.

Sadie thrust hard against the knife. She did not want to touch it.

She pushed her hands against the knife and the knife hard against Jim's side.

Three blades—as slender as blades of grass—as sharp as flint and steel could make them—sprang out, all on one side of the handle.

Three blades with Sadie pressing hard against them, went into Jim's side.

Now Sadie's eyes stared blank again. She did not even draw back her hands to wipe the blood that followed the knife blades.

Sadie sat empty again, following her mind. Past Tomorrow— past Always—past Never.

It never came back to Yesterday nor came through the caves of Hate again.

The Wind slept.

Yesterday was lost.

Stones for Bread

Uncle Dan saw John when he suddenly cut across the street.

John did not look at his uncle.

"What ails that young fool!" Uncle Dan snorted to himself. "Wish he'd a remembered to bust across the street 'thout speakin' the time he come a runnin' to me to borrow that sixty dollars ten months ago! And I ain't seen him but twice since! Ef he ain't seeing me today—I ain't seeing him neither! Reckon it's 'cause he's workin' on his dirty job he don't want to see me! Who ever heard tell of men working at being social workers *anyhow*!"

Uncle Dan began taking wider and longer steps. His pail and mop, shiny across his left shoulders, bumped from side to side. He was going a few blocks from the six buildings where he worked as janitor on Chandler Avenue to the four buildings he kept on Buckham Road.

Dan gave a second glance after John.

"Boy looking kind of worried! Wonder—!"

Dan reached a drugstore and went in and called up his wife, Mary. She was back on Chandler Avenue still scrubbing. Between them, they took care of twelve buildings. Between them they garnered three hundred dollars a month, working day and night for it.

"Mary." Dan always shouted when he talked over a telephone. "I just seed young John a walkin' round this way! Looked kinder worried to me!"

"Bound to look worried!" his wife replied dully. "His ma and his wife's ma and pa and all of them is having some kinder meetin' this morning to settle some mess he and his wife had. John just call me. All goin' to Margaret's!"

"Lawd-ee! Guess I better go over there."

"What for? They ask you?"

"Naw! But Margaret can get to acting the fool so easy!"

"She your sister! Stay away 'til folks send for you!"

"Naw, Mary! I been itchin' to set up with ole Peter Jackson ever since John married his Lucy! Always yellin' 'bout what his daughter is used to and what she ain't used to. What's any pullman porter's daughter got to be used to? He ain't no millionaire!"

"You ain't got no business breakin' in there, Dan!"

"You better come on down to Margaret's yourself, Mary! You know ef I lights into him and Margaret both I might bust wide open! They both is the dog-gummedest!"

"I ain't fixin' to have nobody ask *me* out of nowhere!"

"Well I'm going! In you come on!"

And Dan hung up. He walked out of the drugstore and hired a taxi because his mop and pail might cause an argument in the car. And anyhow, he wanted to get into the fight as quickly as possible.

Dan was like that.

Back at home, Mary scrubbed a little longer.

"Wonder what they doing?"she asked herself aloud after a while. "Wonder ef Dan and Margaret is both acting the fool?"

Mary tried to finish her scrubbing.

"Guess I better get together and go down there and hold Dan down!" she decided finally.

She washed her face, put on a clean cotton house dress and some cotton hose. Then she dug down in the last coil of springs in a broken davenport some tenant had given them and drew out two ten-dollar bills.

Then she went out and took a taxi, too, and hurried to join the conference.

John had really not wanted to see his uncle or anyone else. He was too busy seeing what he had just left at his own house.

He had waked up that morning in his three rooms and bath in a "Thank-God-for-ham-and-eggs-and-a-job-and-a-home" mood.

John was twenty-five. His father and mother had seen him through enough schools to rate a degree. When everything was folding down and the Relief Commissions were unfolding every-where, John managed to land a job that paid one-hundred twenty-five dollars a month with the local commission.

Lucy, his wife, had been through practically the same steps, and twenty-four found her with a degree—a job with the same local Relief Commission held in her own name—and John for a husband. Lucy held her job under her maiden name so that if ever the threat of only allowing one person per family to work for the commission became a reality—she would get by and they would lose nothing.

They had reckoned every detail of their future using their combined salaries as the basis.

"We'll pay for the furniture—travel—get a good car—buy a house." They had planned.

Someday—someday—perhaps—they would have a child.

Maybe.

The child would come after everything was paid for and both Lucy and John owned very complete Vogue and Esquire ward-robes.

They dressed well and talked well and lived far better than their own parents had lived at their age.

Lucy and her careful diction, her carefully cultivated manner-isms of dress and living—was to John all that his parents had meant when they told him again and again all during his growing years: "Marry a nice girl! Marry a girl that's educated and refined and nice looking!"

So Lucy was nice looking and educated and refined.

And Lucy was self-centered and did not know how to manage money. Her mother had made her believe all her life that Lucy need not bother too much about any of the details of housekeep-ing because Papa and Mama wanted to devote all their time and means to their only darling: Lucy.

That is what Papa and Mama wanted to do.

So Lucy could do her nails and keep them done and could have her hair waved and keep the wave in it a long time because she never held her face over a washtub of steaming water or put her hands in a dishpan either.

Anyhow—John married nice-looking educated and refined Lucy on $125 a month and they went to keep house.

They had no maid.

One-hundred twenty-five dollars does not keep you and a maid too! It does not pay the gas and the light and the rent and pay for just so many clothes after you marry as you bought before plus all the meals in drugstores and restaurants because nobody cooks at home.

No money was in John's pockets continually. It got so that when he saw Lucy each month with another dress and still another pair of shoes he began snapping at her before he said "Hello" to her.

And they had only been married seven months.

Yet—John had managed to wake up with a "Thank God" mood the morning Uncle Dan saw him.

He had lain in bed stretching a second when he realized Lucy was not beside him.

She must be in the bathroom. She was not in the living room nor the kitchen. He only had to turn his head to the right to see all over the living room and to the left to cover the kitchen completely.

Slight sounds of agony came suddenly from the bathroom.

John bounded to the door.

"S'matter, Lucy?" he called through the door.

The low sounds of agony became shouts at once.

"I'm vomiting! I'm vomiting!! That's what!!!"

John was dazed for a moment. "Must have been something you ate!"

"Something I ate!" Lucy tore the door open and walked out surprisingly strong. "I vomited yesterday at work! I didn't tell you last night—and now this morning—this morning—as soon as I stepped on the floor it started again!"

John repeated stupidly. "Must have been something you had for lunch yesterday!"

Lucy fell across the bed. "Shut up! I'm sick. Ooh! I'm afraid! I'm afraid! It may be—it may be like Susie Smith last year!"

"You mean—a baby? Gosh! Gosh!!" John was as loud now as Lucy.

Seeing John down, Lucy immediately went lower.

She cried and cried and cried and cried.

John put an arm around [   ]

But his *arm*, weighted with his own worry, fretted her.

She shook off his arm.

"If our rent were only twenty-five dollars a month for these three same rooms as it was when whites lived here—I could manage without her salary." John was thinking. Then he spoke aloud: "That Jim Christensen—that Swedish case worker from Mapledale lives with his folks and he and his wife are using their salaries to build a place of their own!"

"Well your folks have four rooms and no place for us! And I didn't marry any man to coop me up in any little tight old hole with his folks!"

"Neither have yours any place for us!"

"Who said they did?"

"Nobody! I was only saying—!"

"Oh keep quiet! You always take every opportunity to insult my father and mother!"

"Nobody's insulting them! I just said they had a small apartment!"

Lucy jumped up. "I'm going home now and see my mother! I'm not going to work! I can certainly go home to my own people alone!"

"Nobody told you to go! I was just thinking that if it was a baby we'd have to move because I can't pay the $47.50 by myself!"

"You could if you were any good! My father always kept us in a good place! We always lived well! Better than any old meat-lugger's folks! Used to nothing!"

All these were wild shots but they hit sore spots in John.

"Lugging meat's as good as lugging white folks' bags any day!" John defended his father's work. "Put me where I am!"

"And where is that? Three tight little old rooms!"

"Well if it is so little we'd better get out of it!"

"I'm getting out now! I'm going this minute!"

And Lucy slammed the bathroom door and dressed and walked over John without speaking.

He went *out* first, though, and called up his mother—told her he wanted to come see her right away—sketched lightly over the problem, called the supervisor and told her that both he and Lucy were retracing some cases before they reported to the office.

Then he set out for his mother's home.

He called Mary, Uncle Dan's wife, after he got out.

Mary was always so matter-of-fact that it had occurred to him suddenly that to call her and say something might give him a chance to talk to someone who always seemed sane.

Uncle Dan was John's mother's brother. Margaret—John's mother—liked to think privately that all she and Dan had in common was parenthood.

"My brother just *will* do that dirty old janitor work," she told people. "I wish he'd get something nice like John Senior!"

Dan could never see where lugging coal differed from lugging meat. Anyhow the coal paid better.

Privately Margaret wished that John Senior had the ready money Dan always had and that she herself had inherited her brother's wavy hair.

But if she talked down her *nose* about Dan's work, she talked further down it about Dan's wife.

Who ever heard of a man with any get up to him marrying a wife who was content to live in white folks' basements full of white folks' cast-offs—a wife who got up at four o'clock in the morning and scrubbed and cleaned all day right beside her husband like a man?

"She never looks like anything! I've never seen her wear a silk dress and she never has her hair done! Never!! Any intelligent woman would have her hair fixed up!"

Margaret had intoned her complaints against Dan's wife all of John's life.

But there was something about that placid black woman who was Aunt Mary that always soothed John, and when his mother would say, "I never could see what made Dan marry Mary!" or even "I don't believe she ever takes a bath!"—John could not tell her—but he knew what Dan had seen.

He always sought out Mary when he was troubled.

And Mary loved John as she would have loved a son if she had had one.

"Believe I'll just save up and leave everything I got to John!" she often thought to herself. "Give one young colored man a head start like these white men get. Fix it so John won't be forty-five before he gets on his feet!"

It was of John that Mary thought that morning as she rode to his mother's.

"Wonder what the trouble is?" Mary kept saying. "Bet it's that gal's fault! She's as big a fool as John's mother to me!"

She sent her troubled thoughts ahead of her to Margaret's where already a room full of trouble and wrong thoughts had gathered.

Already in Margaret's living room were John and his mother. She sat in an arm chair and he stood behind her, first on one side, then the other.

On the couch, nearly prostrate as befitted one in deep trouble, was Lucy with Lucinda, her mother, and Pete Jackson, her father.

Lucinda was another Margaret. People of this type have the same by-the-yard thoughts about God and man.

Only on one point did they vary: Lucinda knew Lucy was perfection itself and Margaret knew God had never created a woman good enough for John.

To Margaret, Lucy was a nice enough girl but she was only the girl who had married John.

To Lucinda and Peter, John was all right—but he had plucked the flower of their existence from their home.

"If he doesn't treat my daughter right—I'll just about kill him!" Peter liked to say.

He would say it as violent as he could—which was not very violent.

Peter was never very anything except a negative nonentity who only added platitudes and subtracted bromides from living.

If he so much as blew his nose or merely scratched his ear, he slid a self-conscious glance out of the corners of his eyes and looked as guilty as if the whole world had gathered around and seen him suddenly naked.

He sat on Margaret's couch and cleared his throat and crossed his legs and his arms and tried to look the man he was not.

Lucinda held her arm at an angle wih her foot that made a protective bat-wing around Lucy.

Lucy cried softly and looked limp but John did not look at her.

For a few seconds no one said anything.

No one knew what needed to be said.

Then Peter cleared his throat one final time. "I—er—hope—that you—" here he peeked his beard jerkily toward John but he was afraid to look at him. "I hope that you intend to do the right thing by our daughter!"

Margaret went immediately hysterical. "The *right* thing! The *right* thing! John always does the right thing by his wife! They are married! What are you talking about?"

Pete recoiled from the onslaught at once: "Oh—nothing! Nothing! I—"

"Nothing! Nothing! Peter Jackson! Don't you dare sit there and call my daughter nothing!"

"My God! What *is* all this?" John asked himself.

The bell rang loudly.

John went to press the buzzer, but before he got to it there was a banging at the door.

John unlocked it.

And Uncle Dan with his mop and pail marched in.

His sister stared at him. "What you doing here?" Surprise made her lapse into her earlier type of speech.

"Jes' came by! Jes' came by! Mary told me you all was in some kinder mess so I came by! Knew John Senior was to work so I came myself to help you!"

Margaret and Lucinda drew up their backs and sat more erect.

"It is no mess—as you call it!" Margaret stated stiffly. John's wife isn't—"

"Don't you go saying *John's wife* isn't anything!" Lucinda began.

John let his eyes rest briefly on Lucy.

Why was she lying back against her mother with her eyes closed? She did not seem nauseated any more.

"Aw Lucy threw up couple of times this morning," John began, "and she got scared and went running home!"

"Where else should a girl go when she is ill but to her own mother and father?" Lucinda shrieked. She exhausted herself in this one question and looked fiercely at Peter.

"My daughter always has a good home with her mother and father," Peter murmured automatically.

"You always talk like a fool!" Dan growled. "Ain't nobody askin' nobody whether your four rooms are good or not."

"Here!" Lucinda began again.

"So it ain't necessary to commence no fool talk! What's the matter with Lucy?" Uncle Dan hurdled his bellow right across Lucinda's interruption.

"She was sick at her stomach this morning," John repeated.

"Sick at her stomach! Sick at her stomach! What call y'all got to have all this yelling 'cause a gal threw up once?"

"Threw up once!!" Lucy came alive. "I'll have you to know—blood, even, was in the—er—matter which came from my system! Oh I—nearly died!"

"Baby!" Lucinda threw her arms around Lucy.

"My daughter is a lady! She is no *gal*!" Peter interposed.

"Aw for God's sake, nigger!" Dan was getting warmer. "Act human!"

"Don't you swear in my house, Daniel!" Margaret found her tongue. "You ought to be civil! You don't need to call names! I hate that word—nigger!"

"Ain't nobody tole me yet what ails this—Lucy!" Dan avoided gal this time.

"Oh mama!" Lucy rolled her face deep into her mother's bosom and began to cry again. "I'm going to be sick again."

Margaret ran out to the kitchen and got the scrub pail. She was not going to have that Lucy *losing* the contents of her stomach on her rug.

Lucy hung over the pail.

Nothing happened.

Some one rang the bell.

This time it was Mary.

How are y'all?" Mary asked as she entered.

Lucinda was settling a pillow behind Lucy.

Margaret was getting real mad!

Mary!!

Neither she nor Lucinda spoke to Mary.

"Good morning," Peter ventured.

John walked up and put both arms around Mary and kissed her.

Margaret sniffed.

"What ails Lucy?" Mary indicated the scrub pail.

"We think—" began John.

"She's going to—" began Peter at the same time.

"We think it's a—baby!" Margaret finished.

"That's nice," Mary exclaimed heartily. "Why ain't that wonderful?"

Lucy began to laugh and cry and heave last night's dinner heartily all at once so everything was active for another full five minutes.

Then Lucy got erect. "So you think that's wonderful! Wonderful! It ought to be you!" she railed at Mary.

"Why I'm too old!" Mary observed mildly.

"Suppose you had to give up your job and you were married to a man who couldn't support you decent?"

"I'd move to a cheaper place! Always said $47.50 was more money than anyone earning little as John ought to pay." Dan unrolled his speech as if he could not wait to get a word in.

"I'd quit buying so many dresses and stuff and try to make it on what he got," Mary told Lucy.

Margaret gave Lucinda a "Do-you-see-what-fools-I-have-to-contend-with" look.

They drew closer together—there, at least.

"What the doctor think?" Mary asked.

"Yeah? What he say?" echoed Dan.

Lucy looked fully at John for the first time.

John looked at Lucy.

Peter looked at his twirling thumbs.

No one said anything.

Mary persisted. "How the doctor think Lucy is?"

Margaret cleared her throat. "Er—er—he hasn't said anything yet."

"Lucy hasn't—" began Lucinda and hesitated.

"That is to say as it were—" Peter unwound.

"Lucy, have you seen a doctor yet?" John asked.

His wife shook her head.

"Heh-heh! Lawd!" Dan gave an up-from-the-toes colored laugh. He walked over to his mop and picked it up. "Been to college, too!" he observed to no one.

John's jaw dropped a little. "I'll take my wife to a doctor," he managed to say.

"I'll attend to my daughter's needs." Peter told John.

"Papa! Papa! You stay out of this!" Lucinda spoke hastily. "You stay out of this now!"

She did not want Peter to pay all the bills.

Had not Margaret hinted to her often that Dan and Mary had money?

"Stay out of man and wife's affairs!" Lucinda repeated.

And nobody laughed either.

Lucinda rose to her feet and began to adjust her coat.

"My Lord!" Mary said loudly. "My Lord," she said louder. "I got to get back to my scrubbing! Look like to me Lucy ain't the first woman what had a baby and ain't likely to be the last! You all worryin' 'bout the food and the rent and the clothes and the God knows what all ain't nobody said nothing was nothing yet! Seem like to me you puttin' your own worryin' where God ought to be. You'll liable to be eatin' chittlins and you liable to be eatin' the richest kind of food! You don't know! God knows what'll happen."

Margaret was finding herself. "Well—I think we ought to wait and see what a doctor has to say, too! Lucy could go to a clinic!"

"My grandson shall have the best!" Peter uttered the words like an alarm clock.

Old Dan gave a short sibilant derisive sound that was like the lowest possible curse word: "Then git on out and start gittin' it for him!"

Peter drew his head back in his collar.

"Now, Poppa! Now!" Lucinda buttoned her coat more quickly. "Stay out of this!"

She really pulled Peter from his seat and pushed him out the door.

Peter better keep quiet!

That young fool might get the idea that he did not have to pay his wife's hospital bills if it was a baby.

Lucinda was just beginning to enjoy the full use of Peter's money without the constant drainage of a growing daughter leeched on to all family expenses.

She meant to keep things as they were.

"I'll give the christening dress. Real silk—and a nice big dinner," Lucinda was thinking. She said good-bye automatically and hurried Peter off. Lucy was left on the couch somehow.

"I'll give the christening dress. Real silk and a nice big dinner!" Margaret was planning to herself.

Mary dug in her pocket "Here, John!" she stuck two ten-dollar bills in his hand. "I didn't know what to expect so I brought you this."

Dan glowed. Mary was such a real woman! He looked triumphantly at Margaret.

"Wonder if John will let me have three dollars of that to pay my electric bill," Margaret was thinking.

"Good-bye Dan!" she said aloud and she gave Mary only a frigid nod.

Her brother and his wife went off together.

John went for his coat.

He would leave Lucy at a doctor's office then make some kind of call just to cover up his absence if ever the supervisor decided to check up on him.

He would make it somehow—if only—he stopped to think: if only what?

If only Lucinda and Peter had had so many children that they could not be ready to swoop into Lucy's affairs like this all their lives!

Yet—if they had had lots of children—Lucy could not have had the things that made her "refined" and "nice." She might have had no education.

Oh well.

John shrugged himself into his coat.

It surely was plain hell being married to someone who was a Mama's darling.

So much darling that there was no room for her to be his wife.
He would make it.

"Come on Lucy," he said and walked up to her.

She got up silently, stiffly, moving like an old woman.

And they went off together. The did not talk together. They
forgot to settle their hats at their usual jaunty angles.

Both were heavy.

Heavy.

Truly—somewhere—they had been fed stones for bread.

Reap It As You Sow It

Now Nola was one of those people who blind their eyes with their desires—seal their hearts with their sins—then consider the Scriptures.

It happens to state clearly in the twentieth chapter of Exodus that you must not lie—cheat—kill—steal—or commit adultery.

It says just plain do *not* do these things.

Nola, though, thought it said: "Go ahead! Do what you want to do! You won't have to pay! Never! No one keeps the books that balance your account of living."

And it is written on every page, "God alone is the chief *accountant*.

He posts and spreads and checks.

His final sheet is never a penny off. And it balances—somewhere—to the last mite—to the last damnable trick you have played.

Perhaps because Frye Street was so little and insignificant in such a big city, Nola thought God had forgotten her and everyone around her.

Nola was one of those colored girls who seem to come from nowhere bringing nothing with them and who are hell-bent on going nowhere as fast as they can live it.

She was tawny, easy-limbed, with enough fundamental good looks to draw the eye when she wanted to. She was twenty-four and there was not a tavern on Frye Street or Grand Avenue that she did not go into whenever she wanted a drink or a man.

Frye Street is that crooked little tumbled red brick place that joins the river to the edge of the city.

Some part of every race from everywhere lives there.

And from Number 11 to Number 49 on both sides of the street, colored people lived.

In Number 12 lived Nola.

At Number 14 lived Mollie and James.

James and his wife Mollie had only been in the city three months when Nola saw them. Some of the dreamy distances of the South they had just left cut them off from the rest of Frye Street.

Mollie was brown and stout wide-eyed and clean country nice looking. Some people would have called her stout and plump. To colored folks on Frye Street she was just plain "blockety." That meant she was fat in odd spots.

James was grey-eyed and ivory colored with brownish hair. Even the Frye Streeters called him handsome.

It happened that James and Mollie took a walk one night. They walked slowly hand in hand, the way they used to follow country lanes—up Frye Street to Grand Avenue, where the El rushed by.

They never went further. They always stopped at the windows of Lowinsky's department store to pick out the clothes they meant to buy if ever James got a job that was steady.

This night they walked and stood—and Nola swung by on her way to one of her taverns.

She cast a casual eye at Lowinsky's—saw Mollie and James—looked again—saw James—and walked up to him.

"Good evenin'!" Nola put just the right amount of down-homey-ness in her voice. "How y'all this evenin'?"

James and Mollie both answered. "Evenin'! We well, thank you."

"My—er—church is givin' a little party at this here number," Nola began hastily. She dug in her purse and produced a blank card. "I clean forgot the tickets but I'll just put the number of the house on here! We want y'all to come. You strangers in the city, aren't you?"

James nodded dumbly. So did Mollie.

Nola wrote the number fifteen. "Right across the street." She pointed down Frye Street.

"That's right 'cross from where we live!" Mollie exclaimed.

"We might walk by there! Thanks!" James told Nola.

"We want y'all to come!" Nola insisted. "Bye!"

And she swung off up Grand Avenue.

"You reckon it be all right for us to go?" the woman in Mollie made her ask.

"Ought not to hurt! Church folks givin' it," James answered.

They were tired of sitting up in one room.

They spoke to no one but their landlady.

It would be nice to meet some church folks.

They walked along Grand Avenue a while, then they turned back and found themselves hurrying—they were so eager to talk to someone new.

Number 15 was really having a party.

A piano was tinkling a Negroid motley. In the center of the room a loose-hung Negro danced.

"These ain't no church folks!" Mollie told James at the front door. "Dancin'!"

"This ain't down home! Church folks dances if they want to in the city."

"I'm going home!" Mollie started back to the door.

"How 'bout some nice barbecue?" a man's voice asked behind her.

"Have some pop?" offered another voice.

Nola was standing beside them with a man who was grinning dreadfully.

"How much?" James began.

"Oh this my treat!" Nola laughed. "Help yourself, y'all!"

Mollie and James were dazed. They ate and drank in a quiet corner in the hall. Nola hovered near them.

Two girls came in the front door.

"Lawd! Look at all the paint on these women's faces!" Mollie started to whisper to James.

"Meet my friends Mr. and Mrs.—What is you all's name?" Nola asked loudly of Mollie and James.

"Smith," James told her.

"Aw what's your first name, big boy?" Nola persisted.

Mollie made an internal recoil at the close touch in Nola's voice.

"James and Mollie Smith!" James supplied meekly.

The girls muttered, "Pleese-ter-meet-cher!"

"Gimme something to drink!" one of the girls yelled loudly. "Ain't y'all got nothing to drink?"

"Have some pop?" Nola stuck a bottle of strawberry pop into the woman's hands.

"What I want with this stuff!" demanded the girl. "Gimme some beer!"

"You must a had too much already!" Nola told her.

"I'm going home," Mollie began sotto voce to James again.

"Have some more pop," Nola told Jim. She passed him a bottle already open.

James drew on it. "Whoo-ee!" he cried. "This stuff tastes like spirits of nitre."

Mollie took his bottle and drank too. "Sure do!" she agreed.

"Tain't no nitre! That's gin!" Nola said.

"I'm going home!" Mollie said it aloud this time. "Church folks don't drink!"

"Who said they did and who said they didn't?" Nola bristled.

"Aw come on! Let's dance!" James told Mollie. "No use to get mad!"

He was enjoying the excitement strange faces produced in him. He did not want to go back to his one room yet.

So they danced out into the front room. After that, James danced with Nola—then with Mollie once more.

Again he danced with Nola.

Pretty soon Mollie found herself standing in the doorway, while Nola and James circled the room and James was laughing and talking to Nola as if he were having a good time.

At eleven o'clock, maybe, somebody put some more gin or whiskey into the pop.

Anyhow, Nola began dancing in the center of the floor by herself. Higher and wilder she stepped until she was trying to see if she could kick over James's head.

Everyone else *herded* along the walls to watch Nola.

Now there are some ladies who will giggle with the best of them from the sidelines where the tame herd gathers, while the life of the party sees if she can kick her pumps over somebody's husband's head.

There are some women who will stand herded up and giggle.

Mollie was not one of those to stand still.

She walked out blindly and followed a narrow hall. It led directly into the little smoked boxes that served as kitchens in Frye Street houses.

Mollie did not know why she had walked into someone else's kitchen at first. Then she saw a large black frying pan on the back of the stove.

Mollie grabbed it and started back up the narrow hall.

Nola's kicks were at superlative heights.

"Bring up some laundry, Nola!" a voice screamed from the sidelines.

And Nola obliged with a wider display of lingerie and tawny limbs.

And James, his face flooded with a shame-faced flush still stood where Mollie had last seen him—in the very center of the screaming women.

Mollie swung the frying pan.

Grease splattered from it across the faces of two women.

"What the hell you doing?" one woman out-screamed the laughing group.

She pushed the pan aside. It bounced off of Nola's shoulder.

The gin and the kicks had Nola entirely off balance.

She collapsed at once. James reached out his arms automatically and she fell into them.

Someone kicked the pan out of Mollie's hands. It fell on a man's toes and he filled the room with wide-mouthed cursing.

Nola lay stunned a second. Then she started to leap up like a cat and beat Mollie.

She could easily have done so.

But, glancing up, she saw into whose arms she had fallen.

So Nola—Nola who could fight anyone in any tavern— pretended to faint and lay heavier against James.

Fierce fighting exploded all over the room. Mollie ran out of the door and across Frye street.

She could hear the clang of the bell on a patrol wagon before she reached her room.

Nola heard the clang too.

By the time the policemen were scraping the battlers into the wagon, Nola had showed James how to drop out of the kitchen window, cut across the back *alley* and saunter along Grand Avenue as if that were all they had been doing all night.

Upstairs in Number 14, Mollie watched panic-stricken as they loaded the patrol across the street.

"Lawd! Guess James'll go to the lock-up too! Wish I never went to that place! That dirty ole woman!"

Mollie fell across the bed and cried.

The door opened.

Mollie rolled over. "James! How come you ain't gone to the lock-up?"

"Oh Nola she done tole me how to git out the back way!"

Mollie sniffed. "Is that that thing's name? That was one low-down crowd of nigger women, wasn't they, James?"

James sat down on the side of the bed and took off his shoes. He said nothing.

"I don't never want to get mixed up no more with them kind of folks! No suh! Not me!" Mollie chattered nervously.

James shook out his trousers and hung them up.

Still he said nothing.

"I ain't never gone to speak to none of them ef ever I meet one of them on the street!" Mollie could not stop talking. "Fighting and cursing and kicking up like some —"

"Shut up!" James roared suddenly. "You done the fightin' yourself! You 'bout kill Nola! You lucky ef the patrol don't back up here and git you!"

Mollie began to scream loudly.

James had to agree that the people were rather low-down and evil: he had to promise that they would move away from Frye Street the next day.

But long after Mollie had quieted and was asleep, James lay awake beside her tingling with the excitement that their party had set in him.

It was all Mollie's fault that anything had gone wrong. She was too countryfied!

Church folks in the city did things country church folks would not think of doing. There was no need of anyone expecting it. He fell asleep promising himself that he would join the church that gave parties like the one he had left.

Mollie and James did not move next day.

They stayed at Number 14 Frye Street.

Soon it became apparent to all the world that Mollie was "expecting." And it became just as apparent to that same world that Nola was expecting to get James for her own. As Mollie blossomed and bloomed—Nola grew bolder and bolder.

It reached the point that James stayed out all night.

It was as easy as a knife through cheeses—a knife of evil through a cheesy nigger-man.

Yet—people do not break off at once from anything. Something hacks and hacks and hacks at the roots that they have sunk into some relationships.

Then they weaken.

They weaken. They totter. Finally they crash down—cut loose with no roots.

It got so that Jim took the money he was supposed to be paying in the hospital each week so Mollie might go in when her time came—he took the money and bought gifts for Nola. James bought gifts and went places—parties—taverns—everywhere—anywhere with Nola.

James acted as if he were indeed crazy about Nola.

One Saturday night, Mollie was hungry.

She had waited since six for James to come home from work. At nine o'clock she was still sitting at the window—too heavy to move, watching everyone who passed.

As she stared, Nola came down Frye Street on the other side.

Mollie threw up the window. "You Nola?" she called. "You Nola!"

Nola halted a second. "What you want?"

"You see James? Where's James at?"

"Now I ain't see him! How I know where he at?"

"You ought to know! You old dirty thing! Running after him all the time!"

"Shut your damn black mouth or I'll come up there and shut it!"

"You let James alone! Let him alone! I'm 'bout to have the child and he ain't paid the hospital nuthin'! Let him alone!"

Nola cursed long and loud. Then she swung away up the street.

Mollie could only stare after her.

She closed the window and started to get up.

It was then that the pain began to knife deep within her. Her time had come.

Her scream brought the landlady running.

"Lawd! Git to the hospital! Let me help you!"

Mollie found enough breath to say, "Can't go! They won't take me! James ain't paid yet!"

"Now ain't that the devil!! Ain't men fools! Racin' and chasing 'round!"

The knife tore into Mollie again and she screamed once more.

"Let me run git Granny Gray! She used to catch babies down home." The landlady panted and ran off again.

Granny Gray came.

She was an old-time midwife. She never heard of sterilization or any particular hygiene. She did all the things she should never have done.

The baby was born at two o'clock.

Mollie died at three.

James came home at four.

The blood, the baby, and Mollie dead on the bed—knocked him sober.

He stayed sober for a while—even after the funeral. He stayed away from Nola, too.

Old lady Jones whose husband was a janitor way uptown in a wealthy white neighborhood, took the baby.

James shifted away from Number 14. He drifted until he found Nola once more.

Nola set about comforting James. She comforted him so well that they were married six months later.

Now after she married, Nola grew very very strange. It may be that she really loved James.

"Look like to me a married woman ought to b'long to some church," she told James one night.

"Yeah."

"I want you should take me to the Loving Lambs up on the corner some night."

James took her.

And Nola got happy and screamed and cried and plucked up her skirts and walked over the backs of the benches when the preaching was going on.

The reverend bellowed: "If only by keeping God's law of love—love your neighbor and all the rest of it—is the only way folks can make heaven—then there's going to be a mighty passel of niggers toasting in hell with the chaff and the goats after the wheat and the lambs get saved!"

Nola fell back against James. "Amen" she cried in agreement.

"Sperits on her," one old lady hollered.

"Dem sperits is *in* dat gal!" sneered another who knew Nola for what she really was.

James had to take Nola out for some air.

Soon after it became apparent to the world that Nola was "expecting."

She stayed at home and cooked and cleaned with that awful scrupulous cleanliness that only a dirty woman can give a place.

Odd, isn't it, how these women are usually so clean about externals!

James worked hard.

They moved from their one-room place to a little four-room house up on Grand Avenue.

Nola forgot about Mollie dying at home with no doctor to help her. She forgot about James Junior—Mollie's baby—knocked around somewhere uptown.

Nola forgot all the men she had dodged and slipped and danced around with.

She thought God had forgotten, too.

He had not forgotten. It only seemed so. It was merely time for the flourishing—the blossoming—the spreading of branches of rich plenty.

Nola's baby was a girl—beautifully bronzed and so lovable that Nola worshipped her.

No dress was too expensive, no hours too late to work for baby Nola.

One Saturday when baby Nola was two years old, her mother dressed her and let the little girl next door take her for a walk.

The two children stopped to play with some other youngsters in front of the door.

"Guess I'll comb my hair and change my dress 'fore I bring baby Nola in!" Nola thought.

She took a mirror and sat by her bedroom window. She combed her hair and smiled at herself as she listened to little Nola's laughing below her in the street.

"Ain't she too sweet! Listen to her!" Nola spoke aloud to herself.

She stood up and moved her chair nearer to the window so that she might the better watch the perky red hair bow dancing along the red gingham dress in Saturday's late afternoon sunshine.

Life was so good! Pretty soon James would be coming home from his job. No relief and stuff for them like most of the colored folks on Frye Street.

James had a good job sweeping sawdust at the Big Market. He would bring home a good roast for Sunday and maybe chops or a nice steak and a piece of ham.

Life was so good.

Nola yawned a "God-life-is-so-everlastingly-good-as-I-know-it" yawn.

As I know it in this body.

Then she stood up.

There was Jim already, turning the corner of Frye Street, his arms crowded with bundles.

She would go down and open the door for him.

She started to leave the room—remembered that little Nola might see her father across the street and run across to meet him.

She had better call out of the windows for the kids to watch her.

Nola lifted the window and saw baby Nola below her.

Little Nola looked across the street and saw James.

A trailer-truck swung around the corner.

Little Nola saw her father.

She did not see the truck. The driver did not see her.

Nola, up in the window, saw the truck coming—saw the baby run out into the street—and she started to climb out of the window, tearing out her clothes and her hair as she went.

The screams of the children as the truck dragged little Nola were all she heard.

As long as she lived Nola swore that she could not jump through that window to die in that moment little Nola was killed.

She could not move.

For a hand—a woman's hand—brown, stubby, plump—with cracked worn fingernails and an old gold wedding band like Mollie's old-fashioned ring—held her.

A woman's hand locked in a steel grasp in that window. The other hand pointed past Nola to the street below. "See! See!! There!! That is the end of loveliness and hope! Right now your misery begins!"

Nola afterwards thought she heard these very words as she followed the pointing of that finger.

That is what Nola swore afterwards.

I do not know.

When you and your conscience are alone with God in some places and there is a reckoning going on—anything can happen.

You can only wonder which was worse: to go off to an unknown world, leaving your first-born newly come—behind you—drawing you ever back to this earth that hurt you most—or living on days and days and days after a dear little body has been put to sleep for the last time—in the ground—away from you.

How must it be to start up night after night, half awake, to go and tuck blankets around a crib that is empty.

Anyhow—the columns were balanced.

The chief accountant had put the last penny in its proper place.

Nola went back to wondering—seeing if the happy content that filled her one Saturday afternoon when she sat by her window—would ever come again.

Men—lots of men—liquor—lots of liquor—nothing filled her again.

Jim took to staying away from a neighborhood where sorrow had laid darkly on him.

Nola fought and cursed and sank lower and deeper.

One night they had to put her in the wagon to take her to the lock-up for breaking all the glasses in Tarry's tavern.

"Nola! Why don't you behave yourself!" the captain asked as he booked her.

Nola hung to the desk so she could look fully into the man's face: "Lawd don't want me to be no good! He won't let me! He ain't never give me no chance!" she answered.

And she believed that she had spoken the truth when she said it.

Light in Dark Places

Footsteps sounded in the outer hall.

That was the boy!

That was the boy—stepping sporty—tapping hard on his heels and dragging each foot.

That was the boy coming to see Tina.

"What'd he say his name was!" Tina worried.

She would have to speak his name when she opened the door!

Aunt Susie was the only one at home but she would tell Ma when she came home from work, "Some fellow came to see Tina and she ain't knowed his right name! Had to ask him at the door," she'd say.

Ma would get real mad.

And when Ma got real mad, she would beat you with the razor strap.

Aunt Susie was eighty and blind and she sat in the old morris chair by the front room window day and night. Her heart would not let her lie down at night very often.

But Aunt Susie heard every sound that flicked through the three-room flat where she lived with Ma—her niece—and Tina, Ma's youngest daughter.

"She even hear a cat walk by on the back fence, I believe," Ma joked sometimes.

Ma did not joke often. Ma had buried Pa when Tina was six months old and had brought up four children alone in the big city. She went to work at six-thirty in the morning and never got home until eight at night. To work as long as that at the distance from the colored section that Ma had to go each day, left little time for jokes.

Ma was edgy most of the time.

It was not eight yet. Ma was not home. Only Aunt Susie and Tina were there. Now Tina was before the mirror in her cerise rayon taffeta trying to get a frantic peek at her self—trying wildly to remember the name of the boy who was coming.

She really should not have spoken to him last Saturday night when Ma had sent her to the Five and Ten.

But it had been so easy. And besides—all the girls picked up fellows when they felt like it.

You saw a nice guy. You just went over and talked to him. Sometimes it turned out swell. That was how Bessie Jones had met Charlie, her husband. Sometimes it turned out rotten. The police had found Sadie Brown knifed to death in an empty flat over on Hoy Avenue. Folks said she had picked up a guy at a dance and gone out with him instead of going home to the room she shared with her mother.

Anyhow—with Tina it had been easy.

They had both put their feet up on a penny scale at the same time.

They had grinned at each other—bantered a bit—then he had sauntered part of the way home with Tina.

"Be seeing you, baby!" he said as he left. "Maybe next Tuesday!"

Tuesday.

Maybe.

She had remembered that all day in school on Monday and earned a flat failure in every class she was in.

High school was too hard anyhow.

Most of the girls left in their first year to work or to marry. Anything was better than messing with the *Odyssey* and parallelograms and quadratic equations and gym.

Tina meant to get married.

Ma had said she would take Tina out of school if she failed and Tina had been failing consistently and persistently since she had been there.

"I'm going to get married," Tina would say to comfort herself. "Some wise guy—nice looking—look good in his clothes—lots of money!"

The boy in the Five and Ten had worn his clothes with an air that Tina thought was swell.

She would have to have time to uncover the rest.

But now—he was coming along the hall.

His name was—

Tina made one last desperate dive into her mind to find his name.

His knock rattled the door.

"Whatcha sayin', baby," he grinned as Tina opened the door.

He swaggered in, throwing his hat down on the table by the door as he came.

"O.K. Whatcha saying yourself?" Tina responded.

For an answer, the boy pulled up his trousers at the knee and sat down on the sofa. He was chewing gum with a steady click.

Neither he nor Tina spoke for a moment.

His eyes were darting quickly back and forth around the room. He could see that no one was in the kitchen. The bedroom was dark. It would not take long to find out if anyone was in there.

The front room, where he and Tina sat was half dark. He had not seen Aunt Susie's morris chair yet.

He meant to be as bad as he could in the time he was there and he meant to waste no time about it.

"Anything gives Luke a good time!" he always boasted of himself.

It is hard to explain what has produced so many Lukes in the colored race. The teeter-totter on the edge of the decencies of living has filled the colored race with so many Lukes.

There has to be too many young people: too few houses: too many things to long for and too little money to spend freely: too many women: too few men: too many men weak enough to make profit of the fact that they happen to be men: too few women with something in them to make them strong enough to walk over weak men: too much liquor: too many dives: too much street life: too few lovely homes: life from the start—too many people—too few houses.

Too many peasants lured out of cotton and corn fields and jammed down into roach-filled bed-buggy rattle-trap shim-shams of [   ] street after street after street of houses fading [   ].

Too many neon signs winking promises of an excitement that never was—promising a good time that will never be.

All this slaps a woman—loose.

All this slaps a man loose from every decent bit of manliness.

Walk through an area like the one that Tina and Luke lived in and all the lost thoughts—the lost decencies of living—grasp you at the throat and choke you long after you have passed by.

Are these the things that made Luke what he was?

Luke sat down, hitched his trousers up further at the knee and—satisfied that he and Tina were alone, produced a box of candy.

"Here's something for you, baby!"

"Gee! Yeah! I will! Thanks!" Tina crowed and held out her hands.

"Come and get it!" Luke bantered.

Tina was fifteen in age only. She fluffed out her hair and her skirts and rose.

She reached for the candy.

Luke reached for her.

The box fell to the floor.

"What's that?" Aunt Susie demanded suddenly from her corner by the window. She had been dozing and the noise startled her awake.

Surprise knocked Luke to his feet.

"Aw it's a fellow, Aunt Susie!" Tina's voice was full of scorn and disgust. "She can't see nuthin'!" she whispered to Luke.

"Can *hear* plenty! Who you whispering to!"

"It's—it's—" Tina began weakly.

"It's Luke Jones." The boy became smart again. "Just stop by to see Tina 'bout some—some school lessons."

"You go to the high school too, young man?" Aunt Susie was fully awake and eager to talk now. "Ain't that nice!"

"Yeah!" Luke smothered his impatience in a bored yawn.

"Well—Tina." He rose to his feet. "Be seein' yah!"

Tina was dismayed. "You going? Just got here!"

If old Aunt Susie would go into the bedroom just this once!

"Sure! I gotta run along!" Luke said loudly.

With his head he pantomimed—beckoning Tina to go into the bedroom herself. He kept talking: "Sure! I got right smart studying to do." He walked to the outer door, opened it slightly, reached down quickly and pushed off his oxfords. "So long!" he called aloud and slammed the outside door.

The bedroom door, only a few steps away, Luke gained in one single leap. His feet in their socks made no sound.

Tina gaped amazement at his performance. She had not moved.

Seeing her so stupefied, Luke swaggered a little.

He was a smart guy! He'd show this dumb kid and her blind old lady!

He beckoned again for Tina to enter the room with him indicating that they could close the door that led to the living room.

And Tina was afraid. She was so afraid she even wished Ma would walk in right that minute. What Ma would have done about a man standing in the bedroom door with his shoes off, nobody knows.

Luke was growing angry. This stuff was wasting too much of his time. He could go other places and have a better time.

Who did this fool girl think she was?

He made a fierce gesture—sweeping in toward the room behind him with his hat.

The hat slipped from his fingers and fell with a soft thud to the floor.

Aunt Susie cleared her throat. "Well!! Too bad your company had to leave so sudden like, Tina! You, Tina?" she called sharply. "Where you at, gal?"

Tina had to try twice before she could speak. "I'm here, Aunt Susie," she finally managed in a half-croak.

The old lady began a chirruping chatty conversation. "Do look like young men now-days would set a-while and talk with a girl's folks like they used to when I was back home. These uns ain't got no manners in the city, seems to me. What was that fell when y'all were talking?"

"A box of candy." Tina was still frozen afraid.

"Candy! Ain't that nice! I want some but I'll wait a while till after your Ma comes. Candy! I thought it was something else! Funny, I get to feelin' sometimes that anything is liable to happen here in this city! That's why I keep my cane right handy all the time. Somebody might break in here."

"What could you do with any old cane, Aunt Susie?" Tina's voice was full of scorn once more. "You couldn't see nohow to hit nobody!"

"I can't see but I sure can hear!" the old woman countered fiercely. "And look here!" she snatched up her cane, she twisted it, and it came apart.

In the handle of the cane gleamed the three-sided blade of an old-fashioned dagger.

"Lawd! Aunt Susie! Put that thing up! Where you git it," Tina gasped. "I never knew you had nothing like that."

"I ain't meant for you to know it." Aunt Susie told her. "Y'all so foolish you liable to go foolin' with it! I keeps it when I'm settin' here in the dark when y'all are sleepin'! And ef anybody's to make any noise around here what they shouldn't I'd just git up and—"

Aunt Susie sprang to her feet and began to march around the room, thrusting her dagger before her.

She thrust straight at the couch where Luke had been sitting.

"Ooh! Don't, Aunt Susie," Tina whimpered. "You liable to hurt somebody."

"Hurt who! Hurt who! Ain't nobody here is they? That young fellar's gone! I just showing you how I can jab this here thing—all over this place and hit anybody what ain't got no business here!"

She continued her march forward, jabbing and slashing all around her.

Luke, gray-faced, stooped automatically to pick up his hat—snatched it—eeled long the door jamb—across the corner of the living room to the outer door.

One wrench, and Luke was racing down the hall to the street—without the shoes.

"Who's at comin' in? That you Mary?" Aunt Susie paused to ask.

"Now it ain't Ma—it's—it's the wind, Aunt Susie!" Tina lied as glibly as she could.

"The wind! How come the wind gone unlocking doors with safety catches?" Aunt Susie began jabbing and stabbing and moved across the room as she spoke.

Tina saw Luke's oxfords. They were strewn directly in Aunt Susie's path. She would stumble over them in another second.

Tina made a quick grab—took up the shoes and ran to the window. "This here window ain't tight as it might be!" She told Aunt Susie.

Tina pushed up the window quickly and threw Luke's shoes out as far as she could.

Hope he gets 'em, she thought to herself. "Old fool!" she said, suddenly fierce. "I locked the window, Aunt Susie."

Sudden panic gnawed at her: suppose Ma was coming in right now and the shoes had fallen on her?

"I'm going to bed!" Tina became frantic; Ma might be coming even now.

"S'matter? Ain't you going to set up till your Ma comes?"

"No I ain't! I'm going to bed and get out of this old place! Some of these days I'm going to get married and stay away from this old place all the time."

"You going to get married! *To* what—*for* what—*with* what, I'd like to know? You talks the foolishest! And shut that outside door! I heard it open and it ain't never shut yet. Cat or snake must a gone in or out! I ain't heard nothing but I felt something whisk by fast!"

"I tole you it was the wind, Aunt Susie."

"And I say it somethin 'sides the wind! Anyhow—*shut* it."

Tina banged the outside door and banged the bedroom door behind her.

Aunt Susie stood still a second, then she crossed the room swiftly and went straight to the bedroom door.

She laid her head against the side of the door and listened.

She could hear Tina moving and rustling around the room.

"Tina crying! She mad! That nigger really gone then! Thanks to the Lord!"

She crept back to her seat, and lifted up her cane. She fitted the parts together once again. Then she stuck it behind her in her morris chair.

She sighed and rubbed her hands against her face: "Oh I wish—I wish—" she said to herself and rubbed her eyes fiercely.

Then she sat back in her corner—waiting again.

Joyce Flynn teaches in Harvard University's interdisciplinary History and Literature program. She is at work on a two-volume study of conventions of race, ethnicity, and class in American theater. The second volume, *The Drama of the Ethnic Renaissance*, will include a discussion of Marita Bonner's plays.

Joyce Occomy Stricklin is the daughter of Marita Bonner. She lives with her husband and son in Chicago, where she is a free-lance photographer.